T0059566

*Superb praise for*

# Jane and the Genius of the Place

"Barron artfully replicates Austen's voice, sketches several delightful portraits . . . and dazzles her audience with period details."—*Publishers Weekly*

"Barron has succeeded in emulating the writing style of Austen's period without mocking it."
—*The Indianapolis Star*

"A gem of a novel."—*Romantic Times*

"Barron tells the tale in Jane's leisurely voice, skillfully recreating the tone and temper of the time without a hint of an anachronism."—*The Plain Dealer*

"Cleverly blends scholarship with mystery and wit, weaving Jane Austen's correspondence and works of literature into a tale of death and deceit."
—*Rocky Mountain News*

"Faithfully and eloquently recreates a time and place as well as the diary voice of one of the most accomplished women of the early 19th century."
—*The Purloined Letter*

"The skill and expertise with which Stephanie Barron creates her series featuring Jane Austen seems to get better and better with each succeeding entry. The author has attained new heights in her portrayal, with Miss Austen as observer, of a fascinating period in English history."—*Booknews* from The Poisoned Pen

*Please turn the page for more praise for other Jane Austen mysteries by Stephanie Barron*

*Extraordinary praise for*

# Jane and the Wandering Eye

"Barron seamlessly weaves . . . a delightful and lively tale. . . . Period details bring immediacy to a neatly choreographed dance through Bath society."
—*Publishers Weekly*

"Barron's high level of invention testifies to an easy acquaintance with upper-class life and culture in Regency England and a fine grasp of Jane Austen's own literary style—not to mention a mischievous sense of fun." —*The New York Times Book Review*

"For this diverting mystery of manners, the third entry in a genteelly jolly series by Stephanie Barron, the game heroine goes to elegant parties, frequents the theater and visits fashionable gathering spots—all in the discreet service of solving a murder."
—*The New York Times Book Review*

"Charming period authenticity."—*Library Journal*

"Stylish . . . this one will . . . prove diverting for hard-core Austen fans."—*Booklist*

"No betrayal of our interest here: *Jane and the Wandering Eye* is an erudite diversion."
—*The Drood Review of Mystery*

"A lively plot accented with fascinating history . . . Barron's voice grows better and better."
—*Booknews* from The Poisoned Pen

"A pleasant romp . . . [Barron] maintains her ability to mimic Austen's style effectively if not so closely as to ruin the fun."—*The Boston Globe*

"Stephanie Barron continues her uncanny recreation of the 'real' Jane Austen. . . . Barron seamlessly unites historical details of Austen's life with fictional mysteries, all in a close approximation of Austen's own lively, gossipy style." —*Feminist Bookstore News*

*Lavish praise for*

# Jane and the Man of the Cloth

"Nearly as wry as Jane Austen herself, Barron delivers pleasure and amusement in her second delicious Jane Austen mystery. . . . Worthy of its origins, this book is a delight." —*Publishers Weekly*

"If Jane Austen really did have the 'nameless and dateless' romance with a clergyman that some scholars claim, she couldn't have met her swain under more heartthrobbing circumstances than those described by Stephanie Barron." —*The New York Times Book Review*

"Prettily narrated, in true Austen style . . . a boon for Austen lovers." —*Kirkus Reviews*

"Historical fiction at its best." —*Library Journal*

"The words, characters and references are so real that it is a shock to find that the author is not Austen herself." —*The Arizona Republic*

"Stephanie Barron's second Jane Austen mystery . . . is even better than her first. . . . A classic period mystery." —*The News and Observer*, Raleigh, NC

"Delightful . . . captures the style and wit of Austen." —*San Francisco Examiner*

"Loaded with charm, these books will appeal whether you are a fan of Jane Austen or not."
—*Mystery Lovers Bookshop News*

*The highest praise for*

# Jane and the Unpleasantness at Scargrave Manor

"Splendid fun!"—*Star Tribune*, Minneapolis

"Happily succeeds on all levels: a robust tale of manners and mayhem that faithfully reproduces the Austen style—and engrosses to the finish."
—*Kirkus Reviews*

"Jane is unmistakably here with us through the works of Stephanie Barron—sleuthing, entertaining, and making us want to devour the next Austen adventure as soon as possible!"—Diane Mott Davidson

"Well-conceived, stylishly written, plotted with a nice twist . . . and brought off with a voice that works both for its time and our own."
—*Booknews* from The Poisoned Pen

"People who lament Jane Austen's minimal lifetime output . . . now have cause to rejoice."
—*The Drood Review of Mystery*

"A light-hearted mystery . . . The most fun is that 'Jane Austen' is in the middle of it, witty and logical, a foil to some of the ladies who primp, faint and swoon."—*The Denver Post*

"A fascinating ride through the England of the hackney carriage . . . a definite occasion for pride rather than prejudice."—Edward Marston

"A thoroughly enjoyable tale. Fans of the much darker Anne Perry . . . should relish this somewhat lighter look at the society of fifty years earlier."
—*Mostly Murder*

"Jane sorts it all out with the wit and intelligence Jane Austen would display. ★★★ (four if you really love Jane Austen)."—*Detroit Free Press*

## BOOKS BY STEPHANIE BARRON

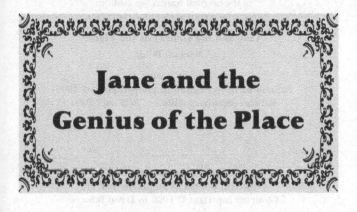

# Jane and the Genius of the Place

*~Being the Fourth Jane Austen Mystery~*

*by Stephanie Barron*

**BANTAM BOOKS**

NEW YORK • TORONTO • LONDON • SYDNEY • AUCKLAND

This edition contains the complete text
of the original hardcover edition.
NOT ONE WORD HAS BEEN OMITTED.

**Jane and the Genius of the Place**

A Bantam Book

PUBLISHING HISTORY
Bantam hardcover edition published January 1999
Bantam paperback edition / February 2000

All rights reserved.
Copyright © 1999 by Stephanie Barron.
Cover art copyright © 1999 by David Bowers.

Library of Congress Catalog Card Number: 98-23803.
No part of this book may be reproduced or transmitted in any form or
by any means, electronic or mechanical, including photocopying,
recording, or by any information storage and retrieval system, without
permission in writing from the publisher.
For information address: Bantam Books.

If you purchased this book without a cover you should be aware
that this book is stolen property. It was reported as "unsold and
destroyed" to the publisher and neither the author nor the publisher has received any payment for this "stripped book."

ISBN 978-0-553-57839-3

*Published simultaneously in the United States and Canada*

Bantam Books are published by Bantam Books, a division of Random
House, Inc. Its trademark, consisting of the words "Bantam Books"
and the portrayal of a rooster, is Registered in U.S. Patent and Trademark Office and in other countries. Marca Registrada. Bantam Books,
New York, New York.

PRINTED IN THE UNITED STATES OF AMERICA

*Dedicated to the memory of Ruth Connor,
whose genius lives on in the places
and people she loved*

*In laying out a garden,*
*the first and chief thing to be considered*
*is the genius of the place.*

—ALEXANDER POPE, 1728
as quoted in
*Observations, Anecdotes and Characters of Books and Men,*
by Joseph Spence.

# Editor's Foreword

BRITISH NOVELIST JANE AUSTEN WAS BORN ON THE EVE of her country's conflict with its American colonies, in 1775, and died only two years after Napoleon's second abdication in 1815; yet the turmoil of England's passage through more than four decades of revolution and warfare is barely evident in her novels. As a result, her fiction has too often been dismissed as superficial or as reflecting the purely "female" preoccupations of domestic life. An Austen scholar might be quick to point out the naval influences in *Persuasion*, or argue that the subtle shifts in social practices and mores that Austen repeatedly chronicles could exist only in the broader context of political transformation—but in the main, her fiction mentions military figures most often as they appear at a ball, and politics not at all.

Austen's letters, however, reveal her to have been anything but ignorant of the affairs of her day. As Warren Roberts points out in his engrossing work, *Jane Austen and the French Revolution* (Macmillan, 1979), the novelist habitually read the London newspapers and commented on the political news reported in them. She followed the battles and engagements of the Royal Navy with avid interest, having two brothers serving in ships of the line, and she spent the entire summer of 1805 near the coastline of Kent—Napoleon's ground zero for invasion.

What a delight, therefore, to discover in this, the fourth of the long-lost Austen journals to be edited for publication, an account of Jane's life during a period known to her contemporaries as the Great Terror. For over two years, from May 1803 until August 1805, Napoleon Bonaparte planned the invasion of England with a passion bordering on mania. He beggared his treasury to build a flotilla of over a thousand ships, massed an army of one hundred thousand troops in the ports of the Channel coast, and goaded his reluctant naval commanders into attempting to breach the remarkably effective British blockade of France. Never, since the Norman Conquest, had Britain faced so serious a threat of invasion from its neighbor; never again, until the Battle of Britain in September 1940, would she confront so potent a military force, merely twenty miles from Dover.

Jane Austen witnessed the denouement of Napoleon's grand scheme from the idyllic vantage of her brother Edward Austen Knight's principal estate, Godmersham Park in Kent. The compelling events of those days—which coincided with Canterbury's Race Week—are here recounted for the first time.

In editing this manuscript for publication, I found Alan Schom's *Trafalgar: Countdown to Battle, 1803–1805* (Oxford University Press, 1990) an invaluable guide to the period. But nothing can exceed the pleasure of my brief walk through the grounds of Godmersham itself, with its sheep-filled meadows rolling down to the Stour, on a hot afternoon in July.

Stephanie Barron
Evergreen, Colorado

# Jane and the
# Genius of the Place

# Chapter 1

## The Figure
## in Scarlet

*Monday,*
*19 August 1805*
~

MISS JANE AUSTEN—LATE OF GREEN PARK BUILDINGS,
Bath, but presently laying claim to nowhere in particular, given her esteemed father's recent death, and the
subsequent upheaval in domestic arrangements—might
never be accused of dissipation. Not for Jane the delights of the *ton*, who may dance until dawn at the most
select assemblies, or haunt the private gaming hells
where hazard is played so scandalously high. At her time
in life—and she is hard on the heels of thirty—there is
something a little unseemly in a desire for modish dress,
or a taste for fashionable watering-places, or a reckless
disregard for social convention. Accustomed from birth
as she has been to the modest lot of a clergyman's daughter, Miss Austen may only witness the habits of her more
materially-fortunate brethren with shocked dismay, and
trust that her fervent prayers—sent Heavenward in all
the humility of a woman mindful of her end—might
serve as intercession between the Fallen and their Maker.

Unless, I observed to myself with satisfaction on the present occasion, the more materially-fortunate brethren determine our Jane to be worthy of a little dissipation-on-loan. A visit to a race-meeting, perhaps, in all the glory of a barouche-landau excellently placed for viewing the horses, a picnic hamper overflowing with good things, and attendant footmen stifling in their livery. There can be few pursuits so conducive to the flutter of an ivory fan or the delicate flirtation of a muslin sunshade. And where but at the Canterbury Races, in the very midst of August Race Week, might one find all the excesses of human folly so conveniently placed to hand?

Within the compass of my sight, I assure you, were any number of incipient scandals. The countenance of more than one gentleman was flushed with wine and the course's promise, or perhaps the anxiety attendant upon heavy betting—for in the decision of a moment, fortunes might be made or lost, reputations sacrificed, and ruin visited upon more than merely the horse.

From the vantage of their gay equipages, ladies young and old flirted with every passing swain, and offered raspberry cordial or spruce beer to such as were overcome by the heat. Our friends the Wildmans, from nearby Chilham Castle; the Edward Taylors, from Bifrons Park; and the Finch-Hattons, of Eastwell Park, in their elegant green barouche, all chattered gaily across the distance separating their parties. Footmen unpacked the heaviest of the hampers, and decanted the spirits from an hundred bottles, while stable lads walked the patient carriage horses under whatever shade might be found.

One dark-haired young woman, tricked out in a very fetching habit of red bombazine, with a tricorn hat and feathers, held pride of place on the box of her own perch phaeton—a daring gesture in so public a gathering, and not for the faint of heart. It was a cunning little equipage, built for speed and grace, and possibly not unsuited to a lady's use in St. James Park—but a rare sight, indeed, among the serviceable coaches of Kent. She drove a pair of matched greys, and led a snorting black gelding behind—or rather, her tyger did. He was a diminutive, crab-faced fellow with a bent back, stifling in gold braid and livery, who sat hunched at the phaeton's rear, awaiting his mistress's commands, and feeding an occasional bit of greenstuff to the snorting black.

As I watched, the figure in scarlet drew a whip-point from her collar and tossed it to an admirer standing at the phaeton's wheel. He caught it neatly and held it to his lips like a spoil of victory; *she* threw back her head and laughed. I might have enquired as to the lady's name, but that I espied my brothers approaching the Austen carriage, and thus dismissed the Fair Unknown without regret. I must confess that even *Jane* will grow weary of fashionable absurdities, when treated to their display for so long as three months.

In June, my sister Cassandra and I shook off the dust of Bath and descended upon Kent, and all the splendour of Godmersham, my brother Edward's principal estate.[1] The change in circumstance has been material, I assure you. My excellent father having passed from this life in the last days of January, the subsequent months were overshadowed by all the gloom of bereavement; and the black hours were hardly improved by my mother's heartfelt wish of quitting Green Park Buildings, in

---

[1] Edward Austen (1767–1852) was third among the eight Austen children. In 1783, at the age of sixteen, he was adopted by a wealthy cousin, Thomas Knight II, from whom he inherited three estates—Godmersham in Kent, and Steventon and Chawton in Hampshire. Edward lived a life of privilege and ease quite beyond the reach of his siblings. In 1812, he took the surname of Knight.—*Editor's note.*

the hope of an establishment more suited to her purse and widowed estate. February, and then March, and even April were allowed to pass away in pursuit of cheaper pastures; but the sensibilities of three women being so far divided on the question of what was vital to our comfort, we could none of us agree. And so we resigned the abominable duty at the first opportunity—my mother embarking upon a visit to Hampshire, and her daughters stepping thankfully into their brother's chaise, sent expressly from Kent for the purpose.

In the great house at Godmersham, no expense is too dear for the achievement of my comfort. All is effected with ease and style, for an elegant mode of living is the primary object of Elizabeth, my brother's wife. There are not many uses for a baronet's daughter, but the steady management of a gentleman's household may safely be described as one of them; and in this, and in the rearing of a numerous progeny, Lizzy gives daily proof of her goodness. At Godmersham I may revel in the solitary possession of the Yellow Room (the bedchamber at the head of the stairs, set aside for my use whenever I am come into Kent), and while away a rainy afternoon with a good book and a better fire in the library's shadowed peace. Here I may be above vulgar economy, and drink only claret with my dinner, despising the orange wine that usually falls to my lot. When Edward's excellent equipages await my every whim, I need not rely upon the hack chaise for the conduct of my business; and if seized by the fever of composition, I have no cause to hide myself away, in constant apprehension of discovery. The grounds at Godmersham are very fine, and include in their compass at least one summerhouse *and* a cunning little temple set on a hill, ideally suited to the visitation of the Muse.

I find my condition in general so enviable, and so entirely suited to my taste, as to make me think with wonder on a certain event of nearly three years ago. Can I have been in full possession of my senses, indeed, to have refused Mr. Harris Bigg-Wither—a man of wealth and easy circumstances, despite his numerous imperfections—simply because I could not esteem him? Utter folly! The indulgence of a fanciful mind! And its bitter reward is orange wine and hired lodgings for the rest of my days.

*"Jane."* My brother Henry, two steps ahead of Edward in their assault upon our barouche, shattered my reverie at a word. "I fear we must desert you this very instant, or we shall never secure a position at the rail. It is the Commodore's final heat, you know, and he is to meet a very telling little filly, Josephine by name, who won her last quite handily. He is to carry four stone six."[2]

Edward—handsome, carefree, and debonair despite the fine beads of sweat starting out on his brow—leaned into the open carriage and kissed his wife. "You look a picture, my dear. Shall our defection make you desolate?"

*Picture* was the very word for Lizzy, with her delicate parasol of Valenciennes lace inclined just so, above her dark head, and the famous Knight pearls shining dully on her bosom. "Not at all," she murmured, with a languid look from her slanting green eyes, "for positioned as you are, Neddie, you quite destroy all our hopes of flirtation. Jane and I can manage quite well by ourselves—until dinnertime, at least, when we shall grow cross and hot and prove quite ready to declare ourselves of your party. Until then, sir, be off! For we want none of your careful ways."

---

[2]  In the late Georgian period, horses of different ages and both sexes commonly raced one another and were handicapped with varying weights designed to level the field. A stone equaled roughly fourteen pounds; from the considerable weight of the Commodore's handicap, we may assume he was being brought down to a pack of less fleet or older horses.—*Editor's note.*

My brother burst out laughing at this sally of his wife's, and kissed her again, to the astonishment of the raven-haired little governess, Anne Sharpe; but all of Kent might observe the pair without contempt, for the Austens' was always acknowledged a love-match. Indeed, Neddie is so amiable, so honestly *good*—and Lizzy so perpetually elegant, without the least pretension to snobbery—that there can be few who must observe their happiness, without wishing them the heartiest good fortune in the world.

"May not I accompany you, Papa?" My niece Fanny bounced impatiently on the barouche seat opposite. She is Edward's eldest child, and very nearly his favourite—a pretty little thing of twelve, with all the advantage of birth, fortune, and connexion to recommend her. "I long to see the Commodore's action!"

"His action, is it? Lord, Fanny, how you do go on. I suppose we have you to thank, Miss Sharpe, for this cunning miss's tongue!"

A look of horror suffused Miss Sharpe's flushed cheeks, and she searched in vain for a word. Fanny's governess cannot be more than two-and-twenty, and however proficient in French and instruction on the pianoforte, is possessed of a delicate constitution. She holds my amiable brother in something very like terror.

"I should not have thought you equal to the mortification of the governess, Neddie," Lizzy interposed quietly. "You are usually possessed of better taste."

"I believe Henry deserves the credit of schooling Fanny's tongue," I quickly supplied, while Miss Sharpe sank back into her seat in confusion. "The children have acquired all manner of cant expressions in the short time he has been with us. I was treated to a sermon on the art of boxing this morning, from little George—who offered to show young Edward his *fives*, and threatened to *draw his cork*, if he did not *come up to scratch*, and I know not what else. Miss Sharpe is hardly equal to Henry's influence. She shall merely be forced to remedy it, when he has at last returned to Town."

"But, Papa—may not I accompany you to the rail?" Fanny persisted, having heard not above a word of the abuse visited upon her favourite uncle.

"The Commodore's action shall hardly be worth viewing, my dear," Neddie said easily, "after the three heats he has already survived. We shall be in luck, does he finish the race at all."

"Nonsense!" Henry cried. "The horse was never fitter!"

"But, Papa—"

"Now, do not teaze, Fanny. You know it would never do. We shall return directly the race is run, for there is sure to be a crush in leaving the field, and the oppression of the weather is fearsome. I will not have your mother tired." And with a forage into the picnic hamper for some bread and cheese, the two men set off for the rail.

Fanny burst into tears and buried her head in Lizzy's lap.

"I suppose," Lizzy observed distantly, while one hand smoothed her eldest's bedraggled curls, "that a finer lady would lament the ruin of her best muslin at such a moment, and shriek for Miss Sharpe to come to her aid. But I have never been very fine in my ways, Jane."

"No," I fondly replied, "only born to an elegance that is as natural as breathing, and that must serve as a lesson to all who meet you. The muslin shall survive, Lizzy, without the intervention of Miss Sharpe."

The governess was in no danger of hastening to her mistress's aid, however, for her interest was entirely claimed by a scene unfolding well beyond the limits of the barouche. As I watched, Miss Sharpe drew a sudden breath, and clasped her gloved hands together as tho' desperate for control. I glanced over my shoulder to discover what had so excited her anxiety—and found myself arrested in my turn.

The lady in scarlet, whom I had remarked some time earlier, now stood upright in her elegant perch phaeton. Her countenance—which in easier moments might well have been judged lovely—was contorted with rage, and she held a whip poised in her right hand. A gentleman stood calmly at her carriage mount, as tho' braced for the issue of her fury; and as I watched, the whip lashed down with a stinging sigh upon his very neck. Beside me, Anne Sharpe cried aloud, and then stifled the sound with her hand.

Lizzy's green eyes narrowed. "Whatever has Mrs. Grey got up to now?"

"Mrs. Grey?"

"The banker's wife. She is capable of anything, I believe—"

"She has just struck the gentleman by the phaeton with her riding whip. Are you acquainted with him?"

"Not at all." Lizzy sounded intrigued. "I have never seen him before in my life. A gentleman from Town, perhaps, come down to Kent on purpose for the races."

"He is possessed of the most extraordinary countenance," I whispered. "But why should she abuse him in so public a manner? I cannot believe he offered her an insult—there was neither heat nor drunkenness in his looks."

Not a commanding figure, to be sure—for he was slight and taut as a greyhound, in his elegant coat of green superfine and his fashionable high-crowned hat. A young man of perhaps thirty, whose auburn hair fell loose to his shoulders, like a cavalier's of another age. In these respects, he looked very much like any other gentleman of breeding who strolled about the race grounds; but in his aspect there was something more: an air of nobility and unguessed powers, that demanded a second glance.

"Perhaps he has declined the offer of Mrs. Grey's favours," Lizzy murmured, "and she could not abide the affront. It would be in keeping with her reputation, I assure you."

As we watched, the scarlet-clad woman pushed angrily past the man she had injured, and hastened from the phaeton. He gazed after her a moment, his countenance devoid of expression, and then drew a handkerchief from within his coat. This he applied to a great weal standing out above the line of his neckcloth; and then, rather thoughtfully, his eyes shifted towards our own. He held our gaze some few seconds, and then, quite deliberately, raised his hat in acknowledgement.

"Yes, Jane," Lizzy breathed, "self-possession and nerve are in all his looks. I would give a great deal to know his name."

"Fanny," Anne Sharpe said abruptly from the seat opposite, "you are crumpling your mother's dress. Do come and sit by me, dear, and partake of the jellied chicken. I am sure this little fit of temper is entirely due to your nerves. They cannot withstand such heat, you know, if you refuse Cook's excellent luncheon."

"Some jellied chicken, Lizzy?" I enquired.

"Every feeling revolts," she said dismissively. Her eyes were still trained on the elegant young man, who had moved off through the crowd in the direction opposite to Mrs. Grey. "I shall never make a patroness of the turf, my dear Jane, for I find the stench of dust and dung very nearly insupportable. Without the parade of fashion that always attends such events, I should be bored to tears."

"Are you perhaps increasing again?" I enquired delicately.

"Lord, no! That is all at an end, I am quite sure," she retorted; but I thought her voice held a note of doubt. Lizzy's ninth child is as yet a babe in arms; but at the age of two-and-thirty, she might expect any number in addition. "Perhaps some raspberry cordial."

I secured her the collation. "Fanny? Miss Sharpe? Some cake and cordial, perhaps?"

My niece raised a tear-stained cheek. "I could not stomach a bite, Aunt Jane, from all the anxiety attendant upon his prospects."

"His *prospects*," her mother repeated in some perplexity. "Whose, my dear?"

"I believe she means the horse, ma'am," Miss Sharpe supplied in her gentle voice.

"Such elevated language! You have been lending Fanny your horrid novels, Miss Sharpe, I am certain of it."

"Indeed not, I assure you, madam—merely Mrs. Palmerstone's edifying letters to her daughters."[3] Anne Sharpe raised eyes full of amusement to my own, and I could not suppress a smile—for we had debated the merits of such writers as Mrs. Radcliffe and Madame D'Arblay for nearly an hour in the schoolroom, with Fanny pleading to borrow my subscription volumes of *Camilla*. I had pressed them, instead, upon Anne Sharpe—and did the governess often resort to horrid novels, I should be the very last to blame her. With the schooling of two small girls in her charge, and limited reserves of strength or health to aid her, she must find in the Austens' exuberance a trial.

Particularly since the Commodore had come to plague us all.

---

[3] Miss Sharp—whose surname Jane was in the habit of spelling variously with or without a final "e"—refers here to a popular work of young lady's instruction, *Letters from Mrs. Palmerstone to her Daughters, inculcating Morality by Entertaining Narratives* (1803), by Mrs. Rachel Hunter.

A fearsome, snorting chestnut steed of nearly sixteen hands, the Commodore might be termed my brother Henry's latest folly. Being a man of some means, well-established in banking circles, and possessed of an elegantly-aristocratic wife in my cousin Eliza, Henry aspires to the habits of the Sporting Set, and has gone in for horse-racing in its most vicious form. Not content with losing breathless sums at Epsom and Newmarket, he has gambled his all on a dearer stake—the possession of an actual beast.

Knowing little of horseflesh, and still less of such points as action or blood, I have been rendered mute in almost every conversation since Henry's arrival in Kent a week ago. He is full of nothing but the subject; and it has been all a matter of furlongs and oat mash and Tattersall's betting room for a se'nnight.[4] The children have caught a dose of the fever; Neddie himself is hardly immune; and never have I found dear Henry's company so profoundly tedious. The flight of his wife, the little Comtesse Eliza, to a shooting party in the North, suggests that she is as impatient for the fad's decline as any of us. And so I prayed that the Commodore might stumble to his ruin in the present race, or perform as wretchedly as a carter's nag, and thus save us all the trouble of adoring him.

"It is too bad!" Fanny was craning over the carriage's side for a view of the course. "In sitting at such a remove,

---

[4] Richard Tattersall (1724–1795) was the foremost horse trader of London. Although deceased by Jane's writing of this account in 1805, the institutions he fostered endure in part to this day. By 1775, Tattersall was providing the newly formed Jockey Club with a room (and his famous claret) for its meetings, and in 1780 he opened a Subscription Room, a club with an annual paid membership, for the laying and settling of bets. The committee that adjudicated betting disputes was known as Tattersall's Committee—the governing body of bookmaking.—*Editor's note.*

we shall be denied the smallest glimpse of the Commodore's triumph. I believe my heart shall break!"

"My dear Fanny." Miss Sharpe laid a gloved hand on her charge's arm. "We are privileged in attending the meeting at all. Recollect that ladies must never approach the rail—it is not the done thing, and is left to the province of such hoydens as may claim neither rank nor breeding among their charms."

"Mrs. Grey may claim rank and breeding, Sharpie, and yet *she* is allowed the liberty of the grounds," Fanny retorted. "I should not be so nice as you are, for a kingdom! Mrs. Grey for me!"

And, indeed, the child spoke no more than the truth. The dark-haired beauty in the scarlet riding habit was strolling freely among the assembled carriages, with the eye of more than one gentleman lingering upon her wistfully. As we watched, she caught the banter of one and returned it playfully, her countenance alive with laughter. The brutal cut of a few minutes earlier was plainly forgotten. She appeared a ravishing young lady of exuberant spirits—forward, perhaps, but entirely in command of her circumstances.

"Perhaps we should read a little of Palmerstone aloud," Miss Sharpe suggested, with a slight note of reproof. She drew a volume from her reticule and patted the empty seat beside her. "Sit down by me, and endeavour to attend. I believe we left off at letter number twelve."

"Mrs. Grey has never read Palmerstone," Fanny retorted darkly, but she sank down next to Miss Sharpe.

"Mrs. Grey is not the pattern I should choose for your conduct, Fanny." Lizzy's words had the tenor of a scold, but I observed her mouth to twitch. "However dashing in moments, Mrs. Grey has *not* been gently reared. She is a Frenchwoman, moreover, and her manners must be very different from ours."

Miss Sharpe commenced to read, in a quiet tone; and

at that moment, I caught a glimpse of scarlet as Mrs. Grey passed to the rear of the governess's bent head. As Lizzy and I watched her wordlessly, she approached a shabby-looking chaise but a hundred feet from our own. It was equipped with neither footman nor tyger, and but for its sweating team of matched bays, appeared all but deserted. At Mrs. Grey's swift knock, however, the carriage door was thrust open by an unseen party within. With a swift glance about, the lady disappeared into the darkness, and the door closed softly behind her.

"Good Lord!" Lizzy murmured. "So Laetitia Collingforth makes Françoise Grey her friend. *This* is news, indeed."

"Has she so little acquaintance among the neighbourhood?"

"I am afraid that Kent has not embraced the Greys as it should," Lizzy replied. "But, then, Mrs. Grey is very young—"

"—and very French," I concluded.

Lizzy nodded abstractedly, her eyes still fixed on the shabby chaise. "That cannot be agreeable, at such a time."

The London papers have been full of nothing but the rumour of invasion the entire summer. Buonaparte's dreaded army, which is said to number some one hundred thousand men, sits but a stone's toss across the Channel from Kent, and many of the less stalwart families among our acquaintance have quitted the neighbourhood for safer regions far from the sea, until the danger should be passed.

"A lesser woman than Mrs. Grey might find her situation awkward," I observed, "and adopt a retiring appearance; but that has hardly been the lady's choice."

Lizzy laughed abruptly. "Retirement would never be Mrs. Grey's preference. I fear she endures our company better than we suffer hers!—Tho' I cannot think why she remains in Kent; London should prove a better field for her appetites and pursuits. Perhaps the country air suits her—or, more to the point, her horses."

"She has set up her stable?" I enquired.

"—And is passionate about the turf. Some one of her racers is entered in the Commodore's heat, no doubt, and thus we may account for her extraordinary behaviour in strolling about the meeting-grounds. She considers herself quite one of the Sporting Set, and spends a fortune, it is said, on the comfort of her mounts."

"Her husband must be in possession of easy circumstances, then."

"Mrs. Grey has never had the appearance of a pauper," Lizzy observed enviously. "I, for one, cannot afford her modiste. My pin money should never run to such sums. You observed the cut of that habit, I presume? The quantity of gold frogging about the neck and bosom? And having displayed it to all of Canterbury, she should never presume to wear it again."

"Well, well." I sighed. "The French are known for their ruinous habits, I believe. Perhaps she shall run through her husband's fortune, and serve as spectacle for us all. We cannot do without a little amusement, the news from the Channel being so very bad."

Lizzy threw me a mocking glance. "We are not all without resources, Jane. Some little money attaches to the lady herself. She is said to be the ward of a French banking family—de Penfleur by name, although her own was Lamartine. Grey married her for her connexions, I believe."

The judgement was callously expressed, but was no more than Lizzy should serve upon any number of her acquaintance. It is rare to marry for love, as my brother has done. Calculation is the more general advocate of worldly alliance, as every baronet's daughter must know.

"She must be new to the neighbourhood," I replied, "for I cannot think I have ever met her before."

"She has been resident in Kent but seven months, and her husband, Mr. Valentine Grey, acceded to his estate only three years ago. You may have heard me speak of it—The Larches. It is one of the finest places in England, Jane. Perhaps we shall pay a call there, one day, if you persist in your fascination for the lady."

I frowned. "The Larches! But is not that only a few miles from Goodnestone? How have we never come to meet them before?"

Lizzy's childhood home, Goodnestone Park, is a lovely old place some seven miles from Godmersham. Her elder brother, Sir Brooke-William Bridges, acceded to the title nearly fifteen years ago, and at his marriage to a respectable young woman, Lizzy's mother retired to Goodnestone Farm a mile distant from the great house. My sister Cassandra has been gone on a visit to Lady Bridges and her unmarried daughters this fortnight, but her letters have made no reference to any neighbours, near or far.

"The Greys do not mix very much in Society, Jane. He is the principal member of a great banking firm—and however genteel a profession, it remains one that many still consider to be *trade*." Lizzy glanced sidelong at this, to see how I should take it; for banker or no, Henry has always been my favourite brother, and I have no patience with snobbery of any kind. "And as Mr. Grey has been resident in these parts only a little while, moreover, he cannot be said to be truly of the neighbourhood."

"No," I rejoined with a touch of irony, "for that he should have been forced to endure his infancy here, and have married the daughter of a local worthy—a Miss Taylor of Bifrons Park, perhaps, or one of the Wildmans of Chilham Castle." Kent, for all its wealth and easy manners, can be a very closed society; it suffers from a touch of the provincial, as every country neighbourhood must.

"Perhaps I have not done as much for Mrs. Grey as I ought," Lizzy admitted, "but I like her too little to further the acquaintance. She is far too young, far too pretty, and far too much of a temptation to the local bloods to stand my friend; such a woman must always be seen in the light of competition. I confess, Jane, that I have withdrawn from the field, rather than tilt with such an adversary."

"Lizzy! You may command any number of dashing young gentlemen with the slightest curl of your finger! You know it to be true!"

"—Unless they have already accepted one of Mrs. Grey's dangerous card-parties," Lizzy retorted. "You can have no notion, Jane, of the fascination the woman exerts. My own brother has fallen victim to her charms; and yet, she cannot be more than two-and-twenty!"

"—With all the cunning of a Countess Jersey," I mused.[5] "And Mr. Grey? He cares nothing for his wife's reputation?"

"Mr. Grey is often from home on business. He maintains a house in Town, and spends the better part of his time there. He is certainly not in evidence today." Lizzy's gaze roved restlessly among the crowd, and her attention was immediately diverted. "Only look! Captain Woodford and my brother!"

"Captain Woodford! Uncle Bridges!" little Fanny cried, and sprang up from her perch near Miss Sharpe, waving a napkin at the pair. "Do come and tell us! How do the horses appear? Is the Commodore stamping to be off?"

[5] Frances, Countess Jersey, was finally deceased by August 1805; but not before her ruthless methods had once enslaved the much younger Prince of Wales.—*Editor's note.*

"They have not yet approached the starter's mark, Miss Fanny," Captain Woodford called jovially as he achieved the barouche, "but I have called upon your champion in his stall, and must declare him in excellent form! As worthy of the plate as any horse lately born. Ladies, your humble and devoted." He swept off his hat with a smart military bow, and we murmured our salutations.

Captain Woodford is a favourite with Lizzy—and did I not believe calculation and cunning quite beneath the daughter of a baronet, I should declare that she intends to secure him for her little sister Harriot. Though well past his first youth and decidedly *not* handsome, being marred by an eye patch that covers half his brow, the Captain is blessed in possessing a sunny nature that renders all misfortune delight, and cannot fail of finding solace in the simplest of pleasures. In Captain Woodford's company one is always assured of good sense, good humour, and honest feeling. I like him the better for his eye patch, as being the outer mark of a life lived honourably in the service of his country.

The Captain is all admiration for Harriot Bridges's fresh countenance, while *she* is wont to blush at the first glimpse of his red coat. And as to rank or fortune, there can be no objection—for she is the daughter of a baronet, and must be possessed of a competence; while the Captain is the second son of a viscount, and holds an excellent commission in the Coldstream Guards, presently quartered at Deal against the advent of the French.

"Lord, Lizzy, but it is hot! Give me some ginger beer like a good sister, and pray do not be telling our mother in what state you found me." Mr. Edward Bridges, Lizzy's younger brother, mopped his brow with a linen handkerchief by way of a courtesy, and accepted the glass that Miss Sharpe proffered. "Woodford and I are just come from a capital little cocking ring set up on the edge of the course, and a pretty penny we lost there, too. I shall depend upon your Commodore to restore our fortunes."

"I might almost hope that you depend in vain," Lizzy retorted, "but that you should apply to my husband for relief from any debts of honour. In either case, win or lose, the Austens must be the making of you."

Her brother smiled roundly, as though Lizzy had uttered nothing like a reproach; and there the matter ended.

Mr. Bridges is a very different sort of gentleman from his companion in cocking, the gallant Captain. A well-made, high-coloured fellow of five-and-twenty, he is bent on spending his purse entire in pursuit of a sporting life. No London fashion may be heralded by *The Gentleman's Magazine* without first being seen on Mr. Bridges's back; no cricket match may be bruited in the neighbourhood, without Mr. Bridges laying a guinea against the odds; no pack of hounds loosed upon the trail of some unfortunate vixen, without Mr. Bridges hot in pursuit on the back of his latest hunter. I relish his absurdities, and find him lively company enough—but I cannot approve him. Long the favourite of his indulgent mother, and lingering still in the single state, he kicks his heels at Goodnestone Farm to the exasperation and expense of all his excellent family. Lizzy, at least, is anxious for her brother's prospects—and has declared that a taste for gaming and fast company will lead him to ruin e'er long.

Despite these storied charms, Mr. Bridges may support at least one claim to sobriety and good conduct—for he is ordained a clergyman in the Church of England, having taken Holy Orders some few years past. He is at present the fortunate beneficiary of two livings: perpetual curate of Goodnestone, which fell in his late father's gift; and very lately, rector of Orlingbury, a parish in Northamptonshire—and one he never visits. In this we may read the reverence of our age: Mr. Edward Bridges, determined Dandy and half-hearted curate!

But perhaps I am too severe. I am quick to detect a convenience, and call it hypocrisy, where another might divine only the usual way of the world.

"You have seen the Commodore, Uncle?" Fanny enquired of Mr. Bridges excitedly. "Is he mad to be off?"

Mr. Bridges then delighted us with the intelligence that the lamentable animal had spent a tolerable half-hour cooling down in his shed between heats; that he had been walked to admiration; and that the quality of his dung was said to be unassailable. Only the famed Eclipse himself could display a sweeter action.[6] A description of the Commodore's chief competitors—who must all be lame, spavined, or doltish in the extreme—then followed, to the delight of Fanny, who declared that Uncle Henry *must* be the champion of the day. Only Captain Woodford saw fit to ruin her hopes.

"I should agree with Mr. Bridges in everything excepting Mrs. Grey's little filly," he said. "In respect of Josephine, I cannot be sanguine. She is a fine-stepping goer, and over such a distance—a heat of two miles—might give the Commodore a fair run for the plate. We shall have some excellent sport when the horn is blown. But enough of racing! You look very well this morning, Mrs. Austen—and your sister might be Diana the Huntress herself, established over the picnic hamper in that becoming habit."

---

[6] Eclipse, a chestnut horse with a white blaze and one white leg, was foaled for the Duke of Cumberland in Windsor Park in the year of the great eclipse: 1764. He was one of the greatest racehorses of all time, and his bloodline is arguably the most important male line in the world of horse racing.—*Editor's note.*

I blushed, for my riding dress was a cast-off of Lizzy's made over to suit myself, and I feared the truth might be blurted out by Fanny, to the mortification of us all. It *is* a lovely summer thing of lilac muslin, with a high collar and scalloped sleeves ending just at the elbow; the train is fashioned long for the accommodation of a lady's posture when riding sidesaddle, a sad encumbrance in the present confines of the barouche, and I am sure that Fanny has trampled it on several occasions at least. My hair had been cut and arranged for Race Week by Mr. Hall, Lizzy's modish London hairdresser, who has been resident at Godmersham for over a fortnight. I had thus abandoned my usual cap, and wore a dashing lilac top hat tied round with a sheer green silk scarf. However cast off by my brother's fortunate wife, the *ensemble* was ravishing; and I felt distinctly elevated in my borrowed feathers. I shall not know how to bear the deprivation when once I am returned to Bath.

"Do not flatter me, Captain Woodford," I managed, "or like Diana I shall prove the ruin of masculine ardour."

"I await your worst, madam," he replied, with an inclination of the head, "for it cannot be more severe than Buonaparte's cannon—and I have steeled myself to *those*, you know, these two years and more."

"Perhaps we should establish Miss Austen at the headlands at Deal," Edward Bridges suggested, "with a sword in one hand and a martial light in her eye, the better to forestall invasion—for a whole company of French cavalry could hardly ignore such loveliness. It must halt them in their tracks, and preserve the nation inviolate."

At my failure to reply, Mr. Bridges threw out his most engaging smile. "I might rescue you then in a dashing manner, my dear Miss Austen, and the both of us be celebrated throughout the country."

The determined silliness of these remarks was entirely in keeping with Mr. Bridges's character; but I adopted a tragic air, as befit a noble heroine. "Not even the prospect of rescue by yourself, sir, shall be deemed too great a sacrifice for my country. But tell me: How does my dearest sister in your wretched hands?"

"Miss Cassandra Austen, when last I had the pleasure of meeting her over the breakfast table, was in excellent looks—tho' entirely cast down at the loss of this race-meeting. She was to remain at the Farm, you know, in attendance upon my sister Harriot, who cannot abide horses in any guise. I offered to smuggle Cassandra out of the house in my curricle, but she affected the vapours at the mere notion of such a scheme, and quitted the breakfast parlour directly."

I could not suppress a laugh at this telling picture.

"You are in wine again, Edward, I am sure of it," Lizzy said in mock exasperation. "Have you led him astray, Captain Woodford?"

"I? Astray? Quite the reverse, I assure you."

"Mamma! Mamma! Only look—there is Mrs. Grey!"

The Commodore momentarily forgotten, Fanny had jumped up from her seat and was craning for a view of the rail.

"Sit *down*, Fanny," Miss Sharpe whispered shrilly, with one hand on her charge's sash. "You will make of yourself a spectacle, child."

"Do observe, Mamma," Fanny persisted, "she has gone quite forward in all the bustle, and intends to o'erlook the race. There is her scarlet habit, not far from Papa and my uncle."

I followed my niece's outflung arm and saw again the dashing figure, late of the perch phaeton. Mrs. Grey had abandoned her equipage and secured a place of advantage quite close to the rail. She was mounted, as though she meant to follow the heat on horseback.[7] Extraordinary! She should be the only lady in the midst of the crush, and exposed to every sort of coarse behaviour—for a race-meeting is hardly the most select, being at liberty to the common labourer as readily as a lord.

But at least she displayed a little sense, in adopting a veil, the better to shield her countenance from the impertinent. Or perhaps the better to invite their gaze—for the black illusion netting, however suited to the disguise of her features, hung jauntily enough from the tricorn hat. Hers was a tall, womanly figure astride the mettlesome beast—the jet-black gelding I had last seen tied to the phaeton. However unseemly her behaviour, however determined her flaunting of convention, I could not fail to admire Mrs. Grey. And pity her, too. Such an one must be *very* rich, indeed—or very unhappy. Only the most extreme sense of liberty, or the utter depths of misery, could give spur to the sort of recklessness she displayed.

"Come, Mr. Bridges," Captain Woodford said, "we must bid the ladies *adieu*, or be denied our place at the rail."

These words had scarce fallen from his lips, when the blowing of a horn announced the horses arrived at the starter's mark, and a murmur of expectation arose from the assembled throng. Mr. Bridges surged forward towards the rail, Captain Woodford in pursuit; Fanny clambered onto the barouche box next to the coachman, Pratt; and even Lizzy gained something in animation.

[7] It was customary in Austen's time for spectators to gallop alongside the competing horses in the final lengths of a race. Though commonplace, the practise was highly dangerous and often led to mishap—either for the mounted spectator or the racehorses themselves, more than one of whom was denied a victory by the interference of an overzealous fan.—*Editor's note.*

"They are off!" Fanny cried, "but I can see nothing—only a sea of hats, and the flash of horses' heads. Oh, you darling Commodore!"

Despite myself, I caught something of the clamour of the moment, and rose to my feet, swaying slightly with the springs of the coach and Fanny's determined energy. A cloud of dust, turned gold in the August sun, announced the vanguard of the horses—they were fast upon our portion of the rail, and I thought that even my disinterested gaze might discern the Commodore's narrow Arab head vying for pride of place with a bay mare. Then, in a flash of scarlet, Mrs. Grey leapt the rail on her fleet black horse.

A cry of "Mrs. Grey!" and "Huzzah!" seemed to break from an hundred throats, and that suddenly, every man in possession of a mount had thrust his way onto the course behind the lady. Like a company of mounted cavalry, top hats blown backwards by the wind, they pounded in the wake of the racing pack—and disappeared around the course's bend.

"Good God!" ejaculated Miss Sharpe.

I turned from the course to see the governess pale and trembling, her hazel eyes fixed on the dust-clouded rail. Presumably she was unaccustomed to such exploits.

"More than one unfortunate shall be unhorsed, Miss Sharpe, depend upon it," I told her. "But do not trouble yourself on a fool's account. They are all very nearly insensible with drink, and shall not mind the bruising."

"Mrs. Grey shall keep her seat, never fear," said Lizzy drily. "She will be safely home and established upon a sofa before the half of them have circled the field."

But Miss Sharpe seemed not to have attended to either of us. Her gaze was still fixed on the course, where the distant splash of scarlet proclaimed the sole woman at the head of the cavalcade. To discern much else was impossible; the Commodore, Josephine, and their competitors in the heat, were swallowed entire in a cloud of dust.

"Are you quite well, Miss Sharpe?" I enquired gently. "You have grown too pale. Perhaps the heat has overcome you. It is well that we are very near to ending so tiresome an amusement—I am sure we should all prefer to be at home."

She sank back down into her seat, and drew a kerchief from her reticule. "Forgive me. A trifling unsteadiness . . ."

The unmounted spectators, like my brothers, had commenced to run along the rail in pursuit of the pack; an idiot's errand, for the pack itself had very soon rounded the final bend of the course, and was bearing down upon the starter's mark. Our heads turned as one— the pounding of hooves announced the approaching triumph—and the bay mare Josephine swept foaming across the finish, with the Commodore hard on her heels.

"Ohhh!" cried Fanny in disappointment.

"Thank God it is over at last," murmured her mother.

And from the trembling Miss Sharpe, came something like a sob.

IT WAS A CHASTENED AND DESPONDENT HENRY WHO rejoined the Godmersham party a half-hour later.

"I am sure that some great mischief has befallen the poor beast." He sagged against the seat cushions and accepted a glass of ginger beer. "He looked off in the near hind. Perhaps the weights—"

"He looked off for the duration of the heat, my dear brother," said Neddie sourly. He was quite winded, and much put out at the devil's chase he had run. "Although I confess my position was too poor to permit of a good view. We should better have gone mounted, like Mrs. Grey."

As tho' conjured by my brother's thought, the figure in scarlet pranced into view near the stylish perch phaeton. She dismounted with a flourish, and thrust the reins at her tyger. Behind her, at a discreet pace, advanced the filly Josephine and her jockey—both looking whipped by the very hounds of Hell, as perhaps they had been. It cannot be comfortable or easy to race in a determined heat, with most of Kent at one's heels.

Mrs. Grey tossed a beautiful gold plate—Canterbury's Race Week prize—into the perch phaeton, with as much disregard as tho' it were a pair of old shoes. She handed a small leather coin pouch to the jockey, and reached a gloved hand to pat the filly's lathered flank. Then, with an insouciance possible only for one who moves under an hundred eyes, she stepped into her carriage, took up the reins, and snapped them smartly over the matched greys' necks. Several of the watching gentlemen cheered. The tyger touched his cap as she turned, his expression wooden; then he and the jockey led their mounts slowly through the milling crowd, in the direction of the stableyard.

"What did I tell you?" Lizzy said languidly. "She shall be established on her sofa while the rest of us are still trapped on the Canterbury road. Detestable woman."

"Do not speak of her, pray." Henry took a long draught. "My dear Eliza will have it that there is nothing like a Frenchwoman for winning, you know—and I declare I begin to be of her opinion. Did you see that grey-eyed jade, Neddie, spurring her mount for all she was worth?"

"I believe Mrs. Grey's eyes to be brown, Henry," my brother absently replied.

"Grey—brown—but upon my word, the Furies ain't in it! I might almost believe her to have cursed the Commodore as he rounded the rail. She has quite the look of the witch about her, however much she affects a veil."

"Now, Henry." I patted his hand. "Let us have no conduct unbecoming to a gentleman. You are to be an example for the children, in this as in so many things. Your disappointment may serve as a cautionary chapter in the annals of the Sporting Life. I see the illustration now, in my mind's eye: A Gentleman Unbowed by the Vagaries of Fortune."

"—However driven upon the poorhouse," he muttered, unreconciled.

"The poorhouse!" I smiled at him conspiratorially, and dropped my voice to a whisper. "Then take comfort, Henry. You shall not travel there alone. The excellent Mr. Bridges is to cheer your solitude, for he named the Commodore as the salvation of all his hopes."

"Am I then to encompass others in my ruin?" Henry groaned in mock despair. "The reproaches that shall be mine! And how am I to face Lady Bridges, his redoubtable mother? I suppose we may expect the unfortunate curate to wait upon us at Godmersham before the day is out?"

"He had better wait upon Mrs. Grey," said Neddie, who had caught something of our conversation. "She is undoubtedly more amenable to charity at present."

"A debt of honour is a debt of honour." Lizzy picked desultorily at the points of her gloves. "No lady would forgive what a gentleman would exact; it does violence to the equality of the sexes."

"You have been reading that wretched Wollstonecraft again," my brother said in exasperation. "I shall burn the volume tonight."[8]

---

[8] Edward refers to *A Vindication of the Rights of Woman*, by Mary Wollstonecraft, first published in 1792. Elizabeth Austen was educated at an excellent finishing school in London, known as "the Ladies' Eton." It may be there that she fostered her interest in women's issues. In 1808, she signed her name in a work written by the radical London feminist Mary Hays.—*Editor's note.*

"May we leave now, Papa?" Fanny implored. "I am most dreadfully hungry."

"Hungry!" Neddie searched in the depths of the picnic hamper. "And not a scrap of jellied chicken left for your fainting father? Scamp!" He pinched his favourite's dimpled cheek. "We shall take to the road directly I secure a draught of ale, Fanny. I have a thirst upon me that would parch the Stour itself."

And so he moved off, intent upon a tankard. Most of the gentlemen of the neighbourhood were roving about the meeting-grounds, exchanging tales of woe or victory; some had placed their money on Mrs. Grey's filly, others on Henry's horse, still others on one of the mounts deep in the pack, who had fared no better than the Commodore. A great deal of hearty laughter and slapping of backs ensued, for which I had little temper; I was fatigued and overheated myself, and longing to be out of my ravishing lilac habit.

"There is my brother Edward," Lizzy observed, "looking bound for the gallows before sunset. You have much to answer for, Henry; I am not sure I should admit you to Godmersham this e'en! Look at the poor fellow—so chapfallen and mumchance! Were it not for the support of Captain Woodford's arm, I doubt he could place one foot before the other!"

And, indeed, Mr. Bridges looked very unwell. His countenance was flushed, his fashionable coiffure disarranged, and his cravat askew. He clutched at his head—which ached, no doubt, from an unfortunate blend of spirits and wine—and muttered indistinguishable words in Captain Woodford's ear. A glance for his sister, and it seemed as tho' he might approach our barouche—until a third man came up with him suddenly, and tore at Mr. Bridges's arm. He was a burly gentleman, with sweeping whiskers and a raffish air; a gentleman I knew of old. Denys Collingforth, of slim means and illiberal temper, who was held in general disfavour by the whole neighbourhood. We should have seen much of the Collingforths, had they proved more genteel, for they lived but a few miles from Godmersham, at Prior's Farm. He was fond of using his fists at the slightest provocation, and was even said to have struck his wife—the unfortunate Laetitia, whose carriage Mrs. Grey had entered only an hour or so before.

I had seen Denys Collingforth in more than one unsavoury moment, during my many sojourns in Kent; and his present appearance argued the immediate precipitation of another. He twisted the sleeve of Mr. Bridges's elegant coat, all choler and ill-humour in a single motion.

The curate gasped, and attempted to shake him off; but he succeeded only in securing both of Mr. Collingforth's hands firmly about his lapels. The gallant Captain Woodford attempted to intervene—and was thrust heavily to one side.

"Lizzy!" I half-rose from my seat. "What *can* Mr. Collingforth mean by such behaviour?"

Her elegant head came swiftly round, and caught the scene at a glance. "Contemptible blackguard," she spat out, "he will draw Edward's cork in a moment."

Not only the children had proved susceptible to Henry's fighting cant.

And draw Mr. Bridges's cork, Collingforth did. A wide, swinging arc of his fist, and the curate fell backwards, blood spurting from his nose. Captain Woodford fell on his adversary immediately, and the three disappeared in a whirling knot of flailing limbs and brightly-coloured breeches. In a moment, however, Neddie had perceived the difficulty—he and Henry raced to the aid of their friends, along with half a dozen others who had no cause to love Collingforth; and the bully was deftly wrenched from the melee.

Muttering an oath, he retired to nurse his wounds. A man I did not recognise—I suppose I may call him a gentleman—threw an arm about his shoulders and said something softly into his ear. The newcomer was dressed all in black, and wore an expression of contempt on his countenance; but his words seemed to calm his friend.

"There'll be the Devil to pay," Collingforth shouted at Mr. Bridges's dusty back; and then shaking his fist, he moved off through the crowd towards his shabby black chaise.

If his wife was within, she did not dare to show her face.

"Well, Lizzy," my brother said as he pulled himself into the barouche, "I believe it is time we turned towards home. This meeting is become almost a brawl, and I will not have Fanny treated to such scenes."

Lizzy's answer, did she contemplate one, was forestalled by a fearful cry. It was a man's voice, torn with suffering and revulsion, as though he looked upon the face of evil and knew it for his own. It came from somewhere behind us.

I turned, aghast, to enquire of Neddie, and saw my own confusion mirrored in my brother's countenance. And then our entire party was on its feet, and the gentlemen had sprung from the barouche, all fatigue and acrimony forgotten. A crowd had gathered at the open door of Collingforth's chaise. I looked, and then turned swiftly to gather Fanny to my breast. Death is not a sight for the young, however sporting-minded.

For spilling from the carriage doorway, arms outflung in supplication, was the figure of a woman. Her streaming hair was dark, her eyes were staring, and tho' the veil and scarlet habit had been torn from her body, leaving her pale and child-like in a simple cotton shift, I knew her instantly for Mrs. Grey.

And knew, with a chill at my heart, that she would never ride again.

# Chapter 2

## *An Act of War*

"GOOD GOD! MRS. GREY, IN COLLINGFORTH'S CHAISE." Neddie threw his elegant top hat into our barouche, and hastened towards the gruesome scene. Henry was hard on his heels.

"Mamma!" Fanny slipped from my grasp. "What has happened to Mrs. Grey? And why is she lying so, in her shift? Does she suffer from a fit?"

Mrs. Grey's face was contorted, her lips thrust apart, and her tongue protuberant; around her neck was a length of red ribbon, such as once must have bound up her long black hair. She had certainly been strangled with it. To gaze upon her was terrible—so much beauty turned horrible in an instant, and utterly beyond salvation.

With a choked cry from the seat opposite, Anne Sharpe fainted dead away.

"Sit *down*, Fanny." Lizzy clutched at her daughter's sash and tugged on it firmly. "If anyone is suffering from a fit, it is your governess, child—and who can wonder, with a charge so troublesome as yourself? Endeavour to behave with a little decorum, while Aunt Jane secures Miss Sharpe's vinaigrette."

I had already scrambled about the carriage in search of such an item, and found it at last in a little travelling case of Fanny's, tricked out with such necessaries as a lady might require. Extra handkerchiefs, a roll of sticking plaster, tiny scissors, and a packet of threaded needles—and, joy of joys, the crystal flacon filled with smelling salts. I waved it under the governess's nose, and watched her snort like Henry's champion.

Fanny was all concern in a moment, and hovered over Miss Sharpe like a little mother; the governess looked quite ill, indeed, but protested that she was entirely well, and struggled to sit upright with something like her usual composure. She accepted a glass of tepid cordial, but kept her face studiously averted from the Collingforth chaise.

For my part, I felt no compunction in regarding the interesting scene unfolding to the rear. My brother had not leapt to the dead woman's side merely from an excess of chivalry—no, in the present instance, such a mark of active concern was absolutely required. The Lord Lieutenant of Kent himself had appointed my brother Justice of the Peace—a capacity in which Neddie had served barely six months. It was an honour without recompense (for gentlemen are never offered the insult of remuneration, as a more common magistrate in Town might be), and tedious in its general description, but quite suited to a man of Neddie's talents and inclination. For tho' my brother has assumed the polish of Fashion—tho' he has moved in the best circles from the age of sixteen, made the Grand Tour with unimpeachable grace, and imbibed all the follies, indulgences, and vices of Society as mother's milk—he was nonetheless reared in a country parsonage, by a father whose chief values lay in application and industry. Possessed now of great estates—and stewards to manage them; of numerous children—and phalanxes of servants, Neddie should decline into peevishness and indolence, without the care of public office as diversion.

And watching him as he knelt over the body of Mrs. Grey, I felt a familiar chill at my heart. I had witnessed such scenes too many times before. For a moment, I might have joined Miss Sharpe, in averting my eyes; but another instant's reflection steeled my resolve. However unpleasant the evil might be, it should encompass all our family; and I could not refuse to help my brother, whom so many occasions had proved so generous to myself. Neddie's superior knowledge of the world, and easy passage among the Great, had used to comfort his shy little sisters; now, it was he who should enter a strange and bewildering land, and *I* who must walk along familiar paths.

The varied experiences of the past several years have opened a new world entire to my understanding; I have endured and survived encounters with a most unscrupulous body of men, without loss of dignity or a very great diminution of reputation; and I could not but be aware now that Neddie's role in the present drama must afford me a greater knowledge of the particulars, than I had heretofore been able to command. It is not that I am prone to a morbid curiosity, or find enchantment and delight in the manifestation of evil, but rather that the power of laying plain a convoluted puzzle—to the greater good of some unfortunate, and the generalised comfort of Society—must have its very great satisfaction. I have not yet learned to despise my curiosity, for all my mother's anxious urging, or the perils of dubious association it brings inevitably in its train. It has been my privilege (tho' some would call it misfortune) to have the unravelling of a few very tiresome knots in the recent past; and in the present instance of Neddie's need, my talents might prove of use.

"What are we to do, Jane?" Lizzy whispered, "for we should not prolong Fanny's exposure to such a dreadful scene. And yet Neddie—"

"—*must* remain," I agreed. "A Justice is required to think of others before his family."

"But, Mamma, how very odd she looks, to be sure!" Fanny stared fascinated at the spectacle near the coach, now virtually obscured by a crowd of the curious. Another instant, and she had mounted to her favourite perch on the box next to Pratt, with the object of gaining a better view.

"Come down at once, Miss Fanny!" Anne Sharpe exclaimed, and took a decided grip on her charge's ankles.

"Perhaps Miss Sharpe and Fanny might pay a visit to the stables," I murmured to Lizzy. "It is not above five minutes' walk, and they could enquire after the Commodore. That should divert Fanny's interest."

Lizzy shook her head decisively. "An admirable notion, Jane, but for the murderer we have loose in the grounds!"

"Murderer?" Fanny slid abruptly back into her seat. "But is Mrs. Grey *murdered* then, Mamma?"

Lizzy gathered her eldest into her arms. "I fear that the lady is dead, my Fanny, but how she came to be so, I cannot say. I should not have spoken until Papa had come to us. Depend upon it, your father shall very soon apprehend the whole."

Fanny's eyes might widen at this speech, and her breath come short; but to her credit, the child evinced a tolerable composure. She neither shrieked, nor fell insensible, nor shuddered as with a dreadful presentiment (as might betray an enthusiast of horrid novels), but turned her soft blue eyes upon her governess and said, "Poor Sharpie. I know you have not the stomach for such things—you were taken quite ill when Caky killed a rat once in the nursery.[1] But then, it *did* squeal most horribly under the poker and tongs, and you *are* a little goose, are you not?" She patted Miss Sharpe's hand. "I cannot think that Mrs. Grey, however dead, was the sort to squeal. And do consider, Sharpie, that my father must presently relieve our fears."

Miss Sharpe kissed Fanny's flushed cheek, and very sensibly produced her chapbook, a serviceable volume in which she has been collecting riddles throughout the summer. The scheme was devised entirely for Fanny's amusement; and in a very little while the two were lost in a familiar exchange, and the danger of hysterics was safely past.

A cicada's trill burst wildly from the copse at the meeting-grounds' fringe—a sudden, sharp keening—and the heat, at the moment, was as oppressive as a lap robe.

"Pray look after the child, Miss Sharpe," Lizzy said abruptly. "Jane and I must speak to Mr. Austen." And with a word to one of the liveried footmen, who had been staring impassively into the middle distance all this while, she was assisted out of the barouche. Immediately I followed.

A knot of men, high-born and low, had gathered tightly around my brothers and the Collingforth chaise. With a tap of her parasol on a broad shoulder, Lizzy won her way to the centre, where Denys Collingforth was held firmly in the grip of two of his neighbours.

---

[1] "Caky" was the nickname Edward Austen's children bestowed on their nurse, Susannah Sackree, who was employed at Godmersham for over six decades. She often served as Jane Austen's personal maid when Jane was resident at Godmersham; she is buried at St. Nicolas's, the old Norman church just south of Godmersham Park, where Edward and Elizabeth Austen Knight are also entombed.—*Editor's note.*

"I tell you, I know nothing!" he spat out. "The jade would no more speak to me this morning than she'd look at a cur in the mud. Too fine for Denys Collingforth, and not above saying it to the world. I never came near her, nor she near me!"

"Then how do you explain, Mr. Collingforth, that she entered your chaise just prior to the final heat?" Lizzy broke in smoothly. "My sister and I observed it ourselves."

The gentleman's mouth fell open, and the colour drained from his face. "Impossible!" he cried. "I was absent from the blasted carriage the better part of the day! Everett will vouch for me—and an hundred others!"

"Where is Mr. Everett?" Neddie cried, with a look of interest for his wife.

The stranger dressed in black, who had supported Collingforth in his dispute with Mr. Bridges, shouldered his way through the crowd. "I am Joshua Everett."

"Are you acquainted with this man?"

"I am. He is Denys Collingforth, of Prior's Farm."

"And did you bear him company at any time this morning?"

"For the entirety of it, sir. We breakfasted at eight, drove out to the meeting-grounds and secured our place, and left a boy to look after the horses."

"That would have been at what hour?" Neddie pressed.

Mr. Everett shrugged, and looked to Collingforth for corroboration. "Ten, perhaps?"

"Half-past. You forget the tankard of ale we drank along the road."

"Half-past," Neddie said, as tho' he possessed a mental ledger of Collingforth's doings. "And then, Mr. Everett?"

"Then we walked about the grounds, gave a look

to the horses, placed some bets with a few gentlemen among our acquaintance—and took up a position near the cocking ring."

"I saw them there," a voice called from the crowd.

"And I," said another.

Neddie nodded swiftly at my brother Henry, who went in search of Collingforth's acquaintance.

"All that would have been prior to the heats themselves, Collingforth."

"Yes. I watched *those* at the rail."

"Your wife did not accompany you this morning?"

"Mrs. Collingforth is indisposed. And with Everett up from Town—"

"I see. And so you insist that there was no one within the chaise when this lady observed Mrs. Grey to enter it?"

"I tell you, Austen, I never returned to the coach until the moment I pulled open this door!" The desperate man glanced with revulsion at Mrs. Grey's rigid countenance. She lay, partly covered with a borrowed shawl, a few feet from my brother, as tho' resting under his protection. "Can not you fetch a surgeon, and close the woman's eyes? How she stares at us all! 'Tis hardly decent!"

"Is there a surgeon present?" Neddie called harshly over the ring of faces.

Muttering, and a jostling to the rear; then a short, round-faced man with a bald pate appeared, bowing to left and right. "Tobias Wood," he said, "at your service, Mr. Justice, sir."

"Very well, Mr. Wood. We shall require your assistance by and by, in removing the corpse to Canterbury. Perhaps for the present, it would suffice to close her eyes."

This Mr. Wood did, with a gentleness of purpose that must relieve the hearts of many.

"Madam," my brother said to his wife with punctilious

courtesy, "you have said that you observed Mrs. Grey to enter Mr. Collingforth's chaise just before the final heat. That would be—" He consulted his watch, and glanced at Henry.

"—sometime before two o'clock," Henry supplied. "I recollect the hour, because it was the Commodore's last race."

"I should put Mrs. Grey's approach to the carriage rather closer to half-past one," Lizzy said clearly. "But you know it makes no odds, Neddie, because Mrs. Grey was certainly alive when the heat was run. We all saw her riding her black at the head of the pack, and afterwards she drove her phaeton out of the grounds. I merely raised the point because Mr. Collingforth seems to have forgot the earlier visit."

"I know nothing of any visit!" he shouted; and a vein in his neck pulsed dangerously. One of his captors lost his grip on the man, and Lizzy stepped backwards as the right arm swung free.

"I perfectly apprehend your reasons for raising the point," Neddie said politely to his wife, as tho' he presided over a ruling in a parlour game. "Did Mrs. Grey knock upon the chaise's door?"

"She did. It opened immediately to admit her."

"So there was someone within?"

"I must assume so. I did not glimpse the face."

"Miss Austen?" Neddie enquired formally of me.

I shook my head in the negative.

"Mr. Collingforth," he continued, "what of the boy you engaged to stand watch over the carriage?"

"Ran off to spend his coin, I must suppose. Such things have occurred before."

"Will the young man engaged by Mr. Collingforth come forward now and tell his story?" Neddie cried.

This time, there was no movement to the rear of

the crowd. Neddie repeated his words, to no avail; and Collingforth looked blackly at his friend Everett. The latter's countenance was as contemptuous as before.

Neddie mopped his reddening brow with a square of lawn and turned once more to the unfortunate gentleman. "Can you offer any explanation for Mrs. Grey's visit to your carriage, Collingforth?"

"I cannot. And as your good lady says, Mr. Justice, it makes no odds. The jade lived to win her race, and carry her plate from the field. How she came to end up here, and in such a state, I cannot say. But I suggest you enquire of the parson, Mr. Bridges, and his fine military friend. Ask them why *they* might have wanted the French trollop dead, and I'm sure you'll hear an earful."

Beside me, Lizzy's fingers clenched about the pearl handle of her parasol, and her green eyes drifted languidly over the assembled faces. Searching for her brother, perhaps, with the barest hint of anxiety.

"You have a marked proclivity for abuse, Collingforth, that you would do well to suppress," Neddie said warningly. "The lady is *Mrs. Grey*, whatever your opinion of her; and I would request that you show some respect of the dead."

Collingforth shot a look full of hatred at the corpse, and I shuddered to observe it. However Mrs. Grey had charmed the gentlemen of Kent, this one had not been among their number.

"Did you invite her to the chaise, Collingforth, and fail to keep your appointment?"

"I did nothing of the kind. I'm a respectable married man."

Someone in the crowd guffawed loudly, and Collingforth cast a bloodshot gaze over the assembled faces. "I'll demand satisfaction of the next man who offers disrespect."

"What about Mrs. Grey?" someone called. "You call what you did to her 'respect'? Where's her habit, Collingforth? You keep it to give to your wife?"

"Silence!" Neddie shouted, in a tone I had never before heard him employ. "I require a fast horse and rider for Canterbury! There's a gold sovereign for the lad who makes the journey in under an hour!"

"I'm your man," cried a fellow in a nankeen coat; one of the stable boys, no doubt.

"Ride like the wind to the constabulary," Neddie instructed him, "and send back a party of men. We will require any number. Where is Mrs. Grey's groom or tyger?"

"Mrs. Grey's tyger!" The cry went up, and was repeated through the swelling ranks; and after an interval, the boy with the bent back was rousted from the stableyard, with the Greys' jockey in tow.

The tyger stopped short at the sight of his mistress, and gave a strangled cry. Then he looked blindly about the ring of men, his fists clenched; saw Collingforth still pinioned; and rushed at him, flailing and pummelling. "Why'd you want to do it, you coward? Why'd you want to go and kill 'er for? She wanted none o' your kind! You couldn't leave 'er in peace!"

Neddie grasped the boy's shoulders and pulled him away. "What is your name, boy?"

"Tom," he said. "Tom Jenkins."

"Why did your mistress leave you behind?"

"She asked me to walk La Flèche back home. Crandall, 'ere, was to walk the filly."

Very white about the lips, the jockey touched his cap.

"La Flèche?" Neddie enquired.

"The black 'un, what she rode in the heat."

"I see. And what road did she intend to take?"

"Why, the road to Wingham, o' course. The Larches lies just this side o' Wingham."

Neddie glanced around him. "Henry! Have you a fresh horse?"

"Of course." My brothers had gone mounted to the race grounds well before our party in the barouche, being eager to see the Commodore into his stall, and survey the course. We had joined them some hours later.

"Then set out immediately along the Wingham road. Mrs. Grey's phaeton must be found, and secured from injury. Ten to one it has been stolen—" He stopped, perplexed. The unspoken question hovered in the air: How had Mrs. Grey come to lie in Collingforth's chaise, quite devoid of her scarlet habit, when we had all observed her to drive out of the grounds a half-hour before? And if she had met with mishap along the road, and her phaeton been stolen—why was her body not lying beneath a hedgerow?

"I shall send a constable towards Wingham immediately I have one," Neddie continued, "but until he arrives, Henry, I beg of you, do not stir from The Larches. If you happen upon the phaeton by some lucky chance, remain with it until the constable appears. Now, Tom!"

"Yes, sir?" The tyger dashed away his tears and endeavoured to stand the straighter.

"Is the black horse in any state for a jog?"

"As fresh as tho' he never was out, sir."

"Very well. You and your colleague—Crandall, is it?—shall bear Mr. Austen company along the Wingham road. If the phaeton is discovered, leave Mr. Austen in custody and proceed to The Larches. Inform the household of what has befallen your mistress. Is that clear?"

"As glass, sir."

"Your master is from home, I presume?"

"He's in London, like always."

"Then a messenger must be sent to him with the news. The housekeeper will look to it."

"Like as not she'll send me," the jockey volunteered. "I usually knows where the master can be found."

Tom glanced at his murdered mistress, who lay so still amidst the dust and the singing cicadas. "What about milady?"

"We shall convey her to Canterbury," Neddie answered gently, and clapped the boy's shoulder. "She must lie for a while at the Hound and Tooth, for there will be an inquest."

"Inquest? But that rogue as did for 'er is standing 'ere, large as life!" the boy spat out, and his fists clenched again. "If I'd been with 'er, as I shoulda been, you wouldn't be looking so easy, Mr. Collingforth, sir!"

"Hold your tongue, Tom," Neddie said sharply. "This is not the time or place for harsh words. The coroner will determine Mr. Collingforth's guilt. You must tell the housekeeper where Mrs. Grey lies—the Hound and Tooth, in Canterbury."

"I'll tell 'em everything," he replied, his face crumpling once more. "They'll want to come and see to 'er."

"I'm afraid that will have to wait until after the coroner has examined the corpse. Now off with you both to the stables!" Neddie's voice was stern—a palpable support, at such a time. "You have a duty that cannot wait."

"Aye, sir." The tyger touched his cap, the jockey bowed, and away they dashed without another word.

"Neddie," Lizzy murmured in his ear, "I cannot like Fanny's situation. Miss Sharpe, too, is most indisposed."

"I shall send you back to Godmersham with Pratt."

"Not until the constabulary arrives," Lizzy replied firmly. "I will not quit the scene until I know how things stand with Mr. Collingforth. I am in part responsible for his discomfiture, but I thought it necessary to speak."

"Undoubtedly. You did well. Jane!"

"Yes, Neddie?" I joined them in a moment.

"I should dearly love another pair of eyes. If you and Lizzy would return to the coach, and from that vantage survey the crowd for anything untoward—the slightest detail that might seem amiss—it should be as gold."

"With alacrity," I said, and slipped my hand through Lizzy's arm.

"And now, Mr. Collingforth," Neddie said, as we turned away, "I must ask leave to search your chaise. Stand aside, Mr. Everett!"

"WHAT A CURIOUS LIGHT THIS SHEDS UPON ONE'S NEIGH-bours, to be sure." Lizzy sighed, as her green eyes roved intently over the equipages drawn up helter-skelter near our own. "There is Mr. Hayes, bustling all his party into a closed carriage, and intent upon his return to Ashford. *He* will not stay a moment, even in respect of the dead— the chance at seizing a clear road before his fellows is too tempting to be missed. Lady Elizabeth Finch-Hatton is pretending to an indisposition. See her there, with her kerchief over her face? I suppose I brought on a fit, by descending from my barouche and approaching the corpse. What a comfort that we need not be so nice, when Lady Elizabeth is on display!"

"I admired your activity, Mrs. Austen," Miss Sharpe said suddenly. "I wished that I might imitate it. That dreadful man required an answer!"

"You observed the lady to enter his chaise as well?"

"Yes," the governess replied, her eyes averted, "but I did not remark her leaving it. I cannot recollect the slightest instance of her passing, in fact, until the mo-ment that little Fanny espied her at the rail—mounted on the black horse, and at the very moment of joining the fray. I shall not soon forget *that*!"

"Nor any of the day's events, I am sure," Lizzy re-plied. "It is quite an introduction, Miss Sharpe, to the elegant delights of Canterbury Race Week. I am sure your friends the Portermans will be appalled, when they hear of it, and shall request your immediate return to London."

Anne Sharpe glanced up at her mistress swiftly, then dropped her eyes once more to the little chapbook.

"I cannot tell the answer to your riddle, Sharpie," said Fanny fretfully, "and I am very hot and tired. When will Papa be done?"

"In a little while, my dear," her mother said, "in but a very little while. Lay your head upon my lap, if you choose, and endeavour to sleep."

While my sister smoothed her daughter's curls, I surveyed the milling crowd.[2] Several of the parties had no intention of awaiting the constabulary, as Lizzy had said. A clutch of horses and harness clogged the gates of the meeting-grounds, and it should be hours, perhaps, before the turf was cleared.

"Tell me of Mr. Collingforth, Lizzy," I said softly.

"Collingforth? He is of no very great account, I assure you. Nothing to do with the Suffolk family, you know—a lateral heir, in the maternal line, who took the name upon his accession to the property."

"Yes, yes—but what sort of character does he possess? Is he the sort of man to conceal a fresh corpse in his carriage?"

"I cannot fathom why *any* man should do so, Jane," Lizzy retorted in exasperation, "much less contrive to discover it himself. Either he is very simple, or very devious, indeed—and my mind at present is divided between the two."

"He seems to hate Mrs. Grey."

---

[2]  It was common in Austen's day to refer to relations by marriage as though they were relations of blood. Although the term *in-law* existed, it was frequently used to describe step relations. —*Editor's note.*

She smiled mirthlessly. "Love often turns to hate, I believe—particularly when it is formed of obsessive passion. Six months ago, perhaps, Mr. Collingforth was very much in Mrs. Grey's pocket. But she tired of him, as she does of so many, and sent him on his way."

"And the affair was countenanced by Society?" I enquired.

"Society, as you would style it, took no notice of either Mrs. Grey or Collingforth. Whatever their form of intimacy, it was quite without the pale of Canterbury fashion. Only Lady Forbes—the wife of the commanding General of the Coldstream Guards—condescended to visit Mrs. Grey after her first weeks in Kent, once the measure of her style had been taken; and Lady Forbes is very young, and cannot be trusted to know any better."

"I see. You said she tired of any number of gentlemen. A motive, perhaps, for her brutal end?"

"Perhaps." Lizzy's slanting green eyes rounded upon me. "My brother must be considered one of them, Jane—Mrs. Grey had him quite wrapped around her little finger—and Captain Woodford, of course. He has been intimate from boyhood with Mr. Valentine Grey, and has frequently called at The Larches."

I glanced at Miss Sharpe's sleek, dark head; her eyes were closed, and she appeared to be dozing. I lowered my voice all the same. "You heard what Mr. Collingforth said of your brother?"

"In company with most of Kent. I wonder where the blackguard has got to? I would dearly love to know what Collingforth meant by accosting him in that fashion, just before the body was discovered. There is something ugly between them, and Woodford, too, if I am any judge of appearances; and such things are so tiresome when they are thrown in the public eye. How I long to shake brother Edward until his teeth rattle in his head!"

Our interesting discourse was broken at that moment

by the arrival of the Canterbury constabulary, come at a gallop, it seemed, from town. They brought in their train a waggon draped in black; I knew it at once for a makeshift hearse.

Neddie strode to meet them; consulted, for a moment, with the man who seemed to be their principal; and this last commenced to bark out orders, dispatching some of his fellows in one direction, and some in another. A few made immediately for the Collingforth chaise.

Mr. Wood, the surgeon, placed his arm under Mrs. Grey's neck, and raised her slightly from the ground. The constables gathered at waist and feet. Neddie looked on, his arms folded across his chest and a line of care etched between his brows. And then Mrs. Grey, her unbound black hair sweeping over the surgeon's arm, was carried slowly to the black-draped waggon. The tide of the curious parted like a guard of honour, and not a whisper or a sigh was heard, as the men struggled forward with their unhappy burden.

"I should like to go home, Pratt," Lizzy said quietly into the stillness. "Let us learn what Mr. Austen intends, and then seek the road without delay."

"Very good, ma'am," the coachman replied. He jumped from the box at once—as he had been longing to do for some time, I am sure—and sought out his master.

Neddie returned with Pratt in a moment.

"There is nothing more for you to do here, Lizzy," he said. "Return to Godmersham with our party, and order a cold supper for Henry and myself. We shall be upon the road some hours, I fear. I ride even now towards The Larches, in the hope that something has been discovered of the missing phaeton."

"Of course," she said dismissively. "Jane and I shall both sit up against your return. But, Neddie—"

"Yes?"

"Can not you tell us something of how Mrs. Grey died?"

"She was throttled with her own hair-ribbon."

"That much I had discerned. But the chaise! How did she come to be there?"

He shook his head. "I could find nothing within that might reveal her history. It is an ugly business—Mrs. Grey being what she is."

"A Frenchwoman?" I concluded.

He nodded. "The danger of her nationality alone should have counselled a greater propriety of behaviour at such a time—but she was never very restrained, as I am sure you observed, and that may have excited the hatred or jealousy of any number of men. I hope to know more once I have seen her husband; but that cannot be until tomorrow."

"You believe her killing an act of *war*, then?"

"In such times as these, with all of Kent in an uproar over the Monster's invasion, I cannot think it extraordinary. She must have been killed on the road, in a chance encounter, when she was quite alone and defenceless. But how she came to be in Collingforth's chaise—"

I gazed pensively at the constables' waggon and its tragic burden. Mr. Wood, the surgeon, had elected to attend the body, and was mounted on the box. Beside me, Miss Sharpe had completed the repacking of the picnic hamper, and Fanny was settled on the seat next to Lizzy. All around us the festive air of a race-meeting was fled, and a line of carriages lengthened towards the Canterbury road. The sedate assemblage of Kentish folk seemed the very last to harbour a political assassin; but other passions might be nearer at hand.

"Mrs. Grey possessed wealth, beauty, and spirit," I mused, "and each might be an insult to a certain sort of man. Or woman, for that matter—for I believe that few among her own sex dared to call her friend."

"And her end is not likely to improve her reputation," Neddie observed. "There is already too much scandal and talk. The disappearance of the lady's habit bears an ugly aspect. I would that her husband were not in Town."

"Unhappy gentleman! To receive such news, in so brutal a manner! No one can deserve such wretchedness."

"Nor such an end," Neddie added. "Tho' God knows Mrs. Grey made any number of enemies in the short time she was among us." He surveyed the tide of his departing neighbours with unwonted shrewdness. "I can think of several spurs to violence, Jane, in the lady's case. A man might wager his purse on the outcome of a meeting, and lose a fortune in the toss; or fancy himself crossed in love, and ready to avenge an injury."

Neddie slapped the barouche's side and nodded to Pratt. The coachman unwillingly lifted the reins.

"And must you charge Mr. Collingforth?" I asked hurriedly.

My brother hesitated, his grey eyes suddenly wary. "As to that—I cannot say, Jane. But I should be happy to canvass the matter at greater leisure, when once we are all together at Godmersham. Henry believes your advice is worth seeking; and I am not fool enough, I hope, to soldier on alone when good counsel is on offer. My experience has never run to murder. The duty *must* be a serious one. It *must* weigh heavily."

He kissed his wife's hand, smoothed Fanny's touseled curls, and then moved off through the thinning crowd towards the glowering Mr. Collingforth. The latter's dark-suited friend, Mr. Everett, had not deserted him; but little of comfort could be derived from so dour a companion. Further observation was denied me, for at that moment the horses started forward under Pratt's metic-

ulous hands, and we were sent back to Godmersham—
like all of Canterbury's ladies, preserved from further
intimacy with what was unpleasant.

In death, it seemed, Mrs. Grey had won what she preferred in life—the companionship of sporting men.

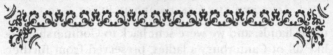

# Chapter 3

## The Unknown Cicisbeo

*19 August 1805, cont'd.*

~

FOR THE COMPLETION OF SEVEN MILES OF INDIFFERENT road to Godmersham, was required nearly two hours. Pratt will never allow the horses to travel at speed, from a horror of dust in an open carriage; and our progress in the present instance was decidedly impeded by the wealth of traffic on every side—most of it hastening from the race-meeting in equal perturbation of spirit. A happier party might have passed the journey in conversation, but Lizzy's thoughts were quite absent, Miss Sharpe's pallor was extreme, and Fanny was nodding in sleep before a quarter of the distance was achieved. We dawdled along between the high Kentish hedgerows while the sun declined into the hills, as silent as though our excellent Pratt conveyed an empty carriage.

From his unwillingness to address the subject, I believed it likely that my brother should arrest Mr. Denys Collingforth. In truth, I could not blame him; a shrewder man than Neddie would hesitate to discharge so obvious a malefactor. But I could not be easy in the determination of Collingforth's guilt. He was an unpalatable rogue, without question; he had spoken roughly of the murdered woman, and looked all his hate in his harsh features; and his carriage had borne the grisly burden of Mrs. Grey's corpse. But Collingforth should be a simpleton, indeed, to discover a body in his own chaise. Had he pursued Mrs. Grey along the Wingham road with murder as his object, he should better have abandoned her in a ditch along with her habit, than returned her to the world's sight. It looked very much as tho' someone else wished Collingforth to hang for the murder—and had arranged events to his liking.

But how had the corpse been conveyed to within the chaise? True, it had been divested of the red habit, and might have drawn less notice—if a corpse clad only in a shift, in broad daylight, could be said to look unremarkable. I did not think it likely, however, that Mrs. Grey had been brought to the chaise while yet alive, *en deshabille*, and strangled within it. Too little time had elapsed between her departure from the meeting-grounds and the discovery of her body, for the effecting of such a kidnapping; perhaps an hour, all told. Moreover, I had heard not a whimper of the poor lady's struggles, and our barouche had sat less than a hundred feet from Collingforth's chaise. The tumult of a race might have covered the deed—but all of Canterbury knew the lady to have been alive and victorious for some time after the final heat.

Revolve the matter of Mrs. Grey as I might, I could in no way account for her end, without the chaise itself having been removed. Upon reflection, I could not vouch for its presence behind our own equipage throughout the period in question—from Mrs. Grey's departure, until Collingforth had thrown open the carriage door. But who might have stolen the chaise for such an intricate purpose? And would there have been time enough to manage the business? It depended, I supposed, on the distance Mrs. Grey's team had already travelled, and where along the Wingham road she had been overtaken.

I should have considered of this earlier, and charged Neddie with examining the ground beneath the chaise's wheels. Some mark of hurried movement *might* have been discerned—

I sighed aloud, and Pratt glanced over his shoulder.

"It's not long now, miss. That be the turning for Chilham, as you'll know."

Chilham—where I had danced on occasion at the modest little Assembly Rooms, and pined in my youth for Mr. Taylor's beautiful dark eyes. He bestowed them upon another young lady more in keeping with his station—his irrepressible cousin, Charlotte—and the two have passed the remarkable family feature to yet another generation. I had called only last week at Bifrons Park, and found all the Taylors thriving.

As I wandered thus among the byways of my youth, the road dipped and swung along an embankment—the hedgerows parted—and we were presented with a fine sweep of country. All the beauty of Godmersham broke suddenly upon me. I suspended thought and sat back in the seat cushions, refreshed immediately by the serenity of the scene.

My brother's principal estate, a fine modern building of rosy brick, nestles like a jewel between two saddles of the downs. Every line of the house as it rises from its deer park—the copses where pheasant thrive, and hares burrow—the enclosed kitchen gardens, and the noble avenue of limes we call Bentigh, that leads sweetly along the river to the old Norman church of St. Nicolas—all must proclaim to passersby, that *here* lives an English gentleman.

I have known Godmersham from the first days of

Neddie's removal here, some ten years ago. I have been privileged to linger within its comforting walls for months at a time, and I regard the place as in some measure my home—and one I must quit always with regret. My own style of living is determined by the scant provision I bring to it; there is a constraint in relative poverty that weighs upon the soul and renders the mind weary. At Godmersham I am always free of penury's burdens, and the interval must be embraced with relief. To leave the place is to be cast out a little from Heaven.

As I considered the relative nature of peace and privilege, Pratt snapped the reins over the horses' backs, and the barouche rolled easily towards the turning for the park. Vivid green hills rose behind the house, shimmering and unvaried as velvet. Here and there a clump of trees broke the evenness of the landscape, rendering both hillside and clump more absolute in their disparity the one to the other. It was a style of beauty first brought to prominence in the last century—a paean to Naturalism, and quite in keeping with my sensibilities.

The Stour murmured a winding course through the meadow, and along its banks the willows trailed, restless in the slightest air. Swallows darted and swooped over our heads as we achieved the turning for the lodge, carriage wheels complaining at the paving's treatment, and little Fanny stirred and sighed. The slanting light of late August splashed gilt over her cheek—and over stone bridge, mown field, and rosy brick—as it turned the air to honey.

The whole was a scene of such measured beauty, in fact, that the horror of death seemed impossible, and the very notion of murder, absurd.

"Are we home, Jane?" Lizzy enquired, rousing herself. "It cannot be too soon. How Neddie must feel the burden of his duty, on such a day!"

"How happy you must be," I returned impulsively, "to

call these fields and hills your home! What richness, in the dull routine of a country life! Is there anything to compare with the peace and beauty of Kent?"

"The dust is intolerable," Lizzy observed, as we pulled up at the door. "I am sure I shall have the head-ache."

Her conviction bore fruit at the house's very entry, and so, calling for her excellent maid, Sayce, my sister was borne away to her room. The rest of us were not to be released without a trial, however—for shouting and jostling in their hurry to be seen, the young Austens tumbled down the steps from the nursery. They had been left behind at the day's outing, as being either too junior or too indisposed—for little Edward was troubled with a persistent cold, which refused to yield to all that the apothecary could advise. The others showed a dangerous inclination towards the same ailment, and with the commencement of their Michaelmas term looming, the older boys could not be too careful.[1] Lizzy had listened to the impassioned arguments of her children the previous night at bed-time. She had consulted with Mr. Green. And in the end, only Fanny—who might suffer a cold the autumn entire, and yet be schooled at home by Miss Sharpe—was permitted the treat of watching the Commodore run.

"Sharpie! Aunt Jane!" the children cried in a tumult. "Is it true? Was a lady murdered at the races, and is Father to find it all out?"

"Edward," I said briskly—for Miss Sharpe appeared, if anything, worse for her journey than she had at its outset—"Miss Sharpe is greatly fatigued. Pray let her pass, and do not be plaguing her with your questions."

Anne Sharpe looked all her thanks, and pressed a

---

[1] Edward Austen Knight's male children attended Winchester College, some seventeen miles distant from his principal Hampshire estate, at Chawton.—*Editor's note.*

hand to her brow. She had been more overpowered by events than any of us. I concluded that she suffered a head-ache more severe than Lizzy's direst imaginings, and ordered her to bed.

"I *am* a little fatigued," she admitted. "Perhaps a short interval—before the children require their suppers—"

"Sackree will see to the bread and milk," I told her firmly. "Pray lie down for a while, Miss Sharpe. You look decidedly unwell."

"I must believe it to be the shock," she said feebly. "That woman—"

"So it *is* true!" Edward shouted triumphantly.

I sank down on the bottom step and set my elegant top hat by my side. "Wherever did you hear such a tale, Edward?"

"He had it from Cook," said his brother George, hopping up and down on one foot, "—who had it from John Butcher, who met a man with the news on his way from the races."

"It was *not* John Butcher, but Samuel Joiner had the news, and *he* met the man in the road," young Elizabeth, a stout girl of five, broke in hotly.

"That is what I said," George retorted. "But—"

"Do not pinch your brother, Eliza," I attempted.

"You did *not* say it was so!" she insisted, "you said it was John Butcher. I heard the whole myself, while I was in the kitchen and Cook was in the yard. If you had gone for the pudding, Dordie, you would know it all, too."

"And *why* were you gone for pudding while Cook was in the yard?" asked Miss Sharpe—suddenly stern and much the pinker for it. "It is the accepted practise to take your pudding at meals, Miss Eliza, and not behind Cook's back."

Both culprits fell silent, their eyes on the ground. It was thus for Fanny to seize the triumphant moment.

"Of course the story is true," she said scornfully, "tho'

neither John Butcher nor Samuel Joiner were within a mile of the race-meeting. I saw it all, Edward, and if you will come into the schoolroom, I shall tell you how it was."

The others fell back in awed silence—and little Eliza burst into tears.

"Come along, children," I said in exasperation. "We shall both tell you the tale. And afterwards, George, perhaps we may have a game of shuttlecock. But you must be very quiet—for your mamma and Miss Sharpe are indisposed."

I smiled at the governess, and bustled the children upstairs. But when I turned at the landing to glance at Anne Sharpe, she still stood with one hand on the rail, her thoughts quite fled and her pallor extreme.

MY DEAREST CASSANDRA, I WROTE, AS I SAT SOME HOURS later at my dressing table, in the solitary splendour of the Yellow Room—and then I hesitated, pen poised for the collection of my thoughts. The hour was late and the house entirely wrapped in slumber. I had opened a window against the still heat of the August night, and my candle's flame dipped and staggered with every stirring of the air. Something there was that hovered over Godmersham—a gathering of violence above my head, that stiffened the very draperies and turned the midnight light to sulphur. Relief might come with the rain—and afterwards, a little sleep; but until the storm should break, I must seek comfort in composition.

When I am parted from my dearest sister by the vicissitudes of Fate or the beguilements of pleasure, it is my inveterate custom to relate the particulars of each day in a newsy, comfortable letter. Two such women, of advancing years and modest society, may generally have very little of importance to communicate; but the habit of conversation, long deferred by absence, will find relief in the written word. A great deal of nothing, therefore, has flown back and forth between Goodnestone Farm and Godmersham Park during the interval of Cassandra's visit to Lady Bridges. I may attest to a voluminous correspondence, regarding such little matters as the progress of young Edward's cold; my continued improvement at the game of shuttlecock; the opinion of Mr. Hall, the elegant London hairdresser, as to the best arrangement of my *coiffure*; and several good jokes regarding Henry's infatuation with his lamentable horse.

But this evening I had matters of a far graver nature to relate, although some part of Mrs. Grey's sad history must already be known to Cassandra—for Mr. Edward Bridges, who could hardly be ignorant of it, should have borne the intelligence to the Farm before me. My sister must as yet be denied the full history of the lady's tragic end, however, for my brothers returned from the race grounds very late this evening, and the details of their grim work were imparted only to myself—Lizzy and the children having already retired.

*You will know, I am sure, of the horrible events that occurred at our race-meeting,* I wrote at last.

I have hastened this letter in the knowledge that you must be suffering under the gravest anxiety for the safety and well-being of all our dear family— but be assured that we are all perfectly well. Miss Sharpe, the governess, was taken ill at the sight of the corpse; but Lizzy and I were hardly tempted to the dramatic, and even Fanny comported herself with admirable coolness. Our brother Neddie was decision and probity itself; he was admirably supported by Henry, and bids fair to conduct the business with despatch. There are further particulars in the matter, however, that will affect those very near to you: Mr. Edward Bridges, his friend Captain Woodford, and, of course, our dear friend Harriot, who must feel for the welfare of both. I thought it wisest to apprise you of matters—and will trust to your discretion in this, as in all things.

Neddie suspected at first that Mrs. Grey's murder might have been spurred by a hatred for the French, she being a citizen of the Empire, a fact that hardly smoothed her entry into Kentish society. Had she been killed along the road and left to the chance discovery of a passerby, that notion might have served admirably; but her being found in Mr. Denys Collingforth's chaise—a fact you will have learned already, in company with most of Kent—must entangle the affair considerably.

Mrs. Grey was seen to depart the race grounds a full hour before her corpse was discovered, quite palpably in the middle of it! Our brother Henry succeeded in locating Mrs. Grey's lost phaeton only two miles along the road to Wingham—her matched greys had been tethered to a tree, and were standing quite docilely at the verge, enjoying the shade. How she came to be torn from her equipage, and returned to the race grounds, is the greatest mystery; the disappearance of her riding habit is another. Neddie has employed a team of local men to search the hedgerows near the phaeton's stand, quite convinced that the scarlet gown was discarded in the underbrush.

Collingforth himself cannot account for the dead woman's presence in his chaise; he was remarked himself to have been distant from it for the better part of the morning, and only returned with the object of departing. He seemed ready to regard the affair as the work of his enemies, and named Mr. Bridges and Captain Woodford as the persons most likely to be accountable for it! You may imagine the sensation this caused in more than one breast; but Neddie bore with the insult admirably, as is his wont, and the uneasy moment passed.

Our brother is too assiduous to discard the political motive, however, merely because another, and more attractive one, presents itself. But Neddie has owned that it is possible that Mrs. Grey's killer—whatever his motive for her death—would wish the world to believe Collingforth responsible. So deep a purpose must argue against the random work of an enemy of the French; and Neddie is forced to the conclusion that he must probe the stuff of Mrs. Grey's life, to learn the reason for her death. The burden must give rise to anxiety. A gentleman less disposed to invade the privacy of a lady cannot be found in all of England!

But to continue—

Neddie enquired narrowly as to Mr. Collingforth's movements—heard the corroboration of his friends—and after a protracted interval, in which he debated the most proper course, enjoined the gentleman to remain in the neighbourhood for the present. The unfortunate Collingforth was then sent home in the charge of his intimate acquaintance, Mr. Everett—a gentleman quite unknown to Kent—while his grisly chaise Neddie retained for a time, to allow of a thorough inspection.

Within the body of the carriage, our brother found little of moment; neither Mrs. Grey's habit, nor a hint as to the identity of her murderer. One gold button from the habit, however, had worked its way between the seat cushions. There it might have lain forever, and forever unremarked, had Neddie not exerted himself to search the interior fully. The presence of the thing must prove suggestive: Are we to conclude that Mrs. Grey was stripped of her clothing in the chaise itself?

Provocative as this gilt trophy might be, however, it is as nothing to those Henry retrieved from Mrs. Grey's phaeton. And now I approach the heart of the matter, Cassandra, and must urge you again to discretion.

The contents were few, and readily observable to the eye—a lap robe against the dust; a hamper of provisions, quite empty; the gold plate presented by the sweepstakes officials; several posies bestowed by the more gallant among her acquaintance; and a novel in the French language.

Henry, of course, seized upon the novel—and proclaimed it to be of a scandalous sort, such as only his wife, Eliza, might scruple to entertain. It is called *La Nouvelle Héloïse*, and I believe is rather shocking—however, the book can be no more surprising than what it was found to conceal. For tucked between two leaves of the volume, Cassandra, was a letter.

Even Neddie's cursory French was equal to the seizing of its meaning. He perused it once—checked several phrases with Henry—and retained the original for further consideration. Mrs. Grey, it seemed, had conducted a correspondence with a gentleman not her husband—and had formed a plan of elopement intended for this very night. The two were to meet at Pegwell Bay, where a boat was to bear them to France.

What remains at issue, my dear Cassandra, is the identity of the amorous gentleman. For no signature was appended to the missive. Might it have been from Collingforth, himself?—And the lady's purpose divined by a jealous rival, who killed her and placed the blame upon her lover? Mr. Bridges, perhaps, or Captain Woodford? (The latter notion must strike everyone but Denys Collingforth as absurd.)

Or were Mrs. Grey's intentions betrayed to her deluded husband? Mr. Valentine Grey was from home this week; but perhaps a timely warning, anonymous or otherwise, drew him back to Kent in an outrage of feeling. It should not be unusual for a man to work his vengeance upon his wife, and charge her lover with the murder.

Denys Collingforth, however, did not comport himself like a lover. Nothing of anguish was in his looks as he contemplated the ravaged corpse of Mrs. Grey. If anything, he appeared the reverse of all that a lover should be. So why deposit the body in *his* chaise?

Or, in the final consideration, was the letter in the novel merely a subterfuge of Mrs. Grey's *cicisbeo*, who intended her end rather than her escape?[2]

The latter seems hardly likely. A disgruntled lover should rather have strangled the lady on the strand at Pegwell in the dark of night, than in the midst of a race-meeting. The letter, for the nonce, must be merely suggestive. It tells us only that *one* among her

---

[2]  A *cicisbeo* was the acknowledged lover of a married woman. In some circles the term was used platonically, to signify a male escort.—*Editor's note.*

friends believed her unhappy enough with her marriage and Kent, to entertain the notion of flight.

Neddie has determined, as you may comprehend, to examine the husband acutely. Mr. Valentine Grey was sent for by express, and is expected at The Larches every moment.

HERE I PAUSED IN MY LETTER TO CASSANDRA, AND SAW again in memory my brother's weary face. It was after ten o'clock when he and Henry returned from the race grounds, and we had the comfortable library entirely to ourselves. Henry threw himself onto a sofa and yawned hugely; Neddie stood in thought by his desk. I had determined not to plague them with questions, being content myself to rest a few moments in my favourite room.

The library, with its five tables, two fireplaces, countless volumes, and eight-and-twenty chairs, is in the newest part of the great house. The first Mr. Thomas Knight added two wings, east and west, nearly thirty years previous; and tho' the entire family is wont to live in the generous space, summer or winter, spurning the chilly grandeur of the more formal drawing-rooms, it sometimes happens that I command the library in splendid solitude. This is a richness not to be carelessly forsworn; for in a house that boasts the frequent presence of nine children—their number increasing with a stupefying regularity—solitude and peace are luxuries dearly bought. But my brother's goodness admits of few limits; he comprehends my need for daily reflection, and the delight I take in the house's privacies; and shoos his numerous progeny to the garden when "Aunt Jane requires her rest."

"And so you are not abed." Neddie swung round and

peered at me from his place by the unlit hearth. "I am glad of it, Jane. I should soon drive poor Henry mad with my mutterings; he has borne with them too long today."

"Not a bit of it." Henry eased off his top boots with a sigh. It should not be remarkable if the feet were swollen, after hours of imprisonment in such fashionable footgear. "I shall be all attention to the despicable business, once I have heard from Jane how the Commodore does."

"He was sold to the knacker not three minutes before your return," I told him with conscious cruelty, "and I doubt he shall make a better meat than he has a racemeeting."

"For shame! The lad was merely weighted too heavily. And he does not like the dust. Give the Commodore a splendid wet muck and he will tear the course to blazes. But truly, Jane—you saw he was looked after?"

I sighed. "A bucket of oats and an hour's rubbingdown. Your groom would hardly do less; I believe he led the nag at a walk the full seven miles between the meeting-grounds and Godmersham, Henry. You have no cause for fear."

"Not for fear, perhaps," Neddie observed, as he flung himself into a chair, "but his concern nonetheless does our brother credit. Yours is a most forgiving nature, Henry; you lose your fortune and mine in backing the beast, and yet are anxious to know whether it ate its dinner well. Were I disposed to transgress and disappoint, I should wish to fall into your hands. I might then be assured of a gentle reckoning."

"Unlike the unfortunate Mrs. Grey," Henry observed. "She certainly met with more brutal treatment."

Neddie regarded him quizzically. "You incline, then, to the theory of a husband pushed past endurance?"

"I incline to nothing," he protested. "She might as readily have been strangled by a broken gamester, mad with backing the wrong horse!"

"Better to have strangled the Commodore, then," I murmured.

Neddie bent his gaze upon me. "What say you, Jane, to Henry's notion?"

"I may say nothing, until I command a greater knowledge of the particulars. Why should you believe Mr. Grey the culprit? Was not he far from the scene, in London?"

Neddie laughed abruptly. "She is as sober as a judge, our sister! If it is particulars you fancy, Jane, then you shall have them. I could not suffer you to remain in ignorance, when all the world will soon be talking of the matter."

He rang for wine, and when it had been brought, consumed a little in silence. It was Henry who related the history of the perch phaeton, its scandalous novel, and the letter it contained; and when he had done, I puzzled a moment over the matter.

"Like you, Henry, I cannot incline towards one theory or another," I declared at last. "We must attempt to ascertain whether Mr. Valentine Grey was indeed in London at the moment of his wife's end—and whether he had reason to suspect a dangerous entanglement with The Unknown. It would not go amiss, either, could we put a name to the lady's lover. But until such things are laid plain, it must all be conjecture. And injurious conjecture at that."

"So we thought as well," Neddie said from his corner. "And having concluded our inspection of the phaeton, despatched the greys to their stable under the watchful eye of the tyger, and charged the Canterbury constabulary with the safekeeping of the carriage—Henry and I proceeded to pay a call upon The Larches."

"The Greys' estate? No wonder, then, that you were so long detained!"

"Indeed. We have tramped through half the neighbourhood in pursuit of justice, and found not a hint of it within fifteen miles of the coast. It has all fled to London, I suppose, out of a terror of French cavalry."

"And did you discover Mr. Grey in savage looks, with pistols at the ready and his housekeeper for hostage, intent upon the defiance of the Law?"

"Hardly. Imagine our surprise, my dear sister, to find Grey as absent as foretold, and the house in possession of strangers."

"Strangers?" I echoed, intrigued.

"Perhaps that is not the correct word," Henry broke in hastily. "But they certainly could not be considered as forming a part of the household."

"Enough of riddles!" I set down my wineglass with decision. "I am not young Fanny, to be diverted at a word."

"Can not you guess whom we found in the saloon, rifling the dead woman's desk for all they were worth?" Neddie's eyes glinted with something too acute to be called amusement.

"I cannot," I retorted helplessly. "I never heard of Mrs. Grey until this morning, and cannot hope to name her intimates."

"Captain Woodford and Edward Bridges," Henry said apologetically, "and both of them much the worse for wine."

"Good God!" I cried; and then, "How can you look so roguish, Neddie? Think what this must mean for Lizzy, if Mr. Bridges's name should be linked in scandal to Mrs. Grey's! And Captain Woodford, too—of whom Harriot has such hopes! It does not bear thinking of."

"I believe it is my Lizzy who has hopes of the gallant

Captain," he amended. "Harriot's feelings, like those of any modest young lady, must be presently in doubt. I cannot be expected to consider of Harriot, if she will not consider of herself."

"Pray, pray, be sensible, Neddie!"

"You disappoint me, Jane," my brother replied drily. "You do not show the proper relish for intrigue. I had expected more, from Henry's account of your doings in Bath last winter. I thought you quite enslaved to a dangerous excitement."

If I threw Henry an evil look, and received an air of insouciance in return, I may perhaps be forgiven.

"Captain Woodford we may explain," I managed eventually. "I understand that he has been on terms of intimacy with Mr. Grey from boyhood, and might naturally wish to be present when the gentleman returned. Perhaps he hoped to shield his friend from the full weight of such terrible news. And Mr. Bridges might merely have accompanied him."

"Tho' they travelled in separate equipages, and seemed distinctly out of charity with one another."

This must give me pause.

"Captain Woodford would have it that they had come to condole with Mr. Grey," Henry threw in, "tho' he could tell us nothing about that gentleman's movements, or when he was expected from London. And poor Mr. Bridges was decidedly red-faced and mumchance—either from the effects of wine or the ruin of his hopes, for I know him to have backed the Commodore to a shocking extent. At first he suggested he would condole with Grey as well, until Captain Woodford abused him to his face for a blackguard and a liar. It would have ended in Bridges calling the Captain out, had Neddie not intervened."[3]

[3] To call a man out was to challenge him to a duel.—*Editor's note.*

"How very singular," I said slowly. "Captain Woodford and Mr. Bridges, to have had a falling-out. They seemed the best of fellows, when last I had the pleasure of conversing with them."

"At the race-meeting itself, Jane?"

"Tho' well before the murder of Mrs. Grey. Our party met with the two gentlemen in the interval before the heats. They seemed most companionable, and joined in their good wishes for the Commodore's running."

"As well they might," Henry retorted gloomily. "Much good it may do them."

"Perhaps the betting aroused their enmity," Neddie mused. "Or Denys Collingforth's insults. He fairly accused them of Mrs. Grey's murder—and before all of Kent."

"But would that cause either to drive post-haste to The Larches?" I protested. "You spoke of rifled desk drawers, Neddie. Certainly you were in error there? The two were surely not despoiling Mrs. Grey's things?"

My brothers exchanged a long look; then Neddie shrugged. "Their appearance at our entrance had all the suggestion of uneasy interruption, Jane. Woodford was bending over the desk, while Mr. Bridges was intent about the lock of one drawer. Whether either man had divined its secrets, I cannot say; but I am certain that was their purpose."

"And could the housekeeper tell you nothing of their coming?"

"Only that they had burst upon her all unawares, when she was already prostrate with grief at her mistress's passing; that they insisted upon admission to the house, and vowed that they would wait for Mr. Grey."

"And so she left them to peruse the contents of her mistress's desk," I muttered. "A considerable liberty."

"I must believe that Mrs. Bastable—the housekeeper—was quite accustomed to seeing my brother Bridges and the Captain at The Larches. To her there was nothing extraordinary in their being granted the freedom of the house."

We considered this unfortunate conclusion in silence a moment, while the willows sighed gently along the banks of the Stour in the darkness. The sound, so generally soothing, drifted through the open French windows like a whisper from the grave.

"Do you apprehend the nature of Mr. Bridges's intimacy with the Greys, Neddie?" I enquired at length.

He shrugged. "It was neither so very great, as to be called intimate, nor so trifling as to pass for the barest acquaintance. Edward would have it that Mrs. Grey was very fond of cards, and when her husband was absent on business in Town, she would often send round to various gentlemen in the neighbourhood, that they might make up her whist table."

"Mr. Bridges played at cards at The Larches?"

"Then no doubt he lost," Henry added.

"It is his chief talent." Neddie rose and turned restlessly before the bare hearth. "But I confess to some anxiety at his presence in that house, and at such a time. I feel scarcely less on Woodford's account. They are both of them honourable fellows—as the behaviour of gentlemen is usually construed."

"Meaning, that they are amiable, good-humoured, feckless sportsmen who should not be trusted with their quarter's pay," I finished. "Either they intended to retrieve their vowels from Mrs. Grey's desk, or some other piece of incriminating paper has given rise to anxiety.[4] A love letter? An indiscretion, too desperate to be revealed to the lady's husband?"

"Perhaps," Neddie admitted.

---

[4] A gentleman's vowels were his IOUs—signed with his name, and binding as a debt of honor.—*Editor's note.*

"Perhaps the lady had a taste for blackmail," Henry threw out.

I started at the word. *Blackmail* will always possess an ugly sound—and I had learned to respect its vicious nature in Bath the previous winter. The rifling of a desk was a natural aftermath of a brutal killing, when the victim of the act had proved brutal herself. Mr. Bridges's behaviour bore all the markings of a man in fear of betrayal. But of what?

Of whatever Denys Collingforth had hinted, in the middle of the race grounds? His object then had been the curate alone, not Captain Woodford—but Woodford had been encompassed in the insult later, the price of coming to the aid of his friend. Perhaps the shadow cast on the Captain's honour had caused the rift with the curate. But the Captain, too, had been discovered bent over the desk—

"I see how it is. This is an ugly business, Neddie."

"And likely to grow worse." He tossed off the last of his wine. "All of Kent may have despised Mrs. Grey; they may have cut her dead in certain circles, and laughed at her in others—but her influence was felt. Her charm was insidious. Her habits and style were bewitching to some. And no matter how the sad nature of her end is resolved, we can none of us hope to avoid the breath of scandal, Jane. We are touched by it too nearly."

He looked then as though he felt all the weight of his commission—hollow-eyed, burdened, and wearied in mind and body. I went to him, and kissed his cheek in silent testament of affection.

"What do you intend to do next?" I asked him.

"I shall endeavour to learn why Collingforth should have killed Françoise Grey," he replied, "tho' I cannot believe he did it."

"You might also enquire who bore a grudge against

Collingforth himself," I suggested. "The introduction of the corpse into his chaise must bear a questionable aspect. It is one thing to murder a woman, and quite another to throw the blame."

"True." My brother took up his candle and made for the stairs. "Pray inform me, Jane, as to the result of your own researches. I am not so callow as to believe you will sit home, quiet and confined, while so much of interest is toward. I will neither enjoin you to silence, nor urge you to the chase—but I will always be ready to listen."

And so our conferences ended, with a solemn procession by candlelight—my brothers to their beds, and I to the Yellow Room's little writing table.

*I would not have you share this intelligence with Harriot for the world,* I cautioned Cassandra now. *Better that she should learn the worst—if worst there is—when it cannot be avoided. But if you should have occasion to observe the two gentlemen, my dear sister—one comprising her brother, and the other her suitor—pray be on your guard. For anything you discern might be as gold.*

I signed the letter, sealed it with some candlewax and my brother's fob, and waited for the storm to break above my head.

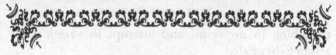

# Chapter 4

## *A Passage with the Bereaved*

*Tuesday,*
*20 August 1805*

~

IN NEARLY THIRTY YEARS OF LIVING I HAVE OFTEN HAD
occasion to observe, that one sensational event may only
be supplanted by another of equal or greater import.
And so it has been with all of us at Godmersham this
morning: Mrs. Grey's brutal murder is quite forgot, and
the agent of her eclipse is none other than Captain
Woodford.

He appeared in the approach to our gates at noon,
arrayed in his full dress uniform and mounted on a dap-
pled grey. I was privileged in having the first sight of
him—for I had profited from the interlude after breakfast, when the little ones were taking turns with patient
Patch, the old pony, to escape to my Doric temple and
my solitude. There in columned shadow I was established with paper and pen, secure in such privacy as I
may rarely command. There I might gaze out over the
chuckling Stour, and watch the growing heat of morning raise a fine mist above the meadows; feel birdsong

throbbing in my veins, and attempt to wrestle Lady Susan to her Fate.[1]

The nature of that Fate is much in question at present, for Lady Susan is not a woman to suffer the vagaries of fortune as willingly as her creator might intend. She is a vengeful and calculating Virago, in fact, and I am entirely delighted with her. Cassandra believes there is something shocking in a woman so very bad; she would have Lady Susan repentant and reformed at the tale's end. But in this we may read the force of sentiment— and the failure of Art to mirror Truth. For I have known a thousand Lady Susans; have seen them sail unremarked through the Fashionable World, their consequence increasing with every fresh outrage. Unnatural mother, adulterous schemer, and treacherous friend—what can such a woman ever know of virtue?

I love her too well, in short, to have her broken for a moral.

My thoughts in this vein had only just borne fruit, in the composition of the novel's final pages, when the sound of hoofbeats on the dusty lane below my hilltop perch alerted all my senses. I half-rose, and peered round a column; observed an officer mounting the stone bridge over the Stour; and set aside my paper and pen. A moment's further study revealed the upright figure to possess an eye patch—and there could not be *two* such at large in the country. Captain Woodford, then,

1  *Lady Susan,* first drafted in the mid-1790s, was never titled or published during Austen's life. Even at the time of its composition, the novel's epistolary form was considered more appropriate to the eighteenth than the nineteenth century. Why Austen abandoned *The Watsons,* which she had begun in 1803 or 1804, in order to finish the more cynical *Lady Susan* is a mystery; but some Austen scholars impute the decision to a persistent depression that resulted from her father's death in January 1805. Despite its flaws, *Lady Susan*'s calculating and amoral heroine is utterly irresistible. —*Editor's note.*

was come to Godmersham, and well before the usual hour for paying a morning call!

If I entertained the notion of a soul burdened with guilt, and advancing upon my brother for the full confession of its sins, I may perhaps be forgiven. I watched with narrowed eyes as the Captain achieved the gates and made his measured progress up the sweep.[2] He did not look a man overwhelmed by grief; yet neither was he galloping as befit an officer charged with the most urgent intelligence. The French were not upon our very doorstep, at least.

I gathered up my little sheaf of paper, secured Lady Susan and my pen in the pocket of my apron, and set off down the slope towards the house.

"CAPTAIN WOODFORD," LIZZY SAID, WITH HER MOST charming smile—the one that is barely a smile at all. "I fear you find us quite abandoned by the gentlemen."

Neddie had left early on horseback intent upon Valentine Grey, while Henry had been charged with learning what he could of Denys Collingforth's affairs. He intended, I believed, to spend the better part of the day drinking ale in the Hound and Tooth, the center of all gossip in Canterbury.

The Captain bowed low over my sister's hand, then inclined his head towards myself. "Mr. Austen is from home? I should have suspected as much. The tragic business at the race-meeting—"

"Indeed," Lizzy returned smoothly. "My husband left the house at eight o'clock, intent upon The Larches. Mr. Grey, it seems, arrived home just after dawn, and Mr. Austen wished to speak with him as soon as might be."

---

[2] The sweep, in Austen's day, was the common name for the driveway.—*Editor's note.*

"Of course. I had not known Grey was returned."
If the Captain felt a moment's uneasiness at the mention of The Larches, he betrayed nothing in his countenance. His entire aspect, in fact, was official and grave, as tho' he moved in a role not entirely his own. He handed Lizzy a furled despatch, tied round with a scarlet cord.

"I had hoped to speak with Mr. Austen himself, but given the pressing nature of the business at hand, can delay no longer. You will comprehend the urgency of this document's contents, I am sure, Mrs. Austen, and see that its instructions are fulfilled to the letter."

But Lizzy was already perusing the despatch, a fine line growing deeper between her brows. "Evacuation orders?" she said faintly. "But is it certain?"

"Nothing can be certain, ma'am, when the enemy is so inscrutable as Buonaparte," the Captain replied. "We merely thought it wisest to discharge these orders among the local gentry, in the event of an invasion's taking place. You apprehend that it would not do, ma'am, to have the populace choking the major routes of any army retreat towards London."

"Retreat," Lizzy repeated. "You have capitulated already, I see."

Captain Woodford gave a short bark of laughter, and glanced at me uneasily. "There is no cause for alarm, Mrs. Austen, I assure you. It is merely wisest to be prepared."

"What has occasioned the present release of these orders?" I enquired. "Have the French been sighted in the Channel?"

"I regret that I am not at liberty to disclose the intelligence," the Captain told me with another bow, "since I am hardly in command of it myself. I may only say that Major-General Lord Forbes was called out in the middle of the night, and told of something that so excited his anxiety, he deemed it best to alert the surrounding countryside. It is everywhere rumoured that the fleet has escaped from Brest and Boulogne—that the Emperor has embarked—and that even now some thousand French ships with cavalry and cannon in their holds are bound for the shores of Kent."

"The fleet escaped? While Admiral Nelson and the intrepid Fly Austen patrol the Channel? Unthinkable!" I scoffed.[3]

"Would that the General might share your fond hope," said Woodford with a smile, "but caution must argue a more present surety. We would wish you to have the chief of your household goods packed and in readiness, in the event you must quit the country on little notice."

"Packing is merely the tenth part of it," Lizzy said abruptly. She crumpled the despatch into a tight little wad. "We are to fire the sainfoin harvest from June, and cull the herds as well?—It shall be a bitter winter in Kent, if every household does the same! And what if we refuse, Captain Woodford?"

"I should not like to have to enforce the orders against your will, madam," he rejoined, "but if my general commands it, I will do so. We cannot have such a rich provision fall into the hands of the French."[4]

---

[3] From his youth, Jane's elder brother, Francis Austen, RN, was called "Fly." He was posted to the Channel station in 1804 as captain of the *Leopard*, and transferred in 1805 to the *Canopus*, a French-built ship of the line under Admiral Lord Horatio Nelson's ultimate command.—*Editor's note.*

[4] Warren Roberts, in *Jane Austen and the French Revolution* (Macmillan, 1979), relates that evacuation plans were disseminated to every household within fifteen miles of the Kentish coast. Godmersham lay some miles west of that perimeter, but perhaps its position along the retreat toward London made it worthy of the Guards' notice. Sainfoin, also known as cockshead, was a common forage plant used as animal fodder.—*Editor's note.*

Lizzy thrust the despatch into my hands, and turned away. "Forgive me, Captain—but I must see that the packing is commenced at once. A household of nine children, a variety of adults, and fourteen in service, may never move but at a ponderous pace. Pray overlook my ill-breeding, and accept a glass of lemonade. Mrs. Salkeld! Mrs. *Salkeld*!"

And so she swept out of the drawing-room, her carriage magnificent, the very picture of an outraged chatelaine. Captain Woodford gazed after her with an air of trouble on his brow, and then smiled ruefully at me. "At least she did not dissolve in tears. For that I am thankful. It is a difficult business, informing the populace of so unexpected a removal. I have witnessed all manner of behaviour in the past several hours—fainting fits, the tearing of hair, and even the threat of violence. One lady I shall forbear to name advanced upon me with a pair of sewing shears!"

I could not suppress a smile. "Poor Captain Woodford! Duty is a difficult master, in the best of times. We must all suffer from its effects. My unfortunate brother feels his burden as cruelly as yourself, I assure you."

At that moment, Russell the manservant appeared in the doorway bearing a tray. Woodford's countenance lightened with an expression of relief. The conveyance of the King's orders must be a parching business.

"Pray sit down, Captain," I said.

He removed his hat, and took a chair, and accepted a glass of lemon-water from Russell. "Little as I enjoy my present orders, I do not envy Mr. Austen his duty. It is one thing to kill another man in battle—that is merely a trick of Fate, the necessity of war. But to murder a woman, in cold blood—and a woman, too, in the full flush of youth! I shall never forget the sight of her dead face as long as I live, Miss Austen."

"I understand you were intimate with the family," I offered gently. "You have my deepest sympathy."

The Captain coloured, and dropped his gaze. "It is true that I have known Grey from our earliest years. We were practically raised in each other's London households and schooled together at Harrow. But as for Françoise—the late Mrs. Grey—my acquaintance was very brief. She had been a bride but seven months."

"So little!"

"You know, of course, that she was connected to an influential banking family in France."

"I heard something of it," I admitted, "but am ignorant of the particulars."

"Mrs. Grey was the ward of the Penfleurs. They are a powerful and prodigious clan, with branches in every kingdom, and a wealth that approaches fable. There are Penfleurs who are princes in France, and Penfleurs who are counts in Naples; Penfleurs who advise the rulers of German states, and not a few who are essential to the Netherlands. Their resources remain entirely in the family, and their credit extends across continents. But remarkably, there were no Penfleurs in England—"

"Until Françoise," I said.

"Until Françoise," he agreed. "I tell you this, Miss Austen, so that you might comprehend the nature of my friend's marriage. It was arranged, I believe, by the elder Penfleur himself, who had the charge of Françoise from infancy; she cannot have been very well acquainted with Mr. Grey, when first she arrived on these shores."

"Did she come to England, then, against her will?"

"I doubt that Françoise Lamartine ever did anything against her will," he replied with a faint smile.

But it could not be surprising, I thought, that in the face of such a marriage—exiled by her family and treated coldly by her husband—she had turned to an unknown lover.

"How very tragic," I murmured. "For so young a woman, and a stranger to Kent, to find her death in so brutal a manner . . . You had no hint of Mrs. Grey possessing any enemies, I suppose?"

He eyed me over the rim of his glass, then set it deliberately on the table. "You are not of Kentish society yourself, Miss Austen, any more than I may claim to be. We are both of us merely visitors to this delightful place, and care little how its intimates may treat us. But that was not the case with Françoise. I am sure that your sister and brother have told you a little of her reception."

"But a coldness on the part of a strange society, in itself, should hardly lead to murder," I persisted. "Surely that is another order of violence altogether, Captain?"

"I have been taught to think so." He rose, and took up his hat. "A sense of what is due to my friend Grey, Miss Austen, must prevent me from speaking plainly. I may only tell you that his wife's enemies were thick upon the ground. You might look no farther than the lady's own household."

I gazed at him narrowly. "I cannot believe you would accuse your oldest friend, Captain Woodford, of doing away with his wife. This cannot be what is *due* to him, as you put it."

"I, accuse Valentine Grey? Impossible!" he cried. "I merely meant to underline, Miss Austen, that Denys Collingforth is hardly the only man in Kent who has reason to think ill of the dead."

"And what *was* his reason, Captain, for despising her?"

Woodford eyed me uneasily. "That is a question best answered by Mr. Collingforth. I am sure your brother, the Justice, has considered of it."

"Mr. Collingforth appears to think ill of any number of people," I observed, as I conducted the Captain to the door. "Had you not been present to prevent it, he should certainly have served our poor Mr. Bridges with violence! You are owed a debt of gratitude in this house, sir."

"Mr. Bridges is possessed of such happy manners as may ensure his making any number of friends," Woodford replied, with a bow. "Whether he is equally capable of retaining them, is another matter. Good day, Miss Austen."

IT WAS ABOVE AN HOUR BEFORE THE CLATTER OF NEDdie's horse, pulled up hard before the door, was heard on the sweep. He looked overheated and cross, and entered the house with a rapid step and the briefest of salutations. After an interval of respectful quiet, and the consumption of a quantity of ale drawn from the barrel in the cellar, good humour and volubility returned.

"I have seen Grey," the Justice announced, as he took up his customary place before the cold library hearth, "and he has seen me. It remains uncertain which of us was most scarred by the encounter—but I shall leave it to you to decide, Jane, when I tell you that the gentleman chose to offer me his glove!"[5]

"Good Lord!" Lizzy ejaculated, and set down the books she had commenced packing. "I cannot think when you have been served such a turn before, Neddie!"

"It is unique in my experience," he admitted, "tho' I am almost ashamed to say as much. Every sprig of fashion is required to have a history of such meetings. It is a poor show I've given you, Lizzy!"

"Pray do not trouble to kill yourself on my account, sir," she replied serenely, and retrieved the books. "Do

[5] Edward Austen refers here to a demand for satisfaction in a matter of honor, in which the offended party usually threw a glove at his opponent's feet or, in extreme cases, struck him with the glove across the cheek. An affair of honor was usually settled at pistol-point. If either party killed the other, the survivor could be charged with murder.—*Editor's note.*

you require breakfast and the witnessing of a will at dawn?"

"Nothing so romantic." Neddie peered at the spines of the volumes she had selected, and pulled several from the box. "Pray leave these, my dear—they had far better be burned with the sainfoin, I am sure."

"Beast."

"What occasioned Mr. Grey's challenge?" I enquired at last, being provoked beyond endurance.

My brother threw himself into a chair and gazed at me idly. "My unwillingness to clap Denys Collingforth in chains, I suspect. But let me relate the whole, I beg, in an orderly fashion. The exercise might do much for the composure of my mind."

And so the Justice undertook to convey the essence of his morning's work: how he had achieved The Larches just after nine o'clock, and found the master of the house breakfasting serenely in his parlour; how Valentine Grey, a compact, powerful man with weary features and the acutest gaze, had appeared in excellent health, despite his broken night. He had enjoined the Justice to take coffee with him in the saloon, and tho' his spirits appeared a little disordered, they were in general composed. A man who looked less the part of a mourning husband could hardly be conceived, Neddie assured us; and from that moment forward, he assumed there had been little of love in the Greys' union.

In the saloon, all was ease and congeniality at first. Grey placidly expressed himself shocked—quite beyond comprehending the event—and wild to see justice done. Neddie said all that was correct and feeling in a man condoling with the bereaved. It was after the coffee, however, when Grey had at last enquired as to the conduct of his wife's case, that the outburst of temper had broken like a thunderclap over my brother's head.

"Do I understand, sir, that you have done nothing to

apprehend the scoundrel responsible for her murder? This is not to be borne!" The widower rose and stood menacingly over my brother, who could not conceal his surprise.

"I am afraid, Mr. Grey, that I am less hasty than yourself. I cannot apprehend a man before I know his name."

"But it is obvious! Collingforth is the man. My poor wife's corpse was discovered in his chaise!"

"In such matters, the obvious may prove a doubtful guide," Neddie returned steadily. "Mr. Collingforth's movements are vouched for by his acquaintance. It seems almost impossible that he should have murdered your wife on the Wingham road, and returned her body to his own chaise. I fear we must look farther afield for the responsible party."

Valentine Grey commenced to pace the length of the saloon in agitation, then halted before French windows giving out onto the gardens, one hand pressed to his brow.

"Can you offer any reason, sir, for your wife's brutal end?" Neddie enquired.

"How can any man be expected to explain such a horror! She must have fallen into the clutches of a fiend!" Grey wheeled to face him, an expression of agony on his countenance so at variance with his earlier behaviour, that Neddie must confess himself amazed. "Can you bear to contemplate it, man? A lady alone—unprotected— quite disregarded by those in whom she placed her trust—"

"Her trust?"

Grey's next words had all the viciousness of a challenge. "Do not deny, man, that she was hated by the entire neighbourhood! Those who should have embraced and protected her as one of their own, rejected her from the first. Do not think I was ignorant of the coldness in which she lived. I saw all, I knew all—and it tore at my heart!"

"Your wife, Mr. Grey, was not entirely one of Kent's own," Neddie countered. "She was a Frenchwoman. In such times as these, her end must be suggestive."

"An act of war, you would say?" Grey laughed harshly. "Impossible. Françoise did nothing to excite a peculiar hatred."

"And yet she is dead," Neddie observed bluntly. "Is it so unlikely that she should be killed by a fool? A simple-minded fellow who resented her triumph at the races, as he resented French victory on the battlefield? Such an one may have thought to strike at the Monster by murdering your wife."

Grey merely snorted.

"You have failed to propose an alternative, Mr. Grey," my brother burst out in exasperation.

"Because there is none that I may offer."

"You can think of no one who might bear your wife ill-will?"

"That is for yourself to determine, Mr. Austen, as the embodiment of the Law. I am told you are the Justice in these parts. Why, then, do I find you at such a loss? Is it perhaps because my wife was merely a *French* lady, that you exert yourself so little?"

Neddie admitted that he began to grow angry. I am sure that he flushed, and controlled himself only with difficulty. But when at last he spoke, it was with admirable coolness. "You have every reason to vent your anger at me, my dear sir. I should far rather you expressed yourself thus in the privacy of this room, than in the public venue of your unfortunate wife's inquest. It was exactly my hope that we might speak in private before that distressing event, which is to occur on the morrow, as there is a matter of some delicacy I had hoped you might resolve."

Mr. Grey went pale. "What the Devil do you mean?"

"I refer to the letter discovered among your wife's effects after her death."

"Letter? What letter?"

Neddie presented the indelicate note from the unknown seducer. Grey read it through with commendable swiftness—he was clearly an adept at the French language—and then crumpled it in his fist.

"I could offer you an hundred such, Austen. There is nothing so very unusual in *this*."

"Indeed?" Neddie rejoined, somewhat surprised. "Mrs. Grey was often in the habit of eloping with gentlemen not her husband?"

Had Valentine Grey thrown down his glove at that moment, he might perhaps have been forgiven. Instead, he merely looked all his outrage, and endeavoured to explain.

"That note is nothing more nor less than a message from one of her French couriers, man. He was undoubtedly sent from her family in Paris, and expected to arrive by packet at the dead of night. It is the custom for couriers to travel in this way, for fear of a cruising Navy ship with little regard for matters of safe passage. But in the event, he was before his time, and met with my wife in this very room, the morning of the race-meeting."

"A courier?" Neddie repeated. "What sort of courier, if I may presume to enquire?"

Grey's impatience was evident in his countenance. "It is a common practise, I assure you, in banking circles—particularly those with branches throughout Europe. Timely intelligence of world events, as you will understand, is vital in matters of finance. My wife was the ward of a powerful French family, the Penfleurs, who in company with other banking houses, such as the Hopes and the Rothschilds, command a service of couriers they may despatch at a moment's notice. Such men carry letters of safe passage across warring borders, and may venture where another might fear to tread."

"A man with intelligence direct from France?" Neddie cried. "—And this man met with your wife on the very day of her death?"

"Indeed. The housekeeper informed me of the fellow's appearance upon my arrival this morning. But he had long since returned whence he came."

"You have no notion of his news?"

"None whatsoever." Grey affected unconcern.

"But is not such a coincidence extraordinary?" Neddie persisted.

"It was the custom for Françoise's family to correspond in this expensive fashion. A private courier is more certain than the mails across the Channel, at such a time."

"I see." Neddie studied the banker's face acutely. "And you did not encounter him along the road?"

"I?" Grey was taken aback. "What should I be doing on the coast road yesterday morning? I was quite fixed in Town, and had been for some weeks. It was your express, which found me at my club late last night, that drew me from Pall Mall as fast as wheels and horseflesh could carry me. I stopped at my lodgings only to collect my man and a change of clothes."

And Grey's man, if he was still to be found, would certainly swear as much, Neddie thought. There was the express rider, too, who could speak to Grey's presence at his club—and any number of honourable clubmen who would have witnessed his play at hazard or loo. But whether Mr. Grey's movements for *all* of Monday might be accounted for, was open to question.

"I wonder if the courier might be located," my brother had mused aloud.

"Neither the courier," Mr. Grey burst out, "nor this note establishing a meeting-place, can have the slightest bearing on my wife's death, Mr. Austen! She was hardly murdered on the shores of Pegwell Bay, but in the middle of a crowded race grounds, where someone must have seen something to the purpose! Did you make enquiries among the spectators? Or despatch a constable to all the major coaching inns, where a miscreant might have taken shelter?"

"One such is even now beating the underbrush about the Wingham road, in search of your wife's riding habit," Neddie replied. "I have offered a gold sovereign to the first man who discovers the gown."

Grey snapped his fingers in irritation. "I give you *that* for your gold sovereign, Mr. Austen, sir! I fail to understand why you have brooked such delay. Had my wife's murderer been pursued in the first moments, I might have seen him hang; but as it is now . . ."

"Then I take it you no longer believe Mr. Collingforth responsible, but some other," my brother observed.

"Collingforth? Who can say? But I will insist, Mr. Austen, that you have been sadly remiss in your duties!"

"Why should Collingforth throttle your wife?"

"You would do well to enquire of *him*."

"Did he bear her any malice?"

"Malice!" A contemptuous snort. "He had eyes for no one but Françoise. The man is a lecher, a blackguard, and a scoundrel—as everyone in Kent, including his wife, must be aware!"

"And so he killed Mrs. Grey because he was in love with her?"

"I should never deign to call it love."

"Did she return his . . . interest?"

"Damn your eyes!" The banker hurled a crystal brandy glass against the stones of his hearth. "The lady lies foully murdered, and you would trample her reputation in the dirt?"'

Neddie was silent an instant. Then he said, "Come,

come, Mr. Grey. If all of Kent knows Collingforth for a scoundrel and a blackguard, they must equally have seen that your wife was what the *ton* would call *fast*. She drove her own carriage, bred her own horses, commanded her own card-parties, and was rarely alone—despite the solitude in which you left her. Only consider of the manner in which she was discovered—quite divested of her riding habit, and hardly in her own equipage!"

A choked snarl of fury from Mr. Grey was the only reply. And at that moment, he threw down his glove.

My brother told us that he regarded it steadily. "If I am truly the first to broach such a delicate matter in your hearing, I am sorry for it," he said, "but depend upon it, I shall not be the last."

Then he retrieved the glove and secured it in his waistcoat pocket. "Let us put off the matter of satisfaction, sir, until your wife's murderer is brought to heel. There is enough of blood in Canterbury at present, without spilling our own into the bargain. Good day to you!"

# Chapter 5

## The Talk of the Town

"AND SO WE ARE TO CONCLUDE THAT MR. GREY'S CHAL-lenge is not retracted, but merely deferred," Lizzy observed. "How very tiresome, to be sure."

Neddie handed her a volume of Montaigne's essays. "I think I may fairly say that the gentleman's bluster is worse than his bite. Do not trouble yourself about duelling pistols, my dear; it shall come to naught."

"Particularly if the gentleman hangs," I added thoughtfully. "Such an exhibition as Grey's, Neddie, must give rise to speculation—it has little of real feeling behind it, and too much of contrivance."

"Spurred by guilt, you would say?" My brother smiled. "Perhaps he merely affects a posture he believes necessary before the world. Grey is, after all, a bereaved husband, and expected to comport himself as such—however little he may grieve for his wife. Such a condition cannot be comfortable. He must suggest outrage, ire, and a desire for vengeance, when, in fact, all he may feel is relief."

"If he cannot feel what he ought, then guilt is natural and just," I returned; "but I cannot esteem him for it. Such unnatural behaviour must appear like deceit, and direct the suspicion of the world against him. Have you despatched a constable to London, Neddie, to enquire into Mr. Grey's movements?"

"One of Canterbury's fellows rode with The Larches' groom in pursuit of Grey last night, and remained in Town to discover what he could of the gentleman. I cannot dispute that Grey was in Pall Mall all evening; but I should be happy to learn where he spent the early part of the day. I do not expect Mr. Grey to betray himself so easily, however, Jane. If he had a hand in his wife's murder—for reasons we have yet to divine—he is not the sort of fool to be discovered."

"My dear," Lizzy interrupted, "if you cannot dispose this morning of the interesting question of Mr. Grey's guilt, perhaps you might bend your considerable intellect to the problems of packing. I should hate to own to any peculiar weakness, but I confess that I find myself quite overwhelmed. We cannot remove the entirety of Godmersham—and yet, what is of so little value as to be left to the French? I am virtually in despair, while you and Jane debate philosophy!"

"A thousand apologies, my dearest," Neddie cried, and knelt beside the box of books. "Surely you have an adequate supply of novels for our amusement? We cannot hope to shift *all* the library's volumes."

"Nor yet the better part of the furniture," his wife agreed mournfully. "There cannot be waggons enough; and besides, I could not answer for the damage along the road. And what of the children, Neddie? Should not they be sent away in safety now?—But what to despatch along with them? Clothes sufficient for a fortnight— or all of the boys' things for the Winchester Michaelmas term?"

"Place the matter entirely in Sackree's hands," Neddie advised. "Miss Sharpe may serve to assist her. You cannot rule every province, Lizzy, tho' the impulse to do so must be strong. As for the children—perhaps they should return to Town with Henry. I believe he intends a removal in a few days' time, and might serve them as escort."

"I could never allow them from my sight in the midst of such uncertainty," Lizzy said with decision. "If we must be forced from our home, we shall quit it together."

"Perhaps I might be of service to Miss Sharpe," I suggested. "I could sort the children's things without danger of confusion. And perhaps my own departure could conveniently be hastened? My mother cannot expect to be welcomed to a household in turmoil. Her September visit should be deferred until an easier time, and Cassandra and I returned to Bath."

"Pray do not consign us all to oblivion in a single paragraph!" Neddie protested. "You excite yourself unduly, Jane. There is no cause to send any of us from home on the strength of a mere rumour."

"You call it rumour?" Lizzy cried. "But Captain Woodford appeared so grave! His aspect very nearly one of defeat! One sight of his sombre countenance, and I was certain we should all be burnt in our beds—and the vexation of it is not to be borne! I have only just received my new gown for tomorrow's Assembly, as you know; and now all such frivolity must be suspended!"

"Not wear your new gown to the Race Week Assembly? Impossible!" Neddie snapped his fingers in dismissal. "I would never suspend any pleasure of yours, for so trifling an affair as an invasion. You shall have your ball, my dear, if Pratt must cut his way through Buonaparte's ranks to achieve it."

Lizzy laughed aloud and cuffed him lightly with a feather-duster. "You must believe me a foolish creature,

Neddie, if you can speak to me so. I might be a child of Fanny's age, and not an old married woman of two-and-thirty. I have quite resigned myself to the loss of the Assembly."

"You mistake, my dear. I merely refuse to be goaded into alarm by an idle report of a courier seen on the road, carrying intelligence that no one has actually heard."

"A courier?" I said, all alive to the word. "The self-same courier of Mrs. Grey?"

My brother nodded. "I encountered Captain Woodford along the Wingham road, a half-hour, perhaps, after his visit here. He told me what his sense of duty must forbid him sharing with a lady—that General Lord Forbes had received warning of the invasion, from a trusty in the service of the Crown, who espied a French courier in the green and gold livery of the Penfleur clan—that is Mrs. Grey's family—flying along the coast road yesterday morning. Early warning of Buonaparte's advance should be as gold on the Exchange, Jane, and the trusty surmised that such was the courier's purpose. The bankers sniff the wind before the politicians feel the storm, as no doubt you are aware."

"But the trusty did not learn the courier's intelligence himself?"

"Are you suggesting," Lizzy enquired in a menacing tone, "that all this effort at removal is so much parade and poppycock?"

"Not at all," Neddie assured her hastily. "Tho' hardly brilliant, Lord Forbes is a careful man. His devotion to his duty is legendary. He believed the moment ripe for a plan of evacuation, in the event that Buonaparte is upon the seas; but nothing certain can be known of the Emperor's movements."

"The General regards this trusty as so worthy of credence?" I asked.

"That I cannot say, being ignorant of the particulars. But I should guess that Lord Forbes has drawn a hasty conclusion, in the belief that no French courier might achieve these shores without the assistance of an invading fleet. He suspects our Navy is routed—but I cannot believe so much. Grey himself assures me that any number of couriers might traverse the Channel with letters of safe passage; and what a man of the world regards as commonplace, a gentleman farmer should never question."

"Then are we to live in this suspense," Lizzy cried, "never knowing whether we are to be turned from our beds?"

Neddie shrugged. "Such are the vagaries of war, my dearest. We might have removed to Town like our more fearful neighbours, several months since, and viewed the present chaos from a position of comfort; but we placed our faith in the protection of the Guards. Woodford informs me that if the French are sighted, the Canterbury beacon tower shall be fired. Until the flames go up in the night, we have nothing to fear; but if the faggots are lit, we must be ready to fly."

"Everything but our writing desks and the silver plate must remain." Lizzy glanced around with regret. "Oh, that I might strangle the fiend Buonaparte myself upon the shores of Pegwell! To think, that he shall have the run of our home—his officers plundering our cellars, his men butchering our pigs, and the rest scrawling careless French boot-blacking in great streaks across our marble floors!"

"If the Emperor chooses to take up residence," Neddie advised, "we may consider ourselves fortunate. He might as easily set fire to the place. Content yourself with a minimal removal, my dear, and pray that we shall find ourselves unpacking the lot, in a few weeks' time. We shall all of us strip to our shirtsleeves, and throw our backs into the endeavour. A few hours may see the worst of it behind us."

"Not if I hope to carry myself with credit at the Assembly tomorrow evening," Lizzy retorted. "A little of the work must be deferred. I cannot expect to do you justice, Neddie (pray forgive the unfortunate pun), without I spend some time under Mr. Hall's hands. Only consider the state of my hair!"

Since Lizzy appeared to distinct advantage, the slight blush of her exertions merely adding to her charms, I could not suppress a smile. "As I have long been the despair of the fashionable Mr. Hall," I told her, "I shall take myself off to the nursery at once, and see to the children's things."

I FOUND THE UPPER STOREYS IN THE THROES OF packing—and a fretful business it was, with far too many female voices raised in a quest for primacy. Mrs. Salkeld, the housekeeper, thought it necessarily her province to carry out Elizabeth's instructions—except in milady's own apartments, where Sayce, milady's maid, was adamant in claiming pride of place. The pitch of argument ran perilously high until milady herself, in her languid voice, banished both women to the ground floor of the house under threat of imminent dismissal.

When I went in search of Anne Sharpe, I found the case no better served in the attics—for among the children's things, Mrs. Salkeld had both the governess and the nursemaid, Sackree, to contend with. I drew Miss Sharpe firmly into the schoolroom and left the two older women—well-matched adversaries of long-standing—to sort out the playthings and smallclothes of nine different children, along with their trunks, bedding, keepsakes, and sundry animals, a menagerie that included three kittens, two grass snakes, and an ailing hedgehog.

"My dear Miss Sharpe," I said, "you must allow me to assist you with the backboards and the instruction books. Surely you cannot expect to manage all this alone!"

The schoolroom is a sparsely-furnished, whitewashed, sloping-roofed apartment tucked into a dormer of the great house. A shelf of stout books was ranged under one window; several samplers lay cast aside on a little stool, and a paint-box—probably Fanny's—sat forgotten on a table. A rage for transparencies several years back had left the windowpanes dotted with a scene or two, and a similar passion for silhouette-drawing had made of the walls an indifferent family portrait gallery— but otherwise the space can have few charms, particularly for one of Anne Sharpe's native elegance. Its windows too small and warped to permit of much air, and its grate insufficient for the extent of the space, the schoolroom is perishingly hot in summer and draughty in winter. Such healthful conditions, I believe, are considered necessary to the rearing of children— who must not be coddled in their formative years, or encouraged in the practise of luxury. I should never charge Neddie or Lizzy with a want of interest in their children's welfare—the number of persons consigned to the little ones' care is testament to their parents' liberality— but I might regard them as suffering from a certain lack of imagination. They rear their children as they themselves were raised—or, perhaps I should say, as Lizzy was raised. Her childhood was a progression from nursemaid to governess and thence to a fashionable school in Town—a period spent almost entirely in the upper floors of Goodnestone Farm. A child of privilege might live the better part of its life in a warren of nursery rooms, sleeping, playing, learning, and dining, all without descending the stairs! Thus are the scions of a baronet raised, in a world quite removed from their parents.

Neddie's case, until he came to Godmersham in his sixteenth year, was very different, indeed—for tho' in our infancy my mother put us all out to nurse with a woman in the village, our childish days were spent in a splendid hurly-burly of crowded rooms and shared beds.

When I gaze at these attics, I cannot help but think that a sensitive little soul might shrink under their influence, as a delicate plant will wither in a gale. How much more might be accomplished, for the enlargement of a young mind, in an atmosphere of cheerful contentment!

"Indeed," objected Anne Sharpe, "you are too solicitous, Miss Austen. I am sure to manage these few things very well alone, and must beg you to turn your energies where they might be of greater use. Pray offer your assistance to Mrs. Austen, who must greatly require it, and allow me to order my province." And then, with a little hesitation— "It is hardly of such moment, you know, if a few primers fall in the hands of the French."

"I only thought that you might be feeling unwell," I returned, "and might require a partner in your endeavour. I suffer myself from the head-ache on occasion, and must pity any of its victims."

Miss Sharpe blushed, and turned away. "I am quite recovered, I thank you. The necessity of quitting this place has entirely revived me. I cannot be low when so much of an urgent nature is toward. And we shall be leaving quite soon! I should not like Mr. Austen to find me behindhand in my work, when the moment for departing Kent is upon us."

I regarded her curiously. There was a slight fever-

ishness to her looks—a hectic tumble to her words—
that seemed at variance with their sense. She spoke of
duty, to be sure—she expressed herself as under an
obligation that might not be deferred—but from her
aspect it almost seemed that she was wild to be free of
Kent. Were the associations of this place, then, entirely
unhappy?

"Mr. Austen believes, Miss Sharpe, that we may exert
ourselves to little purpose." I eased onto a child's wood-
en bench, a sampler furled in my hands. "It is by no
means certain that Buonaparte is to invade; indeed, the
merest rumour appears to have animated the General's
anxiety. My brother has given no orders for the children's removal."

"I do not understand," she faltered. "We are not to be
evacuated, then? We are not to leave for London in a few
days' time?"

"As to that—I cannot say. I am sadly denied a full
knowledge of the officers' intentions. We must abide by
their instructions, of course—pack up our belongings
and make ready to flee, in the event that all our calculations are hollow." I smiled at her encouragingly. "Were
it not the sort of conduct unbecoming to a lady, Miss
Sharpe, I should suggest we lay a little wager. For who
knows what will be the outcome? It is ever the way when
Buonaparte has the ordering of events. The best-laid plans
are torn all asunder."

"So it seems," she replied unsteadily. "So it has always
proved, in my unhappy life."

"Miss Sharpe—"

"Pray leave me, Miss Austen, to attend to this chaos. I
am sure you have trunks enough of your own to fill."

It was undoubtedly a dismissal, and one that brooked
no refusal. I left the governess, her countenance grown
agitated and pale, to the business of the backboards and

books; and wondered very much as to the cause of her distress. Nothing so simple as a disgust for Mrs. Grey's murder could account for it. But I was hardly on such terms of intimacy as to invite Anne Sharpe's confidence. She moved presently in deeper waters, and must breast the current alone.

"AND SO YOU HAVE SEEN MR. GREY," HENRY SAID GAILY, when the footmen had served the first course of dinner and retired to the kitchen passage.

"And he has seen me," Neddie replied. "A less satisfactory meeting between two men of interest to one another, I cannot conceive. But come, brother—you have been cognizant of his banking practise some few years. What is your opinion of Grey?"

Henry shrugged. "I have formed none, Neddie. I cannot claim to be intimate with the man."

"Intimate! I do not know of anyone who is—excepting, perhaps, Captain Woodford, who I believe has known Grey from a boy."

"Grey is not the sort to encourage intimacy," Henry said thoughtfully. "He is of a taciturn, unbending disposition, and keeps his own counsel."

"But what is his reputation in Town?"

"He is a member of White's, of course. I should imagine that is where the groom found him last evening." Henry set down his fork and tasted his wine. "Or rather, he may often be seen among its clubmen, but whether any of them are likely to call Grey friend, I cannot say. Perhaps George Canning—"

"Canning? The Treasurer of the Navy?"

"The very same. He is a very deep file, George Canning, and quite in the confidence of Mr. Pitt. He is also a passionate gardener—and it is this that endears him to

Valentine Grey. I suppose you have heard of Grey's interest in exotic plants?"[1]

"I have heard very little of Mr. Grey," Neddie replied grimly, "and I now comprehend how unfortunate such ignorance must be, in the present circumstance. I begin to think I have led too retiring a life."

"But what of his character, Henry?" I pressed. "You have painted a very dry portrait, indeed! It is nothing like the quixotic fellow our brother encountered this morning!"

Henry studied me with interest. "Quixotic? I should say rather that Grey is calculating and shrewd. He is of a resentful disposition, and possessing considerable powers of intellect and energy himself, despises those of his fellows whose talents are inferior."

"His good opinion, once lost, is lost forever," Lizzy remarked from her end of the table.

Henry smiled at her. "Grey prizes loyalty and honour above all else. Such traits must serve him well in matters of business; but where ties of a more personal nature are concerned, I should imagine they would prove difficult to bear."

"Little wonder, then, that his wife could not love him," I murmured.

"They do seem an ill-matched pair," Henry conceded, "but they are not the first to find themselves tethered for life in an unequal harness."

[1] George Canning (1770–1827) served as Under-Secretary of State in 1796, and as Treasurer of the Navy from 1804–1806. As such, he had virtually no authority over naval organization or policy, which was administered by the First Lord of the Admiralty, but he was responsible for matters of naval finance in Parliament. This included the salaries of naval captains, the naval budget, and the disposition of the Secret Funds—monies set aside for the purpose of espionage, and unaccountable to Parliament.—*Editor's note.*

"Mr. Grey spends the better part of his time in London, I believe. Does his trade prevent him from moving in the first circles? Or has it proved a sort of entrée? What are his pursuits? His interests and ambitions?"

Henry was engrossed in the consumption of a quantity of buttered prawns. "I should hardly call Grey's sort of banking a *trade*, Jane. He inherited a vast concern second only to Hope's, unlike your jumped-up scrivener of a brother."[2]

"Surely you exaggerate," Neddie broke in.

"The fate of England sometimes hangs upon Grey's influence, brother." An unwonted expression of seriousness had suffused Henry's countenance. "He has any number of the Great quite comfortably in his pocket, and may move among them as an equal. Grey is the sort of man who might go anywhere, and meet anybody— but to my knowledge the Fashionable World commands none of his respect. He is the ornament of no particular set, tho' many would claim him. He is much in the affection of Mr. Pitt, but spurns the Tories as liberally as he does the Whigs; he was once spoken of as a likely advisor to the Treasury, but disdains the connivance of public office. And with the Prince, thank God, he will have nothing to do."[3]

Mr. Grey sounded remarkably like another gentle-

[2] The House of Hope was the powerful and influential Scots banking concern based in Amsterdam. Hope financed, among other things, Napoleon Bonaparte's government and campaigns. —*Editor's note.*

[3] William Pitt the Younger (1759–1806) was in his last months of life in August 1805. As minister of the Treasury, he was also prime minister of England. A brilliant, lonely, and calculating political genius, he was the foremost Tory of his generation and a lifelong adversary of the Prince of Wales. He was also an alcoholic, and his liver failed when he was forty-seven. He was carried, dying, from the House of Commons in December 1805, and died early in 1806.—*Editor's note.*

man in my acquaintance, Lord Harold Trowbridge—
and I wondered, for a moment, whether the two were
acquainted. Knowing a little of their characters, it was
impossible for me to consider either man the *friend* of
the other. Such subtle calculation as animated the spirit
and understanding of each, did not easily lend itself to
intimacy. They should rather be allies, or foes.

But then I checked my fanciful portrait of Grey before
it was half-formed. In ignorance of one gentleman's character, I employed another's as pattern—and did grievous
harm, no doubt, to the merits of both.

"If the mastery of neither politics nor Society is Mr.
Grey's object," Neddie persisted, "to what, then, may we
ascribe his ambition?"

Henry shook his head. "Therein lies the chief of the
man's power. He is a mystery to all but himself."

I sipped Neddie's excellent claret, and allowed my
thoughts to wander among the tantalising shades of
Henry's conversation. The blustering vagaries of Valentine Grey—his insistence that his wife was chaste—his
urgency in proving himself a man bereaved, and yet the
absence of feeling behind his words—all rose in my
mind with the force of argument: disputed, confused,
uncertain as to issue.

"And his wife, Henry—the wife he appears to have
banished to Kent," I said. "Was Françoise Grey merely an
impediment?"

"The lady was certainly a pawn, I believe, when she
was affianced to Valentine Grey—it was a marriage of
houses rather than hearts. It is indisputable that Grey
owes to his late wife a considerable part of his present
resources. The Penfleur family may command the fortunes of a continent, and in marrying Françoise, Grey
acceded a little to their power."

"And placed himself under the thumb of an empire,"
I observed.

Henry's eyebrows shot skywards, and he pushed away his plate. "I should never describe Grey as under anyone's thumb."

"Then you fail to consider clearly of the matter," I retorted. "Such a material bargain is never struck, without it is of benefit to both parties. The Penfleur family would be unlikely to part with their ward—and all the weight of their influence—for the paltry return of an estate in Kent. We must assume that Mr. Grey was to further the Penfleur interests in England."

"A delicate business, in time of war," Henry said.

"Perhaps he tired of his obligations," Neddie suggested, "and thought to be rid of them with his wife."

"But why throw the blame upon Denys Collingforth?" I objected. "Why should a man so wholly unconnected with Grey's concerns, be made to suffer for his infamy—if, indeed, he did away with his wife?"

"Perhaps because Collingforth is in no position to defend himself," Henry said wryly. "The man is entirely to pieces, and all of Canterbury knows it. Not a tradesman for miles has been paid by the fellow in months, and they say his pockets are to let to a host of creditors in Town."

"As bad as all that?" Lizzy murmured. "How very shocking, to be sure, to number such folk among one's acquaintance! Were Collingforth possessed of a title, or a position of some consequence, he might weather the storm with becoming grace; but as he is of a vulgar turn, and his wife little better, there is nothing to be done for them."

"They tell me in the Hound and Tooth that the man has run through all his wife's money, placed a mortgage on Prior's Farm, and faces certain ruin, now that Mrs. Grey is dead."

"Was she so much his protectress?" Neddie enquired sharply.

"As to that, I cannot say—but Collingforth's creditors might have allowed him a little more room, but for the fear of a murder charge. They are presently besieging Prior's Farm, and the bailiffs cannot be far behind." Henry hesitated, toying a little with his wineglass, then continued apologetically, "There are those who would say, brother, that you should better have clapped Collingforth in irons when you could. Circumstanced as he is, there is very little else for the man to contemplate than flight to the Continent. Indeed, some are asserting that he has already effected it."

"The Devil he has!" Neddie cried, and at Lizzy's faint moue of disapproval, added, "My dear, a thousand pardons. Brother, *who* would have it that Collingforth is fled?"

Henry shrugged. "Everyone and no one. The intimates of the Hound and Tooth, you understand, are most liberal with their words and chary of their proofs. I only repeat what is commonly held. I must leave you to sort out the business."

Neddie threw down his napkin, pushed back his chair, and commenced to pace the length of the dining-parlour. Lizzy sat even more upright in her chair, and regarded him with the liquid green gaze of a cat.

"It is too bad of you, Henry," she whispered in an aside. "You have quite put him off his turbot. I will not have the mutton spoilt."

"Tell me what you know of Collingforth's black-coated friend," Neddie commanded. "The inscrutable Mr. Everett."

"Ah!" Henry cried, and his countenance lightened. "There you have hit upon a malignant fellow, indeed! Everett had not been in Canterbury a day before it was generally circulated, that he is an arranger of prize-fights—which, tho' quite beyond the pale of the law, are much patronised by the Quality. Everett represents the interests of a champion, a bruising mulatto by the name of Delacroix, who hails from Martinique."

"But what can such a man have to do with Denys Collingforth?" I enquired.

"Collingforth has a passion for boxing, as he does for every game of sport, and has lost a fortune in betting around the ring. Men like Everett may always be found in the neighbourhood of such an one; for a susceptibility to the sport enslaves the purse as well as the man."

"But there was no prize-fight at the Canterbury Races," Neddie objected. He had ceased to pace, and now sank back into his chair. "Some other purpose must have drawn Everett hither."

"I believe he was forced to quit his lodgings in Town for a while," Henry replied. "A matter of some delicacy, only vaguely understood by the regulars at the Hound and Tooth. I surmised a brush with the law, and a desire to lie low; a sudden inspiration as to his friend Collingforth, and a hasty descent into Kent. I should not be surprised if an arranger of prize-fights was hardly ignorant of the coarser pursuits of his company—the fixing of cards and games of chance, and the ruin of innocent young men in gaming hells. I have seen an hundred Everetts in my time, and may now discern the type."

"Then we must conclude that the better part of Collingforth's trouble springs from debts of honour," I ventured. "His intimacy with Mrs. Grey is in part explained."

"Excellent, Jane!" Henry cried. "Depend upon it, you shall always provide the elegant turn of phrase that moves a tale along. I was coming to Mrs. Grey directly."

"Then pray do so at once," Neddie broke in. "This wandering among the byways of the Sporting Life grows tedious."

"Mrs. Grey, as we know, had her own affection for the Sporting Life. A certain coterie of Kentish gentlemen enjoyed the privilege of high play at her tables. It seems that as lately as the spring, Collingforth counted himself among their number—and that he lost heavily. Mrs. Grey held a fistful of Collingforth's vowels—and showed no sign of forgiving his debt."

"Then he should hardly mourn her early death," I said slowly. "I wonder whom else she numbered among her debtors?"

Henry shrugged. "Any amount of local bloods. The lady liked to win, and she possessed the Devil's own luck. Fully half the men of Canterbury were laying bets on the Commodore yesterday, in the hope of improving their fortunes—but to my dismay, they merely bargained further into ruin."

"And there was Mrs. Grey, exulting in her win, while their hopes turned to dust and ashes," Lizzy observed. "Lamentable behaviour, I must say."

"But incitement to murder?" I protested.

"Why not?" Henry's tone was rueful. "The notion has been no stranger to my own thoughts. At least ten times this morning I have considered whether a bullet to the head might not be the kindest service I could render the Commodore, if not myself."

"Henry!"

"It has been a purgatory merely to move about the town, Jane, I assure you. One young buck, who was far too much in wine, went so far as to suppose a collusion between myself and Mrs. Grey—with the Commodore's jockey throwing his race, and all the losses redounding somehow to my benefit. Or to Mrs. Grey's, had she lived— I cannot be entirely certain."

"But to return to Collingforth," Neddie urged. "Surely the death of his chief creditor must relieve his circumstances?"

"I am very much afraid that the loss of merely one among the company, can do little to repair his fortunes."

"A desperate man might kill for revenge, in the belief he had nothing to lose," I said.

"—particularly if he may so construct the murder scene as to divert attention from himself," Neddie added.

"The body in the chaise?"

"Of course. Only a fool would dispose of his victim so obviously—or a very cunning fellow, indeed. From the moment of Mrs. Grey's discovery, we have been struck by the implausibility of the body's lying as it did. We have endeavoured to clear Mr. Collingforth's name, and hardly credited the notion of his guilt—"

Neddie's words were cut short at the entrance of the manservant, Russell, from the kitchen passage.

"Forgive me, sir," he said with a bow, "but there is a constable just arrived from Canterbury. He is most insistent that he be seen. I have informed him that the second course is not yet served, but he refused—"

"Yer honour!"

A spare, bandy-legged fellow pushed past the footman and sprang lightly into the dining-parlour. "I've come fer yer gold sovereign, and I won't take no paper fer it, neither!"

A length of soiled cloth unfurled from his hands, its gold frogging glinting in the candlelight. Lizzy gasped, and Neddie started to his feet.

Mrs. Grey's scarlet riding habit.

# Chapter 6

## *What the Habit Revealed*

~

NEDDIE MOVED TO THE CONSTABLE'S SIDE AND TOOK THE gown from his hands. He whistled softly under his breath. "What is your name, my good sir?"

"Jacob Pyke, yer honour, and a Kentish man from four generations."

"Then I must assume you are familiar with the country, Mr. Pyke."

"I knows it as well as me own wife's arse, sir."

A choking sound from Lizzy, hastily covered by a cough.

"Mr. Pyke!" Neddie said sharply. "There are ladies present."

The constable scraped a bow, and leered all around. "Beggin' yer pardon, and I meant no harm, I'm sure, it being a common enough saying."

"And where did you discover *this*, Constable?"

The man's eyes shifted from my brother's face, and he began to worry the cap he now held in his hands. "In a hedgerow, yer honour, along the Wingham road a ways. 'Twas rolled in a piece of sacking, and thrust well back under the brush, so's not to be seen, like."

"Then how did you happen to discover it, Mr. Pyke?"

An expression of astonished innocence, so false as to cry foul, suffused the man's countenance. "Why—I were told to look for it, yer honour, same's every man jack in Kent. Poking about the leaves and such-like I were, with a long stick, and I comes to a largish lump what don't push back. 'Ho, ho,' I says to myself, 'that there lump ain't a branch nor a bramble no more'n my hand. That be a lady's gown, that be.' And I had it out on the end of the stick."

"I see." Neddie sounded amused. "I commend your dedication to duty, Mr. Pyke. And the sacking?"

"Yer honour never said nothing 'bout wanting no sacking," Pyke countered belligerently. "It weren't in my orders, and I can't be held accountable. Besides—the lad wanted it fer a remembrance, like."

"The lad?"

Mr. Pyke took a step backwards, and looked about him wildly. "Just a lad," he said, "of no account howsomever. He happened to be passing when I unrolled the gown, and begged for the sacking to show his mates." Betrayal was in every line of Constable Pyke's frame, and I surmised that the unfortunate lad—whatever his identity— had found the riding habit while larking in the hedgerow, and had turned it over to the first constable who came in his way. A finer sense of honour had animated the boy than should ever compel his elders; but presumably he had thought the sacking a sensational item enough— knowing nothing of Neddie's gold sovereign.

My brother sighed, and studied the man before him closely. "I should like to see this place," he said, "where you found the riding habit."

"Don't know as I could find it again, yer honour," the

constable protested. "It's nobbit a bit of hedgerow, same's any other."

"I should like you to be waiting along the Wingham road tomorrow morning, all the same," Neddie advised, "in expectation of my appearance. We shall go over the ground as closely as may be. And now, Mr. Pyke, pray be so good as to return to the kitchen. You shall have your gold sovereign, and some supper for your pains."

The man looked all his relief at Neddie's words, and bobbed a salute as he disappeared into the passage. My brother hastened to his library, where he kept his strong-box; and the exchange concluded, we heard no more of Mr. Pyke.

"Henry and I shall forgo the Port this evening, I think," Neddie said as he reappeared, "and beg you to join us immediately in the library. We must learn what the habit may tell us."

THE HABIT'S SECRETS, AT FIRST RECKONING, WERE DISappointingly few. Not so much as a drop of rusty brown stained the scarlet, that might suggest the spilling of blood—but as Mrs. Grey had been strangled with her own hair-ribbon, this was not to be expected.

We spread the gown on one of the library's long tables, and made a thorough examination of its folds. It was much creased, but hardly dirty, excepting the dust at the hem that must always accompany a foray out-of-doors; and perhaps some splashes of mud acquired in the lady's enthusiasm for the mounted chase. No tears or rents did we find, that might suggest a violence in the removal, other than a space at the back where one gold button was missing.

"Strange," Neddie muttered. "The button is found in Collingforth's chaise, but the garment from whence it came is left lying in a hedgerow. Was Mrs. Grey stripped of her clothes in the chaise itself, and the gown thrown aside later on the Wingham road?"

"That does not seem very likely," Lizzy replied. "I must believe we refine too much upon the gold button. It may have nothing whatsoever to do with Mrs. Grey's brutal end—she might have lost it in a trifling way, when Jane and I observed her to enter the chaise well before the final heat."

"Very true," Neddie said thoughtfully, "but it must rob my observation entirely of its honour, my dear!"

"One thing is certain," I added. "Mrs. Grey cannot have removed the habit herself. Such a quantity of buttons running from neck to waist should require the offices of a maid—or an intimate friend."

"We must assume, then, that she received assistance," Neddie said briskly, "—and that she knew whoever killed her."

"But why remove the gown at all?"

I stared at Henry wordlessly. "I am all astonishment that a man such as yourself—a Sporting Gentleman, and a man of the world—requires the explication of a spinster. Having heard a little of Mrs. Grey's reputation, surely you may form an idea of the circumstances."

My unfortunate brother opened his mouth, blushed red, and averted his gaze, to my profound amusement.

"As to *that*—I believe I shall await the coroner's report as to the state of the body," he replied. "But you mistake my meaning, Jane. I am perfectly well aware that a riding habit may prove an impediment to certain types of sport, and it is possible that Mrs. Grey divested herself of the garment with exactly the intention you suspect. But why remove the habit from the scene of the corpse's discovery? Why not leave it where the body was found?—If, indeed, the lady was even killed in Collingforth's chaise. And if she was not . . . how should her murderer transport a corpse, dressed only in a shift, under the eyes of all Canterbury?"

I had asked myself a similar question only yesterday. "I had believed the point was moot. We must assume that the murderer shifted the chaise—either to intercept Mrs. Grey on the Wingham road, or to transport her cooling body."

"Pretty tho' the plan may be, dear Jane, it cannot explain the disposal of the habit. Why should the murderer bother to thrust the thing under a hedgerow, if it bears no sign against himself?"

"Then let us dispute the matter less," Neddie broke in, "and examine the habit more."

He fetched his quizzing glass from the desk, and pored over the scarlet stuff. Lizzy ran her fingers thoughtfully along the hems, as tho' calculating the cost of its gold frogging, while Henry began to count the trail of buttons rather hurriedly under his breath. I merely stood by and surveyed their endeavours with a bemused expression. At length Neddie perceived my inactivity, and looked up.

"Yes, Jane?"

"It is the custom for ladies who ride, as you know, to carry nothing on their persons, not even a reticule. Their hands must necessarily be reserved for the control of the reins. And yet Mrs. Grey, travelling alone yesterday as she did, must have carried some provision about her. There are no pockets let into the seams of this gown; therefore I suggest you look for one concealed in the interior—perhaps within the lining."

"Excellent thought!" my brother cried, and seized the gown immediately.

"Not at the waist, dear," Lizzy advised him, "for it should never do to carry coins below the breast. I would survey the bodice itself."

And there, in an instant, we found what we were

seeking—a small pocket of cloth, let into the bodice's lining, quite invisible from the gown's exterior and only large enough to hold a trifle. Mrs. Grey, it seemed, had employed it to conceal a piece of notepaper. Any coins or bills she might have held had long since disappeared.

"Quickly, Neddie," Lizzy cried, with something closer to animation than I had ever observed in my brother's wife, "spread it out so that we all might see." The note was dated hurriedly, and rather illegibly, *19 August 1805*— the very date of yesterday's race-meeting.

*Ma chère Françoise—*
*You must know that I am a man run mad. If you do not consent to hear me, I will have but one recourse. Oh, God, that I had never seen your face! The Devil himself may assume just such a form, and move with such wanton grace, and yet remain the very soul of evil.*
*I shall be waiting in my chaise before the final heat is run. A word, a look, will tell me all—my salvation or destruction, equally in your hands.*

It was signed Denys Collingforth.

"Good God!" Lizzy ejaculated, and sat down abruptly in a chair. "So it is all a pack of lies! Collingforth *did* communicate with Mrs. Grey at the race-meeting, and the result was her furtive visit to the chaise. He must have seen her there. They must have spoken. And when she refused to meet his demands, he killed her in a rage!"

"You forget," I said gently. "We all observed her, large as life, an hour after the visit to Collingforth's chaise."

"What is that?" Lizzy snapped her fingers dismissively. "The scoundrel merely awaited her departure, and pursued her along the Wingham road. We have divined it all an age ago—we merely lacked sufficient proofs. The cowardly rogue, to discover her corpse himself, and protest an innocence that must be the grossest falsehood!"

"But why divest the lady of her habit?" Henry persisted. "I cannot find the sense of it. Did he suspect her to retain the tell-tale note, he might merely have searched the body for it. Depriving Mrs. Grey of her clothing, without destroying the letter, can have served him nothing."

"Perhaps he could not conceive of the cunning bodice pocket, and in his haste, merely disposed of the clothing as a surety," I suggested.

We were silent a moment in contemplation.

"I cannot like it," Neddie declared, and commenced to turn before the library's windows. "As my dear Lizzy has said, the note must strike at the very heart of motive. Whether he speaks of unrequited love—or unforgiven debt—Collingforth betrays an ungovernable passion; and the violence of his feeling might well have ended in murder."

"You must expose him to the coroner, I suppose?" Lizzy enquired faintly.

"I have no choice."

"But you *will* inform Mr. Collingforth of your discovery before tomorrow's inquest," I said. "Common decency would urge such a small consideration. He must be afforded a chance to explain himself."

Neddie did not immediately reply, but stood in a sombre attitude before the open windows. No breeze stirred the dark hair that fell artlessly across his brow; and if he perceived a little of the twilight scene beyond the glass, it was not reflected in the blankness of his gaze. Heavy thought, and warring duties, and the weight of care sat hard upon my brother's countenance. Then at last he wheeled and crossed to his wife.

"I fear, my dear, that regardless of the hour I must ride out to Prior's Farm, and destroy Collingforth's complaisance entirely. It is too grave and too ugly a business, to await the inquest in the morning." He kissed her hand

and looked to Henry. "Will you ride with me, brother? I cannot like the Kentish roads at present. Between the unknown murderer and the French invader, a man might find his death in any number of ways."

"I should ride with you in any case," Henry retorted, "as you very well know. But I wonder, Neddie, where you think to find Mr. Collingforth. As I intimated at dinner, he is believed to have fled."

"We must begin at Prior's Farm, and follow where the trail might lead. Do not sit up in expectation of our return," Neddie called to his wife, "for we shall be very late upon the road."

**Wednesday,
21 August 1805**

~

WE DID NOT SIT UP IN EXPECTATION OF MY BROTHERS' return, but tho' I followed the mistress of Godmersham to bed in an hour's time, neither could I sleep. The unhealthy excitement of the past two days quite robbed me of tranquillity, and so I took up my pen and the little book of unlined paper I keep always about me, and set down this account of the day. My candle-flame barely flickered in the torpid air, and but for the scratch of the nib in the breathless room, the great house was unnaturally quiet. I had not doused the light a half-hour, however, before the hallooing of the porter at the gate, and the clatter of horses' hooves on the sweep, announced the gentlemen's return.

I hoped for a full account this morning, but was most tediously put off—for when I sought the breakfast-parlour at ten o'clock, I found only Lizzy in possession, and a very cross Lizzy, indeed.

"Your brothers are already gone, Jane," she said over her teacup, "for the inquest is to be at noon, and Neddie *would* search the hedgerows with that detestable man Pyke, before he might face the coroner with something like self-possession."

"Then let us hope that Pyke has consulted his lad," I returned, "that Neddie's efforts might end in something."

"You do think of everything, Jane." Lizzy set down her cup and dusted her fingertips for crumbs. "I am sure that Neddie should be lost without you and Henry to give him spur. I required him to return to the house before venturing into Canterbury, by the by, in the event you wished to accompany him. . . ."

Lizzy's natural delicacy prevented her from adding the words, ". . . *since you have made such a habit of inquests of late,* "and I mentally praised the excellent breeding of baronets' daughters. I settled myself into a chair.

"Tea, Daisy, I think—and perhaps some toast."

"Very good, miss." The housemaid bobbed vaguely in my direction, and quitted the room with obvious reluctance. I leaned conspiratorially towards Lizzy.

"What of Collingforth and the interesting note?"

"I could get nothing from your brother—except that Collingforth was not to be found at Prior's Farm, and his wife has not seen him since Monday e'en. Neddie says that she was quite distracted, and fainted twice in a quarter-hour."

"Did they show her the unfortunate note?"

"Why else should she faint?"

"I suppose we must conclude the hand to be Collingforth's, then. And Mr. Everett?"

"—was naturally your brother's next resort. But when Neddie arrived quite late at the Hound and Tooth, it was to be greeted with the intelligence that Mr. Everett had settled his bill some hours since, and had quitted the place entirely."

"Then it is as Henry feared. Collingforth and Everett have fled in terror of the Law."

Lizzy nodded expressionlessly. "I confess your poor brother has taken it quite to heart. He feels himself to be excessively to blame, and utterly in neglect of his duty—however little any of us should tell him so."

"You may be certain that Mr. Grey will not be so forbearing."

"This flight cannot help Collingforth's chances before the coroner and his panel," Lizzy added.

The passage door swung open, and Daisy's young face appeared over a tray of tea and toast. I accepted it gratefully, and poured out a cup.

"It must look like an admission of guilt," I agreed. "But I wonder—"

"You cannot believe him innocent, Jane!"

"A wider experience of the world has taught me, Lizzy, that I am capable of believing any number of things. Denys Collingforth might be a murderer, it is true—or he may be merely a man pushed past endurance, by an unhappy congruence of circumstances. Ruined by debt, and now suspected of murder—what desperate fellow, unsure of his chances, might not resort to flight?"

Lizzy considered this in silence, while I consumed a quantity of toast. Godmersham's stillroom was evident upon the table, in an admirable preserve of quince, that I knew I should long for in the relative deprivation of a Bath winter.

"I suppose anyone might have murdered the woman, and placed the note in her bodice," Lizzy observed at last.

"But the handwriting?"

My sister shrugged. "Let us suppose that Collingforth sent the letter after all—that he sent it well before the events of Monday, and the note survived in Mrs. Grey's correspondence."

"But Monday's date is inscribed above."

"It is a small thing to forge a date, Jane—hardly of the same order as the forgery of an entire note."

"Very true. I confess, Lizzy, that I had no notion you possessed so cunning a mind. You display a decided talent for subterfuge, and were Neddie aware of it, he should never trust you farther from home than Chilham."

"I have spent the better part of my existence in deceiving my friends," she returned with complaisance, "and if you betray me to the world, Jane, I shall deny you the freedom of Godmersham forever."

"Your secret is safe with me. But there is one point on which I should like your opinion. A note of Collingforth's, placed to advantage and quite out of context, should serve, like the body in the chaise, to throw suspicion far from the actual murderer. But why conceal the note in the habit? Why not leave it in Mrs. Grey's dead hand?"

"Perhaps to underline its plausibility," Lizzy offered. "Two such items, found together, might appear excessive. But placed at a distance, and discovered by individual parties, entirely without reference to one another—"

"Admirable." I partook of the last bit of toast with regret. "The coroner is unlikely to exhibit so much imagination, however."

"You comprehend, Jane, that our notion is only possible if we suppose the murderer to possess an intimacy with Mrs. Grey's correspondence." Lizzy refolded her napkin and arranged it beside her plate. "Someone of her household, perhaps."

Or someone familiar at least with her desk. The image of Captain Woodford and Edward Bridges in the lady's saloon the night of her murder filled my mind. But I only gazed at Lizzy speculatively.

"You *are* in a fever to indict Mr. Grey, my dear. And the poor man has done very little that we know of, to deserve it!"

"He had the shockingly bad form to marry that woman in the first place," she replied caustically, "and to challenge my husband in the second. I cannot like him, Jane, however little I love poor Collingforth."

"We must hope that *somebody* loves poor Collingforth," I observed, "for the coroner most certainly shall not."

# Chapter 7

# A Canterbury Tale

*21 August 1805, cont'd.*

~

NEDDIE AND HENRY RETURNED SOON AFTER BREAKFAST, shaking their heads at the duplicity of men in general, and Constable Pyke in particular. The fellow had drunk the better part of his sovereign in the Hound and Tooth, and was utterly insensible at the appointed hour for meeting. My brothers dallied along the Wingham road for some time, expecting Pyke at every moment. A breathless boy proved their messenger instead—trotting along the hot and dusty road with the constable's regrets. Mr. Pyke was indisposed, and Neddie's errand for nothing.

"Lizzy assured me that you would wish to attend the inquest," he said to me now, over a cooling glass of lemonade, "and I have returned to Godmersham expressly that Henry and I might convey you into Canterbury in the barouche."

"You are very good—"

"Do not tell me that you intend to refuse!" He set down his glass with an emphasis that might have shattered a lesser piece. "Am I to be sent on a fool's errand every hour of the day?"

"Of course I should be happy to accompany you into Canterbury," I said quickly. "I might complete a few purchases towards my toilette, before tonight's Assembly."

"I see that Lizzy was entirely mistaken in your character," he returned, amused. "She was convinced you should be drawn to the macabre deliberation as a fly to jam."

"It is just that I have learned to despise the coroner and his panel, Neddie."

"You are acquainted with Mr. Wing?"

"Of particular coroners I may say nothing. Mr. Wing, and his merits or detractions, are entirely unknown to me, as I am sure you are aware. It is just that every instance of a coroner's judgement I have seen, has proved so fallacious and, indeed, injurious to the parties concerned, that I dread to countenance another by attending."

"Strong words, Jane. Unless I am very much mistaken, Mr. Wing and his panel shall return the only conceivable verdict in the present case."

"—That Mrs. Grey was murdered, and by Denys Collingforth."

"Can there be any other construction placed upon events?"

"You know full well, Neddie, that there can."

He was silent a moment.

"Given how little we truly comprehend of what was toward, any judgement at present must be the grossest presumption. What is required is *time*, and sufficient proofs, if the guilty party is to be charged. That must be true whether Mr. Collingforth is eventually revealed as that party or no."

"You are suggesting I should request of Mr. Wing a postponement."

"As Justice, you might be heard."

"But Valentine Grey is most insistent that the burial be effected at the soonest moment. In this heat, the decay of the corpse must be advanced; and yet the coroner's panel must view the body before they are empanelled. Any delay will be most unfortunate for all concerned."[1]

"That is true. You must do as you think best, of course."

"I must confess that I long for a swift judgement against Collingforth," he replied with becoming candour. "The man is already fled, and quite unlikely to be discovered; he cannot suffer from the charge. It is the judgement, in fine, that all of Kent expects. Valentine Grey would be appeased. I should feel that I had discharged my duty, and there would be an end to the affair."

"Until you found yourself lying wakeful at night, besieged with a thousand doubts as to the body's disposition," I said. "Why was it returned to the race-meeting at all, much less to Collingforth's chaise? That, and an hundred other questions, should plague you until your final hour."

"God preserve me from a prescient woman!" Neddie exclaimed. He drew his watch from his waistcoat. "Let us summon the carriage, Jane, and set about the wretched business."

WE MADE OUR WAY DOWN THE CANTERBURY ROAD UNDER a blazing sky, with the Stour very low in its banks, and a

---

[1] It was considered necessary for a coroner's jury to view the corpse, in order to form a judgment about the manner of death. This practice was later abolished, and replaced with medical examiners' sworn testimony.—*Editor's note.*

haze of insects hovering over the bent heads of the meadow flowers. Already a shelf of cloud hung over the Kentish downs, replete with the false promise of a shower; I knew these clouds of old, and dismissed them as false friends. If Napoleon's hordes had truly embarked for Kent, as the London papers would have it, then Fortune sailed with them. No furious wave should guard the chalk cliffs, or howling wind send the flotilla to oblivion; the French might make the crossing unharassed but for the few leaking, timeworn vessels of the Royal Navy's Channel fleet.

As Neddie's bays jingled their harness, and snorted at the dust, I considered of my brother Frank, and the daily perils he endured. His circumstances must be uppermost in my thoughts, far more than the invasion's threat to Kent; for if the Navy were overwhelmed, and Frank cut down by a French gun, it mattered little what hole we bolted to. The Kingdom would capitulate in a matter of days.

Such a surge of melancholy was unlike my usual spirits, and I detected the effect of the oppressive weather—the lurking, ominous portent of the heat, as though even the air above Kent awaited the thunder of cannon. Activity was the best remedy for such thoughts; but the fever of packing was done, the delights of dressing for the Assembly still ahead; I could hardly do better than to expend my energies in a trip to town.

Canterbury is a place that I have known and admired for almost half my life. Its soaring fortifications, so thick that ten men might walk abreast, and the spires of its venerable cathedral rising above its prosperous shops and houses, must proclaim its storied place in English history. Crowds of the penitent and the hopeful still choke the narrow streets on high holy days, while those who would profit by the pious, hawk their relics and bits of the True Cross under the shadow of the cathedral gates.

It was to the West Gate we proceeded this morning, for tho' the Canterbury gaol is some miles distant, in Longport, the constabulary's offices are housed hard by the gate, in a crabbed and swaybacked Tudor building desperately in want of whitewash. A few steps along the street stood the Hound and Tooth, where the inquest was to be held.

"We shall call for you at White Friars, in two hours' time," Henry assured me. This was the elegant house belonging to Mrs. Knight, Neddie's adoptive mother, not far from the cathedral close. I was always happy to visit Mrs. Knight, who had shown such good sense in reverting Godmersham to my brother well in advance of her own death; for she had been willed a life interest in the estate, and might have presided in Lizzy's place a decade or more. In Canterbury, however, she might learn all the news of her friends without stirring a step from her door; she had the comforts of ready provision, without the care of an estate.

"White Friars, in two hours' time," I repeated, and Henry handed me from the barouche. I watched the coachman's impatient progress down the crowded High Street, until the carriage had turned in at the Hound and Tooth's stableyard; then my gaze drifted back along bow-windowed shopfronts and came to rest upon the curtained first floor of Delmar's Rooms. Here was the scene of this evening's ball—where Mrs. Grey, and all her deceits, should be forgot for a time. Tho' my purse had grown thin from so protracted a visit in Kent, I intended to make as fine an appearance as my means and years would allow. A new pair of long silk gloves, at the very least, was quite essential—and perhaps an ornament for my hair. I turned with a little skip of pleasure, and went in search of the linendraper.

· · ·

"MISS AUSTEN! *JANE!*"

The voice was Harriot Bridges's—so very like Lizzy's, and yet lacking her languid elegance. Harriot, tho' four-and-twenty, retained all the claims of youth, and might betray the breathlessness of sixteen in her accent. She hastened down the length of the draper's shop, still clutching a card of lace, and embraced me as an old friend.

"Harriot! You are blooming. And does my sister accompany you?" I enquired, with real pleasure. All resemblance to Lizzy ended in her sister's voice; for Harriot's hair was a light brown, and her eyes were blue—where Lizzy was a graceful column, Harriot was a cheerful rolling-pin.

"She does not, I am sorry to say. You find me quite alone—excepting my brother, Mr. Bridges, who consented to drive me into town. But how delightful to find you here! Have you completed your purchases? And what do you think of this lace? I confess it is rather dear—but quite bewitching, when I consider of my drab old gown. I might sew it along the flounce in a quarter-hour, and feel myself the queen of the Assembly!"

I had learned long ago that Harriot rarely required an answer, or valued an opinion; she was content to swim in an easy flow of conversation that was as unconsidered as it was constant; and so I merely smiled, and nodded, and hovered at her elbow, while she flitted among the shop's fine stuffs like a bee in a full-blown border. It was part of her enchantment to be as wanting in guile as a child; men found her rosy plumpness and inveterate good humour utterly bewitching; she was constantly in request among the wide acquaintance she cultivated in Kent. It was merely a wonder, I thought as I found her laughing over a length of sprigged muslin, that she had not been snatched up by Captain Woodford long ago.

"And how does Mr. Bridges?"

Harriot pulled a face. "Very ill, indeed. He is fretful and tiresome and hovers about the house until I think I shall run mad! It would be one thing if my brother managed some pleasant conversation—if he endeavoured, at least, to be charming—but he mutters barely a word, and only then when he is spoken to. I thought Cassandra might have the taming of him—he was prodigiously civil to her last week, and seemed to exert himself a little, as he rarely does when we are just a family at home—but he has fallen mumpish of late, and can barely be stirred to exercise his horse. Did I not know Edward, indeed, I should think him to be suffering from a Dreadful Presentiment."

"A Dreadful Presentiment?"

Harriot looked over her shoulder, and attempted an air of gravity. "He seems a man goaded past endurance, Jane. He can neither submit to the confinement of the Farm, nor find courage to venture beyond it. He has not been farther than the lane into the Park, in fully two days!"

"How extraordinary." Mr. Bridges was the sort of gentleman who was never to be found at home. Fishing, playing at cricket, cocking, or riding were his usual pursuits; but Harriot's description suggested he was ill. "He consented to drive you into town today, however?"

"On account of Mrs. Grey's inquest. My brother was most insistent that he should attend—the duty of a clergyman, he said, tho' I believe that is so much stuff. When has Edward ever considered the duties of a clergyman before his own comfort?"

There would be no proper answer to such a comment; and the speaker being Harriot, happily none was expected. But her words must give me cause to wonder. Edward Bridges was behaving like a man in fear for his life—and his behaviour might be marked from the very day of Mrs. Grey's death. He bore watching.

"Does Mr. Bridges intend the Assembly this evening?"

"Oh, yes—as does Captain Woodford!" Harriot cried, her countenance reddening.

"Captain Woodford? You astonish me, Harriot. From his aspect yesterday, I was certain he should be mounted in a beacon post somewhere along the coast, searching the horizon with his one good eye, and single-handedly in defence of the French."

"How can you speak of him so?" she said reproachfully. "I am sure I can offer him nothing but respect. Such wounds as he has suffered—"

"Yes, yes," I rejoined, "but only consider how ludicrous, Harriot! At one moment the Guards would have us dismantle entire estates, and in the next, they are dashing about the floor of Delmar's Rooms, as tho' Buonaparte might be bested in a quadrille!"

"Captain Woodford assured me that it was a question of honour," Harriot told me stiffly. "General Lord Forbes would not have the populace alarmed, by an appearance of anxiety on the part of his men."

"How like a man of the General's talents," I muttered, thinking of Neddie's sainfoin harvest put to burn; but the irony must be lost on Harriot.

I PARTED FROM LIZZY'S SISTER IN THE HIGH, AND TOOK my separate way to the circulating library. I selected one of Maria Edgeworth's novels—*Castle Rackrent*—then turned my steps towards Mrs. Knight at White Friars, a quarter-hour before my brothers were expected. I might sit for a decent interval with the older woman, and regale her with Fanny's exploits and the progress of my nephew Edward's cold, without prolonging the visit beyond what was comfortable.

To my surprise, however, the housemaid informed me that Mrs. Knight was not at home. I was enough an intimate of White Friars, however, that I was invited very civilly within, and offered a glass of wine and a slice of lemon cake. When Neddie and Henry called to claim me, I was thus established in all the splendour of an empty apartment, with an aspect giving out on a late-August garden, quite engrossed in my book.

"This is living fine, indeed," Neddie cried. "Poor Collingforth is charged with murder, and you can do nothing but consume a quantity of cake!"

I closed my book and surveyed him narrowly. "Lizzy has informed me that you are invariably peevish when suffering the pangs of hunger. Call for some more cake, I beg, and tell me of the inquest. Was Mr. Grey in evidence?"

"He arrived in haste, some moments after the jury had viewed the remains of his wife. Mr. Wing, our coroner, actually called Grey to the stand—but he could offer little concerning his wife's death, beyond attesting that he was absent from the country at the time."

"And did Mr. Wing enquire as to his movements?"

"He did not. A gentleman's word, after all, is his bond." Neddie could affect the ironical nearly as well as myself. His own man in London, it seemed, had not yet returned with the desired intelligence.

"You presented the note?"

"And had the pleasure of witnessing Mrs. Collingforth called. The coroner thought it necessary she should attest to her husband's hand—which she did, albeit in an inaudible tone. She looked very ill."

"She fainted," Henry supplied.

"Of course she did," I returned impatiently. "It was expected by everyone in attendance. But I am astonished that she should admit to recognising the hand. Even the most truthful of wives might be forgiven a prevarication, in such a cause."

"Perhaps Laetitia Collingforth has other feelings,

somewhat less expected in a wife," Neddie suggested delicately.

"Such as—a desire for revenge against her husband?"

"She has been made to look a fool before her neighbours."

"True," I said. "But what of the letter in French, discovered within the scandalous novel, Neddie? Did Mr. Grey still maintain that it was sent by a courier?"

"Of course. Any other admission—such as the existence of yet another lover—should serve to cloud the waters. For whatever reason, Mr. Grey desired a swift conclusion to the day's events. He was not inspired to confuse the coroner's judgement. And as we know, Jane, Mrs. Grey *did* receive a courier."

"—Tho' not on the shores of Pegwell Bay," I mused.

"You have neglected to mention the lad," Henry prodded.

Neddie frowned. "It cannot hope to serve Collingforth's case. But perhaps Henry should inform you, Jane. I had stepped out when the lad was called."

"The lad?"

"An undergroom of James Wildman's," Henry supplied. "He had been left to hold the horse while Wildman circulated among the crowd. He was positioned only a hundred yards, perhaps, from our own coach."

"I remember Mr. Wildman's equipage," I said; and indeed, the dark blue fittings of the carriage's interior were elegant in the extreme, as suited the master of Chilham Castle.

"The lad professes to have seen a gentleman unknown to him, enter Collingforth's chaise."

"Could he describe this person?"

"He could not," Henry said, "and being just then distracted by some orders of Wildman's, he did not observe the gentleman to depart. Some time later, when he chanced to look again at Collingforth's chaise, it was to find Mrs. Grey on the point of quitting the interior—presumably after her conference with Collingforth himself."

"Or the unknown gentleman," I said thoughtfully. "And is this boy to be credited?"

Henry shrugged. "Wildman would have it that he comes of a respectable family, in the Castle's employ these many years, and that he has never been known for a fanciful nature."

"How very odd," I said slowly. "It is as tho' Collingforth's chaise was to let for the use of any number of passersby. Are we to assume, then, that Mrs. Grey was acquainted with the stranger? And that she met him by design within the borrowed chaise?"

"I should not be surprised to hear it," Neddie replied. "Nothing that lady did while alive can seem extraordinary now in death. She was accustomed to liberties and behaviours that, in another, might seem inexplicable."

"What did the coroner make of the stable lad's words?"

"Very little, it would seem, since he returned a verdict against Mr. Collingforth."

"Recollect, Jane, that all this is said to have occurred before the final heat," Henry observed, "when Collingforth is known to have been at the cockpit, in company with his friend Everett. He was seen and recognised there by a score of his acquaintance; but, of course, it is immaterial where Collingforth was when Mrs. Grey was yet *alive*."

"It is clear, nonetheless, that despite her husband's protests, there is a man in Mrs. Grey's case," I declared. "That man is hardly Denys Collingforth. Wildman's groom should have recognised so near a neighbour. We must apply ourselves, Neddie, to learning the name of the Unknown Cicisbeo without further delay."

"Why should you exert yourself, Jane, for a rogue like

Collingforth?" my brother asked me curiously. "He is dissolute, nearly ruined by gaming and drink, and he is said to treat his wife abominably. You are hardly even acquainted, and can certainly bear him no affection."

"But I am increasingly convinced that someone has endeavoured to place his neck in a noose," I replied, "and I cannot bear to think that such malevolent cunning should go undetected, much less unpunished. That is all. Call it a simple desire for justice, if you will."

"Or the desire to outwit a foe," he retorted. "I swear you might almost be a man at times. No wonder you are the despair of our mother, Jane."

"She may have Cassandra to console her," I said. And smiled.

# Chapter 8

## At Delmar's Rooms

~

HOWEVER RIDICULOUS I MIGHT FIND THE GUARDS' DECISION to attend the Race Week Assembly, I could see nothing reprehensible in my own participation. I dearly love a ball. And the crowd that moves so indolently through the smart Delmar's Rooms, tho' hardly as fine as the most select society of London, is nonetheless a glittering parade. There is *that* about the company—a liberality of means, a refinement of experience, an elegance of conduct and expression—that must lift the meanest participant to a more elevated plane. It is all too likely that such delights will prove depressingly rare in my future life; my father's death can only reduce my modest fortunes still further; and as the decade of my thirties opens, I must be but too sensible of the continuing diminution of my looks. It is a melancholy picture—one that might thrust me entirely into despair, were I not possessed of those inner resources without which a woman is nothing. However retired my future days, I will have my wit to sustain me—the secret sarcasms of my pen, that must subject even the greatest to my power, unbeknownst to themselves. I shall have long walks in sun and shadow with my dearest sister, Cassandra. I shall have desultory hours of practise on a hired and indifferent piano. And on occasion, courtesy of Neddie and Lizzy, I shall have the illicit pleasure of a Canterbury ball.

While life may still offer a good-size room, braced with roaring fires and a plethora of wax candles—while "The Comical Fellow" or "The Shrewsbury Lasses" still thread their delightful chords through the babble of conversation—while some hundred couples of a nodding acquaintance, and a full detachment of the Coldstream Guards, exist as it were for my pleasure alone—I cannot fail of enjoyment. Let melancholy be banished for another day, when I am too-long marooned in the rains of Bath, and the regrets of my vanished youth.

And thus, heedless of murder and the threat of invasion both, I pinned the shoe-roses to my slippers this evening, adjusted my muslin shawl, and allowed myself to be borne away to yet another scene of dissipation. I had not been arrived five minutes, before I felt my morals to be thoroughly corrupted.

That this was the result of gallantries easily paid, from at least three gentlemen in my general acquaintance, might readily be imagined. I entered upon the scene in the company of the Godmersham party—Neddie, Henry, Lizzy, and myself—with every expectation of pleasure. I wore a borrowed gown, made over in respect of the current season, that became me almost as much as it had graced Lizzy two summers before; my hair had been cut and dressed in curls all about my forehead, courtesy of the obliging Mr. Hall; and despite the closing of that decade beyond which a woman is commonly believed to cherish few hopes, I knew myself to be presently in good looks. I shall never again possess the bloom of eighteen; the bones of my face have sharpened of late, particularly about the nose, as tho' the flesh is stretched too tightly over it, and my complexion is coarser than it was ten years ago. But several months' trial of the air of Kent, taken in daily doses through long country walks, *will* have their effect; and despite the worry of advancing French hordes, and a commensurate anxiety for the safety of my naval brothers, my eyes were as bright as though I were embarked upon my very first ball.

"The Godmersham party! At long last!"

Mr. Edward Taylor advanced upon us with arms outstretched, as befits a very old acquaintance. Those dark eyes I had so long ago celebrated, and mourned upon his betrothal to another, were alight with anticipation and scandal; little else of his former self could be traced in the present figure. Age will take its toll, even among the wealthy of Kent; and the object of my girlhood dreams was become florid and balding. But his ample waistcoat was a testament to the excellent management of his household at Bifrons Park—and so I judged Edward Taylor happy, and excused his fall from grace.

"You have had us all on tenterhooks, man! Thank God that you did not forgo the Assembly." Mr. Taylor seized my brother Neddie's arm. "Is the fellow Collingforth laid by the heels? The matter quite resolved already? Or shall you have recourse to the authorities in London?"

"Don't look so dull and stupid, my dear," Lizzy murmured in Neddie's ear. "He is enquiring about the Grey woman's murder."

"I had perceived that much, Lizzy," Neddie returned,

and bowed to Mr. Taylor with careless grace. "You astonish me, Edward. I had hoped that at least you—who care nothing for horseflesh, and never venture farther than your own spring in such heated weather—might have escaped the tide of Race Week gossip. But if even Mr. Taylor is not immune, I must resign myself to being the object of every eye."

"So that's the way of it, is it?" Mr. Taylor rejoined, not to be deterred. "You intend to tell us nothing?"

"The ways of Justice, like the secrets of the marriage bed, are best enshrouded in silence," Neddie intoned.

Mr. Taylor merely snorted at this, while Lizzy laid a hand caressingly on my brother's shoulder. "Poor lamb," she crooned, "you *shall* be led to the slaughter. I give you a quarter-hour, my dear, at the hands of your dearest friends—and then we shall see how enshrouded your tongue may be. Come along, Jane."

And so I fled in Lizzy's bewitching train, bobbing and nodding to a multitude on either side, to take up a position just below the musicians, where we might observe the gathering company. I expected my sister Cassandra, and Harriot Bridges, among them; and was impatient to converse at long last with the former.

Lizzy snapped open her ivory fan—a gift from my brother Charles, when *Endymion* was in the Mediterranean—and began to waft a humid air about our faces. I do not believe there is a lady living who can carry off dark grey silk so becomingly as Lizzy. The new gown—so long expected from her modiste—had been ordered a month previous, during a flying visit to London; and with its cap sleeves, fitted bodice, and extraordinary turban of jet and feathers, it looked admirably suited to the wardrobe of a queen. Lizzy is in the last days of mourning for her eldest sister, Fanny Cage, who departed this life in May; but her dark colouring makes even the dusky shades of grief appear to advantage.

"Good God, it is *hot*," she murmured. "Every sensible young lady will be slipping into the garden for a turn in the moonlight before the hour is out. How unfortunate that such a recourse is denied to *me*. You, however, might avail yourself—having neither a husband to detain you, nor an anxious regard for your reputation."

"And with whom would you have me take a turn, Lizzy?"

"Anyone might do for a little moonlight," she said, shrugging carelessly. "It conceals a host of sins, and lends an aura of grandeur to the most common physiognomy. Take my brother, Mr. Bridges, for instance—he can look quite well-made with a little shadow to lend him substance."

"I understood from your sister Harriot that Mr. Bridges was indisposed. But perhaps it has passed off, if he truly intends the ball this evening."

"My brother is nothing if not inconstant. He considers it as chief among his charms—being of a turn to mistake an unpardonable weakness for an amiable disposition."

"You are severe upon him."

"The Reverend Brook-Edward Bridges is the sort of man I cannot help but despise," she rejoined sharply. "He believes the world exists to sustain his follies, and ask nothing of him in return. My brother was spoilt as a youth, and age has merely made him indolent. He sponges on my mother and my husband for the relief of his debts, and is foolish enough to believe that he might prevail upon an excellent woman to make his fortune in marriage. Yes, Jane, I am severe upon him—for he has disappointed me these fifteen years at least."

I smiled, catching at but a part of her diatribe. "And which lady is so fortunate as to deserve the honour of Mr. Bridges's attentions? She cannot possess less than ten thousand pounds, I daresay—tho' as the son of a baronet, he might endeavour to look still higher."

"Oh, Jane—have you not seen? Have you not understood?" Lizzy was too well-bred to cry out in exasperation, but the murmured words carried a singular vehemence. "My brother intends that either you or Cassandra shall be his bride. If Cassandra's visit to Goodnestone fails of the desired result, you shall be sent for next week, as a second string to his fiddle. It matters not to Edward which of your hearts he engages; it merely suffices to secure one or the other."

I could not reply for fully five seconds. My heart pounded in my chest with indignation, and the blood rose to my heated cheeks, while speech was left entirely at bay. Lizzy, for her part, retained the serenity of her air—I imagine she might as easily plot regicide behind that extraordinary countenance—and murmured a greeting to a passing acquaintance.

"There is Lady Elizabeth Finch-Hatton," she observed, "shockingly underdressed as usual. I cannot think what she finds to admire in the spectacle of her own bosom. Her husband certainly does not—he will already be settled at whist. And there is her daughter, the feckless Louisa—a not unpretty sort of girl, but distressingly wanting in understanding. I expect them to descend upon Godmersham tomorrow—did I mention as much? They always take us in on their return to Eastwell Park; it has become quite the Race Week custom. I shall have to order a good dinner, regardless of the threat of the French."

"You cannot have spoken seriously just now, Lizzy," I muttered purposefully in her ear. "You can only have intended it as a poor sort of jest."

"—You would refer to my brother's hopes? I should never sport with *those*, my dearest Jane. I find them too tedious to provide of much wit. But I suspect I have distressed you. I did not intend it. I thought that one of your penetration would have marked Edward out long ago."

"Mr. Bridges is certainly a gallant gentleman," I managed, "but as for having the slightest pretension to the affections of either Cassandra or myself—"

"I must confess that in making you both his object, my brother has not simply consulted himself. The alliance is my mother's dearest wish—and this has, in great measure, served to guide him."

"Lady Bridges desires the match?"

Lizzy's superb green eyes glanced at me sidelong. "I perceive that you are all astonishment, Jane. But you must know that as to fortune, my mother is hardly particular. Her anxiety is all for Edward's welfare. She fears he will end by fleeing to the Continent, pursued by his numerous creditors, does he fail to secure a sensible wife. Lady Bridges is aware that, however slim their resources, the Austens have always been possessed of sense. She could not fashion a better helpmeet out of whole cloth, did she even possess the power, than yourself or Cassandra."

"But we have barely a pound to spare between us!" I protested. "How can we be expected to secure Mr. Bridges's fortunes?"

"Ah." Lizzy sighed. "How, indeed? I have represented as much to Mamma. But she will hear nothing against either of you. My brother's circumstances, however presently involved, shall be speedily arranged by Lady Bridges herself, once his betrothal is announced. Provided, of course"—and here the green gaze turned calculating as a cat's—"that Mamma approves of his choice."

"Good God!" I cried. "Can it be possible? Mr. Bridges to marry an Austen, simply for the relief of his debts?"

"Neddie gives the preference to you, Jane," Lizzy said by way of reply, "because you are merely five years Edward's senior, and because Cassandra is so tenacious in the single state. She might have had our good friend Mr. Kemble, of Chilham, these three years for the asking; and yet she shows not the slightest inclination to marry."

"And where do you place your wager, Lizzy?"

"I consider that you are far less likely to be cozened by a popinjay than any woman alive," she replied, "and from the accounts I receive of poor Edward's progress with your sister, I cannot think that Cassandra will yield. It is a hopeless case, is it not? My brother must look to the Continent by and by."

I studied her narrowly. The beautiful face was serene and unruffled as always—but graced with a palpable gleam of humour. "You enjoy this too much, Lizzy."

"I suggest that you do the same," she countered, "for my sister Harriot and the long-suffering Cassandra are even now entering upon Mr. Bridges's arm. Forewarned is forearmed, is it not? Allow me to introduce you, Jane, to Mr. George Farquar, a gentleman of my acquaintance."

And so I took a splendid turn with the engaging Mr. Farquar, the second son of a baronet who, like most of the Fashionable World, had once loved Lizzy Austen, nee Bridges, to distraction. In honour of that vanished passion, he was kind enough to engage me for the next two dances—and in return I submitted to a maddening discourse on the finer points of racing. Mr. Farquar was mad for horseflesh in any form—kept a string of hunters and coursers himself—would be gratified to learn my opinion of Doncaster versus Newmarket, et cetera, et cetera. He had come up from London especially for Race Week, and would be gone again in a few days' time for the next round of meetings at Epsom—and thus spared me the trouble of caring for him at all. With Mr. Farquar I might flirt with impunity, and little danger to either of our hearts. He was so obliging as to commend my style of dress and the manner of my dancing; and so we parted a half-hour later, with approbation on either side.

The interval between the final strains of one dance, and the commencement of another, was marked by a little excitement—a ripple of conversation that went round the room, and died away into nothing, at the entrance of a gentleman and a stranger, dressed all in black. If I thought immediately of the elusive Mr. Everett, the comparison must be odious—for the stranger was possessed of considerable countenance, where Everett was not, and carried himself with an air of easy self-assurance that argued superiority of rank and fortune. Within moments of his appearance, a report was in general circulation about the room—he was Monsieur le Comte de Penfleur, the heir to a considerable French banking fortune, and raised as a brother to the late Françoise Grey. He had arrived only lately at The Larches, in readiness for Friday's funeral rites; and despite the deepest mourning, had insisted upon seeing something of Canterbury society.

Mr. Grey had not elected to accompany his guest.

I watched him move across the room—a slim, elegant figure with a knife-thin nose, ash-blond curls falling across his brow, and disconcertingly pale eyes. There he stood near a potted plant, and bent low over the hand of a bashful young lady—there, by the table of ices, he clicked his heels at a puffed-up worthy—but correct and elegant as his appearance must be, I could not ignore the arrogance of his manner. Monsieur le Comte might move freely among the enemy, but he loved us not at all. Whatever his purpose in coming to the ball, he was under no illusion as to his reception; *politesse* from the English was all very well, but he had known Françoise Grey, and must be aware of her treatment at the hands of Kentish society. We should not be too easily forgiven.

A quarter-hour of idling among the throng that lined the walls must bring the Comte at length to my brother, Neddie—and there, I espied a subtle change in the Frenchman's manner and countenance. Gone was the supercilious air; a certain rigidity, as of discomfort, now marked his movements; he was become guarded and circumspect. I surmised an eagerness to speak that must be at war with a natural reticence; and knew him to be taking Neddie's measure, even as my brother took his in turn. At length the two gentlemen moved off towards one of Delmar's anterooms, where the self-absorption of the card-players might serve as foil for conversation.

Only one woman at the Assembly, I observed, had worn black in respect of the departed—young Lady Forbes, the bride of the Guards' commanding general. She was a pretty little thing, not much above nineteen, with the golden hair and sweet blue eyes of a china doll. But the innocence of her features was quite at variance with her dress—which was a daring costume more suited to a woman of the world. A circlet of black satin wound becomingly across her brow, and her dusky silk gown—as sheer as a mourning veil—fell in dramatic folds to the floor. She might have been Electra, or some other queen of tragedy, and a certain consciousness of effect was evident in the way she clung about Captain Woodford. In one hand she held a square of lawn, the better to dab at her eyes; in the other, a vinaigrette, in event of sudden swoons. Of her husband Major-General Lord Forbes there was not a sign. Perhaps he was a slave to the card-room.

Captain Woodford's single-eyed gaze, now bent upon his fair companion, now roving the room in search of some means of escape, came to rest at last upon myself. He smiled in acknowledgement, and nodded; I returned the courtesy. Just then I espied Lizzy, with her sister Harriot in tow, idling along the edge of the dance floor near the Captain—and his attention was immediately seized. Woodford abandoned Lady Forbes with a bow, hastened to Lizzy's side, and begged Harriot's hand for the dance just then commencing. With a blush and an averted gaze—but no apparent disinclination—she followed him to the floor.

"Miss Austen?"

I tore my eyes from the interesting pair, and was presented with one of Captain Woodford's fellow officers.

"Might I have the pleasure of this dance?"

To my delight and surprise, I discovered that I was much in request, and that full two hours went by before I had a moment to consider of the rest of my party, or indeed of my sister Cassandra. That she was less happy in her experience of the ball was evident from the pained expression with which she greeted Mr. Edward Bridges's attentions. He had elected to station himself by her side, her constant and insidious acolyte; he would fetch her a fresh glass of punch, or see her well-supplied with muffin, and she was utterly martyred to his cause.

The reason for my constant solicitation on the dance floor was soon made plain, however, by the repeated suppositions, cunning asides, and barefaced questions about Mrs. Grey's murder to which I found myself subjected. Neddie's role as Justice had rendered the entire Godmersham party the object of general fascination and enquiry. We were all to be besieged; no one was immune; and so, with an inward bubble of amusement, I set out to learn at least as much as I divulged.

Mr. Goldsmith tells us, that when lovely woman stoops to folly, she has nothing more to do but die; but when she stoops to be an object of scandal, murder is equally to be recommended as a clearer of ill-fame. Much of Kent was at pains to find Mrs. Grey more amiable in death, than they had ever acknowledged her in life; and I must wonder if the elegance of the Comte de Penfleur's address, and the loftiness of his title, must do away entirely with his adoptive sister's reputation. Collingforth, on the other hand, was everywhere declared the worst of fellows—his wife too foolish even to be pitied; and by the end of my third dance, it was evident that he had been judged already and despatched to the gallows by the neighbourhood at large.

Mr. Valentine Grey, however, was decidedly the object of general pity—the sort of pity that is as much knowing contempt, and that must render all condolence an outrage. As to Mr. Grey himself, the reports of his character I was afforded this evening were so at variance with one another, I could not make him out at all. Some would have it he was a shrewd and cunning fellow, too deep to have his measure taken; others that he was a *naïf* who cared for nothing but his remarkable grounds at The Larches. As to his banking concern and its practises, the neighbourhood opinion was even more divided; and I was forced to conclude that the Greys, however fascinating, were very little known in Kent.

Except, perhaps, by one person: Captain Arthur Woodford.

I had consigned the first dance after supper to the gallant Captain. As the supper-room crowd began to thin, I looked about for his battle-scarred figure. He was so much the object of the ladies' attention—single men of excellent family and a respectable commission being hardly thick upon the ground—that I was surprised to find him deserted by the fair sex. He stood, rather, in the closest conversation with Mr. Edward Bridges.

My first assumption—that the two had made up their quarrel—was swiftly dispelled. Mr. Bridges hardly looked easy; he was awkward in his stance, and white about the mouth; while the Captain, whose words were too discreet to be overheard, spoke with a vehemence that argued some heat. On catching sight of me, however, he broke off abruptly, and parted from the curate without the slightest farewell. Mr. Bridges fairly flung himself from the room, as tho' all the imps of Satan were upon him.

"I have not forgot you, Miss Austen, as you see," the Captain cried.

"I am gratified, Captain, that the French have not monopolised all your attention," I returned with a curtsey. "I thought you should have been despatched to the coast, to talk peace or exchange prisoners, as the occasion demanded; and yet here I find you, as fine and easy as tho' Buonaparte had never been born!"

"Lord Forbes should choose poorly in sending me to the coast, Miss Austen," he replied, "for I never talk peace, particularly in French, and I rarely take prisoners." He bowed, and held out his arm; I slipped my own beneath it, and allowed him to lead me to the floor.

"You despise the French language? Then I suppose you have been denied the acquaintance of the Comte de Penfleur," I said as we took our places in the line of couples. A poor command of Mrs. Grey's native tongue might have inhibited the Captain's intimacy with the lady—and surely precluded him from having authored the letter concealed in *La Nouvelle Héloïse*.

"I was so fortunate as to make the gentleman's acquaintance this morning, on a visit of condolence to The Larches," Woodford replied, "but happily, his English is most accomplished."

"And have you made it a policy to abhor an enemy tongue?"

"I have kicked my heels twice in a French prison, Miss Austen, awaiting the necessary exchange," he replied, "and on both occasions, my lamentable efforts at the mastery of French were the despair of my captors.[1] Indeed, I was returned to England post-haste that they might no longer have the burden of hearing me—and thus have never felt compelled to augment the lack."

I laughed at him then, and abused his stupidity like the coquettish Miss I presumed to affect; and wondered all the while whether the Captain might be believed. A man who had endured the tedium of capture, in the company of French officers of equal rank (for so Woodford presumably was housed), should hardly have failed to learn something of the language. Was this a subterfuge, intended for the benefit of the Justice's sister? Had the Captain written the interesting letter, and suggested a flight to Pegwell Bay? And had his friend Mr. Grey discovered the whole, and murdered his wife in a jealous rage?

I could not determine whether Captain Woodford was the sort of man to make love to his oldest friend's wife; or to shield that friend, in a matter of murder. But perhaps he knew nothing of Françoise Grey's end—perhaps he merely suspected her husband guilty of a horror—and hoped that Denys Collingforth might hang for all their sins.

But I had been too long silent; it was not done, in the midst of a dance; and so I clutched at the thread of our conversation.

"And what did you think of the Comte de Penfleur?"

---

[1] It was the practise during this period to hold enemy officers in lodgings that befit their status as gentlemen, and to exchange them for captured officers of one's own army at the first opportunity. —Editor's note.

The Captain's countenance turned, if anything, too careful. "He is all right in his way, I suppose—for a Frenchman."

I laughed in delight. "So much praise for an enemy, from a captain of His Majesty's Guards, may be termed a veritable encomium! And may I ask, sir, upon what grounds this weighty judgement was formed?"

"A little conversation only, I confess. I conveyed my sentiments of condolence, of course—assured the Comte of my affectionate respect for the late departed—and expressed my outrage at the manner of her death. He was almost overcome at such a demonstration of goodwill—I saw the tears start out in his eyes, Miss Austen—and could not speak for several moments. But he then assured me that he bore the people of Canterbury no ill-will on account of the murder; that such shocking episodes might be met with daily in the streets of Paris, and one accepted one's Fate as it was served. We exchanged a few pleasantries—the dry weather, the state of the roads—and then I took myself off." He hesitated. "I pray you will not relate what I have said to any of my colleagues, particularly my commanding officer. Lord Forbes should be most put out, was he aware I had met with a Frenchman recently disembarked from the Channel, and yet had failed to learn the state of the French flotilla from his very lips. I could not think it likely, however, that the Comte had observed anything to the purpose—he had crossed in the night—and I did not like to encroach upon his mourning."

"I admire your delicacy of feeling, Captain," I murmured. "It must be unusual in a seasoned campaigner. You were at The Larches some little while, I collect?"

"Not at all," he replied hastily, as tho' to admit otherwise might be to court censure. "I had not been sitting with Mr. Grey a quarter-hour when the Comte arrived, and in considerable style, too—a coach and four, shipped over from Calais, with liveried servants mounted behind. After the exchange of remarks I have already recounted, I thought it best to make my *adieux* and leave them together; Grey was very much put out, I believe, at the Comte's descent upon the place. He had not been taught to look for it."

If Mr. Grey had murdered Françoise, he should hardly welcome a visitation from the Penfleurs. Questions impossible of answer might well be asked, and the comfortable resolution the widower desired, tediously deferred.

"I had not understood that Mr. Grey was on poor terms with his late wife's family," I hazarded.

Captain Woodford would have shrugged, I think, but for the movement of the dance. As it was, he half-began the gesture, and arrested it only awkwardly. I suppressed a smile. Many a gallant fellow may move without hesitation on horseback, and be completely undone by a line of couples. "I should say rather that he was disconcerted, Miss Austen. He had had no word of the Comte's intentions. Are you at all acquainted with Mr. Grey?"

"I am not."

"He dislikes surprises acutely, and has done so from a boy. The pleasure of an event is never increased, he says, and the inconvenience must be considerable."

"Then he is a man of whose sense I must approve," I said. "But perhaps the Comte prefers to disconcert. I have observed him to effect it on several occasions this evening."

"His adoptive sister was much the same," the Captain replied; and not without a wry amusement. It was the first instance of real feeling I had glimpsed through Woodford's façade, and it intrigued me greatly. *Here* was the affection that he had professed so carefully; here was the regret I had half-expected.

"I observe that you are wearing a black armband, Captain. I commend you for it," I said. "Mrs. Grey may have found more champions in death than she ever claimed in life, but the sincere among us shall always know her *true* friends."

"Thank you," he returned quietly, "but you do me too great honour. I was less Mrs. Grey's friend than perhaps she deserved—or certainly, than she had reason to expect. I believe I thought always of Grey before his wife; and the claims of one friendship may have superseded the other."

"Was it so impossible to be a friend to both?"

He hesitated. "Not impossible, perhaps—but fraught with difficulty. The Greys were not in accord, Miss Austen, and allegiance to the aims of one might often be perceived as betrayal of the other."

"It is a common wisdom to find attraction in divergent characters, but I have always believed that like minds are the most compatible. The world in general exists to divide the sexes; every convention of society and employment must render them strangers the one to the other. Let us pray, then, at every wedding, for a union of heart and purpose."

He smiled almost apologetically. "It is possible to be *too* much alike, Miss Austen. When a lady of strong character and implacable will is forced to live in harness with a gentleman of equal temperament—and when those two must divide their loyalties between warring countries— no, Miss Austen, they cannot be in accord."

"And so you wear the crepe in respect of your friend, and not his late wife?"

"I suppose I honour them both—and the difficult choices they sustained. It is a tragic story, however one regards the deceased. And the public scandal alone must be a trial to one of Grey's retiring temperament—" The Captain broke off, and bit his lip. "I have heard that the London papers are already come into Kent—that they have flocked to the race grounds, and have bent their draughtsmen to the depiction of lurid scenes—a representation of the corpse tumbling out of the chaise, under the startled gaze of the crowd."

"Can it be?" I cried, incensed. "Only think what all her family must suffer!"

"I confess I can think only of Grey," Captain Woodford said heavily. "He must feel his wife's loss most acutely."

Must he, indeed? Nothing in the Captain's previous words, nor yet my brother's report of the banker, had led me to suspect real feeling for his wife.

"Your friend might be allowed to feel the burden of tragedy, Captain," I observed, "and perhaps the weight of scandal; but knowing as little of Mr. Grey as I do, I cannot presume to read his heart. What he feels in respect of his late wife must be closed entirely to me."

He studied my countenance with a slight frown. "You speak as tho' he were a man without heart, Miss Austen. I may assure you that is not the case. A truer man than Valentine Grey never lived."

"Forgive me. I intended no disrespect of your friend. But I find that he has moved so little in Kent—and his character is so little understood—that in general I can form no opinion of him. I know that he is possessed of a sharp temper, and stands ready to challenge even so mild a gentleman as my brother to a duel; but beyond this, I can say nothing."

Captain Woodford came to a halt opposite, as the tune wound to a close. He bowed abstractedly, and I curtseyed. Then he said, "Mr. Grey has actually challenged your brother to a duel?"

I affected a carelessness I could not feel. "Over some trifle discovered among Mrs. Grey's belongings. A letter, I believe, and written in the French language. Whatever the missive contained, my brother believed Mrs. Grey intended flight—and so incensed her husband at the suggestion, that he demanded satisfaction. It ended, however, in nothing. The heat of argument must be deferred, in respect of the search for justice."

"Naturally," Captain Woodford murmured. But he said it as an afterthought, his mind clearly bent upon other things—this letter, perhaps, of which he might know nothing, or everything. Had it been the letter he sought, in Mrs. Grey's saloon the night of her murder?— Or did he suspect something of the author's identity, that must turn his soul to ice?

Regardless, he neither moved nor spoke, while all around us the couples drifted away. At length I said gently, "Captain. Captain!"

He came to his senses, then, and offered his arm; but as I slipped my own within it, I found that the superfine wool was damp with sweat. From the heat of his exertions? Or the weight of apprehension? "Are you quite well, Captain Woodford? Perhaps you should benefit from some punch."

"Forgive me, Miss Austen—but my mind is so much taken up with the claims of duty—the threat of invasion—"

"And the niceties of a public ball," I rejoined with a smile. "At such a time, I cannot think it the wisest thing the Guards have done. But I suppose Lord Forbes believes it necessary to his officers' comfort—or his lady's."

Captain Woodford's lips twitched. "It is not in my power to support the General where his lady is concerned. He should require the strength of several, I fear. But in truth we are meant to serve as example to the populace, Miss Austen. While an officer is engaged in so honourable a duty as the dance, can the Kingdom's security be in question? Never!"

"Did you dance on the shores of Pegwell Bay, Captain, I might better believe you."

To my surprise, the Captain's countenance turned suddenly grave. "Pegwell Bay? Of what interest should Pegwell Bay be to me?"

"Is it not the expected landing-place of the French navy?" I enquired, surprised. "I had always heard that it was. Indeed, my brother—Captain Frank Austen, of the *Canopus*—was tasked with the drafting of a report to that effect not two years ago. He surveyed the Kentish coast, and hit upon Pegwell as the very place for invasion. There are no heights for the enemy to gain there, you know, and the tides, I believe, are favourable for a landing."

When Captain Woodford still said nothing, however, I added in a more subdued tone, "—But perhaps the Army's calculations have undergone a change."

His single dark eye narrowed; then a slight confusion overcame him. The Captain had, perhaps, heard Pegwell spoken of—had thought that any number of places along the coast might serve the French equally well—was not aware that the environs of Ramsgate had fallen so much into general expectation—and would caution me against a too-free canvassing of military affairs.

"For if the entirety of Kent expects the French to land at Pegwell—and the intelligence makes its way to Boulogne—how much better for the Emperor, Miss Austen, if he should land to the south while we are all massed in the north! Better to leave him in doubt of our intentions, as a cat will do with a mouse. We cannot say too little upon the subject. Particularly with a Frenchman in our midst."

It seemed that I had stepped where a lady should not—into the deep waters of strategy and deception—

but I could not retreat without a final bold strike. "It may be dangerous, indeed, to speak too freely in such times as these. Mrs. Grey, you know, was quite familiar with Pegwell—and we would none of us wish to suffer *her* Fate, Captain, now would we?"

# Chapter 9

## A Matter of Movements

I WAS NOT THE ONLY PARTY WHO BANTERED TOO FREELY this evening, on subjects military and otherwise. The entire Assembly was conversant with a rumour to which I had barely attended—regarding the projected movements of the Coldstream Guards.

It was Cassandra who told me of it, as we sat established over our ices during the ball's waning hour. I must say that my sister did not look very well this evening, but perhaps the duties of the sickroom at Goodnestone Farm would tell upon anyone, particularly when coupled with the necessity of packing for evacuation.[1] But she had put on her best pink gown—a colour I should never attempt, given the habitual flush of my cheeks— and her hair, though deprived of the ministrations of

---

[1] Harriot Bridges's elder sister, Marianne (1774–1811), was an invalid from childhood, and was at this time bedridden. Much of Harriot's time was spent attending her, and Cassandra was assisting in the duty while resident at Goodnestone Farm.—*Editor's note.*

Mr. Hall, had been curled and arranged by Harriot Bridges's maid to admiration. Nothing was wanting, in fact, except animation and spirit. I saw the lack, and felt a stirring of anxiety. Perhaps the assiduity of Mr. Bridges's attentions had at length worked upon even so steady a heart as Cassandra's! Perhaps she was even now in an agony of doubt—uncertain whether to accept him or no. In light of my father's death, *any* match might appear as salvation, for one of Cassandra's limited resources.

We had fought our way towards one another through a sea of exhausted and overheated bodies—ladies with drooping headdresses and soiled white gloves, and gentlemen with florid complexions and dampened brows. However hard it might seem to endure such festivities in winter, when one is scantily clad and subject to every window's draught, I must own that I prefer a January reel to the most elegant August country dance. A roaring fire and a vigourous turn about the floor will entirely make up the deficit in natural warmth—but not even the excellent ices of Canterbury may relieve the insipidity of a Race Week ball.

"It is the talk of the neighbourhood," Cassandra confided, her spoonful of ice arrested in mid-air. "The Grenadier Guards are to march from Deal to Chatham, while Captain Woodford's First Coldstream Guards, and the First Scots—or is it the Second?—are to march in turn from Chatham to Deal."[2]

"I suppose it shall make a change from dancing," I replied, "but I cannot think what they mean to effect, by the simple exchange of men. Is the appearance of soldiers about the fields of Kent intended to impress the

[2] The projected troop movements took place on August 30, 1805, as Jane reported in a letter later written from Goodnestone Farm.—*Editor's note.*

Emperor Buonaparte, as he surveys us from the Channel? Shall we seem to be awash in red-clad men, and drive him back upon the shores of France out of terror at the sight?"

"They will pass within a stone's-toss of Goodnestone in their way," Cassandra added, ignoring my barbs. "The country is all alive with what it might mean, Jane—sudden intelligence, perhaps, from France, of the Monster's landfall. If it were to be near Deal, only seven miles from the Farm—if dear Lady Bridges and all her household were to be driven from their beds—I do not think I could bear it! But, of course, I shall assist them in any way that I am able, with Marianne and the packing."

"You had much better bring them all to Godmersham and leave the packing to the French," I said crisply. "I wonder Neddie did not consider of it before. But we have been served with our own plan of evacuation, my dear, and only yesterday morning. The gallant Captain Woodford brought it himself."

"Captain Woodford! I cannot help but like and admire him," she said with a sigh. "There is such an expression of goodness in his looks—and the severity of his wounds must argue for the nobility of his character."

"Does Harriot admire him as much as her whole family?" I gazed out over the floor, where a few straggling couples clung determinedly to the final measures of a dance. Among them were certainly Lizzy's little sister and the Captain, her white dress a delicate counterpoint to his dashing military colours.

"I wish it were in my power to say," Cassandra mused. "On this subject, Harriot cannot be open. There is too great a difference in our ages—nearly ten years—and tho' much thrown together of late, we have never enjoyed the intimacy of sisters. But I suspect her heart to be a little touched. It would be unfortunate if the Guards were to be ordered out of Kent entirely."

"Or the Captain himself run through with a French sword somewhere between Chatham and Deal," I observed callously. "He might at least declare himself to Harriot before the unhappy event, so that she might cherish her interesting state. A girl who is only the *object* of a hero's regard, has never the *éclat* of a bereaved intended."

"Jane! How *can* you!"

Too late I remembered Cassandra's own condition— the loss of her betrothed some eight years before. I bit my lip, and wished my own bitter humour might be kept in better check. But too late! The words were said; and I should not declare them orphans now.

"I speak so because I must, my dear. A degree of general indifference is the only surety against peculiar pain. What a lot of people are killed in these wars, to be sure— and how fortunate that one cares for none of them! If Fly or Charles should be struck on the quarterdeck by a French twenty-four-pounder, a part of me would go over the rail at their side."

"Do not speak of it, I beg," Cassandra said softly. "I know that you have borne a great deal of late—the loss of Mrs. Lefroy, and our own dear Papa—but you mourn too much for them, Jane. They would not wish it so. Papa, I am sure, did not regret his life in leaving it."

I nodded blindly, my gaze obscured by a sudden film of tears; and then turned the conversation with effort. "And so the Guards are to march from Deal! I wonder how much Major-General Lord Forbes really knows— and how much he merely hazards?"

"I am sure that all such manoeuvres are so much Blindman's Buff," Cassandra replied, "tho' Buonaparte would have us all believe him omniscient, and as infallible as Rome. The gentlemen of the neighbourhood, including Mr. Bridges, are in an uproar over the intended troop movements—for it is rumoured they shall come but a day or two before the commencement of pheasant season. The sportsmen are all alive with the fear that the birds shall be disturbed—flushed from their manors, or poached out of hand for an infantryman's dinner."

"It should not be surprising that the credit of our neighbours' game-bags must come before the safety of the Kingdom," I said with conscious irony. "*Apropos* of manoeuvres, my dear, how have you fared in your skirmish with the sporting Mr. Bridges?"

Cassandra blushed and averted her eyes, a perfect picture of consciousness. "Mr. Bridges! Aye, you may well laugh at my persecution, Jane! I should like to know how *you* should fare against the weight of his blandishments, for a fortnight together! Mr. Bridges is excessively teasing. Did you observe that I was forced to stand up with him for full three dances this evening? I only escaped a fourth by pleading the head-ache."

"Three dances! That is very singular, indeed," I observed mildly. "Another man might consider it *too* particular—but perhaps he believes that his being Lizzy's brother must do away with such nice distinction."

"He is not so very much our relation, Jane, as to make me forget what is due to propriety," Cassandra said with some distress. "Do not think that I am ignorant of his object. He hopes to secure my affections—and he has made himself repugnant in the process! Where once I might have found his gallantries flattering—his poses amusing—his wit even tolerable—he is become entirely disgusting! There is a lack of sincerity in all he says that has made his society intolerable."

"Poor Mr. Bridges!—To have lost that interest he particularly hoped to secure. Did I not feel moved to laugh at him heartily, I should pity him a good deal."

"I was much taken with the import of your last letter," my sister confided, in a lowered tone. "I must assure you, Jane, that Mr. Bridges has hardly been easy since Mrs.

Grey's death. He barely speaks a word, and never leaves the house, unless it is to accompany myself or Harriot on some trifling errand. And yet, you know he was never to be found within doors if he could help it! There were weeks on end, when no one at the Farm had the slightest idea of his whereabouts, or whether he should be home to dinner! The change is very marked."

"Perhaps he cannot bear to be parted from *you*, my dear."

"Do not teaze me, Jane. It is very unkind in you, I am sure."

I pressed her hand in apology and said, "You believe the change in his behaviour to date from Mrs. Grey's murder. Can you detect any reason for his seclusion? Has he let fall the slightest syllable that might explain his extraordinary conduct?"

"He moves as tho' in the grip of fear," Cassandra replied, with utter seriousness, "and I have even thought, indeed, that he half-expects to suffer Mrs. Grey's fate."

My eyes widened. "Mr. Bridges, to be torn from his riding habit and strangled with his own hair-ribbon? Impossible!"

"Jane!"

"Forgive me. I could not suppress the notion. But what could possibly give rise to such a fanciful dread, Cassandra? Who should wish to murder Mr. Bridges?"

My sister glanced knowingly about the room before she answered. "Mr. Valentine Grey."

That the reserved and ill-humoured banker should have the slightest idea of the curate's existence, was amusing in the extreme; and I confess I laughed out loud.

"Is it not obvious?" Cassandra cried. "You told me yourself that Mr. Bridges was found in the lady's saloon, on the very night of her murder, rifling the drawers of her writing-desk. He was desperate to secure the letter discovered between the pages of the scandalous French novel—the letter that proposed a meeting at midnight on the shores of Pegwell, and a subsequent flight to the Continent."

"But does Mr. Bridges possess a passable command of French?"

"Naturally! All the Bridgeses are most accomplished in that line!" In her enthusiasm for her theory, Cassandra abandoned the last of her ice and leaned towards me eagerly. "I am certain that he believes himself the agent of Mrs. Grey's end—that his dangerous passion for the lady precipitated her death at the hands of her husband, and that Mr. Grey merely awaits a suitable opportunity to serve vengeance, in turn, upon her lover! Mr. Bridges cannot know that his letter was found among the lady's things. He fears only that he is discovered by the husband, and dares not stir beyond the Farm's threshold."

"—Except to attend the inquest," I amended slowly. "He would desire to learn everything that was known of her end, of course."

"Is it not a delightful idea?" my sister prodded.

"It is not without its merits, Cassandra. But why, then, should Mr. Bridges quarrel with Captain Woodford? Or stand idly by, while Mr. Collingforth is charged with murder?"

"As to that, I cannot tell," she replied with a shrug. "I cannot solve all your mysteries for you, Jane. I am placed to disadvantage, marooned at the Farm. I shall hope to do better, when once we have exchanged our places."

"It is quite a settled matter, then, that I shall go to Goodnestone Farm? Pray—when is the delightful prospect to take place?"

"Whenever Mr. Bridges has proposed, and been refused," Cassandra said wickedly. "I cannot be expected to remain within the bosom of the family, once *that* regrettable episode is sustained."

"When may we expect the elegant curate to come to the point? I have my packing to consider."

A sudden stiffening in Cassandra's looks alerted me to a subtle change. Her gaze was fixed a few inches above my head, and that the self-same Mr. Bridges now hovered there, all civility and attention, I immediately surmised. I turned and found his good-natured, slightly anxious face bent upon us both. I say bent—for the height of his collar points, and the stiffness of his cravat, rendered any but the most exaggerated movements from waist to neck impossible.

"Miss Austen!" he cried. "And the delightful Miss *Jane* Austen! How well you both look this evening, I declare. That such beauty and wit should be united in *one* lady surpasses all experience . . . but that two such, and claiming the same family name, should so subjugate us all to their charms . . ."

"Mr. Bridges," Cassandra broke in, "I must suppose you are come to tell us that the carriage is called. You are very good."

"Not at all! A decided pleasure—and only exceeded by the honour of escorting you home at the close of these delightful festivities. Or should I say—back to the Farm, which, although not your home, must be, I hope, very nearly as dear to you as though it were. That it might prove even dearer in future, through the accomplishment of a certain change . . ."

Cassandra's countenance, I fear, offered no encouragement to the gallant performer; and so he was suffered to dwindle into silence under the glacial influence of her gaze. He merely bowed to me, and offered my sister his arm, and thus the unfortunate pair moved off through the thinning crowd. I pitied Cassandra, but reserved some measure of the feeling for myself— for that Mr. Bridges would soon bring the matter to a point, and as speedily earn his refusal, I little doubted. It would be but a matter of days, then, before I should be despatched to the Farm in Cassandra's stead. And I should hardly meet Mr. Bridges's attentions with my sister's steady tranquillity. I had not the recourse to a headache complaint; for I was commonly acknowledged to be in riotous good health.

"LIZZY," HENRY BEGAN AS WE SETTLED OURSELVES WITH some exhaustion in the Godmersham carriage a quarter-hour later, "have you heard what your young brother is up to? He has actually waited upon Major-General Lord Forbes in the card room, in a matter of pheasant-shooting!—Was pleased to bring the General's attention to a rumour of the Guards' troop movements, and expressed his concern that the marching men might entirely rout his birds! The cheek of it all! Can not you put a word in your brother's ear?"

"I am sure the General gave him a dressing-down," Lizzy returned languidly.

"In too subtle a manner, I fear, for Mr. Bridges's understanding. Lord Forbes informed him that if only the *birds* were routed, he should consider all of Kent but too fortunate."

Neddie's sharp bark of laughter cut through the darkness of the coach. "And how did the young popinjay take it?"

"He suggested an alternative route for the troops—through the hayfields to the west, which he represented as a course that might save several miles."

"And ensure the crops' ruin," Neddie said with satisfaction. "I am sure the General knew how to express his gratitude for young Edward's sage advice."

"He was too much engrossed in play, to lend Mr. Bridges more than half an ear," Henry returned, enjoying the moment hugely, "but I believe he took the point under consideration; for I observed him not a half-hour later, in a frightful rage, with poor Captain Woodford as his object. Lord Forbes was displeased, it seems, with the general knowledge of his manoeuvres. All of Kent may command it; and if *we* are apprised of the Guards' plans, can Napoleon's spies be in ignorance? While the General marches to Deal, the Monster will throw his troops quite elsewhere."

"I doubt it was Captain Woodford who published the intelligence," I mused, "but I should not vouch for Lady Forbes. She has quite the look of a woman who enjoys a sensation—and herself at the centre of it, above all things."

"She is quite the persecution of poor Woodford," Lizzy murmured. "Were it not for the deference he owes his commanding officer, I am sure he should shake her off in a trice; but she *will* hang upon his arm, and regard him as her personal pug-dog, to be petted and spoilt for show."

"You observed once that Lady Forbes was intimate with Mrs. Grey," I said. "On what was their friendship founded?"

Lizzy waved her fan, a gleaming arc of ivory in the darkness. "On a mutual love of finery—of spending more than they ought—and of a desire for shared confidences. There is little that occurred in the Army's Officer Corps, I am sure, that was not known at The Larches an hour later. Lady Forbes is the kind of woman who delights in confiding secrets."

"And Mrs. Grey, in possessing them?" I added thoughtfully. The notion of blackmail was never far from my mind, when I considered of that lady. What might she not have known regarding Captain Woodford, for example, that should thwart his career in the Army?—Or of the spendthrift curate, Edward Bridges, whose luck proved so ruinous at her card-table? She should be unlikely to toy with them for money; she possessed enough of it herself. What, then, had been her object? What form of pressure had she employed? And was her interest merely a malicious delight in the unhappiness of others—or had she a greater object in view?

"Mrs. Grey's relation is a secretive sort, as well," Neddie observed from his corner, as the carriage jolted down the road. "I could not make the Comte out at all; but I quite liked him, all the same."

"The Comte de Penfleur! A very elegant gentleman, indeed." Lizzy was all approval. "But I cannot think it the wisest thing you have ever done, Neddie, to closet yourself fully an hour in his company. All of Canterbury must be alive to the interest of your *tête-à-tête*; and all of Canterbury will be chattering even now."

"It is clear, at least, that the Comte attended the Assembly solely with our conversation in view. He is greatly distressed at Mrs. Grey's death, and cannot feel sanguine with Grey's management of it."

"*Grey's* management?—But Grey is not the Justice responsible," I cried.

"No more he is," my brother replied comfortably, "and the Comte de Penfleur was relieved to hear of it. He was circumspect enough, for the first quarter-hour; but he unbent a great deal, and intimated almost too much, for the remaining three. I should judge him much attached to Françoise Grey; profoundly distrustful of her husband; and anxious that her murderer should not go unpunished."

"As he believes Denys Collingforth will," I added.

"He cares nothing for Collingforth, unless he be guilty—and it is quite clear, from his manner of speaking, that he cannot believe him so. Mr. Grey is too eager to charge poor Collingforth with the murder, for the Comte's liking."

"How very intriguing, to be sure." Lizzy sighed. "It has quite a Continental flavour to it, Jane, almost of a tragic opera. I am sure the stage shall be littered with the dead and dying, before the final curtain is rung down—do not neglect to inform me of how it all ends. For the present, however, I must *implore* you, Neddie, not to forget that the Finch-Hattons are to be at dinner tomorrow. We cannot neglect what is due to our friends, however tedious they might prove, merely because of invasion and murder."

My brother laughed aloud, and kissed his wife's gloved hand, and was content to pass the remainder of the drive in reflective silence.

But I very much wondered, as the shades of night flitted disconsolately past the carriage windows, how greatly the Comte had been attached to his adoptive sister—and whether it was *he* who had written that letter, in agonised French, to urge a meeting at Pegwell Bay.

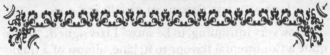

# Chapter 10

## A Desperate Diversion

*Thursday,*
*22 August 1805*

~

I SET DOWN MY ACCOUNT OF THE BALL IN THE EARLY hours of the morning. Once in bed, I tossed and turned until the rain broke before five o'clock, and brought a cooling breeze through the open window. I rose not three hours later and took tea in my room, where I might collect my thoughts before the rest of the house had stirred.

Breakfast at Godmersham is never before ten o'clock, although the children are served in the nursery far earlier. By the time our indolent Lizzy is dressed and abroad, her numerous infants are long since out-of-doors—under the supervision of Sackree, the nurse, or the long-suffering Miss Sharpe. There had been talk yesterday of an expedition with the gamekeeper, in search of wild raspberries; we should have clotted cream and fresh fruit for the Finch-Hattons at dinner.

I found the breakfast parlour quite deserted of life when at last I descended, and was allowed the consumption of tea and toast unmolested. Afterwards I hied myself to the little saloon at the back of the house, which serves the ladies of Godmersham as a sort of morning-room; here my sister Lizzy keeps a cunning little marquetry desk, well-supplied with a quantity of paper, pens, and sealing-wax. I settled myself to compose a letter to my mother—who has been happily established these several weeks in Hampshire with our dear friends, the Lloyds. She was to come to us in September, and together we intended a visit to the seaside at Weymouth. I very much feared, however, that the pleasure-trip would be put off, from a superfluity of French along the Channel coast—but saw no reason to alarm my mother. She is given to the wildest fancies at the best of times, and should require no spur at present from her youngest daughter. One source of consolation I found at least: the Lloyds took no London paper. Mrs. Austen should thus be preserved in ignorance of the sailing of the French fleet, a circumstance devoutly to be hoped. Did the rumour of invasion happen to reach her ears, she should demand her daughters' immediate removal into Hampshire—a prospect I could not regard with composure. The society of Kent was too beguiling, and the matter of Mrs. Grey's death too intriguing, to permit of a hasty departure.

My letter, as a result, was full of a great deal of nothing—a recital of the delights of Race Week, absent the interesting events of the meeting itself. I spoke of Henry's horse, of Henry's disappointment, of the scene at the grounds and the Assembly soon after—all without the slightest mention of the scandalous sensation that had torn Canterbury's peace. Such a letter, being a complex of subterfuge and delicate evasion, required considerable effort; I devoted a half-hour to the task, and had just determined to spend the rest of the morning with the admirable (if tiresome) *Sorrows of Young Werther*, when my industry was abruptly interrupted.[1]

The sound of a horse's hooves galloping to the door—a man's voice, raised in anger—the protest of the servants—perhaps it was another constable, come post-haste with news? I threw down my volume and stepped into the back passage.

A gentleman I had never seen before was crossing the chequered marble of the hall with a rapidity that argued extreme necessity, or a violence of temper. He must pass by where I stood to achieve the library—his obvious intention, as my brother Neddie was generally to be found within after breakfast—but aside from the briefest glance at my face, he offered no acknowledgement or courtesy. Tho' hardly above medium height, the stranger was powerfully-built, with a beautifully-moulded head and greying hair trimmed far shorter than was fashionable. Something of the regimental was writ large in his form; or perhaps it was the air of battle he wore upon his countenance. I should judge him to be about the age of forty; but perhaps it was the weight of care that had traced years upon his looks.

The manservant, Russell, sped desperately in his wake, protesting, "But, sir! I cannot be assured that Mr. Austen is *at home*!"

"And where else should he be, man?" the stranger cried. "For he is certainly not about his duty!"

He paused by the closed library door, however, and allowed Russell to thrust it open.

"Mr. Grey, sir, to see you."

I suppose I should have surmised as much; but, in fact, I was quite thoroughly routed in my expectation. How anyone in Kent might describe this man as a *naif*—

---

[1]   The Romantic novel by Goethe, presumably read in the translation.—*Editor's note.*

or even remotely under the thumb of his young wife—was beyond my comprehension. Valentine Grey was not a man to be bent to any woman's pleasure; he would never be dismissed to his lodgings in London, and made a fool of, the length of Kent; nor was he to be whipped into submission, as Françoise Grey had managed with at least one gentleman at the Canterbury Races. Here was a figure of energy and decision, a formidable adversary and partner. Had she quailed in her heart, the wild French miss, when presented with the man who was her husband?

Valentine Grey, in short, was not what I had expected. The library door snapped shut behind him.

I slipped out of the saloon and made my way through the passage to the kitchens, and from thence to the still-room, where a stout garden trug and shears sat innocently on a table by the garden door. I took them up, as though intent upon the culling of flowers for this evening's dinner—and stepped outside quite unremarked.

After the dim quiet of the saloon, the force of morning sunlight was like a blow against the cheek. I had come away without my bonnet. It was this sort of behaviour, my mother was forever reminding me, that brought freckles to the neatest complexion. But I cared little for such things at present; my complexion was spoilt beyond repair, and had been these three years at least. I hastened towards the swath of cornflowers and lavender that ran riot on either side of the library's French windows, pausing to clip a stem or two from each nodding plant. Neddie had thrust open a window to admit of the breeze; and the murmur of voices rose and swelled before ever I attained my object.

"You can be at no loss to understand why I have come."

"Indeed, Mr. Grey, I am unable to account for the honour of seeing you here. Pray sit down."

"Thank you—but I prefer to stand."

There was the sound of a man pacing; an impatient expulsion of breath; and I had an idea of Valentine Grey come to rest before the barren hearth, and staring unseeing into the grate.

"Then pray tell me how I might be of service," Neddie said, "for I perceive that you are greatly distressed."

"Who would not be, circumstanced as I am?" From the sound of it, Mr. Grey had wheeled to face my brother. His next words had all the viciousness of a challenge. "You have spoken with the Comte de Penfleur, sir!"

"I was so fortunate as to make the Comte's acquaintance last evening—yes," my brother acknowledged.

"And what sort of lies has he been telling you?"

"Lies?" Neddie could affect astonishment as readily as any of the Austens. "I cannot think why the Comte should lie to me, Mr. Grey—a virtual stranger, and one charged with the resolution of his ward's murder. But perhaps you may enlighten me."

"Because he is a blackguard of the worst sort—a cunning insinuator, a seducer of other men's wives, a man without scruple or bar to his malice. Because he hates me as surely as he breathes, Mr. Austen, and has made it his object in life to destroy me."

In another man, such language might have sounded preposterous—the stuff of a Cheltenham tragedy. Grey's quiet vehemence, however, spoke all his conviction; he said nothing more than what he believed to be the truth, and had suffered beyond endurance. —Or so I concluded, as I bent low over a clump of lavender.

"You speak of the Comte de Penfleur who is even now resident in your house, Mr. Grey?" My brother's voice was incredulous.

"I do."

"You welcome such a man into your home—a man

you regard with contempt and abhorrence, a man you acknowledge as your enemy?"

"My wife is dead, Mr. Austen, and will be buried tomorrow." Grey's words fell with infinite weariness. "I cannot deny the head of her family admittance to the rites. The Comte arrived, I may assure you, with the intention of removing Françoise to the Continent for burial. It is only due to the extreme heat of the weather, and the advanced decay of the corpse, that she is allowed to remain here. Indeed, had the Comte been capable of swaying his father a year since, Françoise should never have left France at all. Hippolyte has charged me most bitterly with neglect, in the event of her death."

"The Comte, I must conclude, was against your marriage?"

"The Comte is in the pocket of the Buonapartes, Mr. Austen, and despises everything to do with monarchy and England. He is too short-sighted to perceive the advantage of financial ties with this Kingdom." Mr. Grey, it seemed, had commenced to pace again—a rapid, purposeful sound that conveyed all his anxiety. "His father, however, understood that progress was impossible, absent the judicious flow of capital throughout Europe—and promoted the marriage between myself and his ward with that end in view. The first Comte de Penfleur, Mr. Austen, was an excellent man. He died but six months ago. His son shall never do him credit."

"I quite liked the Comte," Neddie offered mildly.

If I expected an oath or a blow—some form of brutal denial—I was disappointed. Valentine Grey laughed.

"Everyone does," he said. "They cannot fail to find Hippolyte everything that is charming. Even those who have cause to know him well—to understand the extent of his depravity—choose not to see the truth. Françoise—"

Grey broke off, and there was a heavy silence.

"Yes, Mr. Grey?" Neddie enquired politely. "You were speaking of your wife?"

"The Comte de Penfleur has what we English sometimes call *address*—the air of authority, of refinement, of self-restraint and confidence. It never deserts him, even in the most hideous of places. And I have seen him in any number of hells, Mr. Austen, to which a respectable man like yourself should never descend."

There was the briefest of pauses, as my brother assessed his visitor across an expanse of mahogany desk. "Why do you tell me all this, Mr. Grey?"

"Because I hope it will persuade you to divulge your conversation with the Comte last evening."

"To what end?"

"The elucidation of his motives."

"You have said yourself that he came to pay his last respects."

"And perhaps to put paid to the delicate balance now existing between our two banking houses. I believe, in short, that he means to ruin me."

Neddie drew breath. "For the crime of allowing your wife to be murdered?"

"—Or for making her my wife in the first place."

"I was never very good at the taking of hints," Neddie observed. "I much prefer a plain-spoken man to a riddling one."

That for Neddie, I thought. It was not for nothing that his patron, Mr. Knight, had seen him schooled in the art of fencing.

"I believe the Comte to have a purpose in discovering how much you know." Grey's voice was as taut as a violin too-strenuously tuned. "He is adept at the drawing-out of the unwitting, through subtle ploys of which they are unaware. He may have learned much from the most trifling of your remarks—and will move in the greatest unease, or the greatest security, depending upon what he believes."

"Indeed? Then he moves in a sharper light than I!" Neddie's exasperation was obvious. "If the Comte is aware of *how much I know*, then he is in possession of the dearest intelligence in all of Kent, not excepting the intended landfall of the French! To what, exactly, would you refer, Mr. Grey? The facts of your wife's murder? Her liaison with Denys Collingforth? The state of your own marriage? Or her affection for her adoptive brother, the disreputable Comte de Penfleur?"

"Remember to whom you are speaking, Austen," Mr. Grey retorted ominously. "I am not a man to be insulted, in your home or my own."

"Then perhaps you might tell me what it is you seek." From the sound of his movements, Neddie had thrown himself into his favourite chair—a wing-backed fortress drawn up near the cold hearth. Grey, however, paced restlessly to the very edge of the room, and peered unseeing through the French windows. The sight of his compact and powerful form looming near my own had the power to strike terror into an eavesdropping heart— and so I threw my back into snipping flowers as tho' my very life depended upon it. I might have been a sheep cropping grass, or an under-gardener tilling earth, for all the attention Grey paid me.

"Appearance to the contrary, Mr. Austen, I loved my wife. My feeling for her was against the force of all reason—I had long known what she was. A spendthrift, a libertine, an unprincipled creature who lived only for pleasure. But I had waited perhaps too long to marry— and when I fell in love, I did so with utter heedlessness. I threw caution to the winds. I sacrificed everything— pride, principle, even common sense—to win Françoise from her family, and at length I prevailed."

"And your wife, sir?" Neddie enquired drily. "She met your passion with an equal ardour?"

"She accepted it as a familiar token; men had been driving themselves mad about her since she was sixteen. But Françoise cared for no one but herself. Herself— and her guardian's son."

"The present Comte."

Grey must have nodded assent, for no sound fell upon my ears.

"It was in part to separate them that her guardian— the late Comte—betrothed Françoise to me. He must have known that once united in marriage, Hippolyte and his ward would destroy the Penfleur heritage. They are—or were—both selfish, headstrong, dissipated characters; neither restraint nor prudence would survive in their household. They could not be allowed to ruin what he jealously nurtured through revolution and the Empire's rise. And so Françoise was despatched to England."

"He sold her to the highest bidder," Neddie said harshly.

"And I was pleased to buy," Mr. Grey returned, without a flicker of emotion. "I counted the purchase cheap, so mad was I to claim Françoise."

But what, I thought, had been the currency of exchange? How much of his own financial house had Valentine Grey consigned to his enemy's bankers?

"The letter that was discovered in your wife's novel, Mr. Grey," my brother broke in. "It was written by the Comte, I presume."

"Of course." Grey dismissed this abruptly. "I knew his hand the moment you showed it me. I merely denied the fact, from a desire to keep everything that was painful at bay. That letter can have nothing to do with my wife's death."

"It may have everything to do with it."

Grey turned. "What can you mean? Even did the Comte intend to meet my wife by night on the shingle at Pegwell, he cannot have been at the Canterbury Races the very same morning. Every sort of caution would inform against it. And why should he kill her, if he loved her enough to plead for flight? It is beyond all understanding."

"Perhaps she refused him."

"Refused him?" Grey's voice was incredulous. "She could refuse Hippolyte nothing, Mr. Austen, from the time she was a girl."

"Perhaps she had learned to love her husband. Perhaps she thought to remain in Kent, and wrote to the Comte informing him of as much. In a jealous rage, he waited upon the Wingham road, and waylaid her coach . . ."

". . . only to lay the blame upon a complete unknown, the absent Mr. Collingforth? It will not do, Mr. Austen; it decidedly will not do. A man of the Comte's cunning would certainly engage for his rival to hang; he should place the blame squarely upon my shoulders, and laugh the length of my road to Hell. Unless—"

There was a troubling stillness, an interval filled with thought. Then Grey said, "Is that what he told you last evening? That I had strangled Françoise, because she had determined to elope?"

"The Comte de Penfleur said very little to your detriment, sir." Neddie's attitude was easy. "He may have intimated a good deal—that you had neglected your wife, that you bore her little affection, and, indeed, had perhaps allowed her to expose herself to the ridicule of the neighbourhood, from a desire to be rid of her through some deplorable scandal—"

"You call this *very little*?" Mr. Grey burst out. "Upon my word, Austen, I should tremble to learn what you consider a great deal!"

"—but he fell short of charging you with the lady's murder. A man of the Comte's subtlety, you may be sure, would never so completely show his hand. We may expect him to work upon me by degrees, until my mind is shaped to his liking."

"You begin to understand him."

"I think I begin to understand you both. Or at the very least—what each of you wishes me to understand."

Here was the steel beneath the velvet glove. My brother would have the gentleman comprehend that he was hardly a fool, to be played with as a shuttlecock between two battledores. He would reserve his judgement until all the facts were fully in his possession, and only then would he act. Neither Mr. Grey, nor the Comte de Penfleur, would be privy to his counsel.

"I do not quite take your meaning, sir. I have been completely open."

"You have presented a very painful picture, sir, of your private affairs—and one that must have cost you something to divulge. I respect and pity you—for the fortitude which allows such a sacrifice of your natural reserve, and for the calculation that has urged it. But as to openness—there, Mr. Grey, our opinions must part company. I regret to say that you have *not* been entirely open."

"Very well." Grey's accent held an intolerable strain. "Endeavour to show, Mr. Justice of Canterbury, how I have deceived you."

"The very morning after your wife's death, you were at pains to discover Mr. Collingforth the culprit; and quite ingeniously, the gentleman's flight and various circumstances conspired to prove you right. The inquest delivered him, *in absentia*, to the Assizes' mercy; and all of Canterbury condemned him as the very worst of men. Leave aside for the moment that his guilt is hardly proved; what is accepted opinion has all the weight of fact in a country neighbourhood, and the Law will always bow to the weight of fact."

"Why should Collingforth flee the country, if he is innocent?" Grey cried.

My brother chose to ignore him.

"Now that the Comte de Penfleur has appeared to mar the scene, and has had the temerity to speak to the local Justice, you have come in haste to my door. For the first time I learn from your own lips, that the interesting letter written in French was *not* from your wife's courier, but from her lover—as I was always convinced. You speak feelingly of your marriage; of the hatred the Comte bears you; and to what purpose?—For if Collingforth is yet the man who strangled your wife, the Comte's intentions regarding yourself can be of no further interest to me."

Grey was silent. I had an idea of the scene: Neddie at ease in his wing-backed chair, fingers bridged before his nose as he regarded the other man; and Grey, stiff and enraged, brought to a halt on the Aubusson carpet.

"You are desperate for a serious diversion, Mr. Grey," Neddie persisted, "but for the life of me, I cannot think why. What would you protect? —Your own neck? It is hardly at hazard. —Your wife's reputation? She never possessed any. —Your banking concerns? Your position in the estimation of the 'Great'? Perhaps; for it is this that the Comte may yet destroy. I should be deeply gratified, Mr. Grey, if you could be *as frank* with regard to your business as you have been regarding your wife."

Mr. Grey must have determined at this point upon quitting the room; there was the slightest rustle from beyond the window, and the sound of my brother rising to his feet.

"I will take what you have said under consideration,

Austen," Mr. Grey said sharply, "but I can offer you nothing further today."

"Very well. I hope I may always be of service." A bell rang distantly in the house; poor Russell would be running, I knew, to show the gentleman to the door.

"And Mr. Grey—"

"Yes?" The voice came indistinctly, from the far end of the room.

"I may assure you of one thing. I *will find* your wife's murderer—and so help me God, I will see him hang."

The assurance may have been of less comfort than Neddie supposed.

WHEN GREY HAD GONE, I PUT DOWN MY GARDEN TRUG— now overflowing with posies already wilting in the late-morning heat—and stepped through the French windows.

"Is he gone?"

"Safely down the sweep." Neddie was engaged in the filling of his pipe, an indulgence he never practised before a lady; but I had an idea of his internal disquiet, and forbore to chide him. Tobacco, I believe, may be a spur to thought as much as a comfort to the nerves, and I saw no reason to deny him the remedy at such an hour.

He settled himself in his favourite armchair and studied me with amusement. "How much of our conversation did you overlisten?"

"Nearly all of it. You were aware of my presence?"

"For the last half-hour. Grey may not have perceived you in his pacing about the room, but in following his figure to the garden prospect, I could not fail of detecting yours." The amusement deepened. "And what is your considered opinion of the fellow, Jane?"

"As you said of the Comte—I quite liked him."

"Yes," Neddie mused. "It is a great failing in this line of work, to undertake to admire or pity anyone. He is made of stern stuff, Mr. Valentine Grey, and might be capable of anything."

"—Of steady industry; of sacrifice in the name of principle; of ruthless calculation in matters of business or state—but is he capable of passion? I cannot believe it."

"He was eloquent on the subject of his wife."

"He spoke well," I conceded, "but more as a man whose passion is dead."

Neddie shrugged. "So, too, is the object of it."

"Real love endures beyond the grave, Neddie, as you very well know. Men may remarry; they may cherish a second wife, and a third—but their feelings remain tender in respect of the departed. Mr. Grey's passion did not survive the first few months of his marriage, I suspect. He spoke as a man who has learned a part by rote."

"You are severe upon him."

"And yet, I cannot believe him capable of deception in an evil cause. He is the sort of man one instinctively trusts, and expects to perform with integrity. He will return again, I am sure of it—and tell you all you wish to know. His conscience will not allow him to rest, until he has done so."

"I hope you are not proved credulous, Jane"—Neddie sighed—"for I have gambled a good deal on a single throw. Grey may as readily determine that silence is his truest friend, and deny me the knowledge that must unlock this puzzle."

The great clock in the hallway began to toll the hour, and Neddie withdrew his watch from a waistcoat pocket. "Behind again," he muttered, and commenced to wind it. "The Finch-Hattons are expected to dinner, and the sainfoin harvest has yet to be fired."

"Bother the Finch-Hattons," I cried petulantly. "What

do you make of Grey's portrait of the Comte? *There*, at least, you must admit he was entirely frank. He went so far as to admit the letter."

"We may judge, then, that the admission suited his purpose—whatever that purpose may be."

"I quite long to meet the interesting Comte," I persisted, as Neddie made for the library door. "Can not you conspire, Neddie, to invite him to take coffee with us some evening after dinner?"

"I shall do better, Jane," he said with a roguish look. "I shall persuade my elegant wife to set the neighbourhood an example, and pay a call of condolence at The Larches. The funeral is tomorrow, at eleven o'clock; but a Saturday visit on the part of the Godmersham ladies would be admirably in keeping with what is due to Mr. Grey."

"And so it should!" I exclaimed. "Dearest Neddie, for considering of it!"

"I am always happy to oblige you, Jane, even in the matter of your morbid taste for bones. I confess myself most impatient to learn your opinion of the devious Comte de Penfleur."

# Chapter 11

## The Improvement
## of the Estate

### 22 August 1805, cont'd.

~

THE FINCH-HATTONS CAME, IN ALL THE HASTE AND
splendour native to the possessors of an elegant green
barouche. They came—tho' not, as commonly expected,
for the dinner hour, but a bare three minutes after the
household had sought our separate rooms to dress. A
tremendous scurrying in the lower passages, an anxious
banging of Elizabeth's door, and the sudden catapult of
Fanny into my bedchamber, alerted me to my doom.

"Aunt Jane!" Fanny burst out in an ill-managed whisper, "you will never guess what has happened! Mamma's
guests are arrived, and a full hour before their time—
and Mamma not even dressed! She begs that if you are
more beforehand, that you might go down and do the
civil for a while. Sayce is only just begun on Mamma's
hair—and you cannot think how droll Mamma looks,
with curls all bunched on one side, and nothing at all on
the other! I thought I should die of laughter, until she
sent me away in a fury."

A fury, for Lizzy, must encompass nothing more than

a penetrating look, and a suggestion that her husband should show Fanny the dressing-room door; but I apprehended the gravity of her condition in an instant. Lizzy with her hair undone is not to be contemplated.

"Help me with these buttons, Fanny." I shrugged myself into a passable dinner gown and presented my back to my niece. "If you can but find my pale blue slippers—I believe your mother's pug has dragged one under the bed—I am at your service directly."

When I entered the drawing-room moments later, the Finch-Hattons stood aloof from one another, in attitudes of flight—for all the world like strangers at a ship's embarkation. There was Lady Elizabeth, her driving shawl still pinned about her shoulders, and an enormous straw hat balanced like a charger upon her head. She had taken up a position near the front windows, which gave out on the entry and sweep, and seemed engaged in a study of her own conveyance. Her husband, Mr. George Finch-Hatton, stood scowling over his pocket-watch, as though the expected ship had failed to make the tide; while Miss Louisa, the eldest daughter, was perched on the edge of one of Lizzy's little gilt chairs, tapping her foot impatiently.

"What good fortune!" I cried, rushing in with extended hands, the very picture of effusive welcome. "We had not hoped for a glimpse of you until the dinner hour! I am charged with offering a most hearty welcome, in default of my brother and sister, who will no doubt be with us directly. And how did you find the road, Mr. Finch-Hatton? Your horses endured this heat tolerably well?"

"Tolerably, thank you, Miss Austen," he said, and returned to his watch with studied indifference.

"Allow me to take your wrap, Lady Elizabeth."

"Thank you, Miss Austen, but I so detest the duty of

wrapping myself up again—particularly when travelling without my maid—that I believe I shall retain it yet a while. Your sister is indisposed?"

"Not at all—and most anxious to see you. She is merely dressing for dinner. I expect her every moment."

"I see. A pity, George, that we have so little time."

"But I thought . . ."

"It is quite impossible for us to stay above a quarter-hour. We are expected at Eastwell tonight. An engagement of Mr. Finch-Hatton's—"

Expected at Eastwell! When they had been expected *here* for dinner! It was quite extraordinary behaviour—almost indicative of a desire to snub my brother. But no—in that case, they should simply have sent a note, filled with regret at the necessity of despising his hospitality. Perhaps it was a family matter, too private for explanation; or perhaps our embroilment in the affairs of Mrs. Grey . . . I dismissed the last notion as absurd.

"I see," I said with an effort, and crossed to the bell-pull. "Perhaps I should summon Mrs. Austen, so that you do not escape her altogether. She would never forgive me."

"If you would be so good—"

It was fully eight minutes by Mr. Finch-Hatton's pocket-watch, I am sure, before my brother and his wife hurried through the door. I endured the interval as gamely as I might—but with little pleasure, I confess. The Finch-Hattons are never a talkative family; in such circumstances, each seemingly lost in a private reverie, they were as mute as sybils. It was impossible to introduce the subject that must be uppermost in all our minds—Mrs. Grey's death; delicacy forbade it. But each of my forays into conversation proved disappointing. Neither the subject of Race Week, nor last evening's Assembly, nor even the prospect of long sleeves for winter dress, could animate the ladies; and as for Finch-Hatton himself—he was preoccupied with pacing off the length of the drawing-room, a habit acquired, I suppose, from his intimacy with architects.

For if the Finch-Hattons are impoverished in speech, they are rich in the passion for improvement. Their estate at Eastwell is never suffered to remain long in one condition—a team of builders must be permanently installed somewhere in the deer park, I believe, as feudal lords once commanded a host of vassals; and there a legion of gardeners is perennially in pursuit of the last word in landscape fashion. The present house—the third to be built on its site—is a fantastical thing, half riding-school and half-Parthenon.[1] Mr. Joseph Bonomi had the designing of it, and managed it in so outlandish a taste—which he persuaded the Finch-Hattons to believe was at once *classical* and *modern*—that it is quite the talk of the neighbourhood, though perhaps not in the manner his patrons intended.

Conceive, if you are able, a largish white block of a building, divided along its front with pilasters and capitals set into the façade; exactly three great windows on one side of the entry and three on the other, and an immense arched portico, nearly three storeys in height, dominating the whole. Cumbersome, inelegant, unlovely, and awkward—but *classical* and *modern* enough in its expression, that Lady Elizabeth might believe herself a citizen of Rome. I have visited the family at Eastwell several times, and can never find that the place has grown in my estimation. It is peculiarly suited to the

---

1     Eastwell Park sat four miles south of Godmersham on the road to Ashford, now the A20. It was the home of the Finch-Hattons until 1893. The house designed by Bonomi was razed in 1926, and its successor is presently operated as a hotel.—*Editor's note.*

humours of its inhabitants, however, who are in general as awkward and inexpressive as their walls. The Finch-Hatton ladies never speak if they can help it, and then only in plaintive tones; the Finch-Hatton men, when not looking at their pocket-watches, prefer to be out-of-doors.

"Lady Elizabeth!" my sister Lizzy cried from the doorway. "What is this I hear of your not intending dinner? Is it possible? And I have had white soup enough for an army simmering in the kitchens!"

"It may yet serve, dear madam, if Buonaparte has his way," Mr. Finch-Hatton observed drily, and thrust his watch at last into his pocket. Perhaps he had placed an idle bet or two as to the time required for Lizzy's preparation. "You look well, Austen," he said to my brother with a bow; "surprisingly well, under the circumstances."

"You mean the evacuation orders?" Neddie enquired smoothly, as though Mrs. Grey had never lived, much less died. "I cannot take them in earnest, however diligently I set the servants to packing."

"Then I pray the Monster may land on my doorstep rather than yours," Finch-Hatton returned. "I hope I shall know how to receive the renegade! I have been drilling my tenants these two months at least; and there is powder and shot enough in the stores to hold off an entire brigade of cavalry!"

"I applaud your foresight, sir," Neddie said, "but I cannot expect so little of our gallant Navy. With an Austen and a Nelson scouring the Channel, the Monster shall not pass beyond a nautical mile from Boulogne."

"But tell me, Lady Elizabeth," my sister broke in, "must you *certainly* go on to Eastwell tonight? If it is the lateness of the hour that concerns you, I am sure there are bedchambers enough."

"Lateness of the hour! It is not above six o'clock. I am

sure that at Eastwell we dine fully as late as you do at Godmersham," Lady Elizabeth returned frostily. "We are never behindhand, you know, in matters of elegance."[2] Lady Elizabeth is the daughter of an earl, a fact she would have no one forget—particularly the daughter of a baronet.

"You! Behindhand! As though anyone could think it," Lizzy returned, with that pale green gleam in her eye that suggested an inner amusement. "I believe that everything at Eastwell is in the first rank of taste—would not you agree, Jane?"

"Entirely," I murmured. Knowing my opinion of the place all too well, Lizzy was cruelly impertinent; but I endured the test to perfection, and betrayed nothing in my countenance.

"Pray tell me," Neddie persisted, "what improvements do you presently undertake about that remarkable place? Not that it could be said to *require* improvement, but I know your artistic spirit too well. It will never rest while the least suggestion of beauty remains at bay."

*Well put,* I silently commended my brother. He had got the notion in one. At bay would beauty forever remain, however desperately the Finch-Hattons pursued it.

"The interior of the house is quite nearly complete," Lady Elizabeth confided, unbending a little, "but for the trifling matter of some painted Chinese papers that are intended for the drawing-room, and are shockingly delayed *en route.* And then there is the matter of the

---

2  Those who possessed country manners (like Jane Austen's parents) generally dined around three or four o'clock in the afternoon. But stylish, fashionable people accustomed to the habits of London adopted the practise of dining at seven. It was considered dreadfully old-fashioned to do otherwise. Hence Lady Elizabeth's sense of slight.—*Editor's note.*

dining-parlour's draperies—I could never be sanguine regarding the shade of pomegranate silk; it seemed to me to border on the tawdry."

"That is often the way with pomegranate," Neddie remarked, with a compelling command of countenance. "One may meet it anywhere—and not always in the best company."

"Exactly! I believe I shall change it out for green," Lady Elizabeth said complacently. "But it must await Mr. Finch-Hatton's present passion, which quite consumes our energies."

Lizzy's brow furrowed slightly in an effort to discern *which*, of the numerous Finch-Hatton projects, Lady Elizabeth intended. "The construction of the foyer's free-floating dome?"

"The dome!" Finch-Hatton himself cried out, as if in pain. "No, no, my dear lady—the dome is quite complete, the most marvellous thing you shall ever observe! St. Peter's is nothing to it! Although it might be accused of wanting in frescoes—but I shall attend to that presently, when the necessary Florentines may be shipped with safe-passage."

"Florentines," Neddie murmured. "Of course."

"What I would speak of, my dear Mrs. Austen," said Lady Elizabeth with her first suggestion of animation, "is Mr. Finch-Hatton's design of the park. It is to be entirely new-laid—approach, prospect, shrubberies, and all!"

"The park?" I could not but be surprised. "But I thought it had been done in your father's time, by Mr. Capability Brown."

"Not Brown himself," Finch-Hatton supplied carelessly, "but one of his journeymen. And as for *Brown*, well—"

"Oh, do not vex me with the name of *Brown*!" cried Lady Elizabeth. "When I consider how much of the Picturesque that man destroyed, with his sweeps of turf, and his little clumps of trees, and his ha-has built up like a moat about the house, I could weep with vexation!"[3]

Lizzy and I exchanged a speaking look. Neither of us could ignore Lady Elizabeth's recourse to the Picturesque. It had become the chief phrase of Mr. Humphrey Repton's acolytes—those who would dot the landscape with scenes both romantic and wild. Eastwell Park, I surmised, would swiftly be turned into a wilderness, with haunted grottoes and abandoned cottages just ripe for a wandering hermit; a lake would be constructed, with an earth-work island, raised expressly for the purpose of displaying a Gothic ruin—all of it quite *modern*, of course. How it would all appear, with the Roman fantasy of a house as backdrop, I could hardly imagine.

"And so you aspire to the Picturesque," Neddie offered, in a dangerous spirit of encouragement.

"How often have I observed to Mr. Austen," my sister Lizzy said provokingly, "that the little copse on our hill is too insipid for words!—That the walled garden lacked all enchantment! That the path of the Stour might be swelled to something greater—an ornamental pond, perhaps, for the siting of a Chinese pagoda! I even appealed to his desire for coarse-fishing—but to no avail!"

[3] Lancelot "Capability" Brown (1715–1783), the supreme interpreter of the natural style in landscape gardening, transformed the English countryside in the eighteenth century. He abolished rigidly geometrical park designs, such as the formal terracing and allées of the French style then predominating, and achieved a free-flowing, bucolic terrain dotted with copses that has come to epitomize the late Georgian landscape.

A ha-ha was an elaborate livestock guard, separating the area of free-ranging parkland from the more formal garden space. It was formed of either a sunken ditch or a raised wall. Maria Bertram, in Austen's *Mansfield Park*, is trapped by a locked ha-ha gate at her betrothed's estate—a symbolic reference to the prison of social convention.—*Editor's note.*

"Perhaps not a *pagoda*," Mr. Finch-Hatton countered doubtfully, "but a smallish ruin, now—"

"And that avenue," Lady Elizabeth added sadly. "Bentley, as I believe you call it—"

"Bentigh," Neddie corrected gently. "It was planted in the first Mr. Knight's time."

"So I assumed," she rejoined placidly. "I am sure it is shockingly old-fashioned."

"I believe the lime trees are over fifty years old," Neddie agreed. His lips were a trifle too compressed, as though the humourous had given way to the insulting. "Nasty, unnatural sorts of things, limes—don't you agree, Jane?"

"My dear," cried Lady Elizabeth, "I truly believe that the Austens might benefit from an introduction to Mr. Sothey! Is it not the very thing? Would it not be a service in the calling of Art?"

"Of course," her husband replied. "You *must* have Sothey, Austen—he is quite the genius of our little place, as the saying goes, ha! ha! I should not order a spade to be shifted, without I consulted Sothey."[4]

"He is your chief gardener?" Neddie idly enquired.

"*Gardener!* Good God, no!" Finch-Hatton cried.

His daughter, the inscrutable Louisa, echoed a shocked and irreverent, "Julian, a gardener? Lord!"

"Mr. Sothey is the second son of the Earl of Matlock,"

---

[4]  It was Alexander Pope (1688–1744) who remarked that nothing could be achieved in landscape design without respect for the "genius of the place"—the governing spirit of a particular landscape. He referred to an idea first stated by Horace, that every place possessed a resident *genie*, that must be propitiated if Beauty was to be achieved. Pope probably intended this to mean a respect for the natural attributes of the terrain; but at times his words were interpreted quite literally as a respect for the resident god. Grottoes were built to house Pan or a water nymph, as at the great gardens of Stourhead in Wiltshire.—*Editor's note.*

Lady Elizabeth assured us. "His mother and I were quite the best of friends, before poor Honoria died. I have made it a little cause, you know, to look out for Julian—to further his interest, and so on, where a word or two might help. Particularly since the Earl went all to pieces in that shocking way, a few years ago . . ."

She left the matter hanging. I had never heard of the Earl of Matlock, much less his shocking ruin; but Lizzy nodded shrewdly.

"It is a pity, is it not, that those who most lack success at the tables, are the very ones who game to their ruin?"

"And his heir is just like him!" Lady Elizabeth cried, as hot on the scent as a foxhound. "The Honourable Cecil Sothey has fled to Switzerland these two years or more, and how he lives no one can say!"

"But the younger son takes an interest in . . . land-scape?" I ventured.

"Exactly so! Julian was always of an artistic disposition—a painter in oils, and put to study with the finest masters of Europe, before Buonaparte quite destroyed the Grand Tour, and the Earl's circumstances brought an end to all education. But dear Julian's taste is entirely beyond dispute, is it not, my love?"

Mr. Finch-Hatton had withdrawn his pocket-watch once more, and was studying it intently.

"*Mamma,*" Miss Louisa cried in a warning tone, "if you do not leave off chattering, we shall be late for dinner at Eastwell. And then what will Julian say?"

"He is presently a guest at Eastwell Park?" I enquired.

"At last!" Louisa exclaimed. "Julian has been all the summer promising to come, and never setting foot through the door! I declare I was quite distracted with disappointment. But there it is! One lady's misfortune is another's good luck. No one will want Julian at The Larches, I daresay, now that Mrs. Grey—"

"Louisa!" her mother interjected sternly. "It does not do to talk of such things. I am sure Mr. Austen is already sick to death of that odious woman. I quite pity you, Mr. Austen. To be let in for such a tiresome business, and in such heat!"

There was a fractional pause. Then my brother enquired negligently—as tho' merely from politeness—"Mr. Sothey was a guest at The Larches?"

"Julian served Mr. Grey as consultant for nearly half a year," Lady Elizabeth confided proudly. "And you know how much the park is admired! There is nothing to equal The Larches in all of Kent—tho' it *is* the Garden of England."

"So I have been assured. I regret that I have never had occasion to tour the full extent of Grey's grounds," Neddie replied smoothly. "But as you are intimate with Mr. Sothey, perhaps you have been more fortunate."

"We were often invited to pay a call," Lady Elizabeth said vaguely, "but that woman, you know—I could never approve her. To pay a visit might lend a certain countenance to her behaviour. And Julian was so very much occupied—but now that Mrs. Grey is dead, it would not do for him to remain in the house. Julian determined to come to us directly, the very day of the Dreadful Event."

"Mamma," Miss Louisa urged again.

"To devote six months," Neddie observed, "to a single estate! Mr. Sothey must have found a great deal to employ his time."

"Mr. Grey, I believe, has a passion for improvement," Mr. Finch-Hatton interjected approvingly.

"And as Grey was called so often to Town, Mr. Sothey must frequently have acted in his stead," Neddie mused.

The implication—that the landscape designer had found more than mere parkland to occupy his attention—was entirely lost on Lady Elizabeth.

"Julian is a very responsible, steady sort of young man," Lady Elizabeth cried, "and if he possessed the fortune he ought, I should never say nay to him! Our Louisa and Julian have known one another since childhood, you understand—I make nothing of any trifling attachment, of course—but, then, one does not often meet with a girl as good-looking; and now that Julian is grown into such a sprig of fashion, all the young ladies are quite *wild* about him."

"Mam*ma*," Miss Louisa wailed in exasperation.

"My dear—the time!" Mr. Finch-Hatton exclaimed.

"And how long will Mr. Sothey be with you, ma'am?" I enquired hurriedly.

"We are so fortunate as to have his undivided attention for several weeks," Lady Elizabeth replied. "We met with him quite by chance at that unfortunate race-meeting, you know, and he told us it would at last be in his power to pay us a visit. I was overjoyed! I declare I could not stop talking of it, until that lamentable woman put flight to every other consideration." This was the nearest approach she would allow herself to strangulation. "But, however, it is immaterial now. We expect Julian for dinner this evening."

"Then you had certainly better be on your way," Lizzy supplied, with her usual good breeding, as though she had never been jilted of a dinner partner herself, nor vexed beyond imagining by the quantity of effort undergone only this morning in the Godmersham kitchens. "I suppose we cannot hope to see you for several weeks, if Mr. Sothey intends to engross all your time."

"As to that—I cannot say, to be sure—but we are to have quite a little dinner gathering at Eastwell on the morrow—should be charmed, if you are not engaged? You might meet Mr. Sothey, go over his plans for the grounds, and judge of his talents yourselves!"

"You are all kindness, Lady Elizabeth," said my brother swiftly. A quelling look to his wife, who might have refused the invitation, went unnoticed by the Finch-Hattons.

"You are too good, ma'am," said Lizzy distantly.

Lady Elizabeth smiled at her with infinite conde-scension. "Tho' Julian *shall* be much taken up with our little place, Mrs. Austen, I am sure that Mr. Finch-Hatton would be delighted to spare him, should you require a consultation about your grounds. I am strongly of the opinion that you should have that Bentley down—and I do not think I flatter myself when I say, that my opinions on matters of Taste are everywhere celebrated."

And so the Finch-Hattons were shown to their barouche-landau, without having taken so much as a glass of Madeira—in a fever, one supposes, to welcome the genius of Eastwell Park.

We watched them the length of the sweep, and when they had crossed the little stone bridge and were labour-ing up the hill to the Ashford road, Lizzy muttered, "Insufferable woman! I quite detest her. Must we indeed go to Eastwell on the morrow? Could not we decline a full hour after we are expected, and afford them all the misery they have served to us?"

Neddie laughed and carried his wife's hand to his lips. "We cannot. You know it is impossible. Such a dis-play of carelessness would expose you to Lady Eliza-beth's scorn; and you could never bear to appear as vulgar as she. I fear that you have been bested by a Gentleman Improver, my dear—and there is nothing for it but to submit."

"It is of no consequence, Neddie." She let fall the drape across the window, and turned away. "They had not been alighted from their carriage five minutes, be-fore I considered the exchange an admirable one. Mr. Sothey must be formed of sterner stuff than we, to con-template a visit of some weeks to Eastwell!"

"Perhaps you underrate Miss Louisa's charms," I suggested.

"The Finch-Hattons generally rate them so high themselves, that one *must* forever fall short," she replied. "But I stand by my original claim. Mr. Sothey is a martyr to a peculiar cause, known only to himself—and is much to be pitied."

Neddie raised his brows expressively in my direction. He was considering, no doubt, the curious fact of Mr. Sothey's departure for Eastwell Park on the very day of Mrs. Grey's murder. We had heard nothing before this of Sothey's presence in the Grey household; and yet so protracted a visit—even under the guise of an estate's improvement—must be remarkable. Valentine Grey had told us nothing of it, nor of his designer's abrupt departure. Was this the matter he would keep dark—the element of the story that required a desperate diversion?

"I quite long to meet Mr. Sothey," I observed, "being but too susceptible myself to every Sprig of Fashion. And the delight of uniting the honour with another tour of Eastwell Park, is almost too much to be borne! —Tho' I doubt I am *improved* enough myself, since last summer, to stand comparison with that noble place."

"Have a care, Jane," my brother advised, as the dinner bell rang. "Lady Elizabeth may appear foolish at times, and suffer from a lamentable taste; but she is not a stupid woman. Even an irony so disguised as yours, cannot entirely escape her notice."

# **Chapter 12**

# *The Bitter Bread of Governesses*

*Friday,*
*23 August 1805*

~

IF THERE IS ANY SORT OF UNPLEASANTNESS TO BE FACED
in the coming day—depend upon it, it will rain.

The heat broke with a vengeance above our heads
about an hour before dawn, lashing the early morning
darkness with a petulant violence. I drowsed under the
persistent patter of raindrops, content to drift in the twilight between dream and waking. I expected the storm
to pass on directly, and leave the world new-washed under an August sun. By nine o'clock, however—when all
but our indolent Lizzy had assembled in the breakfast
parlour—a steady deluge veiled the meadows from our
sight. The dun-coloured grasses were flattened with the
pelting drops, and the willows at the riverbank were
streaming like a mermaid's tresses.

"The Wingham road will be a morass of mud," Neddie pronounced with decided gloom. "Such a day for a
funeral!"

"—And such a funeral for the day!" Henry added. "It

is well you go in black, brother—for the wet cannot mar such a shade."

Neddie returned no answer; Henry's caprice can prove a sore trial, at times.

"I believe I shall bear you company, Ned," he added, after an interval. "It would never do to send forth the Justice without a proper escort. I might be your outrider, and lend a certain style."

The Justice in question surveyed his brother's fawn-coloured riding breeches and elegant salmon-and-green waistcoat with a critical air. "I declare you look almost Roman, Henry. The very thing for a Papist rite. Do not alter the slightest particular, I beg—excepting, perhaps, the addition of a black armband."

Mrs. Grey was to be interred in the family vault at The Larches itself, with an elderly Catholic priest pressed into service. Where such a man had been found in the cathedral town of Canterbury, was a question best left to Mr. Valentine Grey; that gentleman must have resources of which we knew nothing.

"I understand," Henry confided to the table in general, "that there was some talk of shipping the body back to France. The French Comte is said to have been most insistent. Grey, however, would have none of it—and so in English earth she will lie. The fellows at the Hound and Tooth could talk of little else."

"You astonish me," I said, over my teacup. "I thought nothing could turn them from laying bets on the fate of Mr. Collingforth."

My brothers set out for The Larches a quarter-hour later, for the service was to be at eleven o'clock, and they would require every moment of the interval. In respect of the mire, they went mounted on two of Neddie's hunters, who might gallop over hill and hedgerow if the road proved impassable. I watched their progress some few moments from the breakfast parlour window—

Neddie's easy hands and graceful seat, and Henry's scrabbling dash. The elder brother could never look anything but the country gentleman; the younger, nothing but a man of Town.

"The post is come, Jane," Lizzy informed me from the door, "and you have a letter from Cassandra. Pray do not stand on ceremony with me; I beg you would read it."

The packet's direction was written remarkably ill; my sister had undoubtedly scrawled it in considerable discomposure of mind. I broke the seal without further apology, and endeavoured to make out the hasty lines.

Mr. Edward Bridges, Cassandra reported, had been besieged yesterday morning by creditors at the very doors of the Farm itself, to the embarrassment of his sisters and the extreme displeasure of his formidable mother. Lady Bridges had dismissed the harried men encamped upon her door, with instructions to apply for recompense to her Canterbury solicitor, a Mr. Bane; and then was closeted with her errant son for several hours. Mr. Bridges emerged, looking utterly wretched, and having furnished his mother with a complete list of his tradesmen's debts, and obligations of honour; his losses at race-meetings, cockfights, cricket wagers, and so on. He was made so thoroughly uncomfortable by Lady Bridges's discovery, that he threw himself on Cassandra's mercy, and begged forthwith for an interview. It seems that Lady Bridges had offered her son little choice: He must marry sensibly, and respectably, and quite soon; and he must marry a lady of whom his mother could approve. Mr. Bridges relied upon Cassandra's compassion—her interest as a friend—her unselfish devotion to the welfare of his family, which all of them had frequently remarked—in short, he drove my sister into the drawing-room corner with the energy of a cattle-herder intent upon his dinner.

Cassandra was thus placed in a most dreadful position. She had been a guest in the Bridges household nearly a month, and had received nothing but kindness at their hands; she had always looked with affection upon the entire family; and she was conscious, moreover, of the peculiar tie that existed between her generous brother, Neddie, and his wife's relations. A sense of obligation must very nearly overwhelm; but she recovered her senses before any hasty betrothal might be forced upon her; expressed her gratitude to Mr. Bridges for his esteem—and refused him.

She wrote to inform me that she would be returning to Godmersham on Monday.

I read the bulk of this letter aloud to Lizzy. To her credit, she retained a tolerable measure of composure, and expressed her feelings most eloquently in the determined shredding of a piece of toast. When I had concluded, she said briskly, "And I suppose that this letter"—pointing with a butter knife to the sealed packet lying next to her plate—"will be a summons from Mamma."

"A summons?"

"For yourself." She broke the seal and unfolded a single sheet of determined script, underlined in places and closed with several flourishes. A moment sufficed to peruse it; Lizzy was familiar of old with her mother's style and purpose.

"It is as I suspect, Jane. You are to return to the Farm in Cassandra's carriage; it shall wait only five minutes to deposit your sister, before flying away with yourself. The coachman's instructions are quite explicit; he is not to return from Godmersham, without he carries you as his passenger."

"Your mother is very nearly terrifying, Lizzy. How did you manage to survive your infancy?"

"She would not have had it any other way, I assure you. We were fairly beaten or cajoled out of every dangerous illness, and never suffered to put on airs. Shall you detest the visit very much, Jane?"

"Not at all. Tho' I dislike being driven from my Yellow Room without even the slightest consultation of my wishes, I think I shall find ample scope for enjoyment. Captain Woodford's troops, you know, are to march directly past the Farm on their highly-secret deployment from Chatham to Deal; I expect a skirmish, or at least a protest, from the assembled pheasant-hunters of the neighbourhood."

"Now be, *be*, serious, my dear Jane. Tho' your visit would do much to soften the blow of Edward's ruin— and ease his relations at home immeasurably—I cannot urge you to go."

"I assure you, Lizzy, that I shall account the favour as the merest trifle. I cannot undertake to accept your brother's proposal of marriage, however. I was always inclined to follow Cassandra's lead in everything, you know; and at the advanced age of nearly thirty, I should not like to diverge from her example."

Lizzy was almost provoked to laughter; she expressed once more her sense of my goodness; and went off to the morning-room to write to her mother. I was left in all the shame of one who knows that her private motives are hardly so noble as her public professions; for I intended to profit from my visit to Goodnestone, in a thorough study of Mr. Bridges's uneasy circumstances. He had earned Denys Collingforth's public contempt, fallen out completely with Captain Woodford, and had moved in fear since Mrs. Grey's murder; now creditors hounded his very door. Such a parade of misfortune could hardly arise from coincidence. I was determined to know the reason for it.

But if I was to quit Godmersham in a few days' time, I must avail myself of its beauties while yet they remained to me. I glanced out the window and perceived that it had ceased to rain. Pale sunshine was drifting lightly over the damp meadow grasses, and glinting along the parapet of the bridge; the prospect was more inviting than it had been in days.

I fairly ran from the breakfast parlour, retrieved my little sheaf of papers and a well-mended pen, and walked out in the direction of the Doric temple. Most of the morning and evening should be taken up in the visit to Eastwell; tomorrow we were to pay our visit of condolence at The Larches; and Sunday could offer only the forced inactivity of a Christian observance, punctuated by the packing of trunks for the removal on Monday. *Lady Susan* had been too long neglected; I should find I had forgot how to put words to paper, did I not exercise my fingers soon.

I SETTLED MYSELF IN THE COOL SHADE OF THE PORTICO, and embarked upon a thorough appraisal of my cunning heroine. I must confess that time has taken its toll on her drolleries; she is too much the figure of the previous decade—indeed, the previous century!—and should hardly please the devotees of the *modern*, like Lady Elizabeth, who prefer their heroines fainting, modest, and utterly stupid. But I write entirely for my own amusement, and Lady Susan persists in her influence over my heart and mind; I cannot quite give her up, tho' I should never subject her to the ruthless eyes of the world, by attempting publication. The censure her activities should win, would then be all my own; and I cannot bear a public tongue-lashing.

I had just taken up my pen to write *I am now satisfied that I never could have brought myself to marry Reginald; &*

*am equally determined that Frederica never shall*—when I observed with an inward sigh that Lizzy, Fanny, and Miss Sharpe were toiling up the gentle rise that led to my cherished retreat. I tucked my papers between the leaves of a novel, secured the volume firmly in my hand, and rose to greet them.

"Aunt Jane! We are taking a tour of the park, for the express purpose of finding out what is wrong with it," Fanny cried. She ran up the last few yards of the slope, grown brown with the heat and intermittent rain, and tumbled panting at my feet.

"I have had a letter in the morning post from Lady Elizabeth Finch-Hatton," Lizzy informed me, as she, too, achieved the temple. "She abjures us most strenuously to visit Eastwell this evening, with the object of introducing Mr. Julian Sothey. We are to be treated to dinner— that is very handsome, since she would take none of ours—but I daresay you shall not like it, Jane. Lady Elizabeth's cooks are as modern as her taste in architecture, and Neddie rarely comes away anything but famished. We shall take a hamper and picnic somewhere along the road, before we are obliged to sit down. How tedious, to travel such a distance in fashionable dress! The roads are certain to be dirty with this morning's rain; we shall be stifling in the closed barouche the entire four miles."

"And what to wear, in respect of both a tour of the grounds and dinner?" I wondered.

"That settles it," Lizzy rejoined immediately, "we shall convey ourselves sensibly in carriage attire, and send our evening things with Sayce in a coach to follow. She may dress us both."

"And what have you learned from your tour, Miss Fanny?" I enquired, with a kiss to the little girl's flushed cheek.

"Mamma is of the persuasion that nothing might be saved—but I do not care two straws for an improver!"

she declared hotly. "They are all for swelling brooks into lakes, and stocking them with nasty fish—and I prefer the shallows of our own dear Stour. I *like* our trailing willows—I think them quite romantic! Do not you agree, Sharpie? Is not a tree that weeps more romantic than anything in the world?"

"It is certainly easier to endure than a lady who does so," Miss Sharpe replied, as she achieved the portico. Her own eyes, to my surprise, appeared puffed and reddened from recent tears. "Good morning, Miss Austen. We are come to destroy your privacy, I fear."

"What is privacy, if not to be destroyed?" I replied with a smile. "Had I known you intended the disposition of the entire park, I should have insisted upon being one of the party. I like nothing better than to strike down an ancient avenue for the sake of a whim. And by all means, let us set the common footpaths in the most winding and artistic—not to mention least convenient—fashion, so that the townsfolk are exceedingly put out in their travels from place to place. One cannot disturb one's dependents too much for their own good, I believe."

"Exactly so," Lizzy agreed, "nor the pilgrims, neither, who must benefit from a certain arduousness in their way.[1] I am forever telling Neddie he disconcerts them far too little. He should consider his deer and pheasant as having a far greater claim than a herd of trespassing strangers; and as for the value of a Horrid Prospect—something as like *The Castle of Otranto* as one may make it—I am sure we might sacrifice an avenue or two for the achievement of such a paragon."[2]

[1] The ancient path of pilgrimage toward Canterbury cathedral ran through the meadows of Godmersham in Austen's day. —*Editor's note.*

[2] This 1765 Gothic by Horace Walpole was read and enjoyed by most of Austen's family in her youth. It was the sort of book she later lampooned in *Northanger Abbey.*—*Editor's note.*

"We may do Mr. Sothey an injustice," I warned. "He may be discovered a man of perfect sense and unimpeachable taste, when once we survey his plans for Eastwell."

"Mr. Sothey?" Anne Sharpe enquired. The climb had certainly not agreed with her; she had gone exceedingly pale.

"The improver, my dear. The *gentleman* improver," Lizzy amended. "I spoke of him only a moment ago. We drive to Eastwell this morning on purpose to meet him. I had hoped that you and Fanny would consent to be of the party."

"Lady Elizabeth is the proud mamma of several little boys, who might teaze and amuse Fanny at once," I added, "unless your abhorrence of improvers, my dear, extends so far as to preclude the delights of a roadside picnic, and a change of dress to follow."

"I believe Miss Fanny has a great deal of study left uncompleted," replied Miss Sharpe hurriedly. "The tumult of packing has thrown the schoolroom into confusion, and we have not applied ourselves in days. Indeed"—with an anxious, unseeing look over the peaceful countryside—"I believe we should make our way back to the schoolroom now. The weather is too oppressive to endure for long; and I would not have Miss Fanny the worse for the exercise."

"Or yourself, my dear Miss Sharpe," I observed. "We must not bring on another head-ache. Where is your parasol? That bonnet cannot shield you enough!"

"Indeed, it is quite adequate at present. The rain has proved most refreshing. But I am afraid that the weather in general does not agree with me of late," she faltered. "It has been at once so dry, and so hot, that I am forever sneezing. My eyes have not stopped watering for days— only observe how reddened they have become."

"You must lie down for an hour this morning with

cold compresses of cucumber," Lizzy told her, "and forgo your needlework for a time."

"Yes, ma'am," Miss Sharpe murmured, and dropped a curtsey. "Come along, Fanny."

"But I should like to go to Eastwell above all things!" the girl protested, as her governess dragged her down the hillside. "I long for a picnic in the woods!"

"It would prove exceedingly damp, I am sure."

"But I should not care a jot for that! Please say that I may go, Sharpie . . ."

I watched them idly for a moment, and then turned to my sister. She was perched on one of the temple's chairs, and looked as cool and elegant in her sky-blue muslin as though she lingered in a mountain glade.

"And what do you make of the governess's secrets, Lizzy?" I asked her. "For she certainly guards them jealously."

"You astonish me, Jane. Can you believe little Sharpie to have a deceitful bone in her body?"

"Not, perhaps, deceitful," I amended, "but retiring. She is a woman who keeps her own counsel, my dear—and at the moment, that is enough to make her ill."

Lizzy said nothing for a moment, her green eyes following the diminishing pair. "Mrs. Metcalfe suggested that there might be something in her nature—unreconciled, perhaps—to her present situation."

"Mrs. Metcalfe?"

"An excellent woman, and an old friend of my mother's. She was the instrument of Miss Sharpe's engagement at Godmersham."

"I see. Miss Sharpe had been employed in the Metcalfe family?"

Lizzy shook her head. "She was brought up from a girl by Mrs. Metcalfe's sister, Lady Porterman. General Sir Thomas Porterman was a great friend of Miss Sharpe's parents, I believe—who died abroad, in a carriage accident, and left the child quite unprovided for. She was raised as almost a sister to Miss Lydia Porterman, but on the latter's marriage last year, Lady Porterman felt it was incumbent upon herself to arrange a situation for Miss Sharpe."

"Raised as almost a sister," I said slowly, "in a very elegant situation; and now descended to a position only slightly above that of a servant. What a sad reversal of Miss Sharpe's fortunes! I cannot wonder that she is unreconciled. It is only through the good offices—and generous purses—of my dear brothers, that Cassandra and I have escaped a similar fate."

"It was improbable, you know, that she should remain with the Portermans forever; she must make her way in the world one day; and the sooner the break was forced, the more quickly she might recover."

"But she has not recovered. How unfortunate that she did not follow Miss Porterman in matrimony."

Lizzy pursed her lips, and fanned herself with a slip of paper I had discarded upon the table. "Can one ever reconcile oneself to so material a change? I am sure it has broken her heart. To be removed from a condition of elegance—a house in Town, a carriage at one's command, and every comfort contrived—the very best circle of Society—and to accept, instead, the instruction of a girl such as Fanny—! Who, however excellent in her way, must be a trial to one for whom every prospect of future delight must seem so decidedly at an end?"

I could offer no reply for several moments; my heart was torn. There are too many young ladies of good family and little fortune, consigned to the near-slavery of the governess trade—a condition neither exalted nor demeaning, but open to both influences, as the temper of the employer's household must dictate. Such women live in a half-world, neither domestic nor genteel, and must suffer a thousand slights, a thousand deprivations, a thousand hopes deferred; they end their days as impoverished as they began, forced to live on a pittance saved from the successive rounds of foolish young girls they have scrambled into a little learning—their own beauty quite wasted, the better part of their youth sacrificed. But for the generosity of my brothers, whose incomes must make up the default of my late father's, Cassandra and I might find ourselves dependent upon a similar fate—urging the haughty and condescending among our near-acquaintance to pay for the privilege of our indifferent French, our accomplishments on the pianoforte, and our claims to such elegance as a few years' residence in Bath might afford us. I shuddered and averted my eyes from the small figure of Anne Sharpe, now several hundred yards beyond the haven of the temple.

"I do not know what to do for her, Jane," Lizzy said quietly. "A little higher, and she might be my intimate; a little lower, and I might be her patron. But as it is—"

"You may only preserve her from further degradation, with the sum of twenty pounds per annum. No wonder she longs to go to Town."

Lizzy glanced at me swiftly. "Does she? I had understood she abhorred London. The dirt—the noise—"

"She was wild to be gone but a few days since. The prospect of packing assured her of the event's achievement. I thought I had denied her dearest wish, when I informed her that a removal was only a distant possibility."

"How very odd," Lizzy murmured. "Perhaps she has had a letter ... an acquaintance returned to London ..." She straightened up and shook the dust from her flounces. "We shall be late for Eastwell, Jane, and much tho' it should give me pleasure to incommode Lady Elizabeth, your brother is correct in believing that I cannot allow her the pleasure of despising me. In any case, we cannot plumb the depths of Anne Sharpe by speculating at a distance. It puts me in mind of the sort of complacent old cats who lined the ballrooms of my girlhood, making matches and scandal between the most improbable of lovers."

"They line the ballroom still, Lizzy," I replied, "and I am in a fair way to joining them myself."

WE RETURNED TO THE GREAT HOUSE, AND PETITIONED Cook for raspberry cordial; it arrived almost directly from the icehouse, beaded with the most delicious moisture, on a silver tray. It was as we had finished one glass, and had determined we must exchange our morning gowns for travelling costumes more suited to the rigours of an open carriage, that Neddie and Henry returned from Mrs. Grey's funeral.

"My dear!" Lizzy cried, with more appearance of animation than was usual for her, "we are on the point of dressing for Eastwell, but cannot stir until you have told us all the news. How was the service conducted? Did the Comte and Mr. Grey come to blows? Who was so judicious in feeling as to attend?"

"Mr. James Wildman—Mr. Edward Taylor—Captain Woodford, of course; Mr. Toke, Mr. Sansible, and a few others not unknown to you.[3] Denys Collingforth failed to put in his appearance, as did your brother Edward, Lizzy; but the former was hardly expected, and the latter we may suppose to have been detained by his duty to his mother. Our Henry, however, was generally acclaimed the most sportingly—if inappropriately—attired."

"And Mr. Grey?" Lizzy persisted. "How did he appear?"

---

[3]   Women never attended funerals in Austen's day, even those of close family members. They were deemed too delicate to support the pain of witnessing an interment, despite the fact that they presided over innumerable deathbeds.—*Editor's note.*

Neddie eased himself onto one of the drawing-room's uncomfortable gilt chairs with a grimace. "We were denied the pleasure of meeting Mr. Grey, my dear."

"You have no pity on my poor nerves," Lizzy scolded him crossly. "Jane and I have exhausted nearly every occupation open to a woman this morning—needlework, novel-reading, and the sketching of a quantity of children"—in this, she exaggerated a little, given the indolence of our employment in the temple—"in feverish expectation of your return. I am sure that Jane wore out her pen entirely in her repeated efforts to sharpen it; and yet she cannot have composed more than two sentences together, in the entire course of the morning! You are unspeakably cruel to serve us out in this manner. Mr. Grey, fail to attend his wife's funeral! Impossible, Neddie! Impossible!"

"Improbable, perhaps—unpardonable, even; but impossible? Not at all. The Larches' housekeeper—an excellent woman, one Mrs. Bastable, and a deft hand at blood pudding, as Henry may attest—informed us directly we arrived that the master was called to Town in the early hours of morning. He is expected at home this evening, however—so your visit of condolence cannot be put off."

"How extraordinary!" Lizzy exclaimed. Her countenance was less composed than I had ever had occasion to remark it. "To ride into Town, when one's wife is as yet unburied, and without the slightest regard for public opinion!"

"We can know nothing of Mr. Grey's regard for public opinion," Neddie objected. "It might be quite strenuously excited by his demonstration of poor taste. Indeed, his concern for the feelings of his neighbours on this point might even deprive him of sleep. You should not judge harshly, Lizzy, without a full knowledge of the particulars."

"Excuse me, my dear, but I know *exactly* how I may judge," Lizzy rejoined tartly. "Such nice distinctions between intention and action, belong solely to the province of the Justice, who must stand above reproach. His wife may indulge all the force of prejudice, and declare Mr. Grey an unfeeling brute."

"Did his housekeeper confide the reason for this sudden journey?" I enquired.

"According to Mrs. Bastable, the master received an express from Town just before dawn, presumably on a matter of business. His journey necessarily resulted from it. To suppose more than this, would be sheer conjecture."

"A pressing matter of business, then, to prevent his attending his wife's funeral. I should imagine it the sort of summons that might not be denied—from a person whose powers must command even Grey."

"There can be very few of those," Henry remarked. "A summons from Prime Minister Pitt himself, perhaps?— Who requires another loan to fund the ambitions of Lord Nelson and our brother?"

"Perhaps we should peruse the London papers," I suggested with a smile, "and find in their subtle hints the reason for so much haste. The Comte, I suppose, was in evidence?"

"He might have been the bereaved husband himself, for all his display of anguish," Neddie replied.

"You thought him insincere?"

"No, Jane—merely less restrained than an Englishman might be. His grief bore every appearance of arising from the deepest sense of loss. He accepted the sympathies of the assembled mourners with becoming grace, and begged us all to take some refreshment in the house, when once the service was over."

"He took nothing himself, however," Henry supplied, "and said even less."

"Did you press him, Neddie, on the subject of Mr. Grey's flight?"

"I did not," my brother replied, "but the Comte suggested freely that he thought Grey's absence arose not from a matter of business, but from a persistent disregard for what was due to his wife—a distaste for the scandal her death had caused—and a general desire to place events behind him."

"The Comte will return very soon to France, I suppose."

"If Grey's wishes are consulted, I am sure the fellow would presently be at the ends of the earth! Not even Grey, however, may entirely control the disposition of forces. A fleet action in the Channel may forestall the departure of his unwelcome guest; and then we may observe how the two chessmen play."

"Provided the one does not place the other in check," I observed—and ran away to dress.

# Chapter 13

## *Talking Politics to a Lady*

*Friday, 23 August 1805,*
*very late in the evening*
~

WE ARE ONLY JUST RETURNED FROM OUR VISIT TO EAST-
well Park, and tho' it is nearly midnight now, my head
is so filled with all that I have seen and heard, that
I cannot sleep without setting down a few words in
my little book. A roving owl calls spectrally through
the darkness while the rest of the great house falls silent; monstrous shapes, born of my candle-flame, dance
against the yellow walls. The maid, stifling a gape, has
undone my best dinner gown and brushed out my hair.
She is gone thankfully now to her bed under the airless
rafters, while I sit at the dressing table in only my shift,
desperate for a breeze that never comes. Another midnight I should be overwhelmed with loneliness, and
dwell upon the follies of my past. But a circle of faces
presently whirls before my eyes, caught in a shaft of
memory; best to capture something of their outline,
before it is dulled with sleep.

It was a large and stimulating party—for in addition

to Mr. Finch-Hatton, Lady Elizabeth, and their five children (two of them very engaging little boys), we were treated to all the Finch-Hatton relations. This included the Miss Finches, Anne and Mary, both unmarried and as voluble as Lady Elizabeth is silent; Mr. Emilious Finch-Hatton, the younger brother; and Harriet, Lady Gordon, the one Finch sister so fortunate as to achieve the wedded state.[1] Her husband, Sir Janison, I liked too little to cultivate; his manner was haughty, as befits a baronet, and he gave way to the temptation to sneer at the foolishness of the Miss Finches more than once. I cannot love a man who despises a spinster.

Of Mr. Emilious Finch-Hatton, however, I formed a better opinion. I was so fortunate as to be seated next to him at dinner, and found him a stimulating companion—but more on that point later.[2]

In addition to our two families, there remained a pair of bachelors: Mr. Thomas Brett, an attorney with expectations of a prettyish estate near Wye, called Spring Grove, whom I believe to be sadly in the thrall of Miss Louisa Finch-Hatton; and the remarkable Mr. Julian Sothey.

Tho' we had journeyed the four miles towards Ashford in expectation of a meeting with the Gentleman Improver, it was in fact several hours before he was

---

[1]   George Finch (1747–1823) added "-Hatton" to his name in 1764, presumably in order to inherit from a lateral family line. His sisters did not take the additional surname, but his brother Emilious did. George was a cousin of the 8th Earl of Winchelsea; upon the earl's death in 1826, George's eldest son, George (1791–1858), acceded to the title as 9th earl. His third wife, Fanny, Countess of Winchelsea, was Edward and Elizabeth Austen's granddaughter; the two families thus eventually intermarried. —*Editor's note.*

[2]   Austen later recounted many of the details of this visit to East-well Park in a letter written to Cassandra on Saturday, August 24, 1805. (See Letter #45, in *Jane Austen's Letters*, 3rd edition, Deirdre Le Faye, ed., Oxford University Press, 1995.)—*Editor's note.*

introduced to the ladies' attention. Upon our arrival at Eastwell just after two o'clock, Lizzy and I were immediately conveyed to a pleasantly airy saloon, with French windows surmounted by an Egyptian frieze, done in quite an extraordinary plasterwork—as tho' Robert Adam had witnessed the excesses of Napoleon's campaign, and thought to reproduce all of Alexandria in a single room. The saloon's prospect gave out onto the garden, which my brothers were rapidly traversing in company with the male Finch-Hattons. They were bound for the stables and a pony-trap, in which they intended to tour the park.

Lady Elizabeth and her eldest daughter were reclining indolently on a pair of sofas, apparently overcome by the oppressive weather and the vexation of dressing for dinner; it was not in their power to rise at our entrance. The Miss Finches, in their neat, spare fashion, were industriously at work upon an extensive fringe, apparently divided between them; little George and Daniel were engaged in playing at spillikins, while Lady Gordon read aloud from a novel. (It was, alas, *The Sorrows of Young Werther;* and perhaps my countenance fell upon perceiving it, for the excellent woman set aside the volume directly we were announced.)

"Mrs. Austen!" Mary Finch cried.

"And Miss Jane Austen!" her sister Anne echoed.

The two ladies abandoned their work and bustled forward, all anxiety for our comfort, as though we had arrived in the midst of a terrible storm, or were fainting from three days' hunger. In the fuss that generally ensued, the quieter salutations of the others were entirely overwhelmed.

"To think," Miss Mary began, "—such excellent friends—travelling all this distance, and in such heat and dust! Entirely too amiable! You find us quite at home—reduced to utter stupidity by the oppressive weather—although Harriet has been so good as to amuse us with *Werther*—tho' perhaps amusing is *not* the properest word, for it *is* a trifle tedious in passages—Louisa was quite reduced to tears of boredom for entire chapters together, although I am sure it is very instructive. It is all the rage in Town."

"Had we only possessed Mrs. Edgeworth's works, or even Mrs. Palmerston's," Miss Anne added, "when Mary and I were girls—but, then, we were very fortunate to be taught so much as a syllable of French, or anything of geography, for it was hardly considered suitable to send *girls* to fashionable boarding establishments, such as our little Louisa has been treated to—and quite the fine miss she has returned, with such elegant taste, and her fingers so harmonious—they quite fly about the keyboard, as I am sure you will agree when she consents to play for us, after dinner. I am certain that Mr. Brett intends to teaze her on the subject of performance, blush how she might—"

"Pray allow the ladies to sit down, Mary," Lady Elizabeth commanded in a quelling tone, "and ring for Hopkins with some punch. I trust your journey was uneventful, Mrs. Austen?"

"Entirely, Lady Elizabeth, I thank you."

"You did not bring your eldest daughter. I had hoped she might be a companion for George."

"How unfortunate, then, that she remained at home! She was excessively disappointed, I assure you. But Fanny's governess thought the journey too unhealthful in such heat, to permit of the treat."

Lady Elizabeth inclined her head, and returned to fanning herself with a rush paddle; from Louisa we received not a word. She appeared engaged in studying the prospect of the garden—or perhaps she was hoping for a glimpse of its improver.

"Pray tell me, Miss Austen, how your lovely sister Cassandra does?" Miss Mary Finch cried. "We had hoped to have the pleasure of seeing her at Eastwell. It has been some months since we were so fortunate. Like yourself, I suppose, she yet retains the single state?"

"She does, ma'am," I managed without loss of countenance. "Her recent period of mourning for my father rendered any change in domestic situation abhorrent."

Miss Mary's expression turned so anxious at this, that I feared she might suffer a fit. "But of *course*—your excellent father—any change would be entirely out of the question for either of you girls—nothing so ideally suited to the comfort of a widow, as to have her children about her—I had entirely forgotten—that is, not *forgotten*, exactly, for who could ignore the loss of so admirable a soul, as the Reverend George? But, then, you are yourself no longer in mourning, Miss Austen, and I confess that your blooming looks put all thought of the dear departed quite out of my head. A charming man—and your brothers so very much like him—we shall have the pleasure of seeing Mr. Henry Austen, I hope, tho' my brother has quite stolen him away for the nonce. You will not take my little enquiry regarding your sister in an unamiable light, I hope?"

"Miss Austen is *from* Godmersham at present, I believe?" Miss Anne interjected, with a conscious look for her sister.

And so I related how Cassandra had gone to Harriot Bridges, with a view to assisting in the care of the invalid Bridges sister, Marianne; how she was expected at Godmersham on Monday, and appeared to be suffering herself from a return of the head-ache complaint that had troubled her ever since her unfortunate carriage accident in Lyme.[3]

---

[3] Jane here refers to events related in the second of the recently discovered journal manuscripts, published under the title of *Jane and the Man of the Cloth* (Bantam Books, 1997).

"So Miss Cassandra Austen went to Goodnestone Farm!" Miss Anne exclaimed. "That is very good of her, to be sure, when she must deny herself all the superior pleasures that your brother's estate may offer. But I shall hope that she has not found her time there *entirely* devoid of interest."

"I believe my brother Edward intended to make her visit as stimulating as possible," Lizzy remarked, without even the hint of a smile. "He is quite a slave to Cassandra's enjoyment, and shall presently turn his devotion to Jane. Jane is to make her own visit, you know, upon Cassandra's departure."

In such asides, punctuated by strenuous Finch monologues and virtual silence from the other ladies in the room, nearly an hour and a half were suffered to pass away, before a nuncheon of cheese and fruit materialised upon a tray. After this was consumed, I gave way to the entreaties of the little boys, and joined them in the establishment of cribbage. Daniel and I had just succeeded in winning several hands from Miss Mary and his elder brother, when an exclamation from the languorous Louisa alerted all our attention.

"Mamma! They are coming across the odious ha-ha! I see Mr. Sothey to the fore."

She rose and crossed to the pier-glass, surveying her reflection critically; then with a complete absence of consciousness, plucked at her golden curls and bit some colour into her full lips. Lady Gordon nearly choked on what might have been a giggle, and I observed the Miss Finches to exchange a significant look—but forbore from betraying my amusement. Lizzy, as ever, was a study in cultivated indifference; and so the Austens acquitted themselves more nobly than Miss Louisa's dearest relations.

A turmoil in the entry announced the gentlemen arrived; a hubbub of voices, and the tramp of feet—and the door was thrown open by one who was a stranger to me, and yet not entirely a stranger at all. I felt in an instant that this must be Julian Sothey, a gentleman of whom I had known nothing but a week before; and yet his face was hauntingly familiar. I studied his figure in vain for a hint as to the scene, the moment of our meeting, and found memory elusive.

Slight, narrow-shouldered, and lithe in all his movements, he conveyed an immediate impression of grace, like a superlative dancing master; but his coat of superfine wool, in a respectable shade of blue, was too well-made to permit of such an impertinence. His reddish hair fell unbound to his shoulders; his wide grey eyes were keen, and heavily-lashed; and a droll expression, as of inward laughter at some private joke, played about his lips. He seemed entirely easy at Eastwell Park—so very easy with his position and circumstance, as to precede his host into the saloon. This must argue a degree of self-importance that could not but be repugnant; but I am prone to form a hasty view on very little knowledge, and urged myself to reserve judgement in the case. Mr. Sothey, after all, was the son of Lady Elizabeth's oldest friend—and must be claimed almost as one of the family.

He was followed immediately by Mr. Brett, an acquaintance of Neddie's of many years standing, and then by my two brothers. The Finch-Hatton gentlemen brought up the rear.

"Julian!" Louisa Finch-Hatton cried breathlessly. "You have been an age in the garden, I declare! And I *longed* to finish my portrait today!"

She appeared an ill-bred and disappointed child, with her lower lip protruding dangerously, but Mr. Sothey chose to disregard Miss Louisa's manner, and approached her directly.

"You know, my dear Miss Finch-Hatton," he said with

a bow, "that I move at your father's whim. I exist at East-well only to serve him, and true pleasure must await the disposition of his needs. But you have been amply engaged in amusement, I am sure—with such interesting friends about you! Might I beg an introduction?"

This last was directed at Lizzy and myself; and recovering her pretty ways, Miss Louisa performed the office of making Mr. Julian Sothey known to the Austens. The unfortunate Mr. Brett—a tall, gawkish gentleman with sparse fair hair and dull blue eyes—hovered like a shade at Sothey's rear, unable to yield the hope of Louisa Finch-Hatton's favour. I saw in an instant that it was heavy work, and pitied him.

"I had the very great pleasure of engaging Mr. Henry and Mr. Edward Austen in conversation, ma'am," Sothey told my sister easily, "while we toured the grounds of the park; and I must rejoice at the chance to further my acquaintance with the rest of the family."

Lizzy inclined her head coolly. "I am to learn in a moment, I suppose, that Mr. Austen has contracted the fever for improvement—and that all of Godmersham is to be thrown in an uproar."

"I cannot conceive that a place which has served as *your* home for so many years, could require any further embellishment of taste or beauty," Mr. Sothey replied. "And certainly none that was within *my* power to achieve."

My sister looked at him archly.

"I am only sorry that we are denied the pleasure of meeting your children," Mr. Sothey added. "Lady Elizabeth was quite determined upon that point—that at least the eldest should accompany you, along with a lady whom I believe is her governess. The child is not indisposed, I trust?"

"How very kind in you to enquire. Fanny is entirely

well, I thank you. She enjoys the most robust constitution. I am afraid Miss Sharpe is hardly equal to her."

"Miss Sharpe?"

"The governess. A charming young woman. It was at her suggestion that we denied Fanny the expedition; she feared the state of the roads, and the present uncertainty in the weather, might prove too much for her; and I could not disagree."

"I see. You accord a governess's opinion so much weight, Mrs. Austen?"

"In the matter of my child's well-being? Naturally, Mr. Sothey. It is expressly to attend to such things, that I engage Miss Sharpe. And now if you will excuse me—" Lizzy turned towards her husband, who stood to one side of the open French windows in earnest conversation with Mr. Emilious Finch-Hatton. A slight breeze stirred the white muslin of Lizzy's dress as she moved to join them, and fluttered the ribbons of her rose-coloured sash; the fall of her dark curls about the nape of her neck was as exquisite as the slight pulse beating at the base of her throat. She embodied the sort of elegance that only years of study may attain; but for all her art, Lizzy invariably appeared artless. It was impossible to imagine her a girl of five, with blackcurrant jam trailing down her apron; impossible to envision her quarrelling to the point of tears with a despicable younger brother. Impossible, even, to form an idea of her in the throes of childbirth—tho' she had accomplished it some nine times. She is the sort of woman who seems cut from whole cloth—a perfection from infancy—intended for nothing lower than the graceful passage of a well-proportioned room. I saw in my sister the unconscious fulfillment of an ideal, and knew it forever beyond my grasp.

But it was Mr. Sothey who put in words what I had only

thought in silence. " 'There is something in a face,' " he said, " 'An air, and a peculiar grace/Which boldest painters cannot trace.' "

I caught my breath. "I am unfamiliar with the author of those lines, sir."

"William Somerville," he replied briskly. "A much-neglected poet. Dr. Johnson was pleased to dismiss him as writing very well—*for a gentleman.*' Being the son of an Earl, Miss Austen, I am often placed in a similar category—accorded merit only in as much as I transcend the general mediocrity of my class. Artists, you know, should never possess the distinction of birth; it ruins them for genius."[4]

The Gentleman Improver undoubtedly possessed what Mr. Valentine Grey had called *address*—that curious mixture of charm and air, without which a man may never be termed brilliant. It is elusive in definition, but unmistakable in consequence; and I may confess myself particularly susceptible to its effect.

"I am glad to make your acquaintance, Mr. Sothey—for I should dearly like to comprehend a little of the genius that has so totally overthrown Mr. Finch-Hatton's taste."

"You make it sound a revolution!" he cried, in mock horror, "and a treacherous one at that!"

"Lady Elizabeth assures us that you are intent upon nothing less than the wholesale destruction of formal pieties—the inversion of the traditional order—and if this is *not* revolution, then what may we call it, sir?"

"I daresay the Whigs have found any number of proxies for such a word," Mr. Sothey rejoined, with a sharp

---

4  William Somerville (1675–1742) wrote those lines in the poem entitled *The Lucky Hit*, from 1727. He is best remembered, however, for *The Chace*, a four-volume poem of Miltonian blank verse that celebrated the joys of hunting. In it, he coined the phrase "sport of kings."—*Editor's note.*

look of interest in his clear grey eyes, "but do not allow me to be talking politics to a lady. Say rather that at Eastwell I hope to correct what has gone astray, Miss Austen, and to support what might only have been dreamt of before—that I aspire to a higher order of Beauty than yet exists—and perhaps we shall find agreement."

"I am sure that even Robespierre once proclaimed a similar faith," I rejoined, "and yet as many heads fell at the guillotine, as noble old avenues under the axe of the improver."

"Good Lord! All forms of governance may decline, I assure you, from neglect as well as revolution; and never so particularly as at Eastwell Park."

"It is well, I suppose, that we have seen the place before your hand has accomplished this transformation," I observed, "for we may then judge more acutely whether anarchy or order has been imposed."

Mr. Sothey threw back his head and laughed. "I perceive that you bear no love for the Picturesque, Miss Austen."

"Julian—" Louisa Finch-Hatton broke in irritably, "pray come and sit by me. I intend to play, and you know that I can do nothing without you to turn the pages."

"Pray allow me to serve you, Miss Louisa," Mr. Brett said hurriedly, "for Mr. Sothey is presently engaged."

He attempted to steer her towards the instrument, but Louisa's countenance assumed a mulish look, and she remained rooted to the floor for the space of several heartbeats. At Mr. Sothey's apparent disinclination to honour the request, however, and his fixed interest in myself, the young lady eventually gave way. From the sound of her strenuous playing, I judged her to be serving out punishment to her excellent pianoforte, that might better have been visited upon her Beloved. The little interval provided an opportunity, however, to seize a chair in one corner of the saloon; and to my delight, Mr. Sothey followed.

"If by Picturesque," I continued, "you would refer to the work of Mr. Humphrey Repton, be assured that I am not wholly ignorant of the style. A cousin of my mother's engaged Mr. Repton to improve his rectory in Adlestrop, and the result, we are assured, is delightful."[5]

"Then I may suppose," Mr. Sothey remarked with a glint of humour, "that a perfectly respectable stream has been forced from its hallowed bed, and constrained to run over graduated terraces; that hills have been formed where there were none before, and surmounted with rustic cottages in which no one—particularly hermits or gnomes, to whom such cottages are invariably ascribed—has ever lived. There is a grotto, no doubt, or a ruin in the Gothic style, ideally positioned for viewing in the moonlight. May we hope for so much as an abyss, wherein the Fate of Mortal Man might be contemplated in peace, particularly on days of mist and lowering cloud?"

I could not suppress a smile. "I believe that my cousin carries the abyss within, Mr. Sothey—and thus must find an outer manifestation of Fate unnecessary. But ruins were entirely beyond the reach of Reverend Leigh's purse, as was the better part of Mr. Repton's talents. He merely served as consultant on the redirection of the sweep, and the clearing of a prospect from the rectory to the village; attended to some terracing, and the placement of a few trees."

5 Jane refers to Adlestrop Park, the home of the Reverend Thomas Leigh, her mother's first cousin, which Repton "improved" in 1802. Jane did not see the transformed park at Adlestrop until the summer of 1806, but apparently the changes impressed her very little. She went on to lampoon Repton's ideas and business practices in her 1814 novel, Mansfield Park.—*Editor's note.*

"Then he has served your cousin admirably," Sothey declared, "and in a better fashion than a fellow with ten times his fortune."

"You are no disciple of Mr. Repton?"

"I am well-acquainted with his views," he replied equably, "but have formed my own along a different path."

"—A *higher* path, you would imply?"

"It is not for me to praise myself, Miss Austen. You may believe me capable of every absurdity—as you appear inclined to do—but pray allow me to possess common sense. Only a brainless popinjay will proclaim his merit before others have done so." His lips twitched irrepressibly, and despite my aversion to the entire rage for improvement, I could not help liking Mr. Sothey.

"Then acquaint me with your views," I urged. "To what does the Picturesque refer, if not to the Romantic Horrors you have yourself described?"

"To the ageless elegance of the art of Europe," Sothey replied immediately. "To the noble symmetry of Italian landscape, as expressed in the canvases of the Great Masters. If I may achieve an hundredth part of the beauty and taste enshrined in the prospect of a Roman hillside, as painted by a Claude or a Poussin, then I shall declare myself well-satisfied."[6]

"You have travelled abroad, I perceive."

"As has your brother, I find. Mr. Austen and I enjoyed a splendid half-hour on the subject of the Grand Tour, and found ourselves much in agreement. I was privileged to study the composition of a landscape, while resident in Paris during the period of the Peace," So-

---

[6] Sothey refers to Claude Lorrain (1600–1682) and Nicolas Poussin (1594–1665), French masters of landscape painting. —*Editor's note.*

they added, "and now apply the principles of the Picturesque to the grounds of my acquaintance."

I was immediately intrigued. "And so you would form a prospect—from this saloon's windows, for example—according to the precepts of *painting*?"

"Is not the prospect a sort of picture? Is not the window a veritable frame?" Sothey cried excitedly. "Consider the view across this garden, Miss Austen. Is it not remarkably flat and unvarying? Does even a single feature suggest its primacy to the eye, and direct the gaze of the viewer to its silent grandeur? I would assert that the back garden at Eastwell is a formless jumble, in which all individual beauties are lost; that the distant prospect, with its barren hills and isolated coverts, must insult the eye with tedium; that trees are required in the foreground, to frame the distance properly, and that a richness of detail in the near-ground is imperative, if the eye is to progress beyond it at all. There is no *path*, Miss Austen, for the eye to follow—no guide to a remoter beauty—no sense, in fine, of picturesque perspective. Allow me to demonstrate the transformation I would intend."

He leapt from his chair, and seized a large quarto volume bound in dark blue leather. This was immediately opened and placed upon my lap; and the vigour of Mr. Sothey's action could not but direct the attention of the entire room. I found that I had drawn a circle of attentive admirers, all craning to peer over my shoulder at the pages of the book—which were in fact illustrations, in breathtaking watercolours. All were signed by the painter in a distinctive, sloping script, as tho' the *S* of Sothey were a sail that might carry its master far upon the sea of fame.

"Have you worked upon Miss Austen already, Sothey, that she must submit to your Blue Book?" Mr. Finch-Hatton cried, in high good humour. "Then we must all be bent to its claims. Pray direct us in the study of your work."

I had been presented with a catalogue of East-well Park, as it presently existed; and for every picture Mr. Sothey had executed an overlay, which showed the improvements that might be effected.[7] In silence, punctuated by exclamations of delight and wonder, the whole party was treated to an explanation of Mr. Sothey's vision; and I must confess it to have converted even myself. Nowhere did I find evidence of vulgarity, or a slavish devotion to fad; not a Gothic ruin nor a felled avenue could I detect, but rather the subtraction of those elements in the landscape that contributed to its confusion—a clarification of its beauties, that by the removal of excess, contributed to a finer definition of the whole. As I turned the pages in company with the others, I could not help but acknowledge Mr. Sothey's Art—his accomplished skill—his inexpressible taste. It might have served the Finch-Hattons immeasurably, I thought, had they possessed a man of his talents in the editing of their *architect*. For if even a small part of Sothey's plan were achieved, the ill-framed house would sit like a pebble in a casing intended for a jewel.

"And how do you like my Eastwell, Miss Austen?" Sothey enquired in a lowered tone, when the attentions of the others had been diverted by the entrance of the little children, fresh from their dinners in the nursery, and bent upon an hour with Mamma and Papa before bedtime. "Does it suit your notions of Beauty? Or have I failed where I would most desire to succeed?"

[7] It is evident that Julian Sothey learned something from Humphrey Repton, however little he agreed with the latter's views on landscape design. Repton, like Sothey, was an accomplished painter who was known for the execution of his Red Books— leather-bound volumes illustrating views of clients' grounds, with overlays of intended improvements.—*Editor's note.*

"I have never seen a place for which Nature has done more, or where natural beauty has been so little counteracted by an awkward taste," I acknowledged. "You have seized the landscape's soul, the park as it might be in Paradise."

"I merely let slip the spirit inherent in these woods and hills," Sothey said. "One can do nothing, you know, without one pays homage to the genius of the place."

"Alexander Pope," I returned. "But I thought he meant only a sort of pagan homage—the construction of a grotto, for instance, in respect of the resident River God. I have been hoping for a glimpse of ours, at Godmersham, these six years at least—for you know we are situated on the Stour."

Sothey smiled. "The more ardent contemporaries of Mr. Pope might interpret his injunctions too literally. But I assume him to have intended something perhaps more subtle—that the imposition of elements alien to a country can never be graced with success. The untamed crags of Derbyshire, Miss Austen, would look sadly out of place in the peaceful folds of the Kentish downs, however Romantic their wild beauty."

He sat back against his chair and regarded me with a serious air; and in that moment—when his countenance was swept clean of wit and artifice, and overlaid with an unwonted gravity—I knew at once where I had seen Mr. Sothey before. The revelation must stop my breath, and spur my heart to a rapid pounding.

He was the young man who had drawn my attention at the Canterbury race-meeting—a gentleman of unflinching dignity, who had taken the lash of Mrs. Grey's whip full against his neck.

# Chapter 14

## A Tale of Assignation

### 23 August 1805, cont'd.

~

"ARE YOU QUITE WELL, MISS AUSTEN?"

"It is nothing, sir," I told Mr. Sothey. "The heat—I felt a trifle overcome—perhaps some air—"

I stood up unsteadily and joined my brother and sister at the French windows. Mr. Sothey bowed, and turned his attention to the pianoforte, where Miss Louisa Finch-Hatton now warbled a beguiling Scotch air.

"Jane, my dear," Lizzy murmured at my elbow, "if we do not escape this instant and dress for dinner, we shall be made to look the completest fools. It would be like Lady Elizabeth to ring the dinner bell early, on purpose to catch us out."

"Never fear, Lizzy," I whispered back with tolerable composure, "your little hint of Thursday—that the intimates of Eastwell dined before the fashionable of Godmersham—was hardly lost on Lady Elizabeth. She will keep us waiting until midnight for her elegant courses, and exult in our famished pangs. You may change your gown ten times over with complete equanimity. But I confess I should be happy to escape. Let us go at once!"

Her green eyes narrowed. "Has the Gentleman Improver routed you so entirely? He *has* a cunning air. Were I disposed to throw my daughter away, I could not do better than Lady Elizabeth. She shall see Miss Louisa eloped to Gretna with her protégé before the summer is out, if she does not take care."

I seized Lizzy's elbow and steered her to the door.

"Pray excuse us, my dear," she called over her shoulder to Neddie, "Jane and I cannot hope to rival the Finch-Hattons in beauty, but must fly this moment if we are not entirely to disgrace you."

Neddie bowed as we quitted the room, the very picture of a dutiful husband; but his eyes were abrim with laughter and the frankest admiration as he gazed after his wife. It was clear from his looks that all Miss Louisa's petulant blonde charms could never sway his devotion to the dark and enchanting. Mr. Sothey's quotation rose unbidden into my mind. *"There is something in a face/An air, and a peculiar grace . . ."* Kent is indeed the only place for happiness, and everyone *is* rich there—but in far more than mere pounds and pence.

I CONVEYED MY APPREHENSION REGARDING MR. SOTHEY to Lizzy as we dressed hurriedly for dinner. Sayce was busy about my sister's hair for some time, and our conversation was necessarily curtailed while the lady's maid was present in the room; it would never do for even so superior a servant as Sayce to carry tales of murder to the servants' hall. But as soon as Lizzy was suitably adorned for an intimate dinner among friends—in a cream lawn gown, sprigged and trimmed in exactly the colour of her eyes; its negligent cut and dampened underskirt displayed her form to breathless effect—I concluded my tale of the silent figure poised at the mounts of Mrs. Grey's phaeton, and the cruel descent of the whip.

"Of course," Lizzy murmured, "I recollect the whole. Mrs. Grey's dreadful end had the power to put flight to every other scene we witnessed that day; and I confess that Sothey's features were hardly clear to me at such a remove. They must have stood an hundred paces from our carriage; and my eyes were never strong. I retained only the memory of a rather spare, gentlemanlike figure, that offered not the slightest protest to her abuse. But tell me, Jane," she went on, turning slightly away from the mirror to face me, "—you cannot believe Sothey capable of Mrs. Grey's murder? And on so slight a provocation as a public insult?"

"I do not know what to believe," I said despairingly. "We can know so very little. Certainly there was a discord between them; and we know that Sothey determined to quit The Larches that very day. No one has thought to enquire where the gentleman should have been, while Denys Collingforth's chaise was upon the Wingham road. How simple for him to borrow it, and ride in pursuit of the woman who shamed him!"

"You believe Mr. Sothey to have been Mrs. Grey's lover, as well as Mr. Collingforth—*and* the French Comte?" Lizzy adjusted the petals of a flower that Sayce had secured in her hair, and surveyed herself acutely in the glass. "The lady certainly made effective use of her time."

"We know that Mr. Sothey was resident at The Larches for nearly six months, and *that*, when Mr. Grey was much in Town," I observed. "In such unusual circumstances, an illicit passion would not be unthinkable. Even Mrs. Grey, moreover, would not dare to strike a mere acquaintance in so public a manner. So they *must* have been intimate. There was a passion to the entire scene, quite subtle but undeniable, that might have borne the parties to any length of indiscretion."

"Even murder? But pray consider, Jane—did not the passion we witnessed emanate from the lady herself, rather than the man you would suggest did away with her? And was it the fury of love denied, or of love *unrequited*? Was there not more of wounding, than rejection, in the blow?"

I considered her words a moment in silence, then studied my sister with a new respect. "I should have to say that the passion was entirely Mrs. Grey's, Lizzy. What impressed me forcibly at the time, was the forbearance in the gentleman's entire manner—the sanguine aspect of his countenance as the crop came down upon his neck. He was like a schoolboy called to reprimand before his headmaster, accepting of what he knew to be both just and inevitable. There was neither fear, nor anguish, nor pleading in his looks—only the calm of resignation."

"I am entirely of your way of thinking, Jane. Let us declare, then, that Sothey had broken with the lady, and incurred her wrath; and thus, should hardly have need of strangling her in her shift but an hour later."

"Your idea of it is quite persuasive," I acknowledged, "but how can one possibly determine what to think? We know so little of the particulars, and even less of the characters involved; how one might be worked upon, and another influenced for good or evil."

Lizzy snatched up her reticule and turned to the door. "However little you may comprehend at the moment, my dear Jane, I am certain you shall know it all in a matter of hours. For what better field than a dinner party for the marshalling of your troops—wit, flirtation, and a penetrating mind?"

• • •

My sister's confidence in my powers was sadly misplaced. We descended to the great drawing-room, which was furnished discordantly in several of the latest fashions: couches of loose silk cushions in the Turkish manner, and chairs whose carved gilt arms resembled swans; the whole ceiling tented with a striped silk fabric drawn up in the center of the room, and suspended from the claws of a bronze gryphon, as tho' Napoleon's hordes had overrun several continents with a view to nothing nobler than a miscellany sale—we found the entire party assembled for a removal to the dining-parlour, and ourselves the tardy culprits. That Lizzy gloried in the tedium she had imposed upon Lady Elizabeth—the smallish conversation, and the covert glances at the mantel-clock—I readily perceived. My sister's countenance was as serene as a summer day, however, as she followed Sir Janison and Lady Gordon to the dining-parlour. The rest of us came after in something of a hurly-burly, there being little of precedence to choose among us; a polite skirmish ensued between Mr. Brett and Mr. Sothey, with the former determined he should carry Miss Louisa down the hall, and the latter far more indifferent to the outcome than the lady might have wished. Henry having engaged to convey Miss Mary Finch, I found myself taken up by none other than Mr. Emilious Finch-Hatton, the distinguished (and unusually voluble) younger brother—a circumstance I was inclined to lament, being intent upon the elucidation of Mr. Sothey. But I bore with the reversal with something like grace—a something that increased to surprise and gratitude, when I learned more of my dinner companion.

To say that Mr. Emilious Finch-Hatton is the younger brother of the house, is to suggest a degree of callowness that is entirely unwarranted. He cannot be less than forty, nor older than sixty; but where the truth of his years might be reckoned, I cannot begin to guess.[1] A grey-haired man of elegant manner, he is quick-witted, lithe of movement, open of countenance, and ready in his laughter. Having known him these many years to be an acknowledged *bon vivant*, as liberal in his habits of expense as his easy manner suggests, I had not suspected him of a more sober interest; but must *now* acknowledge deception as Mr. Emilious's most subtle talent.

Having established me correctly at the lower end of the table, he settled himself to my right. "I have long looked forward to this summer's meeting, Miss Austen, from the desire to speak with you regarding a mutual acquaintance," he began, as the napkins were unfurled, and the wine poured.

"I cannot think whom you mean, sir." And, indeed, Mr. Emilious and I could never be described as moving in a similar set, excepting those rare occasions when the claims of duty bring us both into Kent. He spends the better part of his days in Town, apparently content to lead a fashionable and sporting life; a widower these five-and-twenty years, he may escort any number of ladies about the routs of the *ton*, without the slightest betrayal of susceptibility. A suspicion of his having met with my cunning sister Eliza, the little *comtesse*, animated me briefly—but Henry would be the most suitable person to receive that intelligence, not myself.

"I *had* understood that you were a little acquainted with my intimate friend, Lord Harold Trowbridge," Mr. Emilious persisted.

I set down my wineglass with an attempt at ease, but the quickness of the blood in my cheek surely betrayed

---

[1] John Emilious Daniel Edward Finch-Hatton (1755–1841) was about fifty when he dined with Jane Austen in August 1805. —*Editor's note.*

a deeper sensibility. "And *has* Lord Harold, then, an intimate friend? Such a singular intelligence must certainly astonish!" I had not received a word from my Dark Angel in fully eight months, beyond a brief message of condolence at the death of my father this January last. A gentleman never writes to a lady of his acquaintance, of course, unless there is an understanding—an open or a secret engagement of marriage—and despite Lord Harold's perpetual disregard for convention, he should be unlikely to expose *me* to censure through a careless impropriety. But he might have paid a call while yet we remained in Bath—he might even have sought me out in Kent, had his regard or his necessity warranted such attention. His evident disinclination, tho' only to be expected from a gentleman of his solitary habits and elusive purpose, had fallen like a shower of coldest rain upon an unguarded head.

I will confess here in the privacy of my little book that I have *missed* our conversations—the intimacy of shared thought, and the ready understanding, so rare between a man and a woman. Lord Harold has never taught me to entertain expectations of a deeper interest on his side— our manner of living is so different, and the disparity of birth too great—but I had come to depend upon the notion of his friendship. This was foolish, perhaps, in respect of a man whose heart and mind are opened to no one; Trowbridge is the sort to profit by an acquaintance, as occasion dictates, and move on without a backwards glance. I had been thrown off, in short, when my utility to His Lordship was done; and I resented the change.

Mr. Emilious, I found, was studying me narrowly as I turned the stem of my wineglass between my fingers; and so I strove for the appearance of composure. "I knew His Lordship a little in Bath last winter. His niece, Lady Desdemona Trowbridge—the Countess of Swithin, rather—and I were thrown much together."

"On account of that dreadful business with the Theatre Royal," Mr. Emilious returned. "You rendered the entire Wilborough clan an inexpressible service, Miss Austen. Trowbridge himself could not say enough of your understanding—and from such a quarter, that must be the highest praise, indeed."

What *exactly* Mr. Emilious had heard of my adventures in Bath the previous Christmas—which had come nearer to compromising my reputation than any of my impetuous forays to date—was left in doubt.[2] I surveyed his countenance for the slightest hint of excessive familiarity—for an odious approach to the indelicate—and could discern nothing but respectful admiration. I drew breath, accordingly, and enquired, "His Lordship is well?"

"My intelligence of Lord Harold is no more recent than March," my companion replied. "We dined together but two days before his departure for the Russian court—and he then appeared much as he always does: a trifle weary of the world and his place in it, but whether due to excessive application, or excessive boredom, who can say? I saw him into the Portsmouth coach the following morning. He was to embark on a Navy frigate, since travel across the Continent is made so perilous for an Englishman. But I am forgetting—no doubt you are well-acquainted with His Lordship's route."

"Well-acquainted? *I?*" Astonishment very nearly deprived me of speech. "But I have not met with Lord Harold these eight months at least."

"I am excessively surprised," Mr. Emilious cried. "I had understood from his latest communication that you were completely in his confidence; that he regarded

---

[2] Jane alludes here to events detailed in the third volume of her recently published detective journals, *Jane and the Wandering Eye* (Bantam Books, 1998).—*Editor's note.*

you, indeed, as one of the few among his friends who might wholly be trusted."

I flushed. "Trust, Mr. Emilious, is a suspect quality in Lord Harold's hands."

"So I comprehend." He was silent an instant, his gaze fixed absently on Lady Elizabeth's hideous candelabra. A faint breeze—or the current of conversation in the room, perhaps—stirred its flames fitfully.

"Are you at liberty to disclose the nature of His Lordship's errand to Russia?" I enquired delicately. "Or does discretion forbid the particulars?"

Mr. Emilious regarded me with calculation, a fine line between his brows; his easy manner was entirely fled. "I am told it is impolite to mention politics before a lady," he said slowly, "but I intend no disrespect to yourself, Miss Austen, in declaring that you have never been accorded that fragile status by Lord Harold. He assures me that you possess the keenest understanding in the world, and are conversant in everything that one must, from convention, reserve solely to the affairs of men."

"I cannot admit to having bagged a grouse, Mr. Finch-Hatton, nor to having sported a pipe of Virginia tobacco; but I may confess to a glancing acquaintance with the London papers."

"You have heard, then, of the Anglo-Russian accord?"

I stared at him indifferently. "Is there anyone who has not? It was ratified, I believe, but a few weeks ago."

Mr. Emilious had the frankness to smile; he glanced involuntarily at his niece, Miss Louisa, and said: "Few ladies, Miss Austen, have the strength to tear their gazes from the fashion plates of *La Belle Assemblée*, in support of news from abroad. I doubt that one in an hundred could tell me what you clearly apprehend—that the Tsar of all the Russias, Alexander the First, has at long last admitted to a distrust of Napoleon, and pledged to stand with England against the French."

"I shall value His Imperial Majesty's pledges the more when once they are put to the test," I observed. "My naval brothers assure me that we must benefit from the exchange, in gaining freedom for our ships in northern waters; Mr. Pitt has long since struck a bargain with Gustavus of Sweden towards this very end—but what good can England hope to return, to the Tsar of all the Russias? Did the French purpose to acquire his snowy steppes, we should hardly intervene."

"But we may serve to further Alexander's dearest interest," Mr. Emilious countered. "The Tsar has long desired the conquest of Ottoman lands to the south of his present borders; and in this, he rivals the French. A year ago he recalled his ambassador from Paris; as recently as May, he was made distinctly uneasy by Buonaparte's seizure of the Italian crown. The fall of the Ligurian Republic this summer has further excited his anxiety. But he bears us no love, for all that; in clasping the hand of the English, Alexander has chosen the lesser of the evils available to him."

"I must believe that the Russian mind is forever closed to the open heart of an Englishman."

"—unless that Englishman be Lord Harold Trowbridge."

I smiled involuntarily. Mr. Emilious was correct; in the Gentleman Rogue, Tsar Alexander's ministers would meet the most inscrutable of adversaries. "His Lordship was instrumental in the accord's completion, I collect?"

"He was—tho' the credit shall go publicly to another. That is only as he would wish; he has quitted the Russian court already some weeks, and at present exerts his delicate influence with the Hapsburg Emperor. For an alliance to stand firm against the French, Mr. Pitt must secure the Austrians at any cost."[3]

"But of course," I murmured, as though the subtlety of the Prime Minister's conduct could never be lost on so keen a female mind. "I must wonder, sir, whether any coalition might avail us comfort, when the French are rumored to have left Boulogne."

"Ah," Mr. Emilious returned; and his eyes glinted. "And yet you will perceive, Miss Austen, that I credit rumour so little, I remain as yet in Kent."

"As do we all. Town can offer few delights in August."

"I hope that I may call upon you one day this week? You are quite fixed for the present at Godmersham?"

"Until Monday, sir, when I shall pay a visit to Lady Bridges, at Goodnestone Farm."

The footmen then appearing to carry out the remove, and unfurl the clean cloth, all discourse was at an end.[4] I had little doubt that Mr. Emilious intended no idle pleasantry in his last remark. He had approached me with a purpose this evening, and had set about to sound my depths. Whatever Lord Harold's intention in directing his friend to my door, it was not of a sort to be broached over the dinner table; and I found myself impatient to know what it was. Indeed, my thoughts were entirely in a whirl: for I exulted—there could be no

---

[3] Presumably, news of the Austrian accord had not reached London at the time that Jane conversed with Mr. Emilious Finch-Hatton. In fact, the Austrians had joined what came to be known as the Third Coalition on August 9, but the passage of news overland was slow and uncertain in time of war, and almost equally so when conveyed by ship.—*Editor's note.*

[4] It was the custom in Austen's day to present at least two courses at a formal dinner, each comprising up to twenty dishes of a variety of vegetables, meats, and salads. When one course was consumed, the dishes were removed along with the tablecloth, which would be relaid for the second course.—*Editor's note.*

other word—in the knowledge that I had not been entirely forgot. Lord Harold elusive at so small a remove as Town, was cause for pain; Lord Harold despatched to remotest Russia, was quite another instance. My spirits, of a sudden, had soared ridiculously; Mr. Sothey, the murdered Françoise Grey, even the invading French—all consigned to oblivion in respect of Mr. Emilious's words.

Patience was to be my trial in the present instance, however. Having devoted the entirety of the first course to the amusement of Mr. Emilious Finch-Hatton, I should accord my elegant phrases to the gentleman seated at my left, Mr. Brett, during the second. When the covers were settled upon every square inch of the table's surface, I turned, and found the poor man's gaze fixed pensively on Miss Louisa Finch-Hatton.

That young lady was seated farther up the table, as suited the eldest daughter of the house; she was placed between my brother Henry and Mr. Sothey, whose interest she had tenaciously engaged, and refused to give up despite the appearance of the second course. Poor Henry looked quite put out, and in the throes of boredom, since his companion to the right was Miss Anne Finch. I perceived that that excellent lady was presently in full flood upon the subject of whalebone corsets, and the mortification of their creaking, particularly for a gentleman. This might be considered a daring launch in Miss Anne Finch's mind. One look at Henry's face reminded me of my duty to Mr. Brett.

"And how do you find the practise of law in Kent, Mr. Brett?" I began, my fascinated gaze fixed firmly on his profile.

He tore his eyes from Louisa and sought my countenance almost blindly. "I beg your pardon? I fear I was not attending."

"You are a solicitor, I believe?"

"I am."

"Then pray tell me, sir—what sense can you make of my brother's unfortunate business with Mrs. Grey?"

"I should rather have called it Mrs. Grey's unfortunate business," he observed, with a quelling look, "and your brother's duty, Miss Austen."

"But of course," I murmured, "as who better than an Austen should know?"

Mr. Brett, I made no doubt, was burdened by an inclination to find all women dangerously forward in the expression of their opinions, excepting his delightful Louisa—who could be counted upon to voice nothing more challenging than a view of the weather, or the latest rage among the *ton*. "Then you have escaped the general fit of curiosity, Mr. Brett, as to the nature of Mrs. Grey's end?"

"If you mean the morbid preoccupation with her death—I can think of nothing less seemly. Curiosity in such a cause must be abhorrent." His eyes strayed involuntarily to Mr. Sothey and Louisa, and of a sudden, I considered the utility of the Green-Eyed Monster. Many a man might be goaded by jealousy, where a judicious reserve should counsel otherwise. I should be very much surprised if Mr. Brett had not already acquainted himself with the chief failings of his rival, the better to combat the latter's power.

"You are entirely correct, of course," I offered mildly, "and I must admire your forbearance. An attorney must be but too susceptible to an avid interest in such crimes; natural inclination would lead you to it, and your talents admirably suit you to the task. The temptation to indulge in theories and solutions must be nearly overwhelming— a temptation that Mr. Sothey, for example, could not be expected to feel."

"No, indeed," Mr. Brett vehemently declared, "Mr.

Sothey's temptations must lie in an entirely different quarter. Neither reason nor propriety can be known to such a man."

"You do not esteem a landscape designer?"

Mr. Brett turned upon me an eloquent eye. "It makes no matter what Sothey styles himself. A scoundrel with neither character nor feeling to recommend him may go by any name he chooses. I hope that I may never esteem a shameless poacher on the preserve of his betters, Miss Austen—a man who would take money for the expression of his merest opinion, and a few dabblings in watercolour! He should be run out of the country on a wood plank; and the sooner, the better, for all concerned."

If Mr. Sothey caught a syllable of Mr. Brett's indignant words, he betrayed not a hint of it; Miss Louisa, I am certain, was too engaged in admiring his voice, to attend to any other in the room.

"What can Mr. Sothey have done, to merit such opprobrium?" I enquired.

"Only such as must make him the enemy of every respectable man in the Kingdom! That he has the impudence to show his face at this table, when the history of his connexion with that regrettable woman must be known to the entire country, surpasses belief! And yet, there he sits, in the most open coquetry with an innocent young lady, as tho' all the sins of lechery did not proclaim themselves in his countenance!"

I allowed his wrath to subside a little, and then ventured, "If you would allude to Mrs. Grey—I had understood that Mr. Sothey was engaged in the household in much the capacity that he is entertained here. As a landscape designer, and the intimate friend of *Mr.* Grey."

Mr. Brett laughed abruptly—an unlovely sound. "That will be the tale he tells, no doubt. But I have seen the evidence of his cunning with my own eyes, and the memory of it is seared upon my brain. I would not call that fellow friend, for any amount of money in the world. He cannot apprehend the meaning of the word; *friend* must be as open to injury as enemy, to Mr. Sothey. He is not a man to be trusted."

"If what you would imply is true," I persisted, "I must wonder at Mr. Grey's permitting him the liberty of his household. Mr. Sothey only quitted The Larches this week, I believe."

"As recently as the day of Mrs. Grey's death. I must think the coincidence quite telling."

"You cannot mean—"

"—that he was somehow responsible?" Mr. Brett hesitated; but even the goad of jealousy, it seemed, was inadequate to a charge of murder. "I cannot know of what Mr. Sothey is capable. But I was privileged to witness his arrival here the day of the race-meeting—having ridden over to pay my respects to the ladies, unaware that the Finch-Hattons were as yet detained in Canterbury. The impression of haste and trouble Mr. Sothey *then* conveyed was unmistakable. He seemed in flight from the Devil himself, if you will pardon the expression; his hat gone, his appearance wild, with a great weal standing out on his neck; his baggage in disarray, and his manservant decidedly put out at the suddenness of the removal. 'Good God!' I cried, upon first perceiving them, 'have the French indeed made landfall in Kent? Has the alarm been sounded?'—for their appearance, Miss Austen, must give rise to every anxiety. Sothey attempted a laugh, but it came out queerly, and with entirely the opposite effect of ease he had intended. 'Merely a brush with a footpad, Mr. Brett,' he declared, 'who visited this injury upon me, before Frick bade him be off, with the persuasion of a pistol.' I saw the manservant, Frick, look swiftly at his master, as if to call him liar; and wondered at the tale. The two disappeared into the house as freely as tho' it were their own, and I turned my mount towards the Canterbury road. But later, when I learned of Mrs. Grey's death, and remembered Mr. Sothey's conduct in that house, I formed my own conclusion."

"You believe that Mr. Grey turned him away from The Larches?" I hazarded. "But surely Mr. Grey was in London?"

"Of course it was not Grey!" Mr. Brett declared, all astonishment. "He was too indifferent to his wife's conduct, Miss Austen, to lose the services of so valuable a consultant as Mr. Sothey. No; I should imagine it was the lady herself who ran Sothey off, because of his infamy."

This last put me entirely at sea. "You suspect Mr. Sothey of having wronged her?"

"But of course! That is what I have been telling you!" Mr. Brett abandoned the last of his buttered prawns and set down his cutlery. "I had arranged to call upon Mrs. Grey a few days before her death, on a matter of business—"

So even the probity of Mr. Brett was open to conjecture. Had the business been horse-trading? Or a pressing debt of honour, contracted under Mrs. Grey's hand?

"—and found the lady from home. I was surprised that she had forgot our engagement, but was told by the housekeeper that a courier had come of a sudden from France, and that Mrs. Grey could not avoid the necessity of riding out to Canterbury to meet him. I was about to leave my card in the entry and depart, when the sound of footfalls in the gravel of the stableyard alerted me. Perhaps Mrs. Grey had returned! I took the liberty of entering the little saloon—" he hesitated. "Do you know The Larches?"

"Not at all," I admitted.

"There are three principal rooms on the ground floor—a drawing-room, a dining-parlour, and a little saloon that gives out on the stableyard. The latter was Mrs. Grey's favourite room, because of her fondness for the stables; she delighted in all the comings and goings of the yard, and might observe them as she conducted her correspondence."

"I perceive that you were an intimate friend, Mr. Brett. You have my deepest sympathies."

He looked surprised—seemed about to speak—and then thought better of what he had almost said. "I cannot admit to a liking for either of the Greys, Miss Austen. They were neither of them the sort to encourage intimacy. But Mrs. Grey could command a remarkable fascination—and the interest of her card-parties was undeniable, particularly for a man without family, like myself."

"I see. And in the little saloon, Mr. Brett? Were you so fortunate as to find Mrs. Grey returned?"

"I was not," he resumed. "Imagine my surprise, when I observed Mr. Sothey—whom everyone had acknowledged as her lover these several weeks—crossing the yard *with a lady's gown hanging over his arm.* He peered around at the stable door, as tho' conscious of my eyes upon him; but I fancy that the fall of light was unsuitable to the detection of my figure in the saloon window. He vanished within the stable; and something about his manner cautioned me to remain. I had no wish to call for my horse at that moment, and disturb Sothey about his business. I waited, accordingly, some moments—and when the door opened again, it revealed not Mr. Sothey—"

"But Mrs. Grey?"

"—a woman I had never seen before in my life," Mr. Brett concluded grimly. "She was mounted sidesaddle, in the gown Mr. Sothey had brought her, and cantered out of the yard directly."

"How very odd!" I said. "And you believe this woman to have been hiding within the stable, quite bereft of her clothes?"

"I can come to no other conclusion," he replied.

"And you could make nothing of her countenance."

"It was eclipsed by the shade of a riding-hat, complete with veil, and could tell me nothing; but I remember that her hair was dark as a raven's wing."

"How dashing of you," I murmured. "You betray a poetic turn in your account, Mr. Brett, that is excessively gratifying. And Mr. Sothey? Did he follow the lady?"

"I watched the door for several moments, but he did not appear; and the housekeeper soon discovering me still upon the premises, I did not like to linger. I called for my horse, all alive to the possibility that Sothey must return to the house at the stable lad's activity; but, however, he did not."

"And so you believe Mrs. Grey to have learned of Sothey's liaison with an unknown woman," I mused, "and to have broken with him on the very day of her death."

"Can there be any other construction placed upon events?" Mr. Brett enquired.

I was silent, but my gaze *would* seek out the clear-eyed countenance of the landscape designer. He was a puzzling gentleman, indeed. I knew little of him, for good or ill—but I thought that there had been nobility in his looks, as Mrs. Grey's whip lashed down upon his neck. Animation and honest pleasure, too, as he spoke of the Picturesque; a lively intelligence, an informed mind. He might charm a thousand ladies less keen in their reserve than myself—and yet he had certainly charmed me. Nowhere had I detected a desire to impose, a false posturing, the telltale marks of deceit.

And if Mr. Sothey were entangled in the Greys' deadly

game—why, then, was Mr. Collingforth fled to the Continent? Had the improver arranged appearances to his liking, and burdened an innocent man with the blame?

I must know more of Julian Sothey before I might be able to measure his talents; and happily, Fate obliged.

# Chapter 15

## A Dangerous Correspondence

**23 August 1805, cont'd.**

~

"Lizzy, dearest," my brother Edward said, as we were settled into our carriage some hours later, "I quite liked the Gentleman Improver. He is a man of information and taste."

"Not at all what one would expect of Eastwell Park," Lizzy replied.

"Then perhaps he shall prove the salvation of it. Did you admire his plans?"

"—The cunning little Blue Book? I thought it quite ravishing, Neddie. I long to have one of my own."

"How delightful. Then you will not object if he rides over to Godmersham one day or another?"

"I object to nothing, provided he leaves our avenue in peace."

"Excellent," Neddie returned comfortably. "I invited him for Sunday. We have never very much to do then, as you know, and might as well spend it in walking about the park as not."

Lizzy settled back against the seat cushions, a dim perfection in the wan moonlight creeping into the carriage; only the creak of the springs and the steady beat of the horses' hooves served to disturb the darkness.

"And you, Jane?" Neddie enquired at length. "Do you despise Mr. Sothey as much as Humphrey Repton?"

"I cannot despise a man of whom I know so little."

"Then this is indeed a reformed Jane!" Henry cried. "I have known you to despise an hundred such at first meeting, for nothing more than a poorly-turned phrase."

"Jane is always cautious when she possesses a dangerous knowledge," Lizzy observed from her corner. "She has detected Mr. Sothey in an indiscretion."

"Have you?" Neddie's voice acquired something more of interest. "Then pray offer it to the general view. My work as Justice should be nothing at all, without a few well-placed indiscretions."

And so I related not only the history of Mrs. Grey's riding crop, but also of Mr. Brett's dubious intelligence regarding the woman in The Larches stableyard, and Sothey's disheveled arrival at Eastwell the evening of the race-meeting.

"You employed your time to better effect than I," my brother observed drily, "for all I learned from Sothey was that he has no interest in the Gothic, and finds the Hermit Cottage a wretched addition to the body of landscape architecture. But how ought we to regard this . . . indiscretion, if such it should be called? For as you have noted, Jane—the man should hardly have strangled Mrs. Grey in a fit of passion, did he precipitate a break in the first place. From your description of the lady's whip-hand, I should rather have expected to find Sothey stripped to his small clothes in Collingforth's chaise, than Mrs. Grey herself."

"Collingforth's chaise," Henry broke in. "Might it not have been Sothey the stable lad saw, entering the carriage?"

"We cannot judge the particulars on so slight an impression," I countered, "nor yet on the evidence of a man like Mr. Brett. He is consumed by the desire to injure a rival—and jealousy working on a weak mind may produce every sort of evil. We must divine the truth as best we can. A direct approach to Sothey, however, is impossible at present; let it suffice to know him better by degrees."

"Unhappily, we lack sufficient time," Neddie said briskly. "Denys Collingforth is fled, and cannot feel the hangman's rope; but if I am not to appear a fool before my neighbours, and the Lord Lieutenant of Kent himself, I must conclude the matter swiftly. I would not have Collingforth charged guilty in Sothey's place—however charming the fellow's Blue Books—if he is guilty of having strangled Mrs. Grey."

Trust Neddie to place his finger on the point.

"Then I would advise a visit to The Larches' stable-yard," I told him. "One groom or another may have observed something to our advantage—Sothey's assignation with the unknown lady, or perhaps Mrs. Grey's discovery of it later."

"Indeed," Neddie said thoughtfully. "And as we are to pay our call of condolence at The Larches on the morrow, perhaps you, Henry, might manage a visit to the stables—being a notable devotee of the turf. I might profitably occupy Mr. Grey's attention, while you interrogate the grooms."

But all thought of Mr. Sothey and The Larches was driven from our heads at our return to Godmersham. A constable had been stationed in the central hall some hours, patiently awaiting our arrival; and the news he bore was shocking in the extreme.

Denys Collingforth had been found along the London road, a few miles from the town of Deal. His throat had been cut, his pockets emptied, and his body sunk with a stone at the bottom of a millpond. Two unfortunate boys, intent upon a swim, had discovered him there—to the horror of their mothers, and the routing of their sleep.

*Saturday,*
*24 August 1805*

~

MY OWN REPOSE WAS SIMILARLY BANISHED, AS THO' A spectral presence hovered about the bed curtains, its wakeful eye trained upon my tossing form. Lord Harold paraded through my dreams, arrayed in court dress and apparently deprived of the power of speech; my father, too, appeared as he had been in my earliest youth—a laughing, lively fellow who talked enough for ten. Perhaps it was his voice that so consumed Lord Harold's; he persisted in reading aloud from Oliver Goldsmith, to the persecution of my senses. I threw back the bedcovers at last, and sat up in the darkness; the great house was utterly still, but for the settling groan of its deepest timbers, and the whisper of a mouse in the wainscotting.

Had Lord Harold prevailed in Vienna? Was he even now upon the wing of his return? Were we likely ever to meet again?

And what of his intimate friend, Mr. Emilious Finch-Hatton? A curious, deceptive, and engaging fellow. He had undertaken to sound my depths, during the course of dinner, for purposes as yet obscure; but I should dearly love to know his meaning. Besieged as he was with convivial relations, Mr. Emilious was unlikely to ride over from Eastwell before Monday, when I should be gone to

Goodnestone Farm; that was most unlucky. I must put the gentleman and his intrigues entirely out of my mind.

Having done so, however, I found sleep no less destroyed by thought. From Eastwell Park it was but a step to our arrival at Godmersham, and the shocking intelligence of Collingforth's murder that had greeted us; and on this, my mind might well be occupied for the remainder of the night. Who had done away with Denys Collingforth? A footpad, encountered at random along the London road? The unsavoury black-clad friend, Mr. Everett, who had vanished from Canterbury without a trace? Or the self-same person who had struck down Mrs. Grey?

For that Collingforth had never strangled the lady was my heartfelt conviction; his own sudden death was too implausible in the event. He had been killed to ensure his silence, perhaps—or by an avenging hand, that could not feel certain he would hang. And of a sudden, I remembered Mr. Valentine Grey's hasty departure for London Thursday night, the very eve of his wife's interment—an extraordinary journey, conceived on the spur of a messenger's summons. Had the man been paid to shadow Denys Collingforth? And having found him, rode like the wind to inform his master, Mr. Grey?

Was it Grey's hand that had slit Collingforth's throat, and weighted his body for the millpond?

The hope of sleep could not lie in such a direction; only one remedy could commend itself. With a sigh of despair I took up my candle, opened the bedchamber door, and lit my wick from the taper left burning all night in the hall. No other recourse was left me: I must immerse myself in the pages of *Werther*, until utter insensibility should descend.

MY BROTHER NEDDIE WAS AFOOT ALMOST BEFORE THE first light had broken. I was roused from my slumber by the sound of men shouting, and the clatter of horses' hooves. When I dashed to my bedroom window, it was to survey a scene of ordered chaos in the stable area below. The rain had commenced once more in earnest, and was driving down in great tearing sheets that churned the yard to mud. Neddie was mounted and intent upon his departure, Henry was being heaved into the saddle by an under-groom, and Mrs. Salkeld stood in their midst holding aloft a swinging lantern. Neddie took from her outstretched hand a steaming cup of what could only be coffee, returned it with thanks, and wheeled his horse.

They would be bound for Deal, some ten miles distant, and a small coaching inn called the Hoop & Griffin, where Denys Collingforth lay cold and lifeless on a bare plank table. Then there would be the tedious work of informing the coroner, settling a date for the inquest, and visiting the thankful widow—conducted in all the mire of dirt and wet. Later should come the hours of fruitless questions, the vexation of never putting name or face to the man's murderer.

I shuddered, and went back to bed.

"I BEG YOUR PARDON, MISS AUSTEN," ANNE SHARPE SAID from the open doorway some hours later, "but I could not help enquiring—your visit to the Finch-Hattons was pleasant, I hope?"

Tho' the governess could know nothing of the death of Denys Collingforth—having already retired by the late hour of our return, and being unlikely to have encountered anyone charged with the intelligence before breakfast—a feverish light animated her countenance. Her hazel eyes were too large in her white face.

"Pray come in, my dear, and sit down," I cried. "You look decidedly unwell. I am sure you must have passed a wretched night!"

"I . . . that is to say, the ill effects of the rain . . . I have never been a creature to endure the sound of thunder. It invariably gives rise to . . . migraine." She pressed a hand against her temple and swayed slightly. I moved to her at once, and helped her to a chair.

"You should not be out of bed," I said firmly.

"No—you are too kind—but it is nothing, truly. I shall be vastly better in a moment, I am sure."

"You were wise to decline the party at Eastwell, for your own sake as well as Fanny's. You could not have sustained the jolting of the carriage, much less the punishment of conversation."

"Punishment, indeed," she whispered, and closed her eyes against the thought.

"We none of us slept very well last evening," I added, with some anxiety for the faintness of her looks. "Our party returned only before midnight, and to news of a dreadful nature. Mr. Collingforth has been found—quite dead. My brothers rode out before dawn to view the body."

Her breath caught in her throat, and she clutched at my wrist almost painfully.

"Is Mrs. Austen yet emerged from her apartments?"

"I do not believe so. You wished to speak with her?"

"It is nothing—a trifle. Any hour will do. But Mr. Collingforth—it was suicide, I presume? He was driven to take his own life, from the bitter knowledge of his guilt?"

"A man may perhaps slit his own throat," I replied, "but he is unlikely to then tie a stone to his legs, and trundle himself into a millpond. No, Miss Sharpe, I must believe that poor Collingforth was murdered, like the late Mrs. Grey—tho' for reasons that are as yet obscure to us."

The governess shuddered visibly. "Good God! That I might be allowed to forget! That dreadful woman—"

"Miss Sharpe—"

"You do not know how her face has haunted me," she cried, staring up at me blindly. "Like a demon, or a witch, in her bloodred dress."

I stared at her, aghast. Something more than a dread of violent death was at work in Miss Sharpe—something that touched quite nearly on Mrs. Grey herself. I remembered, of a sudden, the little governess's marked reserve at the race-meeting, and her horrified regard for the lady's corpse. Had not her present fever commenced as Mrs. Grey's life ended?—Perhaps they had met before, in Town, when Anne Sharpe was more the lady's social equal, and the girl had despaired at meeting with her again in such reduced circumstances.

"Can not you tell me what this is all about, Miss Sharpe?" I enquired gently.

The governess stiffened, and regained something of her composure. "You are very kind, Miss Austen," she replied, "but I assure you I merely suffer from the head-ache."

"Then Dr. Wilmot should examine you." I turned briskly for the door. "Mrs. Austen wishes to consult him in respect of young Edward, who is not at all improved in his fever; and if the physician is summoned on behalf of one, he might as well have the dosing of us all!"

Miss Sharpe half-rose from her seat and clutched at my arm. "I beg of you, do not disclose my indisposition to Mrs. Austen. That, of all things, I could not bear."

"But, my dear—"

"Can you not perceive that she already believes me decidedly unsuited to the governance of her children?"

Miss Sharpe cried fiercely. "She thinks me a poor, troublesome creature, too delicate for the trials of education. I do not know why she has endured me this long. I shall be turned out without a reference, before a twelvemonth is complete; and how I shall manage *then*, when all my friends have deserted me—"

"You must calm yourself, Miss Sharpe." Alarm sharpened my tone, and she winced as tho' a blow had been struck. I sank down by her chair. "Indeed, you distress yourself unduly. I am certain that my sister can find nothing to abhor in your considerable talents; she speaks very highly of your accomplishments, and is full of admiration for your success with Fanny—whom we all know to have arrived at a most trying age. You are to be congratulated, rather than dismissed!"

The governess shook her head, and all but stopped her ears at my words, as tho' I had subjected her to the most thorough abuse; she declared herself unworthy of such kindness, and very nearly intent upon giving notice, so acute was her sense of failure. I attempted to reason with her further; but at length, determined that the wisest course was to put her to bed—and thither she was sent, with orders to take some tea on a tray, and a stern injunction not to set forth until her spirits were entirely recovered.

When I had seen her safely into her bedchamber, I sat a little while in my own; and considered of Miss Sharpe. Broken rest or a case of the migraine could hardly explain so elevated a condition of nerves. She looked quite wild, as tho' all peace was fled from her heart forever. She had certainly been most unwell since the day of the race-meeting. Was that a mere matter of unlucky coincidence—or the working of a deeper evil? She could have had nothing to do with Mrs. Grey's end. The very notion was repugnant—and fantastic in the extreme, for Miss Sharpe had been seated opposite myself for the duration of the heats. Something in the day, however, had destroyed all her complaisance. Only the next morning, she was ardent in her desire to exchange Kent for London. Her disappointment at the failure of the French to overrun the country must be instructive.

Such signs and tokens I revolved for their meaning a while longer—and then quitted the bedchamber in search of my niece Fanny.

I found her in the passage outside the kitchens (the children's favourite haunt), attempting to keep a shuttlecock aloft with the help of young William. A well-feathered shuttlecock shall always have the power to tempt me; I am a proficient of the battledore of old; and so I joined the children straightaway, to their screams of delight. On several occasions we kept it aloft with three strikes of the battledore, and on *one* memorable instance, for *six*. And when at last the cock had fallen behind a mountain of bundles left standing in the hall—the work of the invasion packers—and defied retrieval, to William's dismay, we all retired to the kitchen itself, to plead for shortbread and lemon-water.

"Fanny," I said, after Cook had satisfied our first pangs of thirst, and gone about the business of dressing a guinea hen, "whatever has occurred to unsettle Miss Sharpe?"

She turned upon me a clear green gaze, so much like her mother's. "It must be an affair of the heart, Aunt Jane, I am certain of it."

"You have read your novels to good effect, Fanny. A romantic young lady will always find trouble to stem from an affair of the heart; but in Miss Sharpe's case, I cannot believe it. She goes nowhere and sees no one—and yet, for much of the past week, she has been decidedly unwell. What *can* have precipitated her distress?"

"Not me," William declared stoutly. "I always run when I see her coming."

"She may go abroad very little," Fanny said carelessly, "but she has had a letter. I know—I saw it."

"You saw her correspondence? For shame, Fanny!"

"Not to *read*," she protested. "Just to see. Russell brought it to the schoolroom, on a little silver tray, once the post had come."

"But Miss Sharpe surely has received a letter before. She must have a wide acquaintance—her previous life having been lived in the world of Fashion. There can be nothing extraordinary in this."

"Oh, Aunt *Jane*," Fanny cried irritably, "you are determined to plague and vex me, you troublesome creature!—Do you like that phrase? I learned it by heart, from one of Madame D'Arblay's works."

"It is admirably put. Madame D'Arblay may always be depended upon for insults in the first style of elegance."

"But what I would tell you, Aunt, is simply this: Sharpie always receives her letters on Tuesdays. They come from her friends, the Portermans. General Sir Thomas and Lady Porterman are excessively fond of her, you know, and correspond most faithfully. Directly she receives her letters, she sets Eliza and me to learning a piece of verse, and composes an answer while we are bent over our books."

"I perceive that Miss Sharpe is a creature of method. Perhaps we may hope for the imposition of order upon your sadly muddled life. I fail to see, however, that her method lends itself to your present theory. There is little of the heart written in it."

"But *this* letter—the important one—came on *Wednesday*, Aunt Jane, which you must agree is contrary to all expectation." Fanny paused to savour her triumph.

"Unless the mails were delayed."

"But it was *not* the usual Tuesday letter from the

Portermans, because the hand was entirely strange; and I saw that Sharpie caught her breath when she accepted it from Russell."

"And did she then set you to learning a piece of verse?" I enquired curiously.

"She stuffed the letter hurriedly into her pocket, as tho' she dared not trust herself to peruse its lines," Fanny confided. "Only consider, Aunt Jane! Sharpie believes her love forever denied—all hope of passion lost—and then, when she had ceased to look for it, the summons comes! He is once more a free man! He longs to press her to his bosom. But she—*she* cannot determine to go to him. She is tortured with doubt. She reads his letter again and again, rising at midnight to study the words by the light of a flickering taper . . . tho' they are already written indelibly on her soul . . ."

"Can not we ask Salkeld to move the boxes?" William broke in plaintively. "I should hate to lose my shuttlecock. Uncle Henry brought it from London, and I am sure that Canterbury has nothing so fine."

". . . and then, at dawn, she burns it in the schoolroom grate!" Fanny declared, with a fine flair for the dramatic.

"She never did!" William cried, "for Daisy never lays a fire in that room in summer."

"Oh, hush, William." Fanny dismissed him with a look of scorn; it must be remarkable that she, a girl of twelve, had suffered the proximity of a boy half her age for so long as a morning's exercise. "You have no understanding of narrative structure, you silly boy. The fire at dawn is essential."

"Yes, dear—but *was* there a fire?" I could not help asking.

Fanny looked over her shoulder carefully, as tho' to foil an observer. "Miss Sharpe requested Daisy to build one on Thursday morning, altho' the morning was fine. She would insist that the schoolroom was damp, and needed an airing, and that a fire would ward off the danger of a chill. I thought it all nonsense, for you know we did not have any rain until yesterday; but when I returned from my dinner in the nursery, I found her kneeling by the grate, with a bundle of letters in her hands. She was burning them, every one."

"Wednesday's letter, as well?"

Fanny shrugged eloquently. "I am sure *I* do not know, Aunt Jane. But it would make a very good story if she had."

I could not do otherwise than to agree with my niece, and considered of Miss Sharpe's furtive behaviour with a mind grown cold with apprehension. Then I charged Fanny not to plague the governess on the subject of her mysterious correspondence, or to confide the nature of my questions; concern for the young woman's well-being alone had animated my enquiry, and I deemed it best that she be left to nurse her trouble in peace. Fanny and William offered a solemn vow of silence, that I fervently hoped would survive the morning; and so I left them to their shortbread, and the promise of the packing-cases being very soon shifted.

I had burned enough letters myself, to know that they were rarely consumed to satisfaction. Ashes from the schoolroom grate might hold the key to Miss Sharpe's behaviour; and the ashes themselves might yet be located, in some safe corner of the scullery. But could I calmly put in train the ruin of the governess's privacy?

A picture of Anne Sharpe's wretched countenance, as it had appeared this morning in my Yellow Room, decided me in an instant. The governess had said that she was haunted by the murdered Mrs. Grey—and I intended to know the reason why.

• • • •

"ASHES?" MRS. SALKELD STOOD ARRESTED IN MID-stride, a great ring of keys in one upraised hand. "Whatever should you be wishing for ashes, miss?" Then, recollecting herself, she added swiftly, "—Not that it's the least bit of my business, I'm sure, and you'll forgive the impertinence. You'll be having your reasons, no doubt. I was just that surprised—"

"I'm afraid that in all the bustle of packing, I burned a few papers I should not," I told her. "I have little hope of any remnant remaining, of course—but while there is the slightest opportunity of retrieval—"

"Ah, you and your little papers, Miss Austen," the housekeeper returned with a comfortable laugh. "Many's the time I've said to Russell, 'How accomplished all the young ladies are today, to be sure! There's that Miss Jane, always scribbling in her little books, what she sews together herself, and laughing to herself all the while.' There's no end of amusement for the young ladies, nowadays—and in your grandmamma's time, I daresay none of the fine misses even knew their letters!"

I merely inclined my head bashfully at this, and begged silent forgiveness of the dear departed Jane Leigh, late the wife of a Fellow of All Souls, Oxford, who had certainly known her letters—and followed Mrs. Salkeld into the stillroom.[1]

"Here is the ash-tub," she said with a gesture towards a barrel in the corner. "We always keep a goodly supply, for the soap-making, as you'll see. I'm sure I cannot tell you, miss, where the ashes from the Yellow Room grate might be; and a deal of work you'll find it to sift the lot."

"Perhaps I might employ a gardener's sieve," I mused, with an eye to the girth and depth of the barrel.

[1] Jane Walker Leigh (1704–68) was Jane Austen's maternal grandmother.—*Editor's note.*

"Then I shall call for the under-gardener," Mrs. Salkeld said decisively, "that he might shift the barrel out-of-doors while he's about it, and save us all a good deal of mess. Do you wait a moment, miss, and I'll send Russell in search of the lad."

I waited a moment—I waited several—and indeed, a quarter-hour had passed, during which the rain failed to dissipate, and the gloom of my task impressed itself forcibly on my mind.

"Are you sure you hadn't better wait for the weather to clear, miss?" Mrs. Salkeld enquired doubtfully, when she had returned from despatching Russell out into the wet.

"You are too good, my dear Mrs. Salkeld—but the anxiety I have caused myself in the destruction of these papers, may only be relieved by immediate activity. I shall take care to don a cloak and bonnet, you may be sure."

"Lord, miss! You may certainly have the loan of mine, which are hanging right within the door."

And so, promising to guard Mrs. Salkeld's property from a wanton besmirching, I met the under-gardener on the back terrace, and commenced my unwholesome task.

A QUANTITY OF ASH, AS ANY UPPER HOUSEMAID WILL own, is never a friend to order. Its feather-weight quality will incline it to rapid dispersal in a wind, while its powdery dirt invades every crevice and pore. On a fine day, my task should have been tiresome enough; but that same quantity of ash, turned sodden from the effects of rain, is positively loathsome. Shelter under the eaves of the house as I might, I was as grimy as a chimney sweep's monkey by the time a quarter-hour was out. What my elegant sister Lizzy should say, did she stumble upon me unawares, I shuddered to think; and if Miss Sharpe should venture from her bed—

Mrs. Salkeld had thoughtfully provided a second barrel, for the transference of the stuff, and a large garden trowel in addition to the sieve. My work was fairly rapid, as a result, and I had not progressed beyond a quarter of the barrel's depth when I began to detect a difference in the texture of the ash. Much of it had been of a soft, light-grey powder—the remains of the hickory logs Lizzy burned in her grate while she dressed for dinner, regardless of the season. But now I detected a coarser substance amidst the fine—several large flakes of stiff rag, scorched yellowish-black at their edges.

I dropped the trowel and removed my cotton gloves, already quite spoilt from the effects of the ash—bent down to lift the fragile scraps from their bed of powder—and laid them carefully to rest in the mesh sieve. Delicate work, with all the pressure of time; for Miss Sharpe might determine her migraine to be fled at any moment, and descend to the servants' wing in search of tea. I schooled myself to calm, and fingered my way through the ash for perhaps another quarter-hour, the rain beating soft as a kiss on Mrs. Salkeld's bonnet. Then, perceiving the ash to be once again of the sort that derived from logs alone—more of Lizzy's hickory, no doubt—I declared myself satisfied and carried the precious bits back into the stillroom.

"Mrs. Salkeld," I called, "I have found success! Russell may retrieve the barrel at his convenience, and convey my thanks to the under-gardener."

"I'll not be a moment, miss," Mrs. Salkeld called to me comfortably from the kitchen passage, "once I've just sent this teapot up to poor Miss Sharpe. Rang for Daisy, she did, and another fire; the cold's that penetrating today, what with the rain."

I left her muttering over the ways of governesses too

fine to work for their bread, and smuggled my burden into the library. With the gentlemen gone, it should be quite deserted of life; for Lizzy would spend the better part of the day dressing in her boudoir, in respect of her condolence call at The Larches.

I am sorry to say that Miss Sharpe's letters divulged little to my plundering eyes. However incomplete the attempt at burning had been, the fragments were well-nigh indecipherable. The power of my own sight is indifferent at best, from the adverse effect of writing and sewing in every manner of light; and it was only through the adoption of my brother's quizzing glass—discarded near a pile of tradesmen's bills left lying on his desk— that I could discern anything at all. What emerged under the influence of a stronger lens was a smattering of letters, that trailed off disobligingly: *aff*—affect? affection? or affable?—*mise*—chemise? promise?—and then, quite starkly, the entire word *death*.

I sat back on my heels abruptly at that, and considered. *My affection for you, I promise, will endure unto death.* That should fit Fanny's reading of the situation. Or perhaps it had said: *Such an affable reception, in your white chemise—I am sure you caught your death!* Or perhaps the fragments were drawn from separate letters, and together would make no sense whatsoever. In either case, the endeavour was hopeless. I had found just enough to tantalise, and too little to enlighten.

I examined the rest of the fragments in a desultory manner, conscious of an allusion that had escaped me. What was it? *Affection? Promise?* Nothing to do with those; they were words so debased by the traffic of every day, as to have lost any charge of meaning. *Death*, then—it must strike any reader dumb with its awful truth. And perhaps the word *chemise*.

Mrs. Grey, indeed, had found death in her chemise.

I shivered from a cold that owed nothing to the rain,

and looked sharply once more at the fragments of paper.

The fractured words, it is true, could tell me little. But I had neglected to consider of the hand.

A firm hand, and yet light in its strokes, like the finest sort of engraving. There was the *S*, scrawled distinct in the—*mise*, like a sail unfurled on a t'gallant yard. I had seen this hand before, tho' only briefly. It was the distinctive sloping script of the Gentleman Improver, Julian Sothey.

# Chapter 16

## *End of a Sporting Gentleman*

*24 August 1805, cont'd.*

~

TOWARDS NOON MY BROTHERS RETURNED FROM THE Hoop & Griffin in Deal—travel-weary, drenched to the skin, and quite put out of humour.

Denys Collingforth's body had revealed nothing of the nature of his murderer, and far too much of the grisly manner of his demise. Henry, I understood from several delicate intimations of the Justice's, had been quite sick for a quarter-hour together, and could not be brought to look upon the corpse again; Neddie had only suffered it through the application of a handkerchief to the nose, and a stout brandy to the stomach.

The cords of the neck were severed quite through, my brother told me, and must have spattered the murderer's clothes in the cutting. Neddie had hired a team of local labourers to dredge the millpond whence the body was recovered, and scour the surrounding underbrush, in the faint hope of discovering the murderer's discarded clothing, which might yet bear a tailor's or a launderer's mark; but he held out very little hope of their discovery. A clever man, who had planned Collingforth's death, might as easily have carried a change of clothes, and burned the bloodied ones along the way. Or he might simply have disguised his sins with a voluminous driving cape until achieving the sprawl of London. There any amount of refuse might be discarded undetected.

"And how was Collingforth's body recognised in Deal?" Lizzy enquired, a faint line of confusion between her brows.

"He had been seen in that town on Thursday morning, by one of his acquaintance—a Mr. Pembroke, not unknown among the Sporting Set. As I understand it, Pembroke makes a tidy profession of cheating at cards, Lizzy; and Collingforth was formerly intimate with him. He espied Collingforth loitering in a doorway in a shabby part of town, looking quite desperate; and as Pembroke could not believe him capable of murder— he had heard the news of Mrs. Grey's death, and the result of Wednesday's inquest—he undertook to shield his old friend. He carried Mr. Collingforth away to his rooms, and kept him there, drinking brandy until after dark. Poor Collingforth was almost beside himself at the news of the charge laid against him, Pembroke said— and they agreed that the best course he might adopt, was to get himself away to the Continent. The Downs anchorage is at Deal, you know—and Pembroke charged his friend with buying a passage on any ship that might soon weigh anchor, and be away. Indeed, he pressed some money upon Collingforth for that express purpose, although he declined the office of arranging the matter for him—Pembroke was loath to entangle himself in the flight of a man charged with murder."

"As he was quick to point out to Mr. Justice Austen," I murmured, amused. "Have you questioned this fellow narrowly, Neddie? He seems entirely too plausible. Might he not have helped Mr. Collingforth into the millpond, for a small consideration between friends?"

"I am before you, Jane," my brother retorted with a smile; "I have learned, independent of Mr. Pembroke, that he parted from Collingforth at ten o'clock. His landlady—an elderly, quite disinterested personage—was required to bar the door behind the two men, and found them utterly disguised with drink. Pembroke met with an acquaintance in the street, who bore him away to a cock-fight, and remained in his company some hours; Collingforth, much muffled as a surety against discovery, set off towards the Downs anchorage. That is the last that Pembroke saw of him—until learning by chance that a murdered man had been found on Friday, and was lying at the Hoop & Griffin, he stopped to view the corpse."

We were all silent an instant, in consideration.

"And so Mr. Collingforth never booked his passage," I mused. "One is compelled to wonder why. Was he afraid of discovery?—Or discovered, in fact, between the time he parted from friend Pembroke, and fetched up at the quai's steps?"

"If the landlady may be believed, and Collingforth was decidedly in wine, he cannot have posed much resistance," Henry observed sombrely. "Two stout fellows—or even one in his right senses—might have bagged him as easily as a bird."

"I cannot think that many of the townsfolk should have recognised him," Lizzy objected. "Deal is above sixteen miles from his home at Prior's Farm! He cannot often have had occasion to go there."

Neddie shrugged. "Denys Collingforth was generally to be found wherever there was a matter of sport—or a wager that might be laid against it. I should not be surprised to learn that he was known, among certain circles, in every town in Kent. And you forget, my dear, that he was a hunted man. I posted an offer of one hundred pounds for his retrieval, unharmed—a handsome sum, in the eyes of many."

"And thus sealed his death warrant," I concluded, "for whoever killed Denys Collingforth had determined that he should *not* return unharmed. Such an eventuality could hardly serve the purpose of Mrs. Grey's murderer. Better he should die, and the whole affair die with him."

My brother went pale. I had spoken without consideration—and now regretted the callous words immeasurably. "Do not blame yourself, Neddie!" I cried hastily. "I would not have you to feel yourself in the slightest regard responsible. You acted as a reasonable man should always think best—and cannot have foreseen the outcome. We may yet discover, moreover, that Mr. Collingforth was killed by a common footpad."

He did not reply, but sat staring at the small gilt table before him, as tho' he saw the dead Collingforth's ravaged face reflected in its surface. Lizzy went to him, and seized his hand; Henry looked at me speakingly, and I felt myself very much to blame. It is always Neddie's way to harbour his injuries, where the rest of us might find relief in a single outburst; and I knew, from the cast of my brother's countenance, that my unwitting blow had gone home.

"What shall you do, my love?" Lizzy gently enquired.

He turned to stare at her blankly, and seemed to emerge from reverie.

"Why—as to that, my dear, I believe I have done all that I can, as Jane so rightly observes. I have despatched a messenger to London, with a request of the magistrates for any intelligence regarding Mr. Collingforth's absent friend, Mr. Everett. I have ordered the constable at Deal to interrogate the captains still anchored in the Downs, in the hope of discovering whether Collingforth attempted to purchase a passage on Thursday night; and I have set another man on the trail of Mr. Grey."

"Mr. Grey?" she exclaimed. "But Mr. Grey was gone to London on Thursday night!"

"—or so his housekeeper was informed," Neddie sanguinely returned. His eyes met mine over the crown of his wife's head. "But I have had cause to wonder, my dear, if his midnight messenger was not from London, but rather a man sent by Mr. Pembroke of Deal, who detained his friend so long over a bottle in the privacy of his rooms. Such an interval might allow of communication with The Larches. Perhaps Mr. Pembroke thought to retrieve tenfold the passage money lent to Collingforth, in a small service to Mr. Grey."

IT WAS WELL AFTER NOON BY THE TIME NEDDIE'S recital was done. He took a small nuncheon, exchanged his soiled clothes for fresh, and rang for Pratt around the hour of one o'clock. Some moments later we set off for The Larches and our call of condolence, in a carriage closed against the final showers of rain. Lizzy was a picture of fashionable decorum—her dark grey dress a trifle warm for the season, but perfectly suited to mourning; and just elegant enough, with a latticework of black satin running about the bodice, and a trim of jet beads capping her white shoulder, to proclaim it only recently delivered from the modiste's. More black ribbon was twined among her auburn curls, and jet dangled from her ears. She had adopted a pert little illusion veil that slanted fetchingly over one eye, and her gloves were dove-grey lace.

For my own part, I had removed the traces of ash from my person; pinned up the straying fragments of my hair, and exchanged my very damp muslin for a dry one.

The period of mourning undergone for my late father being so recently at an end, I boasted no less than *three* gowns suitable for the occasion—and detested every one of them. The sight of dusky cloth must always evoke the most painful memories. I spurned them all, and borrowed a lavender muslin from my sister's store, left behind when she removed to Goodnestone.

"How far is The Larches, Lizzy?" I enquired, as the chaise slowed to skirt a daunting puddle.

"Not above five miles, I should think. We might achieve it in half an hour. You shall like to revisit the neighbourhood, Jane—it is not far from Rowling, a place you always regarded with affection."

Rowling! I had not thought of it in an age; it might be a word from my vanished girlhood, and to speak it again thrust me swiftly back in memory. It is a smallish house— little more than a cottage, in fact—that sits about a mile from Goodnestone Farm. Neddie and Elizabeth spent their earliest years at Rowling, before old Mrs. Knight made over Godmersham to Edward, and removed herself to White Friars. I had spent some weeks at Rowling when I was twenty; it was there I learned to admire Mr. Edward Taylor's beautiful dark eyes, and tried to forget the hazel ones of a certain Tom Lefroy. I had danced the Boulanger at Goodnestone Farm, and walked home in the dark under a borrowed umbrella. At Rowling I had begun my work upon *Elinor and Marianne*, and struggled with the burlesque of *Susan*. Such a place must always linger in memory as fondly as dear Steventon—the scene of youthful hopes and dreams. So many of them dashed.[1]

---

[1] *Elinor and Marianne* was published in 1811 as *Sense and Sensibility*. *Susan* was sold to a publisher in 1803 but did not reach print as *Northanger Abbey* until 1818, after Austen's death. Steventon was Austen's birthplace; she spent the first two decades of her life in Steventon Rectory, which was later razed.—*Editor's note*.

"How I wish that we might have time to walk around the garden," I said wistfully.

"You shall have walking enough at The Larches," Neddie reminded me. "There is not a finer showplace in Kent."

"Particularly now that Mr. Sothey has had his way with it," I observed.

We proceeded then in silence, for Lizzy was not of a disposition for idle chatter, and my brothers were too weary to keep their eyes from closing. Tho' I would have given much for their opinion of my morning's discoveries—the curious fact of Mr. Sothey's handwriting, on letters destroyed by the governess—I could not feel it wise to canvass the matter so soon. My own part in disturbing the ashes was suspect enough, and open to censure; but I hesitated to expose Anne Sharpe to the contempt of her employers. Lizzy should be unlikely to look with favour on a governess familiar with intrigue; she would not scruple to dismiss a woman whom she considered unsuitable for the instruction of her daughters; and that I might be the agent of Anne Sharpe's ruin, was more than I could bear.

I could conceive a perfectly innocent explanation for the entire matter. Anne Sharpe had been taken much into Society during her years with the Portermans, and it was not incredible that she should have met Sothey somewhere, and formed an attachment. Fortune being scant on either side, the two might have considered it imprudent to marry, and determined to separate. Miss Sharpe came to my sister, in the regrettable role of governess, while Mr. Sothey was left to barter his talent for the arrangement of landscape. The gentleman might quickly have thrown himself into new things, new acquaintance—including his *affaire* with Françoise Grey. Miss Sharpe's heart, however, may have proved unequal to her sense of duty.

She had borne with her disappointment tolerably well, until the morning of the Canterbury race-meeting. There she must have witnessed, in company with myself, Mrs. Grey's stinging rebuke of her *cicisbeo*. The outrage! The betrayal! The mortification! And then, in the privacy of her own room, the desolation of loss. It should be enough to pique the sensibility of any well-bred young woman.

That Mr. Sothey had discerned his Anne in the Austen carriage, I little doubted—his marked interest in the Godmersham nursery, so evident during our conversation at Eastwell, was now explained. The mysterious letter that Fanny perceived on Wednesday would have been his communication; and no answer to it arriving— no Anne Sharpe appearing at the Eastwell dinner on Friday—he would necessarily have been at a high pitch of nerves. Whatever Sothey wrote to the governess, it had precipitated a different reply than he had expected, for she had ordered a fire as early as Thursday and destroyed the entirety of his correspondence.

But would a young lady, bred to the most delicate sense of duty, have consented to correspond with such a man, absent some private understanding of marriage? Had Anne Sharpe, in fact, been secretly *engaged* to Mr. Sothey?

Then his attentions to Françoise Grey—and the subsequent public rupture at the Canterbury race-meeting— were despicable, indeed. What if Anne Sharpe had somehow precipitated Mrs. Grey's anger? And incited Julian Sothey to murder?

Fantastic as the notion might seem—the merest flight of fancy—one consideration must lend it weight: Mr. Brett's disturbing glimpse of a woman with raven hair emerging from The Larches' stables. If that lady had been Anne Sharpe—

"Here we are at last, Jane—tho' well before I expected,"

Lizzy murmured. "No one but Pratt may manage a team so nobly through the mud, to be sure! And how fortunate that the rain is ended—you shall have a delightful prospect of the valley as we approach."

I thrust aside Mr. Sothey and his amours—consigned Anne Sharpe and her secrets to a safe compartment in my mind—and prepared for delight.

NOTHING MY BROTHER HENRY HAD TOLD ME OF VALENtine Grey's consequence had urged me to believe The Larches a modest little place. My brief impression of the late Mrs. Grey—bold, dashing, and devil-may-care—had done nothing to dampen expectation. A woman may only flout convention when she commands sufficient power, either of rank or fortune; Françoise Grey had commanded both. I knew that her home would be in the first style of luxury. To this I was indifferent—one great house richly furnished may be very much like another. It was the grounds of The Larches alone that utterly deprived me of speech.

One approaches the place by a winding drive, that runs for some time through rolling Kentish downs; clumps of trees, in the style of Capability Brown, dot the greenest meadows, and an arched bridge surmounts the river perhaps a mile before the house. In this, there is nothing to astonish—Stourhead or The Vyne[2] might

[2] Stourhead was the ancestral home of the Hoares, a wealthy and ennobled family of bankers whose chief passion was the creation of a classical pleasure-ground running to over a thousand acres. There is no record of Austen ever visiting Stourhead, but as it sits a short distance from Bath, she may have done so. The Vyne, in Hampshire, was the ancestral home of the Chutes, and best known for its hunt; Reverend James Austen, Jane's eldest brother, was an intimate friend of the Chute family.—*Editor's note.*

boast as much—and even the prospect of The Larches itself, first perceived around a turning of the drive, is only as noble as any other modern villa of its type. I could cry out in delight, and admire it as I have done any number of places, without feeling moved by a deeper beauty; it required a walk around the remarkable park, before I was completely overcome.

One enters the grounds from a terrace running perpendicular to one side of the house; a series of steps leads to a gravel path, that descends through a wood; and after a period of winding among larch tree, and beech, underplanted with the rarest specimens of rhododendron and azalea, the wood opens out to reveal a plunge of valley, its sides steeply planted with every variety of growing thing, massed in the most pleasing arrangement of colour and form. Below lies the river, now swelled to something greater—a lake, in fact, that is spanned at its narrowest points by first a bridge, and then a ferry. Emerging from the trees, on promontories of their own, and offering rival views of the valley's charms, are three temples—dedicated to Philosophy, Science, and Art.

I rested several moments under the portico of the last, surveying the fall of ground before me, and the ferry boat plying its oars between the near shore and my own; and rather wondered that Mr. Grey had neglected to raise an altar to the god of Mammon—his consequence and his garden both being dependent upon it. But these thoughts seemed ungenerous in the face of such beauty; and besides, the gentleman in question stood silently near me. It would never do to excite his contempt when we had progressed so admirably towards a better knowledge of one another.

But I forget myself, and proceed apace to Mr. Valentine Grey, when I had better have begun with his housekeeper.

Our excellent Pratt pulled up before the house in due course, and we found one Mrs. Bastable standing in the open doorway, as tho' in expectation of our visit. She was quite magnificent in an old-fashioned gown of black lawn, a starched white apron, and a ribboned cap; and she bobbed a cold curtsey as Neddie handed my sister from the carriage.

"Good morning, madam," she said, in a colourless voice, "it is very good to see you at The Larches again, and after so long a period. You have been well, I trust?"

"Perfectly, Bastable, I assure you," Lizzy said in a tone of faint amusement. The woman's implication was hardly lost upon her; she had been rebuked for neglect of the dead mistress, and for descending like a vulture upon the funeral-baked meats. "You do not know my sister, Miss Austen, I believe."

I was treated to a similarly chilly courtesy, and ushered into the house.

Immediately upon entering, my eyes were drawn to the figures of two men—Mr. Valentine Grey, who stood grim-faced and stalwart next to his friend, Captain Woodford; and the Comte de Penfleur, who was established almost indolently upon a settee. Now that the rain had ended for good and all, a watery light played about his fair hair as tho' in benediction. The Comte must have felt the weight of my gaze; his own came up, and searched the room—only to pass indifferently over my unremarkable countenance and fix, with some earnest study, upon Lizzy's glowing one. But I was denied further occasion to observe—some few of our acquaintance were present in respect of the dead, and demanded recognition. Charlotte Taylor of Bifrons Park was there, with her eldest daughter, tho' not her husband; the Colemans, from Court Lodge, stood nervously in a corner; Nicolas and Anna-Maria Toke advanced immediately to pay their respects. It was heavy work, I own; a little awkwardness, in respect of the occasion and Neddie's role, was inevitable. Cordial as the feelings of all towards our party might be, there was nonetheless a little reserve; my brother must be viewed in *this* house, above all others, in the capacity first of his commission— and only secondarily as a valued friend. We others, as probable parties to his counsel, were treated with an equal respect; and so we were left a little apart, while our neighbours eyed us sidelong, and hurriedly concluded their visits.

"Mrs. Austen!" Charlotte Taylor cried, "how very well you are looking, to be sure. Such a cunning employment of jet beads! I do not know when I have seen a more ravishing gown, to be sure. Pray pirouette a little upon the carpet, that we might observe the flounce!"

"You are too kind, Charlotte," Lizzy replied, without the slightest suggestion of a pirouette. "I am pleased to find you thriving. Mr. Taylor is well, I trust?"

"Oh, Edward is never less than stout," she cried. "He quite puts me out of countenance. How am I to contrive a visit to Bath, when he will not suffer from the gout? Now tell me how you like my gown!"

Lizzy surveyed the apparition—a striped green silk, with a perilous quantity of soutache about the sleeves and hem, and smiled faintly. "It suits you admirably, Charlotte."

"It *is* handsome, I think, but I do not know whether it is not overtrimmed; I have the greatest dislike to the idea of being overtrimmed; quite a horror of finery. I must put on a few ornaments, naturally; I should look naked otherwise; but my natural taste is all for simplicity. A simple style of dress is so infinitely preferable to finery."

"Indeed," Lizzy murmured.

Delicately, I began to edge away, in the direction of a fine Italian landscape that hung against one wall.

Charlotte Taylor on the subject of simplicity was not to be endured; she was constitutionally unfit for the task, and *must* be insincere.

"But I am quite in the minority, I believe," she went on. "Few people seem to value simplicity of dress—show and finery are everything. I have some notion of putting such a trimming as this to my white and silver poplin. Do you think it will look well, Lizzy?"[3]

The landscape artist had captured a distant prospect of an ancient hillside, surmounted by cyprus and a few tumbled columns; the mood was one of desolation and peace, a glorious past recalled, and now thankfully put to rest. Mr. Sothey should have found it admirable—the very soul of Picturesque—but whether congenial as a back garden, I could not presume to say. With a little start, I recollected that Mr. Sothey had probably known this picture well—he had frequented these rooms at The Larches for some months, and might almost have regarded them as his own. What had occurred between the Greys and the improver, to precipitate his hasty flight? And how did Mr. Grey regard Julian Sothey now?

"Lizzy," my brother Neddie was saying to his wife, "you must allow me to introduce the Comte de Penfleur."

I turned, and was in time to catch the Frenchman bending low over my sister's hand. "It is an honour, madam," he said. "Rarely have I seen such beauty and elegance united in the figure of a woman—particularly so far from Paris."

"You are too kind, sir," Lizzy replied coolly, "but I am afraid that your experience of England is regrettably narrow."

[3] Austen later ascribed almost exactly these words to one of her more insufferable characters, Mrs. Elton, of *Emma*. Perhaps her extended caricature of that lady is taken, in part, from Charlotte Taylor.—*Editor's note.*

*"Au contraire."* He released her hand.

"And may I present my sister, Miss Austen," Neddie said, with a faint frown for the Comte.

I curtseyed, and the Frenchman bowed. "I should have detected the family resemblance anywhere. You have quite the look of your brother Henry, Miss Austen, particularly about the eyes. His character, I imagine, is somewhat less deep; he has the look of a *bon vivant,* while your own aspect is more of reserve and understanding."

"Indeed?" I replied, amused. "And are you a student of character, monsieur?"

"I am a student of humanity," he replied with great seriousness. "The infinite variety of human expression and inclination is endlessly diverting, would not you agree? Particularly in England, where the national character is one of suppressed emotion. The necessity of schooling one's impulses to conform with an imposed convention is accepted here without question; but the result must be a soul eternally at war with the self. One cannot find happiness without a disregard for convention, Miss Austen; in France, the Revolution has taught us this."

"I see." Such a philosophy at work on Françoise Grey might have done incomparable mischief, but from the glow of his looks and the ardour of his phrases, the Comte must intend only good. Thus are all revolutionaries formed. "It has been my observation, monsieur— and I, too, am a student of character—that the flouting of convention, particularly for a woman, may often lead to great unhappiness."

"In England, perhaps," he mused, "for there is little room for the expression of the self. In England, yes, such a policy might be difficult—and bring unhappiness, even, in the short term—but eventually the joy of living by one's lights would undoubtedly prevail."

"Provided one survived so long," I murmured. "And have you travelled much in England, monsieur?"

"The hostilities have prevented me from visiting as often as I should have wished; but there was a time—around the year 'two—when I nearly made England my home. I have the widest experience of the country and its Fashionable Set; and thus I may protest with some energy"—turning smoothly to Lizzy—"that you are too modest, Mrs. Austen."

"A mother of nine cannot be thinking any longer of her own beauty," Lizzy said indifferently. "She had far better look to her daughters'."

"In such cases," Neddie broke in somewhat tartly, "a lady has not often much beauty to think of."

"*Nine* children?" cried the Comte. "But you must have been married very young!"

Lizzy merely inclined her head without reply—not for her, to be trapped into revealing her age—and turned the conversation without a flicker. "The late Mrs. Grey, monsieur, was a paragon of style. Nothing in Canterbury was equal to her; nothing, indeed, in all of Kent. She was an adept at conveying the thousand little differences between a French manner of life and the English; and we shall not soon forget her. You have my deepest sympathies."

Admirable, I thought—she had managed to suggest a respect for the lady that she had never felt, without the slightest hypocrisy of word or look. Nothing she had said was open to dispute; and it might be heard in any number of ways, according to the inclination of the auditor.

"You are very good," the Comte replied. "I was often troubled by the tone of my Françoise's correspondence—she appeared to live in such wretched loneliness and isolation—but to know that she was not entirely without friends is a considerable comfort. Indeed, in having made the acquaintance of your excellent husband, Mrs.

Austen—and now yourself—I feel I have secured my hope that justice shall be done. Mr. Grey does not command the will of every gentleman in the country, I find."

"Upon my word, Hippolyte, you place a great deal of confidence in your own charm," Mr. Grey said wryly from behind the Comte's back. "Do you believe for a moment that by flattering his wife, you may convince the Justice that I murdered Françoise? This is not France, where insinuation will pass for statecraft, and influence suborn common sense."

He spoke just loudly enough to be audible to most of the room, and the pleasant murmur of conversation among the assembled guests died abruptly away. We were left standing in a little island of quiet, with barely a head turned in our direction. No one should have dreamt of suggesting in public that Valentine Grey had ever raised a finger against his wife; to have the gentleman propose the worst himself, was indelicate in the extreme.

Then Captain Woodford laid his hand easily on Grey's shoulder, and drew his friend away; the two men adjourned to a decanter standing on a demi-lune side-table. Mr. Grey poured out a drink, and tossed it back; Woodford spoke low and urgently into his ear.

Charlotte Taylor rose to leave, her cheeks flushed and her eyes averted from Lizzy. She grasped her daughter's hand firmly in her own, and made her *adieux* in a breathless accent. Anna-Maria Toke was swift to follow.

"My apologies, madam, for this little unpleasantness," said the Comte de Penfleur. "I have learned to expect it in Mr. Grey's household; but I shall not trouble him for very much longer."

"You are returning, I collect, to France?" Neddie enquired.

"I hope to be able to cross from Dover early in the week, perhaps as soon as Monday. There remain a few . . .

uncertainties, however. I might be prevented by circumstance from embarking for some time. But I believe I shall remove this evening to an hotel in that town, in expectation of my passage; it cannot do to remain in a house where I am regarded with so much suspicion and dislike."

"Are you familiar with Dover, sir? I should recommend the York House among the coaching inns; the Ship cannot be relied upon."

"Thank you, Mr. Austen—but I always put up at the Royal. I have already written to the landlord to bespeak my room, and shall be gone in a matter of hours. You may reach me there, should the occasion require it; and I depend upon you, sir, to convey the slightest detail regarding Mrs. Grey's affairs. You know how deeply I am concerned that the man Collingforth, or"—with a significant look over his shoulder at Mr. Grey—"*whoever is responsible,* should not go unpunished."

So the news of Denys Collingforth's murder had not yet reached The Larches. It could not be far behind us, however; there is nothing like the country for the rapid communication of what is dreadful.

"Perhaps you would be so good as to afford me a little of your time this morning, monsieur," Neddie replied, "when the duty you owe these visitors is done. I have recently been placed in possession of some intelligence that may prove of interest to both Mr. Grey and yourself."

"Indeed?" the Comte cried. "And may I ask—"

"My deepest sympathies, Monsieur le Comte," said Mrs. Coleman with a bob.

"Deepest—that is, I am very sorry for you, indeed," muttered her husband, and with a hand to her elbow, steered her towards the door. The little party, it seemed, had run its course; only the Austens and Captain Woodford were left in possession of the saloon.

"You are not leaving, Austen?" Valentine Grey enquired of my brother in a lowered tone. "There is a matter regarding which I greatly desire your attention."

"I am at your service, sir," Neddie replied, "provided you may afford me a little of your time for the communication of some urgent news."

Grey glanced about the thinning room, his eyes drifting indifferently over the Comte de Penfleur. "Then I suggest we repair to the library."

"I would beg that you allow the Comte to accompany us."

Grey frowned. "Is that necessary?"

"What I would say must necessarily concern him."

"Very well." The banker turned for the door abruptly. "But he shall not be privy to *my* words. He may listen to the Justice, and pack himself off to Dover. Bastable!"

The housekeeper appeared in the doorway, an affronted expression on her countenance. Presumably she preferred the master to ring for a maid, rather than to shout like a common publican. "Yes, sir?"

"Pray be so good as to summon a lad for the purpose of conveying our guests around the grounds," he said impatiently. "They may be some time at it, and will require refreshment in the temple. Have you adequate shoes, Mrs. Austen?"

"Perfectly, sir, I thank you."

He eyed Lizzy's elegant slippers. "You shall be swollen and blistered before a quarter-hour is out; but no matter. The park does not give up its beauties so easily; they must be teazed into submission, like a spirited woman. And you, sir? What is your pleasure?"

This last was directed at Henry. He had been most intent upon the study of a very fine snuff-box abandoned on a marquetry table, but lifted his gaze at Grey's address, and said in as colourless a voice as possible, "My shoes are perfectly adequate to your grounds, Mr. Grey, if that is what you would know. My stockings, perhaps, might be thinner; and as for my smallclothes—"

Grey threw back his head and laughed with undisguised delight. There was a difference in his manner of behaving this morning, from what it had been in his interview at Godmersham; he was at once reckless and carefree, grim and abandoned. It was as tho' a great weight had been lifted from his shoulders, or as tho' he found himself in the thick of battle, and had wagered his all on the toss. Intriguing. His entire air suggested a man with nothing to lose, and everything to defend.

"Come into the library, Austen," he said, "and send the rest of your family out into the garden. Unless the weight of your brother's smallclothes prohibits the tour."

"I believe they should be admirably suited to visiting the stables," Henry offered mildly. "I quite long to see the filly Josephine at closer quarters. You may have heard, Mr. Grey, that your late wife's horse bested my own at the Canterbury Races, on the very day of her tragic . . . accident."

There was the briefest of silences. The Comte de Penfleur adjusted his cuffs, a look of abstracted pain upon his countenance. Then Grey said, "I should be happy for you to inspect the filly, Mr. Austen. The bulk of the stables will be sent down to Tattersall's in a matter of weeks; and if, having seen Josephine, you wish to make an offer for her, I should not be loath to consider it."

"You would *sell* her horses?" Penfleur cried, all complaisance fled.

"I cannot send them out of my sight fast enough," Grey replied, with a bitter emphasis.

"Then I shall take them all!" The Frenchman's face had reddened, and he walked slowly towards Grey, his hands clenching slightly.

The banker regarded him with undisguised contempt. "I regret to inform you, monsieur, that they are not for sale."

The Comte tore his glove from within his coat and dashed it in Grey's face. The other man neither flinched nor dropped his gaze from Penfleur's; but breathing shallowly, as tho' an iron band constrained his lungs, he said, "I beg you will ignore what the Comte has just done, Mr. Austen. It can have nothing to do with you; and I should abhor your interference in so delicate and private a matter."[4]

"Just as I should abhor the necessity of mounting a watch upon your movements, Mr. Grey," Neddie replied steadily, "or yours, Monsieur le Comte. I have no wish to post men outside your door all night, for the prevention of a dawn meeting; so pray retrieve your glove, sir, and let us hear no more about it."

"You saw how he insulted me." Penfleur's voice, in that instant, was colder and more deadly than I could have imagined. "I cannot allow such abuse to go unaddressed. My honour—"

"—cannot have been abused by a simple truth," Neddie protested. "Mrs. Grey's stables are presently not for sale. They shall be under the gavel at Tattersall's in a matter of weeks, and did you wish to appear in the ring, and place your bids with the rest, I am sure you would be heard as readily as another. Now, may I suggest, gentlemen—as Mrs. Bastable has appeared with the lad who is to guide the ladies—that we repair to the library? The Comte must not delay on his road to Dover; and the news I would communicate is decidedly pressing."

---

[4] Magistrates (and, by extension, Justices of the Peace in country neighborhoods) were charged with preventing public demonstrations of violence. This included prizefights, which were illegal, but was particularly aimed at duels—which were conducted, of necessity, in the greatest secrecy.—*Editor's note.*

Neither Grey nor the Comte offered a word in reply; the malevolence of their mutual regard was chilling. The banker was the first to turn away, and at last the Frenchman followed him through the door.

He did not deign to retrieve his glove.

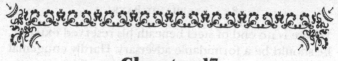

# **Chapter 17**

## *Warring Theories*

~

I WAS SEVERAL HOURS IN LEARNING THE NATURE OF THE
interview among the three men, for the tour of the gardens so transported Lizzy and me, that we quite forgot
the ugly scene. We traversed the wood, and descended
into the valley, and allowed the ferryman to ply his boat
for our amusement. Then we sent the gardener's lad
away, and perched in some chairs arranged amidst the
columns of the Temple of Philosophy.

"I cannot believe that Mr. Grey is very well-acquainted
with Aristotle," Lizzy observed, wrinkling her nose, "nor
yet with Heracleitus. And yet he installed those massive
figures of them here as one might pose a favourite
grandfather above the drawing-room mantel. It is quite
an extraordinary taste. One has an idea of them come
alive at midnight, and discoursing on the nature of
eternity."

"Perhaps Mr. Grey possesses talents of which we know
nothing."

"I quite pity the little Françoise," Lizzy said idly.

"There is no end of steel beneath his reserved exterior; he should be a formidable adversary. Hardly congenial for one bent on having her own way, and wild for amusement. I wonder she did not desert him long since."

"For the Comte?"

"Ah, the Comte." My sister smiled. "He is thoroughly reprehensible, is he not? Too clever for his own good; too careless of his morals for safety; and too intrigued by the effect of his meddling in the peace of others."

"Whether he cared a jot for Françoise or no," I agreed, "he should attempt to destroy Grey's happiness for the sheer satisfaction of it. The contest, I suspect, has always been between the two gentlemen; the lady was merely a token. Grey first won a critical round, in securing Françoise's hand, and the Comte thought to rout him entirely by eloping with her at the last."

"Penfleur is not a man who endures his losses, Jane. He will have his satisfaction in everything—including the matter of the horses."

"I tremble for Henry, does he attempt to offer for Josephine."

"What ridiculous creatures men are." She sighed. "As tho' honour were a stuff one could fashion and discard, like the latest modes! Poor Neddie will be dozing in Mr. Grey's sweep for most of the night, in terror of a dawn meeting."

I was only half-attending to her, for a lone figure traversing the iron bridge had caught my eye. "Is that Henry come in search of us? Or—yes, it is Mr. Grey!"

"You are far too intrigued by the man for safety, Jane," she observed. "He is possessed of a deep and impenetrable character; and such an one will always prove of fascination to yourself. Take care."

"Perhaps he shall presently strike into another path," I suggested.

But the gentleman did not; he strode through his

pleasure grounds as tho' intent upon a single object—the retrieval of ourselves. "I believe our time in Paradise is at an end."

"Then do you go to meet him, my dear," Lizzy said, "and turn back for me at the ferry landing. I am far too fatigued to walk back to the bridge, and you know these slippers should never support it. Detestable Mr. Grey—he is far too correct about everything; and for that, I shall not forgive him." She turned her sunshade towards the offending apparition, and gazed out over the lake.

And thus was I thrown to the wolf.

"THE LARCHES IS A REMARKABLE ACHIEVEMENT, MR. Grey. I must congratulate you most sincerely."

If my faltering words were inadequate to the beauty everywhere around us, my companion did not choose to quarrel. Indeed, all trace of his former belligerence had fled; his countenance was as easy as a child's released from illness. Whatever the nature of his interview with Neddie, the result had proved of benefit. Or perhaps he derived such solace from his grounds, that more melancholy considerations were banished.

"I can never be unhappy while the park remains," he replied, as tho' reading my thoughts. "It is a peace unparalleled, a balm for wounded spirits, a little paradise on earth, Miss Austen—and when I am away, I long always to return."

"How unfortunate, then, that your business calls you so frequently to Town," I rejoined. "For when we leave what is precious to the care of others, we endure a peculiar pain."

He frowned at that, and studied my countenance for some falseness—a desire to prick his vanity, perhaps, by alluding to the dalliances of his wife, of which all of Kent must be aware. But my aspect did not betray me; I had uttered the sentiment as a simple truth; and Mr. Grey at last accepted it as such.

He offered me his arm, and we continued along the path towards the ferry.

"Mrs. Austen was overcome by the heat, you say?"

"Nothing so grave. Elizabeth is a stout walker, but her slippers are less equal to these paths than my more sensible boots. I came prepared to admire The Larches, from the praise I had heard everywhere of these grounds; and to admire, one must first be able to see."

A faint smile was my reward. "I have known any number of fools to praise from utter blindness, Miss Austen."

"That will always be the general case," I said calmly, "but with very great luck, Mr. Grey, you may occasionally encounter a taste as brilliant as mine. I blush to admit it—it is most unwomanly, I own—but I have never been called a fool. I have long suspected it is the chief reason that no sensible man will marry me."

To my gratification, Mr. Grey laughed aloud. "Men of sense, whatever you may say, do not wish for silly wives."

"How mortifying," I replied. "And I had doted on the notion! You force me to the conclusion, sir, that some other charm is lacking."

"Then I should be horsewhipped, Miss Austen. How may I make amends?"

"By conveying me to that little temple on the hill. I failed to achieve it with my sister."

"—who even now awaits us anxiously."

"It must be her deprivation, then, for adopting fragile shoes."

"Very well. The prospect of the house from that vantage is magnificent."

He led me swiftly to the portico of the domed Temple of the Arts, and we stood in silent amity, with all of The Larches falling away before us. Here was no oppression of August heat, no desiccated air of a season wearied beyond imagining; all was verdant and singing with the voices of a thousand birds.

"How glorious!" I cried. "I wonder you can bear to live within four walls, Mr. Grey, when all this beauty lies without them."

He did not reply, and his expression was remote.

"And all this you have done, in the space of a few years," I continued.

"I cannot claim so much," he returned abruptly. "The Larches was my father's passion before me. The construction of this valley the lake you observe—are entirely his own. Such growth of trees could never be accomplished in a few years, as you must know. What I have done is small, indeed, compared to my father's accomplishments—I have pruned where his hand was excessive, and added what his sensibility could not envision."

"Mr. Sothey, I believe, was your consultant?"

He raised an eyebrow in surprise. "You are acquainted with Sothey?"

"A little. We dined with him last evening, at Eastwell Park. The Finch-Hattons are old friends."

"And what did you think of him?"

I hesitated. His tone imparted nothing of his own opinion. "I thought him a man of understanding and wide knowledge of the world, possessed of considerable taste. But I can judge no further; his character wants openness, and of deeper qualities I could form no opinion."

"Reserve must be natural in a fellow whose every expectation was blasted by an unworthy father," Mr. Grey observed. "I must assure you that Julian Sothey is the very best of men, Miss Austen. I esteem him as a friend, naturally; but as a man of education and honour,

I can place none other before him. If there is anything of real beauty to be found at present in The Larches, I am sure it is due entirely to Mr. Sothey."

"Then you are fortunate, indeed, sir." That I managed a reply at all was remarkable; my thoughts were in a state of discomposure. I had suspected that Mr. Grey should despise Julian Sothey as his wife's paramour; but this heartfelt testimonial must blast my assumptions. "You have been acquainted with Mr. Sothey for some time, I collect?"

"No, indeed. His family and mine moved in very different circles. I might have had the purchase of his father's notes at one time or another, but any ties of a social nature were not to be thought of."[1]

"Was Mr. Sothey's father so very depraved?"

Grey smiled grimly. "I am too familiar with the more common forms of depravity, Miss Austen, to be a sober judge of it in others. Let us simply say that the Earl had offended deeply, among those whom it is not wise to offend, and placed himself outside the pale of good *ton*."

"I see. His son, however, is not so abandoned."

"His son possesses such an amiable temper, as must endear him to everyone." This was said without the slightest hint of irony, as might be natural in a cuckold; and again, I found cause for wonder.

"Lady Elizabeth Finch-Hatton certainly makes Mr. Sothey her protégé," I said. "I suppose you formed an acquaintance with the gentleman in just such an household."

Mr. Grey hesitated, as tho' debating how much might be said. "I first met Sothey through a mutual friend, Miss

[1] It was common for creditors holding notes of indebtedness to sell the paper at a deep discount. Those who purchased the notes on such terms did so as a sort of speculation on the eventual repayment.—*Editor's note.*

Austen—Mr. George Canning, a present member of Government. No doubt you will have heard of him."

Quite recently in fact, I thought in silence; and blessed my brother Henry. "Mr. Canning! He is a great enthusiast for exotic plants, I believe?"

Grey's careworn features lightened. "And something of an authority on landscape design. We share a love of the obscure and the exotic, Miss Austen—and Canning has directed me in the trial of many specimens rare in this northern clime. When I expressed a wish of cultivating the American azalea, it was he who commended Sothey as my greatest friend. I have never found occasion to regret the acquaintance."

"I should have liked to have seen the azaleas in their season," I said.

"You, too, are an admirer of the exotic?" my companion enquired seriously.

I coloured, and passed off the question with a laugh. "Not at all, I assure you. I merely find pleasure in the English landscape, sir, and all its myriad beauties."

"Then perhaps you may be so fortunate as to return to Kent in April, when my azaleas are at their finest flowering." He secured my hand within his arm, and led me firmly from the temple's steps. "But now, I fear, we must relieve Mrs. Austen's anxiety; the hour grows late, and her husband will be every moment expecting her."

We descended once more by the hillside path, and found that Lizzy was already come in search of us. I was glad of her company on the return to the house; her elegant remarks were a foil for silence. Reflection, however, availed me nothing. I was plagued with questions on every side, for which experience could provide no answer.

•   •   •   •

"SO GREY CAN BE CHARMING WHEN HE CHOOSES," NED-die said thoughtfully, when the dinner things had been cleared away and we had assembled in the library. Henry had taken up the London *Times*; Lizzy was established over the teapot; and I had begun to pick desultorily at my work. Neddie, however, was restless; he paced before the empty hearth like a man who badly wanted occupation. Had he been of a reading turn, I should have instantly recommended *Werther*. It is remarkable how much service even a dissatisfying book might render—tho' not, perhaps, in the manner its author intended.

"How did you like him, Jane?" he enquired, coming to a halt by my chair.

"Very much. He is not a man to recommend himself on first meeting, perhaps—but one whose character rewards with more persistent application. He was gracious in conversation and frank in his remarks; there was neither haughtiness nor vulgarity to despise in his manners. I cannot believe him capable of a conscious deceit; but even had I witnessed nothing of the scene in the saloon, I should suspect him to be familiar with violence. He is ruthless in matters of principle, I should think, and in the safeguarding of his own concerns."

"This is a formidable picture, indeed!" Neddie cried. "How, then, Jane, do you account for his ingenuous belief in Sothey's character?"

During the course of our return to Godmersham, I had conveyed the substance of my conversation with Grey. "Either Mr. Grey is more adept at dissimulation than I should give him credit for being, or he knew nothing of Mr. Sothey's dalliance with his wife."

"We have only Mr. Brett's malicious tongue to credit for the idea, after all," Neddie mused.

"Then why the whip against the neck, in the middle of the Canterbury Races?" Lizzy protested.

I shrugged. "Perhaps the lady was surfeited with the

American azalea. But I admit, Neddie, that I cannot make the matter out at all. I must learn more of Mr. Sothey, before I may judge rightly."

"And you, Lizzy?" my brother enquired, turning to his wife. "How did you find Mr. Grey?"

"I liked him well enough," she said languidly, "for another woman's husband. He is too lacking in drollery and wit for my taste; but his coat was very well made, and the gloss on his Hessians unexceptionable."

"Henry?"

My brother glanced up from his newspaper and frowned at us all. "To the praise of unexceptionable Hessians, what may I possibly add?"

"Very little, of course," Lizzy rejoined smoothly, "your own being incapable of comparison. No man who persists in valeting himself, can expect to rival Mr. Grey. Henry must take as his example my brother, Mr. Bridges— who has driven himself to the brink of ruin, in pursuit of a well-polished boot. I have quite lost count of the number of men Edward has engaged to dress him, or the various formulas of blacking and champagne, assured to bring his leathers to a mirror-brightness. It is not the most noble of callings, perhaps; but as a means of passing time, it may serve as well as any other."

"Enough of Henry's boots," I cried. "You delight in teasing us, Neddie. You know very well that we are all agog to learn how Mr. Grey received the news of Collingforth's murder. Did he betray any prior consciousness? Is it likely he was privy to the deed?"

"As to that—" My brother's eyebrow lifted satirically. "Mr. Grey had the poor taste to congratulate me on the unfortunate fellow's death, and said that he was very well pleased with the swiftness of English justice. He then offered me a brandy, despite the heat of the afternoon—as tho' we had accomplished nothing more dreadful than the blooding of a fox."

"And how did you answer him?"

"I refused the brandy, of course." Neddie threw himself into his favourite chair, not far from the open French windows, and raked one hand through his hair. "But truth to tell, Jane, I felt deuced uncomfortable. Grey's complaisance surpassed everything; he was as easy as tho' the wretched business were entirely resolved, despite the questions that must arise to torment one. I pointed out that Collingforth's guilt was in no wise proved—that the complications of the chaise and the timing of his wife's death could not be gainsaid, and urged Grey to be less sanguine. But he replied that he had no doubt that Collingforth was responsible, and had found his just deserts at the end of a knife."

"And the Comte de Penfleur?"

"He served himself the brandy without recourse to Grey."

"Neddie!"

"I observed his hand to tremble as he unstoppered the decanter. I should say that the Comte was greatly put out. He surmised that the matter would be concluded with Collingforth's murder, and the truth of Mrs. Grey's end remain forever uncertain."

"He is determined in his belief that Grey was responsible," I said, "tho' he is loath to accuse him directly."

"Ah! Not so loath as you assume," Neddie cried with satisfaction. "Now we come to the intriguing part—the scenes enacted with the gentlemen in private."

We gazed at him expectantly. Even Henry set aside his paper.

"I was treated first to an interview with Valentine Grey. He was most uncomfortable, when it came to the point; and told me that he believed his information to be entirely *de trop*, now that Collingforth was dead; but in the interest of justice, he could do no more than his duty. What he would tell me must grossly expose his wife;

indeed, the discoveries he had recently made had quite astonished even himself, who must be thoroughly acquainted with her character—"

"Hah!" Lizzy snorted. "As tho' any man might comprehend the nature of his wife."

"—but he had found occasion, in recent days, for a thorough review of her possessions and correspondence."

"Naturally," I murmured. "A man of greater courage (or less), should have burned the whole without the briefest glimpse. Mr. Grey is at last revealed as pitiably human! He has probed the wound, and rubbed salt in its depths."

"Well?" Lizzy enquired impatiently. "And what did he find?"

Like a conjurer, Neddie produced a sheaf of folded rag from within his coat, and presented it with a flourish. His wife visibly recoiled.

"*That* is her private correspondence? Her husband actually displayed it to you? But how despicable!"

"It is entirely in French," Neddie replied without a pause, "and, I am assured, entirely from the Comte de Penfleur. It was to prevent the letters from falling into that gentleman's hands that Mr. Grey undertook to read them at all. And what he discovered distressed and confounded him."

"Then they *were* lovers," I said.

"Not in the least," Neddie replied. "Or if they bore one another any affection, the letters betray little sign. They were partners, Jane, in a very grave collusion—the securing of information regarding the movement of troops along the Kentish coast, for the edification of His Imperial Majesty, Napoleon Buonaparte."

Henry slapped one hand excitedly against his thigh.

"—Or so Mr. Grey was forced to conclude, after reading these letters," Neddie added. "He tells me that they are filled with Penfleur's instructions regarding the management of Mrs. Grey's friends—Captain Woodford and Lady Forbes being at the head of the list, and your brother, Mr. Bridges, Lizzy, trailing doubtfully at the end."

"Edward?" she cried incredulously. "What might *Edward* possibly have known, that should be of interest to Buonaparte?"

"A very great deal. His friend Woodford, you know, was in the habit of confiding snippets of intelligence to his most intimate friends, that should never have left he officers' mess; and Mr. Bridges must naturally have been the recipient of these. What Woodford might, in a moment of caution, hesitate to impart to Mrs. Grey, his friend had no compunction in relating. I imagine his being privy to the Army's secrets must have greatly increased Mr. Bridges's sense of importance."

Lizzy drew breath sharply, and looked the most indignant I had ever seen her. "Fool," she muttered, "he will be the undoing of us all."

"Lady Forbes, for her part, is a silly little gossip who should have delighted in communicating her husband's schemes," Henry observed quickly, as tho' to divert Lizzy's attention.

"—Such as the intended troop movement next week between Chatham and Deal," I added, as comprehension dawned. "All of Kent is in an uproar regarding the disruption of the pheasant-shooting; and Major-General Lord Forbes was quite put out at the report's circulation. Captain Woodford himself cautioned me against speaking too freely."

"I suppose Mrs. Grey's fascinating card-parties were a means of securing information?" Henry said.

"At first," Neddie conceded. "But I have an idea that over time, the gaming debts were themselves a useful tool. They secured Mrs. Grey's hold on her unwilling friends. As the possessor of any number of vowels, she might choose to extend her debtors' credit, or even for-give a sum entirely—for a small consideration."

"How brilliant!" I muttered. "And yet, how dangerous in the extreme. She ran a severe risk, did any of her vic-tims determine to be free of her."

"It is possible that the lady was subtle enough, that few among them comprehended what she was about. But perhaps one at least perceived her object."

"Denys Collingforth," I said.

"Exactly."

I rose, and commenced to turn the length of the room in considerable perturbation of spirit. "But if Col-lingforth resisted the lady's power, and threatened to expose her, should not Mrs. Grey have done the murder, rather than end a victim?"

Neddie observed me in silence, his own expression guarded. I puzzled it out still further, and then wheeled to face him. "Do you credit Grey's suggestion that he knew nothing of his wife's activity? Or are the letters all a subterfuge, to place his enemy the Comte in the gravest peril of his life, and clear his own concerns from every stain of treason?"

"That is exactly what I cannot determine," my brother replied grimly. From the cast of his countenance I knew that I had spoken aloud his governing obsession. "It was to that end—the illumination of Grey's character—that I solicited the opinion of each of you, regarding the man. I cannot make him out at all. Another fellow, upon learning that Collingforth was dead, should have left the matter of his wife's espionage for the grave to swallow—should have burned the evidence at midnight, and re-joiced in the vagaries of Fortune."

"Unless he feared the Comte's power, in ways we have yet to discover, and thought to place his head in a noose," Lizzy observed. "Did Grey urge you to arrest the Frenchman?"

"He did not. I told him forthrightly that I could not, in all conscience, place charges on the force of accusation alone; I must peruse the correspondence myself, and form a judgement independent of Grey's. He accepted as much."

"Mr. Grey is a careful man."

"I did promise, however, to have the Comte watched."

"Penfleur had departed already for Dover?" I enquired.

"His carriage was at the door, when at length I emerged from Grey's study; and it was then that the Comte drew me aside, to urge me most passionately to pursue justice in Mrs. Grey's cause. He had reason to believe that Mr. Grey was involved in a very deep game, regarding a delicate situation of international finance; that his arrangements—which reached from the Americas to Spain and Amsterdam—might reasonably be construed as treasonous; and that it was not inconceivable his beloved Françoise had discovered the whole. Mr. Grey had never borne his wife the slightest affection, and when forced to the point, had secured his empire and his reputation through the murder of his wife."

Henry whistled. "That's playing the matter very close, indeed. The Comte de Penfleur *is* a cool fellow."

"Or a very desperate one," Lizzy retorted calmly. "It is possible, Neddie, to form a simple idea of how the murders were effected. Let us suppose that matters fell out as Mr. Grey has suggested. Denys Collingforth was pressed for what he knew, and pressed by his creditors; he grew tired of living in thrall to Mrs. Grey, and formed a pact with his friend Everett—a shady character, by all accounts—to support him in a dangerous act. He lured the lady to his chaise at the race-meeting with the letter discovered in her riding habit, and informed her of his intention to expose her; when she defied him, he drove out along the Wingham road after the race and killed her. He neglected, however, to discover his letter on her person, and simply disposed of the riding habit entirely as a safeguard against discovery. The Comte de Penfleur arrived the following day, thwarted in his hopes of an elopement and insecure in his liberty. He would have known, from Mrs. Grey's letters, that Collingforth—in whose carriage her murdered body was discovered—was the least docile of her charges. The Comte undertook to buy intelligence of Collingforth's movements, while diverting attention from his own nefarious doings, by suggesting to the Justice that *Mr. Grey* was the murderer. The cardsharper, Pembroke, reported Collingforth's presence in Deal to the Comte; the Comte despatched his minions (or killed Collingforth himself; the point is immaterial); and poor Collingforth's silence was purchased at the cost of his life."

We regarded her with some wonder. As a theory, it was not entirely without merit.

"But why return Mrs. Grey's body to the race-meeting grounds, and risk the gravest complications?" I protested. "Why not leave her in her phaeton on the Wingham road?"

"Because he had secured his friend Everett's word as to his absence from the chaise throughout the racing," Lizzy said calmly, "and could not be secure if her body were discovered elsewhere. Collingforth hoped, perhaps, that the incongruity should linger in our minds, and prove his best security of innocence."

"Admirable!" Neddie cried. "Upon my word, I am ready to accede to it myself!"

"Excepting," Henry broke in, "for the considerable weight that may lie behind the Comte's words."

Neddie and I both frowned in perplexity.

"He may have spoken no more than the truth," Henry persisted.

"Regarding what or whom?" Neddie cried.

"Speak plainly, Henry, for the love of God," I added, in exasperation.

"In perusing the *Times*, Jane—which you admirers of country life only rarely look into—I have been powerfully reminded that we have entirely ignored the fact of Mrs. Grey's courier."

Neddie threw up his hands in disgust.

"Her courier?" I prompted.

"—The elusive fellow from France, in green and gold livery, who was charged with the most pressing intelligence. The courier who arrived on the very morning of her death, and may unwittingly have precipitated it."

"I like your theory not half so well as my own," Lizzy murmured, and stretched as comfortably as a cat. "It lacks simplicity."

"We believed it possible that the courier came to warn of a French invasion." Henry waved his furled newspaper like a martial baton. "But no invasion has occurred. The watchtowers stand unfired. Evacuation is put off. Has it not occurred to you, Neddie, that the news for Mrs. Grey must have been entirely otherwise?"

"Grey himself has said that her family often chose to communicate with her in such a fashion. Perhaps the man was charged with delivering the Comte's final letter—the proposal of elopement we discovered in *La Nouvelle Héloïse*."

"Or perhaps it was in your friend Mr. Grey's interest to suggest as much."

"I do not understand you, Henry. Why should Grey conceal the nature of his wife's intelligence?"

"Because it threatened the security of his banking concern, his reputation, and, indeed, his very life."

"What do you know?" Neddie reached unconsciously for his clay pipe, and felt in his pockets for a pouch of tobacco. Lizzy took the pipe from his hand without a word and set it aside.

"I know nothing at all, I assure you," Henry protested, "—but I might suggest a good deal. Grey is certainly involved in a very deep game, as the Comte has observed. Did you learn nothing from the state of his household?"

"The Larches? I thought it charming."

Henry snorted. "*Charming*. Perhaps it was. But I should very much like to know, brother, what sort of difficulties the man has incurred, and how he hopes to extricate himself without the most public scandal!"

"Scandal?" Lizzy echoed. "I should have thought the murder of his wife scandal enough for the present."

"I refer to the conduct of Mr. Grey's business," Henry retorted. "I had not spent above an hour at The Larches, before I knew that his firm is extended to the breaking point."

"How can you say so?" I enquired. "Certainly Mr. Grey maintains a considerable estate. The maintenance of the grounds at least must exact a fortune. But his circumstances appeared quite easy."

"And yet he employs no housemaids," Henry observed. "Mrs. Bastable is required to perform the slightest office. The condition of the stables, moreover, is appalling—the boxes have not been mucked out since Mrs. Grey's death. When I enquired as to the cause, I was told that the master had refused an order for bedding, and turned away the better part of the stable lads. As a result, it was impossible to discover anything of Julian Sothey's assignation with an unknown lady in the stable-yard. No one with the slightest pretension to knowledge had been retained in service."

"Such a dismissal of staff might be very much to Mr. Grey's purpose, did he intend the sale of Mrs. Grey's string," I argued, "but I cannot see how it reveals his circumstances to be hopeless."

"Have you any idea of the quality of the blood in Grey's stables? It will be the sale of the decade. He stands to make thousands of pounds. And from the look of things, I should say that he is desperate for funds."

"Perhaps he cannot bear to be reminded of his wife's passion for horseflesh," Lizzy observed, "and merely hopes to dispose of her stock in the most efficacious manner possible. I see nothing of scandal in *this*."

"Then perhaps the London papers shall convince you." Henry tossed the *Times* onto the sofa beside us. "Examine the notice at the bottom of page three, I beg. It concerns Mr. Grey closely."

Neddie, Lizzy, and I bent our heads over the sheet, and endeavoured to make it out.

" '*Dutch banks fail to back French securities,*' " I read slowly. " '*Government loans feared in default.*' "

"Read on," Henry said.

" 'The Secretary of the Treasury, Mr. Pitt, is gravely concerned by yesterday's decision on the part of the House of Hope, Scots bankers resident in Amsterdam, to refuse the French government further security.[2] While the confusion of our enemies is devoutly to be wished, in the halls of commerce as well as on the battlefield, the delicate state of the Imperial treasury must threaten relations of finance throughout Europe, and devolve to this kingdom's ultimate disadvantage. In light of this consideration, Mr. Pitt has sent an envoy to Amsterdam for consultation.' "

I raised my head from the broadsheet. "And how might Mr. Pitt's conduct of business concern Mr. Grey, Henry?"

He rolled his eyes in impatience. "Grey is allied to a French banking family, Jane, and his resources must in part be theirs. If Buonaparte has gone to Amsterdam for credit, and been *denied* by so great a house as Hope, then we must assume that the French banking establishment

---

[2] The Prime Minister always held the portfolio of Secretary of the Treasury. As a member of the cabinet as well as its leader, he was thus *primus inter pares*—first among equals.—*Editor's note.*

has exhausted its capital. Furthermore, the government itself can offer nothing as security for its desired loan—or nothing that Hope will accept. The Comte de Penfleur must be aware of that much. As to what else he knows or suspects, I cannot say."

"You believe Grey to have invested heavily in the French government, at the behest of his wife—funds that Buonaparte has presently exhausted?" Neddie demanded.

Henry shrugged helplessly. "Who can say? But if Grey's stables appear so neglected, only consider the state of the Emperor's!"

"But Buonaparte has a stranglehold on much of Europe," I cried, in disbelief. "Surely he might plunder any number of coffers."

Henry hesitated, then shrugged. "I cannot undertake to say. I have heard rumours in the City that the French government is bankrupt, but I dismissed such talk as a mixture of bluster and hope. I can dismiss it no more."[3]

"The French, bankrupt?" Lizzy's voice was a study in disbelief. "But I have seen the plates of the Empress's coronation gown, Henry. She did not appear in rags, I assure you."

"The cost of the coronation, and the building of some two thousand ships, might well beggar a greater nation than France. Add to all this, the maintenance of an army left standing nearly two years along the coast, in readiness for a Channel crossing; the necessity of defending a far-flung border; and the spirit of excess that has animated the French court now these many months—and I think you may look for a bankrupt quite easily."

"It is something," I mused, "that the Monster should

---

[3]  The ears of the City's businessmen, in this instance, were keener than Henry Austen knew. By mid-August 1805, Bonaparte's funds were completely exhausted. No relief, either from bankers or allies, was forthcoming.—*Editor's note.*

ruin himself with England as his object. All of Europe must thank us for the issue; and I for one shall wish Buonaparte thrown into a debtor's gaol. But, Henry—if Buonaparte is bankrupt, the war must be very soon at an end! Only think what that might mean for our brothers!"

"An end to all advancement up the Navy list," Henry said brutally.[4] "But do not be so hasty, Jane, to dismiss His Imperial Majesty. Buonaparte has saved himself a thousand times before, and in far worse circumstances."

"Perhaps he looks to improve his fortunes through an assault on the Bank of England," Neddie said idly.

"Perhaps." Something of heat had died out of Henry's countenance, and been replaced by an expression of care. "I dearly wish that we knew how it was. I fear I shall have to desert you tomorrow, and return to Town."

"Sunday travel, Henry?" I teazed. "You have lived too long with the Comtesse Eliza, and her careless regard for propriety."

"Go to *Town*, in August?" Neddie cried. "Surely nothing can be so serious as that!"

"Mr. Pitt certainly believes so. This news will already have affected the 'Change; securities will be all a-hoo by Monday morning, and every man of finance intent upon reading the world's tea-leaves. I dare not linger another day."

I rose and extended my hand to my favourite brother. "It seems that Mr. Pitt knows what he is about. I expect you shall be off before dawn—but pray send us word,

---

4   The navy list was a ranking of commissioned officers, the lowest being post captains, that showed their relative seniority. One moved up the list by rote, as vacancies occurred above through retirement or death. The list also contained the names of commissioned ships, their class, number of guns, and complement. —*Editor's note.*

Henry, if any whisper of Mr. Grey's perilous affairs should reach your ears."

"I should never fail you in a matter of gossip, Jane," he returned, with something like his usual charm; and so we parted.

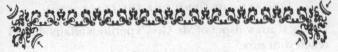

# Chapter 18

## Dutch Wool and
## Spanish Lace

*Sunday,*
*25 August 1805*
~

THE ILL EFFECTS OF YESTERDAY'S RAIN HAVING COM-
pletely disappeared by nine o'clock this morning, we
walked through the venerable old avenue of limes and
yews, called Bentigh, to St. Nicolas Church for services. The air under the spreading boughs was light
and refreshing, and spoke at last of the turn towards
autumn; a meadowlark sang of the summer's decline;
and our family party—a considerable parade, comprising children, some part of the servants, Mrs. Salkeld,
Caky, Miss Sharpe, Neddie, Lizzy, and myself—was un-
reasonably gay. The little ones skipped and turned
somersaults, until returned to a sense of their duty by
the imprecations of nurse, governess, and mother; I
felt almost compelled to run behind them, and sing
aloud of the glorious day. It was to be my last at Godmersham for a time; on the morrow I departed for Goodnestone Farm.

"And to think that Mr. Sothey would have our avenue

down!" I cried to Neddie. "You shall defend it, I hope, at sword's point if necessary."

"We cannot know what Mr. Sothey intends for the park, until he has toured its extent, and offered his opinion," my brother returned. "Do not be in such a haste to despise the man, Jane, before he has partaken of Sunday dinner!"

"Sunday dinner?" Miss Sharpe enquired, in a low voice.

I turned swiftly and regarded her. "I had forgot, of course. Poor Miss Sharpe. It seems you are the last to learn of everything! Mr. Sothey, the estate improver presently at Eastwell Park, intends to visit Godmersham this morning. He is to tour the grounds."

I kept my voice deliberately free of any peculiar emphasis, but the governess was too little mistress of her feelings to disguise her discomposure. She drew a sharp breath and halted in her steps. Had an opportunity of escape presented itself, I am sure she would have seized it; but a recognition of the oddity of her behaviour presently impressed itself, and she walked on. No word did she offer in explanation; Anne Sharpe was clearly disinclined to bestow any confidence regarding the Gentleman Improver. I supposed she might take her secret to her grave.

The old churchyard of St. Nicolas is a quiet, peaceful place. The edifice itself is Norman, dating to the thirteenth century, and is perched on the bank of the Stour above what had once been that river's principal ford. The ancient stones lean crazily over the humped earth of the graves; the wind sighs in the willow trees, and the murmur of water calls like a nymph from beyond the leaded windows. I have grown to love the little church, so unlike the bustle of Bath's imposing edifices; in as humble a house as this, one might feel closer to God Himself. But Anne Sharpe seemed impervious to the place's charms; her countenance was utterly wretched.

"I am sure you will approve of Mr. Sothey, once you are a little acquainted with him," I said, as we reached the vestibule, and the children fell decorously into line behind Fanny. "He is everything that is charming; and so decidedly possessed of genius! I quite liked him."

"There can be no occasion for my meeting with him," the governess replied. "He will be abroad with Mr. Austen in the park for much of the day, and I have a great deal yet to attend to in the schoolroom—the threat of invasion is hardly passed. And Fanny must be heard, in the reading of her Sunday lesson; then there are the little ones' dinners to attend to—I cannot fall in his way."

I affected puzzlement. "Have you some cause to dread this meeting, Miss Sharpe? You cannot have heard ill of Mr. Sothey!"

She looked me full in the face at last, with such an expression of anguish that I felt myself a very false friend, indeed. "I neither know nor care what Mr. Sothey is, Miss Austen," she said clearly. "I ask only to be allowed to care for my charges in peace. Now let us go into the service, if you please; everyone will be remarking upon our absence."

"Of course," I replied, and allowed her to pass.

"JANE," MY BROTHER CALLED, AS I WALKED TOWARDS THE little saloon after breakfast. "Might I beg an indulgence?"

"How might I be of service, Neddie?"

He steered me into the library and quietly closed the door. "I would dearly love your assistance in the matter of Mrs. Grey's correspondence. It has been years since I had occasion to translate any French, and I find that I progress only slowly."

"My own French is indifferent—I make no promises—but I should be happy to exert my wits in the attempt."

"If you do not find the duty loathsome—" He studied me anxiously.

"Loathsome? I should find it diverting in the extreme."

"Very well. I thought it only wise to enquire. Lizzy was so decidedly put off by the idea of disturbing another lady's privacy, that I thought perhaps you . . ."

"I am *not* a baronet's daughter, Neddie," I replied firmly, "and have looked into correspondence not my own, on more than one occasion heretofore." If the ashes of Anne Sharpe's letters rose accusingly in my mind, I did not betray as much to my brother. I settled myself near one of the great tables that divided the room, and looked at him expectantly.

"I have arranged them by date, a tedious job in itself; there must be nearly thirty of them, Jane, running from the month of Mrs. Grey's arrival in Kent—that would be just after her marriage, in February—until the middle of August."

"Seven months of correspondence from the Comte de Penfleur," I mused. "Let us call it one letter per week, with an occasional bonus of two. Hardly the ardent work of a lover; more the perfunctory stuff of a business arrangement. Perhaps Mr. Grey is correct in his fears. Have you read any of them?"

"I managed to decipher these"—he waved several sheets of creased paper vaguely—"but the writing is so fine, and what with the crossing of the lines . . . I shall be weeks perusing the rest."

I took the letters and leafed through them. Neddie was in earnest; most of the pages had been narrowly inscribed, with the sheet turned to the horizontal, and the original message crossed with a second text. I should not have suspected the Comte of economy in the matter of paper; but perhaps he feared the suspicions of Mr. Grey, did his wife's demand for postage mount too high.[1] All the sheets were signed, I observed, with merely the letter *H.* So that Mrs. Grey might dismiss her correspondent as an old schoolfriend, still resident in France?

"And what have you discovered?"

"He speaks a great deal of millinery," Neddie said unexpectedly. "There is a quantity of talk about Spanish lace, and whether Mrs. Grey should be able to find it; some discussion of Dutch woollens, as well, and whether the quality is so reliable as English. It seems Spanish lace and Dutch cloth are devilish hard to come by in France at present; tho' I cannot think why."

"But it is France herself that embargoes such goods from trade with England!" I exclaimed. "Can you possibly have read it aright?"

He shrugged. "Perhaps my French is more lamentable than I thought."

"Or perhaps Mr. Grey is mistaken in the identity of his wife's correspondent. Recollect that we have only his assertion these letters were written by the Comte at all."

"As to that—" Neddie searched among the papers on his desk, and retrieved another sheet of paper, slightly soiled and equally creased. The seal was identical to those already laid before me, and the hand could not be more like. "This is the letter discovered in Mrs. Grey's French novel, which—"

"—Mr. Grey has *also* chosen to identify as the Comte's."

[1] In Austen's day, the recipient of a letter paid the postage. —*Editor's note.*

"—which matches the writing on this scrap of paper, Jane," Neddie persisted patiently, "given to me by the Comte. It bears the direction of his inn at Dover, the Royal."

"Very well. The Comte has chosen to style himself 'H,' and speak only of millinery to his ladylove. I suppose there are histories recorded that are yet more extraordinary. We must assume it is a sort of code."

"Pray examine the letters yourself, Jane, and attempt to form an opinion. I shall be greatly in your debt."

"Do not deceive yourself, Neddie. It is *I* who am under the greatest obligation. I have not been so diverted by a puzzle since the weeks before our father's death; and I make no apology for profiting so grossly by Mrs. Grey's murder. This will be the first disinterested service she has rendered to anyone, in life or death."

TWO FULL HOURS WERE REQUIRED FOR THE REVIEW OF the correspondence. It was a tedious business; the Comte—our duplicitous "H"—was possessed of a fiendish hand, very nearly indecipherable. The elegance of his phrasing further confounded his despoilers; we were at pains to untangle the ravishing verbs from their dependent clauses, and must own to a head-ache after only a part of our work was done. But it proved, in the main, to be as Neddie had said—repeated discussions of lace and wool, and the most efficacious arrangements for the procuring of each. On rare occasions, the Comte commended his Françoise for her management of this friend or that—*I am pleased to observe the progress you have made in securing the affection of Mr. Collingforth*, for example; or, more interesting still, *Captain Woodford appears unsuited to his task; I would suggest you discourage his visits.* And gradually, about the month of June, another name crept into the letters: that of Julian Sothey.

*Mr. Sothey's interest in your well-being must always ensure him a warm place in my heart. . . . Mr. Sothey is possessed of a peculiar aptitude for gossip. I was charmed by your report of his conversation with Lady Forbes. . . . Mr. Sothey's influence with your husband might do much towards the securing of our lace. Pray exert your charms towards this end, ma chère Françoise, for it appears that your own influence with the gentleman is limited.*

Mr. Sothey, it seemed, had been a gratifying tool in Mrs. Grey's hands. How useful the Gentleman Improver should be, to a woman of her inclination! He knew everyone, and was welcome everywhere; he overheard the counsels of the Great at their very dinner tables. Where Mrs. Grey's sex and very foreignness should be a bar to a certain sort of male intimacy, Mr. Sothey was trusted and admired by the men of his acquaintance; before *him*, they should always be open. Had he understood, at last, that he was being worked upon—and confronted Mrs. Grey at the Canterbury Races? Was this the break that had sparked the lady's fury?

"Neddie," I said abruptly, "pray consider the phrases I have translated. They are drawn from several of the Comte's letters, despatched during the course of June and July. I do not doubt that we shall discover more such, in the month of August."

He read them, and a frown gathered on his brow. "Do you suppose Sothey to have been aware of the delicacy of the information he conveyed? Or that Mrs. Grey intended to use him against her own husband?"

"I cannot undertake to say. A man in the grip of infatuation, might do anything to win the favour of his lady; he might offer her the dearest intelligence, without a second thought as to the wisdom of the impulse. And, too, we know so little of Mrs. Grey herself—how subtle her manipulation may have been, and how patiently effected, week by week."

"But can Grey have been blind to such a passion in his friend, or its consequences? Is it possible he should overlook Sothey's attempts to influence himself?"

"We rarely suspect a friend of the heart—a man whose integrity and opinion we esteem—of employing our affections for particular ends," I observed. "It requires a doubt of intimacy, to reveal the snake."

"That should make Sothey's betrayal all the more abhorrent." Neddie considered a moment in silence. "But perhaps we read too much into these words, Jane. Sothey might be worked upon from any number of causes. He may have cared nothing for Françoise Grey— but possessed as ruinous a taste for gaming as his father. That should easily place him in her power."

"It should not be surprising," I agreed. "Such things are said to run in the blood. But what was he intended to procure, Neddie?"

"Gossip?"

"His charm and brilliance—his inclination for discourse—and the ease with which he moved among the houses of the Great, should provide him with a considerable fund of knowledge. But that appears to have been the least of his talents. He is specifically intended by the Comte to secure some Spanish lace, and arguably from Mr. Grey."

"But what is the lace intended to signify?"

"Money, Neddie," I replied with decision. "Recall what Henry has suspected, and what the Comte himself has said. Grey has a scheme under consideration, that must encompass the great banking houses of Europe; it is the only way in which Mr. Sothey might be of use to Penfleur."

"But was not the Comte already Grey's partner in a Continental concern?" my brother protested, bewildered. "Why should he have need of subterfuge?"

"Because the intended use of the funds, my dear,

should ruin Mr. Grey were it suspected. He should be accused of treason, or worse; and until the funds are secured, he must never be allowed to suspect the gravity of his betrayal."

My brother whistled. "You suspect that Grey is to bankroll Buonaparte's invasion of England?"

"I can think of nothing else that should require such delicacy of arrangement and preparation. Only consider, Neddie—Françoise Grey was forced into a loveless marriage, for the express purpose of winning her husband's resources. Let us hope that she eventually failed—and was murdered as a result."

"And if she succeeded?" A fine beading of sweat stood out on my brother's brow. "What then, for Grey and the security of the Kingdom?"

"That is a question," I said drily, "that I suspect you must put to Mr. Grey."

MY BROTHER MIGHT HAVE MOUNTED HIS HORSE AT THAT very moment, and ridden off in the direction of The Larches, had he not been prevented by the appearance of the Gentleman Improver. As it was, he was forced to be content with a hastily-scrawled note, despatched by messenger to Valentine Grey, that required that gentleman's presence at dinner—or if the banker were otherwise engaged, for coffee afterwards.

It was hardly Mr. Sothey's fault that he thus interrupted our counsels at a most inauspicious moment. He had arrived in good time—at a quarter past one o'clock—and looked so delighted at the prospect of his visit, that I could hardly believe him capable of a conscious deceit. He was elegantly dressed, and as cool in his appearance as tho' the short ride had no power to discomfit him; praised everything from the plasterwork in the hall, to the arrangement of the rooms, and would stay within doors only long enough to pay his respects to Lizzy, before proposing that we should all walk out and survey the grounds.

To my surprise and delight, Mr. Emilious Finch-Hatton had ridden over from Eastwell in company with the improver.

"Miss Austen!" he cried, bending low over my hand, "it is a pleasure to see you again. I have had a letter from our mutual friend, that would not delay of its communication to you; and so I have imposed upon Sothey and yourselves, in presuming to invite myself to dinner."

"You will always be welcome, sir, as I believe you know." We were awaiting Lizzy's appearance on the stairs, in stout boots better suited to walking than the slippers she had sported all morning, before crossing the Stour. Mr. Sothey had judged the prospect from the Doric temple's height ideally suited to an initial survey of the grounds; and there we should commence our tour. "Lord Harold is well?"

"He is as well as any man may be, who has been denied a glimpse of his native shores for six months together. He found success in Austria, I understand—the Hapsburgs will stand with England and Russia—and is presently embarked for Amsterdam."[2]

---

[2] Austria's alliance with England and Russia on August 9 concluded the building of what was termed the Third Coalition. It was thrown into conflict with Napoleonic France soon thereafter, at the Battle of Austerlitz, December 2, 1805. Bonaparte triumphed, and was ceded considerable German and Italian territory at the Treaty of Pressburg, which was concluded later that month. Austria's ties to England were then severed completely, and she was forced to pay forty million francs as indemnity to France.—*Editor's note.*

"Amsterdam?" I echoed. "As Mr. Pitt's personal envoy, perhaps?"

"I believe Lord Harold presently enjoys that honour."

"Then he is charged with the thankless task of persuading a Scots banker to lend, where all confidence is lacking." Unless, I thought, Trowbridge is too late—and Mr. Grey's funds have already rescued the French crown.

"You have been reading the *Times*, I see," Mr. Emilious observed with a twinkle. "You may soon discover some interesting items in its columns, I believe—but I shall say no more, at present."

We had been walking all this while to the end of the sweep; had passed the lodge, crossed the Canterbury road, and were fetched up at the little foot-bridge over the Stour.[3] The tedious uphill climb to achieve the temple next engrossed our attention, and Mr. Emilious—being better suited to the consumption of an elegant meal, than the scaling of more Picturesque heights—could hardly be expected to spare breath for my amusement.

"Capital!" Mr. Sothey cried, his face aglow. He stood under the temple's portico next to my brother, who was also flushed with the exercise. Lizzy had adopted a chair. "The house is nobly positioned between this rise of the downs and the hills against its back; and with the Stour bisecting the narrow valley, it is a most bucolic scene. That cottage away to the right, with the road winding up to it, is a dependent's?"

"It belongs to the gamekeeper," Neddie said, "for the deer park runs up through the far downs; and that

---

[3] Present-day visitors to Godmersham will be slightly confused by this description. The Canterbury road Jane describes is now the A28, and was rerouted well after her death (in the 1830s) beyond the far bank of the Stour. The Doric temple now has the road to its back, rather than standing in contemplation of it, as in Jane's day.—*Editor's note.*

building behind the house, midway up the slope, is the ice house."

"Your farmland is where?"

"To the south."

"I see. Adjacent to the church?"

"Just so."

"That avenue, I collect, is your usual path to Sunday service?"

"We have traversed it already twice today."

Mr. Sothey shaded his eyes with one hand against the slanting light of the westering sun, and turned first north and then south, towards Chilham Castle. "It is remarkable, however, how little space was accorded the pleasure gardens, given the expanse of the park, and the commodious impression afforded by the rising ground. It is unfortunate that the river runs so close to the road, and the road so near to the gatekeeper's lodge. There is an impression of confinement, of claustration, at that end of the estate, that is most unfortunate. The garden paths running down to the limes only increase that sensation, if you will observe; for they are without exception unvaryingly straight, and must serve as boundaries rather than avenues of escape."

Neddie's eyes narrowed, and his lips compressed.

"I rather wonder at the original builder's intent," Mr. Sothey mused, "in placing the house at right angles to the river and the road."

"Perhaps he found a southern exposure, and the prospect of the downs and the church, more pleasant than that of the highway," Neddie said tartly.

"Perhaps—but as you see, it increases the crowding of the sweep and the lodge immeasurably. Those are kitchen gardens, I suppose?" Mr. Sothey gestured towards two enclosures at the north end of Bentigh.

"They are," Neddie replied. "An estate cannot hope to function without them. They have served us amply for

more years than you can claim, Mr. Sothey." There was
a faint note of belligerence in his tone, as tho' the improver's observations were felt as a personal attack.

"My dear sir," Mr. Sothey said swiftly, "you must not
take it amiss if I prod and prick your sensibilities here
and there. It is always difficult to work against the force
of habit; we are creatures of convention, as you very well
know, and despise the merest hint of change. It is essential, however, to comprehend the daily employment of
these grounds, and the manner in which the work of the
estate might be improved, and made compatible with its
visual delights. I shall demand to know a great deal from
the kitchen maids—how often they use certain paths,
where the villagers are wont to trespass, and whither the
Austen ladies delight in roaming, in the pursuit of exercise. All this must be understood, before anything of
improvement may be achieved."

"And so the genius of our place is a kitchen maid?" I
enquired, amused. "I tremble to think what might occur,
if the nursemaid is not appeased!"

Mr. Sothey threw back his head and laughed. His
remarkable auburn locks rippled in the sun; and I was
struck at once by the vigour and openness of his looks—
he might have been Gabriel, surveying the Lord's kingdom. "I should have said the *genie* of Godmersham was
Demeter, Miss Austen—the drowsing hum of the birds
among the grain speaks only of harvest to my ears; but
we shall know better with time. Perhaps the resident
spirit is one of water, and sings through the stones of
the Stour; or perhaps it wanders among the lime trees,
plaiting violets in its hair."

"Then pray take care you do not destroy its natural
haunt," Neddie broke in.

"Heaven forbid!" Mr. Sothey cried. "I cannot think
that *destruction* is the wisest approach to Art. You are

happy, Mr. Austen, in the possession of an estate where natural beauty and a wise hand have achieved much; the essentials of the place are so good, that a very little effort may offer considerable rewards."

Neddie did not look appeased; there was a stiffness to his demeanour, and a caution in his air, that argued opposition to anything Mr. Sothey might counsel.

"I should like to sketch the approach from the Stour," Mr. Sothey said with decision, "and then ascend to the ice house. We might profitably traverse the garden paths afterwards, and examine the avenue of lime trees. They are of considerable age, if I do not mistake?"

"Indeed," Neddie replied, "and are regarded with affection by most of the populace."

Happily, Mr. Sothey was too little intimate with my brother to read his humours in his looks; Lizzy and I were not so fortunate.

"It was ever thus," Lizzy murmured to me. "You cannot think how many months together I was forced to urge the abandonment of your brother's periwig, and the laying aside of the powdering horn, in favour of his delightful hair! I believe a twelvemonth at least was required to achieve it; and now he would have it the change in fashion was all his own thought, and as natural as breathing. It will be the same with Mr. Sothey's views, I am sure."

"Let us hope that Mr. Sothey does not advise the felling of Bentigh," I replied, and prepared to follow the gentlemen down the slope.

It was just as we rounded the northern side of the house, and prepared to ascend to the ice house, that we fell in with Anne Sharpe.

She had been walking some time with Fanny and young Lizzy—the two girls had taken their dolls for an airing, and were just returned to the house intent upon refreshment. The exercise had improved the governess's looks; there was colour in her cheeks, and a brightness in her eye, that had been lacking for some days. She wore a simple day dress of pale pink muslin—her best, put on in respect of Sunday service, and not yet exchanged for another; and her dark hair peeked out from the depths of her bonnet, with all the gloss of a raven's wing. It was commendable, I thought, that she had ventured out-of-doors, despite her fear of meeting with Mr. Sothey; perhaps my warning had served to prepare her, and afforded a measure of strength.

"Miss Sharpe!" my brother cried. "How have you liked your charges today? They are easier to manage, I warrant, when the air is fresh and the sun in good regulation!"

"We are all very well, sir, I thank you," she replied with a curtsey, "only a trifle tired. We have walked to Seaton Wood and back." She kept her eyes trained on Neddie's face, as tho' she could not trust herself to look beyond; but her appearance was one of tolerable composure.

"So far!" Neddie cried. "Then I am sure you have carried my little Lizzy nearly half the distance." He caught the child up in his arms, and kissed her.

"Not at all, Papa," she said stoutly. "I was promised an extra bit of pudding with my supper, if I achieved the walk alone."

"How very wise of Miss Sharpe. But I am forgetting my manners—I do not believe you are acquainted with our guests, Miss Sharpe. This is Mr. Sothey, and that is Mr. Finch-Hatton; Miss Sharpe, my daughters' governess."

She curtseyed again to the two gentlemen, who doffed their hats; and I glanced quickly from the improver to the governess to observe how Mr. Sothey took the introduction. I expected a certain reserve; a circumspection, even—but he defied expectation as always.

"I am privileged in being very well-acquainted with Miss Sharpe," he said with a bow, and the keenest look in his grey eyes. "We were so fortunate as to spend some weeks together in Weymouth, last year, while she was yet with the Portermans. Your friends are in health, I trust?"

"Very well, sir," Miss Sharpe replied, in a barely audible tone. Her cheeks had flushed crimson from mortification; she must be suffering agonies of discovery before her employer—for never, at any mention of Mr. Sothey's name heretofore, had she admitted to the acquaintance. I felt for her, and could have abused Mr. Sothey for stupidity to his face.

He moved towards her slowly, until a very little distance separated them. "And are you equally in health and spirits, Miss Sharpe?" he enquired softly. "Or has something occurred to trouble you?"

"I believe I should be returning to the house," she replied, and took Lizzy's hand. "Come along, Fanny. We deserve our lemon-water, after such vigourous exertion; and then perhaps we shall rest a little, until dinner is served."

"Until dinner, then," Mr. Sothey said, raising his hat to Miss Sharpe.

"I always take my dinner with the children, sir," she replied distantly; and with a nod to Mr. Emilious, moved off across the lawn.

Mr. Sothey watched her go without another word. There was a compression to his lips, and an intensity in his gaze, that argued strong emotion; but he remained as ever under perfect regulation. The suspicions of the entire party must be awakened against him; even Mr. Emilious seemed to observe his friend narrowly; but the improver turned towards us all with a smile, and said gaily: "How oddly she has arranged her hair, to be sure! I have never observed anything like it. She is very much changed since last summer—quite fallen off in looks. I should hardly have known her again."

# Chapter 19

## Baiting the Trap

### 25 August 1805, cont'd.

~

"I HAD EXPECTED MR. VALENTINE GREY TO DINNER,"
Neddie observed, when the servants had withdrawn
and we were established over our boned trout and jellied fowl, "but he has disappointed me, alas. We must
endeavour to talk affairs of state without our most
knowledgeable partner."

From a hurried conference with my brother in the
drawing-room before Mr. Emilious led me to the table, I
had learned that The Larches returned no reply to my
brother's note. If this was cause for anxiety, Neddie
betrayed no sign; Mr. Grey might have gone up to London, on a matter of business, and failed even in receipt
of the message. But on the morrow, Neddie vowed, Mr.
Grey must be found and questioned regarding the matter of Spanish lace; for events looked to have taken so
grave a turn, as to make my brother doubt the extent of
his own authority.

"Mr. Grey?" Julian Sothey enquired, with an eager
glance. "How I should have liked to have seen him! I

came away from The Larches, you know, on the very day of his wife's tragic death; and have never been so fortunate as to meet with Grey since. He was in London at the time, of course; but I am greatly remiss in paying my respects. Circumstances prevented my attendance at Mrs. Grey's funeral—and in short, he will think me an odd sort of friend, do I not pay a call of condolence very soon."

None of us assembled at the table, I imagine, should have broached the subject of Mrs. Grey directly to the improver; and his raising it himself, in so careless a fashion, must give rise to wonder in more than one quarter. Neddie was taken aback, and even I was at a loss for words; but Lizzy's self-possession, as always, was equal to everything.

"You may have one source of consolation, Mr. Sothey," she said, "in the felicity your sudden descent upon Eastwell Park brought to Lady Elizabeth. She was never more astonished, she told me, than when you assured her it was within your power to pay your longed-for visit. She was quite unable to account for the honour of seeing you, having considered you quite fixed at The Larches."

This last required some reply. Some men might have coloured and looked confused, or hurried themselves into too-fulsome explanation; Mr. Sothey merely laughed. "Lady Elizabeth, I believe, is the most generous of my friends—for never have I appeared on her door-step, a lost and masterless cur, that she has not received me into her household without the slightest demand for explanation!"

"We have grown so used to Sothey's turning up like a bad penny," Mr. Emilious Finch-Hatton observed, "that he might almost have a bedchamber set aside for his perpetual use! But in this instance, Mrs. Austen, I fear that Lady Elizabeth has unconsciously misled you. Sothey informed *me* of his intention of quitting The Larches some weeks before the day he intended, but I neglected to relate the fact to my sister. I cannot excuse such neglect; I may only plead the coincidence of a summer cold, that rendered me so wretched as to ignore everything that did not have to do with myself. Lady Elizabeth's confusion at the races and likewise her surprised delight, were entirely of my making."

"I suppose her chief fear at present," Lizzy said with a slight smile, "is that Mr. Sothey will be gone as suddenly as he came!"

"Experience has taught her, madam," that gentleman replied, "that I am rarely to be found in the same house for many weeks together. I consider myself quite fixed at Eastwell Park for the present—but should events conspire to divert my attention, I should be gone in a matter of hours!"

"You endeavour to make inconstancy appear a matter for pride, Mr. Sothey," I objected, "but it will not do. A man of your reputation cannot so lightly risk the world's good opinion. An appearance of sober dependability must be your best friend at present, when many might wonder at your quitting The Larches so precipitately."

He shrugged almost indolently. "My work there was done. To have remained longer would have looked very odd, indeed."

"Despite the circumstance of sudden death in the household?"

Mr. Sothey smiled. "You forget, Miss Austen, that Mrs. Grey's murder was the merest coincidence. I had fixed on the date as my intended departure long before, as Mr. Finch-Hatton will attest; my bags were packed and stowed in the chaise I drove to the race-meeting."

Perhaps so much was true; but I thought the improver's gaze too steady, and his expression too fixed, to permit of easiness. Neddie, I knew, was observing him acutely; and finding his reliance upon Mr. Emilious instructive. Would Mr. Sothey have come to Godmersham, I wondered, without his wise old watchdog?

"Circumstances, it seems, prevented even Mr. Grey from witnessing his late wife's interment," Lizzy observed. She, at least, was enjoying the exchange. "With so near a relation absent from the rites, Mr. Sothey can hardly charge himself with neglect."

"Grey, absent from the funeral rites?" Mr. Sothey cried. "You astonish me, Mrs. Austen! I should have said he would sooner cut off his own arm, than fail in respect of so important a duty."

"Mr. Grey was called from home on Thursday evening," Neddie told him, "on what appears to have been a matter of business."

"I suppose only such a claim as that might sway Mr. Grey," Mr. Emilious observed. "But I cannot stand in judgement of his actions. He is the most honourable man I know of, in either the financial or the political line; and if he felt himself compelled to be from home, he undoubtedly had his reasons."

"You are acquainted with Mr. Grey?" I enquired, surprised. "I thought he moved but little in Society."

"Say rather that he is the acquaintance of a very old friend of mine, Miss Austen, and you shall have got it right." Mr. Emilious's countenance was as bland and charming as ever, but an acuteness had come into his pale blue eyes that warned me away from suspect ground.

"I may hazard a guess as to the friend's name," I said slowly, as an idea took shape in my mind. "Is it Mr. George Canning, by any chance?"

"The very man!" Mr. Emilious cried.

"Mr. Grey happened to tell me of his acquaintance with the gentleman. Indeed, Mr. Sothey, he credited Mr.

Canning with his introduction to yourself, and could not praise the gentleman enough. I suppose you have all met, at one time or another, around Mr. Canning's table."

"Just so," Mr. Sothey said. He affected an easy good-humour, but I do not think I flatter myself in declaring that he was considerably disconcerted, and not a little put out. It seemed that George Canning possessed other qualities besides those of clubman and exotic plant enthusiast—qualities more suited, perhaps, to intrigue and subterfuge. He was, after all, Treasurer of the Navy and an acknowledged confederate of Lord Harold Trowbridge; Mr. Emilious had informed me of the fact himself. Oh, that I might avail myself of Lord Harold's resources, and know exactly how things were!

"So Grey was from home on Thursday evening," Mr. Sothey mused. "It was hazardous to be abroad that night, I believe. Is it true, Mr. Austen—are you able to divulge so much—that Mr. Denys Collingforth was murdered in Deal on that very evening?"

"He was," Neddie replied imperturbably. "I suppose the intelligence has travelled swiftly from Prior's Farm, and is presently the toast of the Hound and Tooth?"

"I heard it first from a manservant of Mr. Finch-Hatton's," Mr. Sothey replied, "but how he came by the news, I cannot say."

"Depend upon it, he had it of the butcher's lad, who learned it of his washer-woman mother, who takes in laundry from Prior's Farm—or some such roundabout tale," Mr. Emilious said comfortably. "Poor Collingforth! And so he was done for as he did."

"Not quite," my brother countered quietly. "Mrs. Grey, after all, was throttled. Mr. Collingforth's neck was cut."

"Really?" Mr. Emilious kept his eyes trained on his

knife, which was steadily applying a quantity of butter to one of Cook's feather-light rolls. "There is no suggestion, I suppose, that he effected the wound himself?"

"None whatsoever," Neddie replied, "since he was discovered bound and weighted at the bottom of a pond." If my brother felt himself to be the subject of interrogation, he betrayed little of his discomfort in his countenance; but I thought Neddie's easy manner was become guarded. "Have you a notion, sir, of the murderer?"

"Why, as to that—it might as well have been Sothey and myself," Mr. Emilious cried, with a jovial look for his companion, "for we were abroad on the very road to Deal, in respect of a dinner with some friends, on Thursday night."

"I should never suspect *you*, Mr. Finch-Hatton," my brother replied calmly, "for your name does not appear in Mrs. Grey's interesting correspondence. You can have not the slightest connexion to the affair, as those documents attest."

There was a sudden, appalled silence; and involuntarily, I closed my eyes. Whatever Neddie had done, was done with calculation; he was not a fatuous insinuator, to trade privileged fact as currency with his guests. He was throwing the letters like a scented bait before a pack of roused foxhounds; and I trembled for the result.

"Her . . . *correspondence*?" Mr. Emilious repeated, with a swift glance at Mr. Sothey. "You have had occasion to look into the lady's letters?"

"Any number," Neddie said airily, "and the names found within it should astonish the neighbourhood, I may assure you!"

"Then I hope you will take care, my dear sir, that they never come to light." Mr. Emilious held my brother's gaze quite steadily. "From what little I know of Mrs. Grey, I am certain she can have said nothing flattering of her acquaintance."

"Then she merely returned a common favour," Lizzy observed idly, "for they certainly had nothing good to say of *her*."

"Upon my word, Mr. Austen—the ladies will think us decidedly dull," Mr. Emilious cried, with a gallant look for Lizzy. "All this talk of dusty matters had better be confined to the Port, had it not? We were charmed to see you at Eastwell, Mrs. Austen, on Friday evening; you have been too chary in your visits altogether."

"Lady Elizabeth shall wish me at the ends of the earth, sir, do I succeed in wresting her improver from her grasp," Lizzy rejoined. "I rather wonder at her allowing you to ride over to Godmersham at all, Mr. Sothey!— But perhaps she sent Mr. Finch-Hatton as a sort of surety against your return. Are you charged with bringing Mr. Sothey to Eastwell unharmed, sir, and well before dawn?"

"Unharmed," Mr. Emilious replied, "but not, I hope, before dawn. Mr. Sothey has so much delight in Godmersham, dear madam, that were it not for a delicacy in appearing forward, I am sure he should express his wish to continue sketching tomorrow."

Mr. Sothey looked sharply at his friend, but said nothing. Lizzy instantly took the hint, and invited them both to stay the night—protested that it should prove not the slightest trouble—the rooms were already made up; and was so gracious in her assurances, and so frank in her delight, that the two men accepted with alacrity. I wondered, as I observed them, how Miss Sharpe should find the addition—but as the governess had held firm to her intention of remaining above stairs, I was denied the chance to observe her.

Anne Sharpe's poor history had paled in comparison, however, with the suspicions now alive against Mr. Sothey and his companion; and I must wonder whether Mr. Emilious Finch-Hatton had *another* object in prolonging his stay, than the improvement of my brother's estate. That Neddie assumed as much—that he had indeed incited the event with his careless talk of letters and names—I read in the studied blandness of his looks; and vowed to sit wakeful far into the night, that I might be witness to everything that should come to pass.

It was nearly two o'clock, and the house had been abed some three hours, when a sound in the gallery outside my door alerted all my senses. It was the hesitant, muffled, and quite obvious fall of footsteps along the drugget—footsteps that endeavoured to disguise their passage, and yet could not avoid the creaking board or the impact of an occasional chair leg. They came from the end of the wing just beyond my Yellow Room; Mr. Sothey had been housed there, with Mr. Emilious opposite. Had I been possessed of cunning, as I now assumed these two to be, I should have descended by the back stair, which depended from the opposite end of the hallway; but as the gentlemen were unfamiliar with the house, they might prefer to go as they had come—by the main staircase opposite Neddie's door.

I waited until the footsteps should have passed, and then threw back my bedclothes and moved as soundlessly as possible to the chair by my door. I put on my dressing-gown and reached for the knob. Another instant, and the doorway yawned wide—I peered out, scarcely breathing, and surveyed the gallery. It was empty of life. Whoever had passed must be presently upon the stairs.

One foot forward, and then another; and at length I had achieved the end of the hall. I must be admitted as possessing an advantage, in having traversed it a thousand times before. Not for me the trespass on a weak board, that should alert my quarry to pursuit. I peered down into the sweeping dimness of the stairs, and glimpsed a single figure bobbing hesitantly before me in the dark—a woman, fully dressed and bonneted, and carrying a satchel. It must be, it could not be other than, Anne Sharpe.

I abandoned caution, and hastened down the stairs in her wake. She turned, and uttered a little cry that was as swiftly stifled by a hand to her mouth. Then she sped rapidly down the remaining stairs.

"Miss Sharpe!" I trained my voice to a whisper, but the words issued forth with all the violence of a shot in the echoing expanse of the marble-floored front hall. She was but a few feet away from me now, and intent upon the front door. As she struggled with the bolts, glancing half-fearfully over her shoulder, I reached her side.

"Whatever can you be thinking of, my dear? To walk abroad in the dead of night, without a single friend to bear you company? You are certainly in the grip of a fit," I told her firmly, and closed my hand over her own. "Come sit down upon this bench, and tell me what you are about."

"Why, for the love of God, can not you leave me alone?" she cried. "But for you, I should have been comfortably away! Away—from all that is painful, from—"

"Julian Sothey?"

"Mr. Sothey is nothing to me, Miss Austen. You quite mistake the matter, I assure you."

"Nothing to you *now*, perhaps. But I think there was a time when he was very dear, indeed."

She went limp, and allowed me to lead her towards one of the little damask benches that lined the entry hall. There she sat down and threw her head in her hands.

"You met at Weymouth and I suppose you fell in love with him there. Did you know that he was in Kent when you accepted the position at Godmersham?"

She nodded helplessly. "We had agreed to a secret engagement, and corresponded faithfully. I used to walk out on the morning a letter was expected, and intercept it in the post. I did not think that Mrs. Austen would look kindly on such a predisposition."

"It bore too much of an affinity for intrigue—yes, I see how it was. And I suppose you met with Mr. Sothey, in the stableyard at The Larches, when Mrs. Grey was abroad?"

Her head came up at that, and a band of moonlight cut across her face. I read the look of shock in her countenance. "I, meet Julian in the stables at The Larches? However can you have devised such a notion, Miss Austen?"

"You did not sometimes visit him there?"

"How should I, who have no mount at my disposal, and am not a great walker, have travelled all that distance? It is above six miles! Impossible! I have never been nearer to The Larches than the Canterbury race grounds; indeed, I never had occasion to observe Mrs. Grey herself, until—" She faltered.

"Until the lady brought her whip down upon the neck of your betrothed," I concluded grimly, "and you knew in an instant that the greatest intimacy must subsist between them. Or feared as much."

"Feared—knew—I cannot tell you which," she replied wretchedly. "I may only say that the most powerful conviction of betrayal then overcame me—and with it, a dreadful sense of shame. I had been treated lightly by a man I thought worthy of my love, and knew myself for a fool."

"Mr. Sothey saw you on that morning, I collect?"

"Our eyes met across the race grounds. You must

recall that he was positioned in such a manner that his figure must be visible to our party; seated in the Austen barouche, I was similarly exposed to his sight. We had not met in over a year, Miss Austen; and at my first glimpse of him, what joy!—to be overcome, so suddenly, by a passion akin almost to hatred."

"He did not attempt to converse with you."

"No," she agreed, "and that alone convinced me of his guilt. Julian is many things, Miss Austen, but he is not a man who may lie in his looks. I knew that he was afraid to meet me, knowing what I had witnessed; and in this I comprehended the whole of the story."

"Perhaps he read only indignation in your countenance, and thought to appease you later, when the first anger should have passed. Did he attempt to write a letter?" I enquired ingenuously.

"He may have attempted much," Miss Sharpe replied, "but any letters I subsequently received, I burned without reading. Perhaps I should have returned them; but I had heard he was gone from The Larches, and did not know the direction at Eastwell. To have enquired it of Mrs. Austen would have appeared too strange."

"I see." Much of my supposition regarding the governess was proved correct—all but Mr. Brett's tale of a dark-haired woman departing on horseback from The Larches' stableyard. Could Mr. Brett be believed? Or was the story the merest fabrication? "Were you surprised, Miss Sharpe, to learn that Mr. Sothey was gone to Eastwell?"

"Utterly surprised," she said in a low voice. "Julian had made no mention of such a removal to me, in his earlier letters—had offered nothing of a new direction, where my correspondence might be sent. In such neglect, Miss Austen, I read a further disregard. It was plain that Julian had tired of me, and wished to be free of all obligation."

"Never say so, my dearest!"

The words burst forth in a cry of anguish, and in an instant, Julian Sothey was upon us. From whence he had come, drawn by the little scene, I could not at first imagine; but he was dressed as fully as Anne Sharpe, as tho' he, too, had intended a midnight flight. He threw himself upon his knees before the governess and seized her hands.

"You see before you, Anne, a heart now more your own than when you nearly broke it a few days ago! Have you any notion of the agony you have caused—the sleepless nights, the endless calculation, the desperate attempts at communication? All for the merest trifle—a misapprehension—the bitter result of a petulant woman's fury! Can you possibly have believed that I should abandon you, my Anne, for the fiend that was Mrs. Grey?"

Anne Sharpe still sat rigidly upon the bench, as tho' turned to stone by Mr. Sothey's appearance; his words had washed over her as ineffectually as a summer storm. "Please, Julian, I beg of you. Do not make me look a fool. Mrs. Grey should never have presumed to strike you, did she not believe you to be well within her power."

"Within her power, perhaps," he replied, "but never what you believe me to have been. Come to your senses, Anne! Is it conceivable I could be other than your own?"

She did not reply, but struggled to free her hands from his; and at that moment, a second voice at our backs alerted all our senses.

"Julian, Julian—must you bring the entire house around our ears?"

I turned, and perceived Mr. Emilious Finch-Hatton. He appeared remarkably easy for a man discovered in his host's entry hall at two o'clock in the morning. Tho' his words suggested chagrin, there was an air of amused calculation about his countenance. I judged that he had only just quitted the library; all behind him was dark.

"Good evening, sir." I contrived to hold my voice steady. "I collect you have been rifling my brother's desk, in a fruitless search for Mrs. Grey's letters. You would have done better to credit him with a degree of honesty you cannot share, when first he informed you that your name was not to be found in their passages."

"Good evening, Miss Austen," he replied with a courtly bow. "As you are so familiar with the lady's correspondence, I need not remind you that my friend Sothey's name is everywhere in evidence. It behooved me to ensure that Sothey's connexion with Mrs. Grey, and her dubious undertakings for the Emperor of France, should never come to light."

"Did you protect him as ardently last Monday, somewhere along the Wingham road?" I retorted.

"If by that question, you would enquire whether I throttled Mrs. Grey, I must answer in the negative. I might offer you my word as a gentleman—but I perceive that you hold me in something like contempt, Miss Austen. More to the point, we are all most abominably situated in this draughty hall. If a full explanation is to be undertaken, I suggest we remove to the library, where we might dispose ourselves in greater comfort."

"The library?" cried my brother Neddie with considerable indignation. He held aloft a taper, and stared at us all from the library doorway, with undisguised disgust. "Say rather the kitchens! I have been standing fully two hours behind these damnable drapes, and I refuse to remain in that room a moment longer! If your sense of honour requires an explanation, Finch-Hatton, then pray let it be conducted in a civilised manner—over a quantity of bread and butter."

"I thought you must be concealed behind the drapes," Mr. Emilious replied companionably. "It was either yourself or a very large rat, that persisted in knocking against the windowpanes whilst we were engaged in rummaging about your desk. Where, by the by, have you hidden Mrs. Grey's letters?"

Neddie turned without a word and strode down the back passage towards the kitchens. Mr. Emilious held out his hand in a gesture of gallantry; and after a moment's hesitation, the rest of us deigned to follow.

# Chapter 20

## *Policies of Love and War*

~

"I SUPPOSE," MR. EMILIOUS FINCH-HATTON BEGAN, AS he helped himself to some of Cook's excellent currant jam, "you are wild to know how I come into this tangled business."

"You flatter yourself, sir," Neddie replied. "For my part, I should be happy to learn so little as the manner of Mrs. Grey's death. Your own machinations are immaterial."

"I should like to know any number of things," I broke in, "and am not averse to hearing Mr. Finch-Hatton. I rather think we shall come to the matter of Mrs. Grey, in time."

"Excellent woman!" Mr. Emilious cried. "Lord Harold has assuredly judged you aright."

"Am I to conclude, then, that Lord Harold is aware of his friend's involvement in an affair of murder?"

"He warned me against you, you know," Mr. Emilious said by way of answer. "He thought you likely to be my worst enemy, my dear Miss Austen. I endeavoured to make you my friend—but alas, events moved well beyond my ordering of them, with the discovery of those letters. Mr. Grey happened upon the correspondence, I suppose?"

"He did," Neddie supplied.

Mr. Emilious leaned forward in some excitement, to the detriment of his shirtsleeves, which were smeared with butter. "Did he tell you where he discovered them? For upon my word, the fellows I had hoped might effect it, were quite pitiful in the application!"

"Mr. Bridges and Captain Woodford?" I surmised.

"The very same. I led those two excellent fellows to believe it a matter of some delicacy, that should compromise the lady's reputation before her husband. Woodford agreed in an instant, from concern for his friend Grey; Mr. Bridges, quite naturally, had other motives. He accepted the task for a small consideration. A man whose circumstances are so thoroughly embarrassed, must be open to almost any application. But I believe the two had a falling-out, over the question of the letters' whereabouts; each suspected the other's motives."

"You are not a man to soil your own hands, I perceive."

"It was hardly a question of *that*, Miss Austen, but one rather of efficiency. It would have looked too odd for Sothey to return to the house, you know, and I had never been an intimate there—but I am getting ahead of myself. Where were the letters discovered?"

"You shall have to enquire of Mr. Grey yourself," Neddie replied, "for he did not think to tell me. That is, if you possess sufficient courage to meet with Mr. Grey."

The older man shook his head sadly over his hunk of bread. "I assure you, Mr. Austen, that you have completely misjudged me. I had nothing whatsoever to do with Mrs. Grey's end; except, perhaps, in the precipitation of it. I was never so fortunate as to meet the lady."

"Tho' you learned much of her, from your associate Mr. Sothey," I supplied. "You had encountered him before, at George Canning's; perhaps he came to you in some distress, once he knew that he had fallen into the woman's power, and was being employed for her own devious purposes."

"I, employed by Mrs. *Grey*?" Mr. Sothey interjected with a bitter laugh. "I fear, Miss Austen, that you have got it the wrong way round."

I looked from the improver to Mr. Emilious, much struck. "You would mean to say, Mr. Sothey, that you went to The Larches nearly seven months ago, for the express purpose of observing Mrs. Grey?"

"It was for that Mr. Canning ensured my introduction to Grey. I was peculiarly suited to the task, Miss Austen, in being an improver of landscape; Mr. Grey, as you know, has a passion for his grounds, and as a result of his recent marriage, was determined to spend much of his time in Kent. Canning—who, in his capacity as Treasurer of the Navy, is charged with the administration of the Government's Secret Funds—had long suspected the nature of Grey's marriage.[1] He believed the lady's family intended to use its influence with Grey to the detriment of the Kingdom's fortunes. You may well enquire how he came to believe this; let it suffice to say that Canning is familiar with the Comte de Penfleur these many years."

"And so he sent you, Mr. Sothey, to spy on the Grey household."

[1] The Secret Funds were monies voted annually by Parliament, and set aside for the government's use. No public inquiry as to their disposition was allowed; and while they were commonly used during the Napoleonic Wars for the payment of spies and the active sabotage of Bonaparte's government, in past eras the Secret Funds had defrayed the debts of royal mistresses, or purchased votes in corrupt parliamentary elections.—*Editor's note.*

Anne Sharpe moaned softly, and covered her face with her hands. Mr. Sothey's countenance wore a fleeting look of pain; but he kept his eyes averted from his beloved. "He did. I had been in the employ of Mr. Canning for some time—ever since the end of peace had enforced my return from the Continent.[2] My reputation ensured my acceptance among the households of the Great; I was thus in a position to go anywhere, and see everyone. My work, I may say, has proved invaluable to Canning and his clandestine office."

"Then at Weymouth—" Anne Sharpe began, with a desperate look.

"—at Weymouth I was charged with the cultivation of General Sir Thomas Porterman," he concluded. "I was *not* charged with making love to his ward—of that you may be certain. It is to my own detriment, and that of my Government, that I have come to care for Miss Anne Sharpe so deeply; but I begin to think the difficulty will resolve itself, with time." The bitterness had only deepened in Mr. Sothey's voice; he certainly believed the governess was lost to him.

"Do you mean to say," my brother enquired, "that the entire seven months you were resident at The Larches, you were working upon the lady of the house?—Endeavouring to win her trust, with the object of defeating the Comte de Penfleur?"

"How succinctly you put things, Mr. Austen, to be sure," Mr. Emilious returned. "Sothey was charged with winning the lady's confidence, and with supplying her with some information that was . . . shall we say, less than accurate. Mrs. Grey became Canning's most useful

---

[2] Sothey is presumably speaking of the period around May 1803, when the Treaty of Amiens between England and France was broken.—*Editor's note.*

channel for the confusion of the enemy; for her sources were so varied, in comprising half the county, and yet so much in conflict with one another, that the Comte could hardly determine which intelligence to credit, and which to discount. Sothey's being so much a friend to Mr. Grey, and so clearly in his confidence, must argue assurance in his regard; whereas the more suspect among the group—such as Denys Collingforth, a desperate man, and Lady Forbes, a very silly woman—might be dismissed. However much truth they managed to convey."

"I must congratulate you on a certain brilliance in your conduct, Sothey," my brother said. "It defies belief. And Mr. Emilious Finch-Hatton, I presume, is your superior in Canning's line?"

"Call me colleague, rather," Mr. Emilious said, "and I am satisfied. Certainly I should never have trespassed so long upon my brother's generosity, by remaining at Eastwell, had not Sothey required the possibility of a bolt-hole. Should the need of quitting The Larches arise, I was to be depended upon. And in the meanwhile, I may say that I served as his occasional counsel. Little that Mrs. Grey had under contemplation was unknown to me."

"But to what end?" I broke in. "The matter of Spanish lace?"

Both men stared, then looked at one another in perplexity. "Spanish lace?"

"That is what the Comte de Penfleur was wont to call it. Neddie and I assumed it referred to considerable monies, of which the French government is in daily expectation. We understood from the letters that Mr. Grey was to be influenced by Mr. Sothey, towards the end of procuring foreign funds—possibly in Amsterdam, or in Spain. But we cannot determine whether the monies ever arrived—or whether Mrs. Grey was killed before the plan was effected. Certainly the continued presence of the Comte de Penfleur in England would argue a doubt."

"As would the failure of the French fleet to invade our shores," Mr. Emilious returned gravely. "There cannot be an invasion, my dear Miss Austen, without there are funds to drive it. You may be assured those funds—whatever Mrs. Grey may have intended—will never arrive."

"The funds were drawn from Grey's bank, I presume?" Neddie's countenance was carefully controlled, but his eyes glittered strangely as he looked at me. He was in the grip, I should judge, of a powerful excitement; while for my part, I felt only a curious lethargy—the result, one assumes, of too much conversation and too little sleep.

"Grey's bank? Good Lord, no!" Mr. Emilious laughed. "He was required to offer surety for the funds' transferal, of course—that is the usual way of things, in such matters of international finance—but the monies were to be shipped from the Americas."

"The Americas?"

"From Spain's colonies, to be exact. You must know that every summer, before the onset of the hurricane season, the Spanish treasure ships set out for Cádiz. They have done so for nearly two centuries, bearing cargoes of silver and pieces of eight."

"But what has that to do with Mr. Grey?" I cried.

"Very little. Pray hear me out, Miss Austen, and all shall become clear." Mr. Emilious looked at me sternly from under his elegant grey brows, and I was forced to submit. I wondered, however, how such a man could ever have formed a friendship with Lord Harold. While the one was bruisingly to the point, the other was tedious in the extreme. Both, I must suppose, were assiduous in the marshalling of fact, however; and in this, their talents might be prized.

"According to her treaties with France, signed over two years ago, Spain is required to contribute six million francs each month to the French treasury."

"But that is incredible," Neddie cried. "How is half such a sum to be paid?"

"I used the term *contribute* only loosely, to be sure," Mr. Emilious replied. "It is the most blatant extortion, at which the fiends of Buonaparte are too sadly adept. But to continue: Spain has failed in its payments for nearly a year, and the French treasury has suffered. There are rumours of bankruptcy, and of an Emperor grown desperate at the cost of power."

"We have heard those rumours," I told him.

"Spain offered this year's treasure fleet in payment of its debt. But you may recall, Miss Austen, that we are presently at war with Spain; and that only last summer, a Royal Navy squadron was so daring as to seize the annual shipment from the Americas, to general lamentation in Cádiz. Spain could not sustain such a loss again. The very stability of the Spanish crown must depend upon its fulfillment of Buonaparte's demands."

"Yes, yes," I returned impatiently. "But what of Mr. Grey?"

"The Spanish crown approached our Prime Minister, Mr. Pitt. They informed him of the difficulties they faced on every side. They spoke of complicated arrangements. They looked for expressions of good faith. The Government could hardly extend an obvious hand of assistance—no more than it should do on behalf of France. But Mr. Pitt believed that an accommodation might be found."

"That being?" Neddie enquired. His voice was as taut as a bowstring.

"The result of these delicate negotiations has been that the Spanish treasure was to be transported this year in English vessels commissioned in the Royal Navy.[3] The money was to be received in Amsterdam, by the House of Hope, which undertook to extend a loan to the French government. Mr. Grey's part in all of this, was to indemnify the British ships, in the event of a loss at sea. A minor role, but a necessary one."

"The House of Hope has recently refused its loan," I broke in, puzzled. "You told me yourself that Lord Harold was sent to Amsterdam, as Mr. Pitt's envoy. Has the entire matter gone awry?"

"I believe that it has gone exactly as was intended," Mr. Emilious replied with satisfaction.

"The treasure ships never arrived," Neddie concluded.

"They struck a reef not far from these shores, and unfortunately were lost. It is a pity that Mr. Pitt chose to consign the treasure to some of the Navy's oldest vessels; but it cannot be helped. With Mr. Grey's indemnification in hand, the Navy might build several new ships of the line, of course, and hardly see themselves the poorer."

"Unlike Mr. Grey," I said, remembering Henry's assessment of his household.

"Oh, you need not concern yourself with *Grey*, Miss Austen. A grateful Crown will make all possible amends, I am sure."

"And the treasure?" Neddie asked.

"—Is presumed to have been lost with the ships." Mr. Emilious Finch-Hatton's gaze was blandly innocent. "How even Lord Harold intends to smooth those

---

[3]  Alan Schom refers to this remarkable instance of intergovernmental cooperation in *Trafalgar: Countdown to Battle, 1803–1805*, but the full story behind events is outlined for the first time here.—*Editor's note.*

troubled waters, I cannot begin to think. But I shall trust, as ever, in his inimitable powers."

To my surprise, Neddie almost smiled. "And we have *this* to thank for the preservation of our peace! They may say what they like of the Tory Pitt—drunkard, idiot, enfeebled dotard—but, by God, he is a man of policy! If England stands another year without a Frenchman on her shores, we shall have Pitt to thank!"

"And now I may inform you of a piece of news I received by messenger yesterday morning," Mr. Emilious said. "The French are reported to be breaking camp at their Channel ports. The mass of armed troops—nearly an hundred thousand men, who have been rotting along the coast for two years—have been ordered to the Empire's eastern borders. It is almost certain that Buonaparte intends war with Austria."[4]

"Austria!" I cried. "And is the Comte de Penfleur aware of the ruin of his hopes?"

"We must pray that he continues in ignorance a little while longer," Mr. Emilious replied. "Else he will be gone from these shores before we find sufficient cause to arrest him."

Neddie consumed the last of his bread, and pushed back his chair from the table. The look of elation had quite fled from his features. "Gratified as I may be by this frank avowal of all your interests," he told Mr. Emilious, "I rather wonder at your revealing so much. You have

[4] Finch-Hatton had early news of the troop pullout, something we may attribute to George Canning and his Secret Funds. As historian Alan Schom points out in *Trafalgar: Countdown to Battle, 1803–1805*, the French government's bankruptcy forced Napoleon to abandon the invasion of England and turn east to Austria, where he believed an easy land campaign would replenish his coffers. His instincts were richly rewarded. The Austrian indemnity alone at the Treaty of Pressburg amounted to forty million francs.—*Editor's note.*

exposed Mr. Sothey as an agent of Government; you have declared yourself to be very nearly the same; and you have disclosed not a little of that Government's policy. To what end, sir? The diversion of our interest? For is it not irrefutable, that Mrs. Grey *died* as a result of your efforts? *Something* alerted her confederates to the failure of their hopes. I have not forgot the French courier that was seen at her house the very morning of her death—revealing, perhaps, the nature of her betrayal. Am I not charged, Mr. Finch-Hatton, with the pursuit of her murderer, and the resolution of her death?"

There was a heavy silence about the table. Then Mr. Emilious said, "I trust you will comprehend, Mr. Austen, the impenetrable nature of espionage. We may never know for a fact who killed Mrs. Grey. It is probable, however, that she died at the hands of the Comte de Penfleur. Certainly he had reason to believe that she had betrayed him; the promised funds failed to arrive, precipitating his own highly perilous journey to these shores; and he may even have suspected that the lady was a victim of her sources."

"It was for this that I quitted The Larches on Monday," Mr. Sothey broke in. "I could not be assured of my own safety, did I remain too long in the household. I learned of the Comte's intended arrival from that self-same courier you would mention, Mr. Austen—and I freely own, I prepared to depart. Mrs. Grey's fury upon learning my intention, precipitated a public attack—"

"The whip, brought down upon your neck," I murmured.

"—but even still, I cannot think she understood the extent of my subtle use of her. She believed me to the last, a poor idiot employed for her own devices; it was I, she thought, who had urged her husband to receive the Comte de Penfleur's letter, begging that he should indemnify the Royal Navy's ships—when, in fact, it was Mr. Pitt himself, who proposed the plan."

"I should not like to be Grey," my brother said suddenly, "does the Comte ever tumble to the truth of what occurred. We must hope, as you said, that he is yet in ignorance of the truth, or Grey's life should not be worth a farthing." His voice trailed away suddenly, and he stared fixedly at Emilious Finch-Hatton.

"Those were almost your exact words, Mr. Emilious." I forced the gentleman to meet my gaze. "—That the Comte must be kept in ignorance a little longer. A Comte in doubt as to the state of the funds was all very well—but a Comte who knew the truth, that he had been betrayed by Mr. Grey and England, should stop at nothing! It was for that—the preservation of his ignorance—that Mrs. Grey was killed."

There was a terrible pause—one filled with horrified implication, as we each of us glanced at the others around the table—and then Julian Sothey thrust himself to his feet.

"Sit down, boy," Mr. Emilious charged him in a deadly tone. "I shall deal with this." Then, in a calmer accent, he said: "As for Mr. Grey's life—you may rest easy on that score. The Comte de Penfleur shall not stir from his rooms, without I learn of it; and Mr. Grey has been called by Mr. Pitt to London on a pretext, expressly for the preservation of his safety."

"So even Grey is as yet in ignorance of the extent of his folly!" Neddie cried. "I can well comprehend it. What man could endure the knowledge that his colleagues and friends had murdered his wife, as a policy of statecraft!"

"Are you accusing me of murder, Mr. Austen? Consider well, before you do," Mr. Emilious said sternly. "You cannot hope to prove such a claim; for tho' present at the Canterbury Races, I was under the eye of my unimpeachable brother, and half a dozen others, for the whole of the proceedings."

"But what of Mr. Sothey? Where was *he*, at the critical hour?"

The improver's countenance assumed the perfect serenity I had last discerned at the Canterbury Races.

"My man will vouch for me."

"Your man! Aye, I am sure he will vouch for anything. But I cannot be so certain he will be believed."

"Come, come, Mr. Austen," Mr. Emilious interrupted in a placating tone. "Is it not far more likely that the Comte de Penfleur murdered Mrs. Grey? I am certain, for my part, that he murdered Denys Collingforth."

"On what grounds?" Neddie retorted, his brows knit.

"—Because he intended that Collingforth's murder should look like the work of Mr. Grey, towards whom he has always harboured the most vengeful jealousy. The crime was committed on the very night the Comte knew Grey to be called away on business. Grey travelled alone; no one might vouch for his route; and the man Pembroke, if questioned, should be taught to accuse Grey as his paymaster. Pembroke undoubtedly sent the news of Collingforth's presence in Deal to the master of The Larches; but I would warrant it was the Comte who received it."

"You know a great deal too much about that man's affairs," Neddie observed.

"It is my duty to know everything that the Comte holds in contemplation, before he so much as conceives it," Mr. Emilious flashed. "Arrest the man Pembroke, Mr. Justice Austen, and see if I have not told you rightly!"

There was a faint whimper, as of a small animal run to earth, and Anne Sharpe reached a trembling hand to my arm.

"What is it, my dear? Do you wish to seek your bed?"

She shook her head, and said in a voice so faint as to be almost inaudible, "I have a duty of my own to perform, or all sleep shall be banished forever." Then, more clearly, "You asked me whether I had ever had occasion to visit Mr. Sothey in the stables at The Larches. Did that question arise from a particular instance you know of, Miss Austen—or from a general suspicion of my behaviour?"

"A particular instance," I replied. "A woman with raven-dark hair was seen riding out of The Larches' stables, a few days before Mrs. Grey's death."

The governess rose unsteadily, as tho' seized with a sickness, and backed slowly away from the table. Her hazel eyes were fixed on Julian Sothey, and the expression of horror in their depths must have filled even him with dread.

"Then it *was* you," she whispered. "I thought that I had been dreaming—a trick of the light and my tortured brain. But I have seen it in memory again and again, wearying my thoughts like a child's rhyming song! If you knew the nightmare I have lived in, Julian, you should have fled the country long since!"

"Anne—"

"Do you not know that I have observed you sit your horse an hundred times, during those happy days in Weymouth? Whether you chose to ride sidesaddle, and wear a long red gown, I should know your seat anywhere!"

—*Did you see that grey-eyed jade, Neddie, spurring her mount for all she was worth?*

—*I believe Mrs. Grey's eyes to be brown, Henry.*

"Of course," I said slowly. "Henry saw what we all did not. Your eyes are decidedly grey, Mr. Sothey—and the lady's eyes were brown."

"I could not believe it true," Anne Sharpe burst out, "but I know now that I was not mistaken! It was you, Julian, who were astride Mrs. Grey's horse in the final heat; and the lady herself was already dead at your hands!"

# Chapter 21

## *The Better Part of Valour*

~

WHAT HAPPENED NEXT WAS TOO SWIFT FOR THOUGHT. Emilious Finch-Hatton leapt from his seat, and would have seized Anne Sharpe by the neck, had not Mr. Sothey been before him; she cried out, and cowered behind the spare form of the improver. Sothey contrived to hold Finch-Hatton at bay, while the latter muttered imprecations through his teeth.

"Fool! She'll have your neck!"

"I care nothing for life, Finch-Hatton," Sothey cried, "if I have not the love of this woman. Can you have understood me so little?"

"I have understood you not at all. I thought you a man of sense, of coldest calculation——not a weak-hearted fool, to be played upon by a girl!" Mr. Emilious wheeled away from his confederate and thrust a kitchen chair violently towards the wall. He seemed oblivious to the look of appalled fascination on my brother's countenance; I, who had long understood what he was, could appear more sanguine.

"You must demand a vow of silence from her, Sothey," he muttered. "Everything—your life, and possibly Grey's—depends upon it!"

"Not to mention the spotlessness of your own reputation," I observed from my position by the table. "I doubt that Miss Sharpe would willingly speak now of what she knows, did her grave yawn before her; but shall you demand a similar vow from ourselves, Mr. Finch-Hatton? Such a request might appear quite reasonable, to a spinster of advancing years, who wishes only to sit quietly at home; but to a man in commission of the peace for the neighbourhood—! One of some standing, too, whose honour must be seen as embodied in his word. I should not like to depend upon such a vow, Mr. Finch-Hatton; but perhaps you shall choose the surest path, and make an end to us all. What does Mr. Sothey advise?"

Sothey simply gave me a long look; then he led Anne Sharpe back to her chair, with a gentleness usually reserved for the aged or the infirm. She went as a condemned woman goes to the block—mute, stiff, and lost to inner contemplation. Her hand, when I touched it, was deathly cold.

"While Mr. Emilious is considering the most proper means of ensuring our silence," I said, "you might endeavour to satisfy my curiosity, Mr. Sothey. I perceive now that Mrs. Grey's murder was the work of some days—the fruit of considerable planning. You were observed to enter the stable at The Larches, and emerge in the guise of a dark-haired woman mounted on horseback, a full two days before the lady's death. I comprehend the necessity of preparation—it is one thing to gallop in pursuit of a pack, as one has been riding all one's life; and quite another to attempt it sidesaddle, and in skirts."

"I did not relish the prospect," he replied. "But I thought it best to be prepared for every eventuality. And

I was proved correct in the event. Mrs. Grey informed me at the race-meeting, that her husband had betrayed her; that her credit in France, and her every hope of a future life, was utterly in ruins; and she beseeched me to aid her in a desperate attempt—the kidnapping and torture of Valentine Grey. She thought to make him divulge the present whereabouts of the Spanish treasure promised to France. I loved Grey too well, and had worked too long in support of the funds' diversion, to accede to such a request."

"And when you refused, she struck you with her whip."

"My negative produced a dreadful passion," he agreed. "She was never a soul under perfect management. I informed her that I could not be a party to so heinous a crime; there were others, no doubt, who would gladly accommodate her."

"Such as Denys Collingforth."

He averted his gaze.

"And so you determined, that for Grey's sake and the sake of your . . . policy, that Mrs. Grey must die. Your careful preparation must be put into play. You waited for her in Collingforth's coach; and when she entered it a little before the final heat—under the observant eyes of the entire Austen party—you strangled her there, with her own hair-ribbon."

"I wonder that you did not hear the struggle," Neddie said.

I shrugged. "For all his slightness, Mr. Sothey moves with considerable grace—I should judge him a man of some strength."

Emilious Finch-Hatton paced restlessly before the kitchen hearth, his hands clasped behind his back. Now, I thought—when the two men were engaged in the relation of their tale—now was the moment to seize and bind them. They had practically admitted to the crime of murder; and yet, Neddie did nothing. Could it be that he was hesitating? Or that he doubted of his ability to prove either man's guilt?

And then I saw that his fingers had closed over a bread knife, and were sliding it by imperceptible degrees towards the edge of the table. I hurried myself into speech once more.

"I suppose, Mr. Sothey, that when the gruesome work was done, you put on Mrs. Grey's habit over your own suit of clothes. You are slight enough to have managed it, and Mrs. Grey was a well-formed woman. You added, however, two items—a black wig and illusion veil, under the brim of the lady's tricorn hat. How did you conceal them on your person, as you walked about the meeting-grounds?"

Sothey shrugged dismissively. "I wore, you may recollect, a prodigiously handsome hat, with a high circular crown. The wig and veil were concealed within, and devilish warm they made it, too."

"Highly necessary, however, for the discouragement of the curious. But you did not mean to be under the observation of anyone very long. Arrayed in the scarlet riding habit, you quitted the chaise; retrieved Mrs. Grey's black horse from her tyger; approached the rail and threw yourself into the heat. That, if I recollect, was ultimately your undoing—for Miss Sharpe observed you jump the rail, and understood the alteration that had taken place, however little she might comprehend or explain it."

"She cannot have the least notion of what she saw," Mr. Emilious broke in wearily. "Your entire history, Miss Austen, is the most extraordinary fabrication of humbug and lies."

I smiled at him faintly. "I thought it unlikely, sir, that Lord Harold Trowbridge should possess an intimate friend; but knowing you now a little, as I do, I comprehend the extent of my folly. You can never have been on terms of intimacy with that remarkable intellect, and yet fail to profit from his example. Accept, Mr. Finch-Hatton, that you have underestimated the Austens; and be satisfied."

"With the filly Josephine triumphant," my brother said to Julian Sothey, "all that remained was to accept the plate with a careless grace, and drive your phaeton precipitately out of the grounds. A mile down the Wingham road, you discarded the habit; but at the last, you thought better of the wig and veil. It would never do for *them* to be found; we should have seen in an instant that it was not Mrs. Grey, but an imposter, who had paraded about the grounds."

"We never thought to wonder what had become of the lady's hat," I agreed. "That was very stupid of us. And what of Mr. Sothey's own? The prodigiously expensive, high-crowned affair, so admirably suited to the concealment of a wig?"

"I tossed it from the far window of Collingforth's chaise, before exiting from the near side, apparelled as Mrs. Grey," he replied in a subdued tone. "It fell into the underbrush at the fringe of the race grounds—you will recall that the chaise was parked at the farthest extent of the carriages—and for all I know, it rests there still."

"The fate of all things cherished and expensive," I observed, "—to be lost at hazard, and well before their time. And once you had driven the phaeton along the Wingham road, I suppose your man was instructed to fetch you?"

"Of course not," Sothey replied. "I walked back to the race grounds. To admit my valet to an intimate knowledge of my affairs should place me in the man's power; and that is not how an agent of George Canning's survives."

"Nor, it would seem, does he survive by placing

himself in a *woman's* power; but that, we may suppose, you could not help. I comprehend it all, Mr. Sothey, except for one thing—why did you choose to implicate Denys Collingforth?"

"I had lived long enough at The Larches to believe Collingforth capable of anything, Miss Austen. He was a man driven by his passion for gaming, and by the pressures his resultant debts exacted; little as he loved Mrs. Grey, he was completely in her power, and should be the obvious instrument of revenge against her husband. I could not allow their conference to take place."

"And, too, Collingforth's chaise was one of the few bereft of an attendant party," I mused. "Not so much as a groom was left to look after the horses. Yes, I see perfectly how it was. A fearful symmetry must dictate your choice."

"I never believed he would be charged with murder," Sothey protested. "The man might name an hundred witnesses to his conduct that day, and all of them at some distance from his chaise. I thought him in the clear."

"Until my brother discovered his message in Mrs. Grey's habit."

"I had no notion she would keep it about her."

I studied him keenly. "So you wrote that summons yourself?"

He bowed his head. "I had seen Collingforth's hand a score of times—he was forever sending little missives, in acceptance of Mrs. Grey's card-parties. It was a simple matter for an artist to affect his hand."

"So simple, in fact, that even his wife was fooled. How unfortunate for Mr. Collingforth! Besieged on every side, he bolted from town, rather than face the coroner—and thus fell a second victim to your schemes. But why weight his body and throw him in the millpond? Should you not have been better served by an appearance of suicide, and a note to that effect, scrawled in his handwriting?"

Sothey's eyes widened. "You cannot believe that I murdered *Collingforth!*—An innocent man! I was never more miserable than when I learned the result of the inquest, and never more relieved than when I was told that he had fled. I thought it a benediction of Heaven, that one man at least might escape the fate of the condemned."

"And when you learned of his murder?"

Sothey threw his hands skyward in a gesture of utter helplessness, then let them fall without a word.

The improver's protest had the ring of truth; but in such a case, who knew what might be believed? A jury of his peers should dismiss his claim without a second thought. The murder of Mrs. Grey would prove him capable of every infamy. And yet, what had he effected, against an avowed spy of the enemy, but a simple act of war? It was to Sothey, perhaps, that we owed the unsullied peace of the Kentish night, and the broken camps along the Channel. Such tangles were beyond my power of resolution; I knew only that I recoiled from the hand that could murder a woman from cold-blooded calculation, when I should not think twice about the death of an enemy soldier, in the heat of battle. There was a hypocrisy in this, that was hardly comfortable; and I read a similar confusion in my brother's eyes.

"If you have quite done," Mr. Emilious Finch-Hatton said, "I believe that Sothey and I should take our leave."

He had risen from his seat, and withdrawn a duelling pistol from his coat; it was a lovely thing, of highly-polished wood, and silver handle. But the ball in its depths should suffice for only one, before Finch-Hatton must reload; and in recognition of this, he had trained the piece upon my brother.

"I suggest you place the knife upon the table, Austen, where I might see it."

It was brilliantly done; had Finch-Hatton chosen to fix upon Anne Sharpe, he could not depend upon Sothey—on myself, and he should risk Neddie's heroics. As it was, my brother stood in all the horror of our regard—and considered, I suppose, of his nine children. He hesitated, glanced beseechingly at me, and then laid the knife in the middle of the worn oak.

"I regret the necessity of such brutal persuasion," Mr. Emilious said sadly, "but dawn approaches, and Sothey's road is a long one. Pray make our excuses to your bewitching wife, Mr. Austen, and assure her that we bear her no ill-will for the nature of this flight. The extended tour of the grounds, I fear, must be deferred for another time."

"There are many forms of justice, Finch-Hatton," Neddie replied carefully, "and Sothey's shall find him. Of your own fate, I confess, I am less sanguine; you have the peculiar ability to remain always on the fringe of the field, an observer of the fray, or perhaps its truest instigator. Such men invariably live long and interesting lives; whether their reputations survive them, is another question. And now, pray get out, before I find a foolish courage, and take your ball in pursuit of the bubble reputation."

Finch-Hatton shook his head, a smile playing at the corners of his mouth. "Pray allow Mr. Sothey to bind you to your chair, Mr. Austen—and the ladies also—lest you hound us on horseback the length of England. We require several hours, I should think, for the effecting of this flight; and we cannot waste a moment. In a very little while, I assume, your cook will be about the matter of breakfast."

And so it was done: Finch-Hatton remained to train his pistol on Neddie, while Sothey fetched some twine from the stillroom; we were bound into our chairs as tightly as knots could hold us, and left with the unpleasant sensation of pigs trussed for the slaughter. Only Anne Sharpe appeared too remote for sensation; she was very nearly in a swoon.

"Anne," Sothey said desperately, as he knelt before her chair, "will not you throw up everything, and come with me?"

She turned from him with such an expression of horror, that his countenance went white. "Can every tender feeling be denied me? Can not you understand what I have effected for my King, my country? —Indeed, Anne, for the love of such an one as you?"

"Do not attempt to claim that you strangled Mrs. Grey out of love for me," she retorted bitterly. "I have never understood what you are. From the first moment of our meeting, I pledged my heart to a creature of my own invention; and I reap nothing now but my just reward."

He would have touched her then, but she shrank away; and in utter silence, he bound her hands.

"Where shall you go?" I enquired, as he came to me.

He merely shook his head. "Mr. Canning, I must believe, will have some use for a desperate man. There are any number of noisome holes throughout the world, where such an one might be hidden—and so die."

When he bent to tie my wrists, I caught his fingers in mine. "Do not give way entirely to despair, Mr. Sothey. If these hands have shed some blood, they have also been the instruments of a remarkable beauty. In your art I glimpsed a little of Paradise; but there cannot be a garden without a serpent or two. I shall not soon forget the beauty of your works, or the genius I have glimpsed."

"My genius, Miss Austen, is akin to Lucifer's; and I fear that he was cast out from Heaven."

"There is something of the demon and the angel in all of us, Mr. Sothey," I replied, "and I know that your angel shall prevail. Let that hope be your guide—the beacon in your darkness—that redemption, and atonement, might come to you at last."

The knots tied, he bowed low over my coupled wrists and kissed the back of my hand. Then, his eyes averted from Anne Sharpe, he quitted the room without another word.

And so they left us.

IT WAS A TEDIOUS INTERVAL, POSSIBLY AS LONG AS AN hour and a half, before the first clatter of feet on the servants' stair announced the housemaids come in search of water. Anne Sharpe could provide no conversation to relieve the boredom of that passage; she was lost in a peculiar torment, that did not admit of speech; and the greatest kindness we could offer, was to respect her silence.

Of Neddie I enquired only once.

"You remarked that there were many forms of justice, and that Mr. Sothey would come to his in time. Of what were you thinking, Neddie? Do you intend to pursue him to the limits of the law?"

"I may risk the wrath of Mr. George Canning," he replied wearily, "and perhaps, even, of Mr. Pitt. I cannot pretend to understand so deep an undertaking, Jane, as was unfolded here before us. But I may discharge one duty upon my conscience—I may inform Mr. Valentine Grey of exactly how his wife came to die."

"You believe him as yet in ignorance?" I cried.

"He should never have handed over her letters," Neddie said, "did he comprehend the ruin he should bring upon his friend Sothey's head. No, Jane—I believe Grey's part in the puzzle extended only so far as indemnification of the Royal Navy's ships. Of his wife's ungentle handling, he can have known nothing."

"—But suspected a great deal," I returned thoughtfully. "Perhaps his conscience, indeed, argued the presentation of those letters."

"And if I know anything of the man's character," Neddie observed grimly, "he shall not rest until his honour is satisfied. It is for Grey to pursue his friend Sothey to the ends of the earth, and settle the account at pistol-point. And to my great relief, Jane, my dear, I shall be nowhere within hailing distance, when the deed is done."

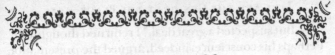

# Chapter 22

## *The Genius of the Place*

*16 September 1805*

~

I HAVE COME AT LAST TO THE END OF MY KENTISH INTER-
lude; nearly four months of dissipation, vice, and the
corruption of high living—a period I relinquish with
infinite regret. Ahead lie all the pleasures of a visit to the
seaside at Worthing, in company with my sister Cassandra, our friend Mary Lloyd, and my widowed and
querulous mother; then the return to winter in Bath, in
temporary lodgings and all the inelegance of reduced
circumstances. I cannot look upon the succession of
months with anything like complacency, nor contemplate the fulfillment of my thirtieth year with particular
satisfaction. I must trust, however, in the vagaries of
Fate—which invariably surprise when one has ceased to
expect them.

I closed my visit to Godmersham as I have so often
marked its extent—by repairing to the little Doric temple across the Stour, and sitting awhile in contemplation
of the beauty of the downs. The lime trees of Bentigh,
it seemed, should proceed in their march unmolested;

so, too, the kitchen gardens, amidst their harried traffic of scullery maids and under-gardeners. The promise of Mr. Sothey's Blue Book was at Godmersham unfulfilled, just as at Eastwell it remained unrealised—to Lady Elizabeth's confusion and pain. Of Mr. Sothey's whereabouts she has learned not the slightest syllable. No explanation of her protégé's abrupt departure has been offered to her—just as none was ever given for his sudden appearance at her door. She professes to believe his desertion immaterial; but thinks her daughter Louisa decidedly ill-used.

Anne Sharpe, who has more occasion to believe herself abandoned, must enjoy the satisfaction of knowing it to be the result of her own design. She has rallied tolerably in spirits, tho' she remains unequal to the challenge of Lizzy's daughters, and has accepted a position with a Mrs. Raikes, who possesses only one little girl. She is to leave Godmersham in January, and I hope that she may find tranquillity in her future employment.[1]

I had much to consider, as I lingered in the late summer air—the conclusion of the tragic business of Mrs. Grey, and the mysterious death of the Comte de Penfleur.

It was while I was suffering the blandishments of Edward Bridges, on the third day of my visit to Goodnestone Farm, that I learned the intelligence of Neddie. My brother enclosed a short note in Cassandra's letter, to the effect that the Frenchman had been found shot through the heart in the middle of a gallop not far from

---

[1]   Anne Sharpe eventually found even one child insupportable, and became a companion to Mrs. Raikes's crippled sister, a position she held for five years. She corresponded with Jane Austen up to the point of Jane's death; Cassandra sent her a lock of her sister's hair as a remembrance. By 1823, Anne Sharpe was the owner of a boarding school for girls in Liverpool, where she remained for nearly two decades. She died in retirement in 1853.—*Editor's note.*

the outskirts of Dover. It is presumed that the Comte met another gentleman there, at dawn, for the satisfaction of some affair of honour; but why he brought no second, who might have exposed his murderer, remains a mystery to all of Kent. Suspicion has fallen on Mr. Valentine Grey, of course—but that gentleman has chosen to say nothing regarding the Comte's untimely end; and there are those—Mr. Justice Austen among them—who maintain that Grey was away in London on a matter of business at the time.

I was so honoured during my week's residence among the Bridges family, as to receive a proposal of marriage from a certain desperate curate—but of my reply, let us relate as little as possible, beyond the fact that it was in the negative. Mr. Bridges's declaration coincided with the Coldstream Guards' secret troop movement towards Deal; and we must assume that only an excess of boredom at being forced within doors, and the most extreme anxiety regarding the security of the pheasants, could give rise to so foolish an impulse.

I have now the distinction of having loved two men, from whom it was my destiny to be parted forever; and of having refused another two, whom it was my destiny never to love. I begin to resemble the interesting career of one of Mrs. Burney's heroines, and cannot expect so much of romance in future.

It was as I was seated over the pages of my little book, wrestling Lady Susan at last to her deserts, that the figure of a gentleman toiling up the hill intruded upon my sight. It was a spare figure, tho' tall and elegantly dressed; a trousered gentleman quite at a loss in the country, whose shoes should never sustain the effects of the previous night's rain. The hair beneath his rakish hat was silver, and the knife-blade of his nose must scream his name aloud as clearly as a hot-pressed calling card. I felt all the rush of recognition—rose, and gained support from the temple's table—breathed deep, and endeavoured to calm the racing of my heart.

And when Lord Harold had at last achieved the summit of Neddie's little hill, I was tolerably in command of my countenance. I might curtsey, and extend my hand, and say with admirable composure, "An unlooked-for pleasure, Lord Harold, indeed! What could possibly bring you to so remote a corner of Kent?—For I assure you, sir, that we know nothing at Godmersham of coalitions and accords, or the subtle employments of diplomacy. You had better turn back by the road you have come, and ask the way to Eastwell Park."

"I *had* intended to pay my respects to Mr. Finch-Hatton," he replied, with an effort to subdue his smile, "but that I recently learned of his posting abroad—to a sinecure in India, much embattled at present. With tigers on the one hand, and mutinous sepoys on the other, who can say how Mr. Emilious shall fare?"

"Having survived the dangerous Miss Austen," I replied, "we may consider him as equal to anything."

Lord Harold threw back his head and laughed—the first genuine expression of mirth I had ever witnessed in that gentleman. Then taking up the pages of *Lady Susan*, and placing my hand within the crook of his arm, he led me back towards my brother's house.

If ever there is a monument built on Godmersham's heights—a propitiation of the local spirit, perhaps—then pray let it be dedicated to the genius of laughter.

If you enjoyed Stephanie Barron's
Jane Austen Mystery,
**Jane and the Genius of the Place,**
you won't want to miss any of the superb mysteries
in this bestselling series.

Don't miss Jane Austen's next
foray into sleuthing!

# Jane and the
# Ghosts of Netley

*—Being the Seventh Jane Austen Mystery—*

by Stephanie Barron

Available from
Bantam Books

# About the Author

Stephanie Barron, a lifelong admirer of Jane Austen's work, is the author of eleven Jane Austen mysteries, as well as the novels *The White Garden* and *A Flaw in the Blood.* She lives in Colorado.